STROKE OF TEMPTATION

LILAH LANCE

TITAN SECURITY BOOK VI

To all the good girls
who know the power of 'that's a good girl'

CONTENT WARNING

There is explicit content, graphic details, mentions of kidnapping, murder, trauma, abuse and adult content in this story.

MISSION BRIEFING

Welcome back to Titan

You are no longer a part of a team.

This will be your first solo mission at Titan

PROLOGUE

SEVEN YEARS AGO

AVANI

TWELVE YEARS OLD

"Be safe you two!" Mum was waving at Alisha and me wiping her eyes. "Oh, don't forget to eat something, Lisha!"

"Love you two, both." Papa was grinning ear to ear, his dark hair and brighter hazel eyes on Alisha. Lish was Papa's favorite and I was Mum's.

He told me Mum begged to have another baby after Lish because she loved her and then she adored me.

My parents were wonderful people.

"Yes, Mum!" Alisha grinned as we waved from the taxi. "Bye, Papa! Do not worry about us!"

"Too late," Mum said with a hint of mock-reproach.

"We always worry!" Papa yelled.

I loved my parents but I felt emotional waving to them like I was embarking on something scary with older sister Alisha.

At twenty, she was much smarter than I was. Prettier.

The apple of my father's eye. And me?

This summer, I had turned twelve and I was going to New York with my sister while my parents stayed behind in Oxfordshire.

Our parents would join us later, Papa had to go see Mum's family.

I adjusted my outfit Mum insisted on and my hair as Alisha smiled over at me looking all cool and sophisticated. "Did you want your headphones?"

I nodded as she plucked them out of her trendy purse. Alisha made everything look effortless.

In how she carried herself, with her jeans and simple t-shirt Alisha still looked like a *cool* girl. I wasn't cool.

I was kind of nerdy and out of place in my own body. A little too round for my own good.

As she handed them to me, she put on her own ready to zone out until we arrived at the airport.

I felt nervous, anxious, a bit of anxiety.

This was my first time away from Mum and Dad and I missed them already.

It ached a little in the spot.

I hated leaving Mum behind. I knew they'd come to the city again but Mum and Dad both had family in the UK they wanted to see.

"Lish?" I shook her leg to get her attention.

"What?" She looked annoyed.

My sister wasn't a mean girl per se. Not really.

Not quite. No.

Alisha just had a different world she existed in.

She was seven years older than me. *Cool*. Articulate.

Boys gathered around her even if she ignored it and girls wanted to be my sister. She always had friends, always had cool things, always had her head in a magazine.

And sometimes she wasn't fond of me encroaching on her time.

I was a bit annoying, clingy, I wanted to absorb Alisha into me. I wanted to be around her all the time. I was a little nervous.

"When did Mum say she would get to New York?"

"I think the end of summer," Alisha said. "I think. Papa says if Mum's family drives him crazy probably sooner."

I grinned. "Do you miss them when you leave home?"

Alisha left home all the time. Not for university but for modeling shoots, shows she did, photoshoots, and lots of cool things I didn't do.

"I think initially, but it goes away once you find your own thing in life. I noticed after the first time, I didn't really care."

"Why's that?" I asked her as the rolling hills passed us by.

She thought about it. "Because...Mum and Papa are always home." She smiled a little at that. "Every time I need them they're there and I know after my shoots I come home to them. So it's not so bad. You'll see." She grinned. "They'll be home before we know it."

I sat back in my seat with a satisfied smile.

They'll be home before we know it.

ALISHA WAS CRYING.

Standing on the bustling Manhattan street, clutching me close, her voice trembled as she spoke into her phone.

The air around us was chilly, almost biting, and I couldn't tell who was shaking more—Alisha or me.

Earlier, I had been talking to Mum when the call abruptly dropped, replaced by a crashing sound. Papa had been driving.

"What's happening?"

Alisha shook her head, pulling me to the side of the pavement.

Her voice quivered as she continued on the phone. "...What do I do? She's here..."

Something dreadful had happened, but I didn't feel the tears that usually accompanied such moments.

Mum always said I was the more emotional one—the weepy sister. If anyone cried, I cried.

Alisha playfully called me a watering pot.

She wasn't like that. She looked different from me, cool and collected.

In secondary school, she mingled with the popular crowd. Cool, aloof, and it wasn't that Alisha wasn't nice.

We were just too far apart in age and she was nothing like my parents.

Her head always in magazines and clothes and mine in books.

Alisha had loved fashion since she'd been a kid according to my Mum.

As she grew older, her modeling career took off, a decision that sparked debates between Mum and Dad—Dad, always proud, claimed his looks had landed her gigs; Mum, protective, worried about exploitation from predators.

Sometimes, I felt like people forgot about me. But I didn't mind. I still liked Alisha, even when we didn't get along.

Since I could remember, Alisha had been vibrant and lively.

A world apart from me. An *extrovert*.

Mum had often joked that she thought she could only have Alisha.

Dad was overjoyed, celebrated having two girls.

After university, Mum and Dad spent time in America, where they fell in love, visiting Dad's family in Chiswick during breaks.

"I understand, thank you." Alisha ended the call, pulling me closer.

Her lip quivered as she scanned the street, searching for something.

"Avani, we need to go home now."

"To Mum?" Why? "Why aren't they coming?"

Alisha's flat in the city was tiny, but it was ours. I liked it.

"What happened?"

"I'll tell you at home, darling. I promise. Let's go home, Avani. We have to go home now." Alisha tugged me into her chest and I didn't understand.

But I did.

Alisha trembled, and I knew something terrible had happened.

Numb and aching, I held on tightly as we rode back in the cab.

Arriving at Alisha's flat, she held me close, gently explaining what had happened to Mum and Dad.

Tears streamed down both our faces. I wiped my eyes feeling like I was in a dream.

"What do you mean...Mum and Dad were in an accident..."

Six weeks passed in a blur of tears and hushed whispers.

At *twenty*, Alisha became my legal guardian, and I clung to her like a lifeline. Alisha changed.

My old sister was gone. The old vibrant girl who snuck outside her window or went out with friends...was gone.

I knew she sometimes went to her room when it got overwhelming not coming out for a long time. When she did her eyes were red and cheeks puffy like mine.

Every moment apart felt like an eternity, and I shadowed her constantly, only parting when she showered.

I needed her nearby, a reminder that I wasn't alone.

I felt like if I left her alone, something would happen to her.

We returned to England, a place once filled with laughter, now shrouded in grief over the loss of our parents who would not in fact ever be coming home.

I still thought about Mum yelling at us to eat and Alisha's laughter as she grinned at her.

Had I told Mum I loved her?

Had I told her about wanting to be like her?

Had I told her I was working hard in school to be her?

I didn't. And I cried. A lot.

I learned if possible, I could turn into a watering pot.

I had always been more sensitive than Alisha.

Mum called me the softer one since I'd taken so long to come into the world. But I felt fragile after losing them.

As we laid Mum and Dad to rest, I felt a piece of myself buried with them. Something in me was gone. I was terrified to move wrong. Like if I did—I might shatter to pieces.

Back in New York, Alisha tried her best to keep our lives normal, but I noticed the strain behind her smile.

The way she held her composure. She'd gotten frightening skinny.

Alisha never said we were struggling, but we shared everything. We couldn't afford expensive salon visits so we didn't cut our hair, Alisha found ways to cut costs with laundry, hygiene, and food.

We never went out.

And my initial idyllic life completely shattered.

But as long as I was with Alisha I didn't mind.

ONE EVENING, I WATCHED HER AT THE STOVE, HER EYES SHIMMERING a little as she stirred a pot of rice, frying up eggs.

It was all we had, the fridge sorta of emptier than usual while Alisha waited to get paid from a job.

"Are you all right?"

"Yes, dear just allergies."

"How was your interview?"

"Brilliant. I got the job."

"That's fantastic."

She had done a round of interviews that week and planned to start a position soon as a receptionist at a hotel.

I remember being hungry that night, almost ravenous as I sat down wolfing down my food. It was only halfway through my plate that I realized she wasn't eating.

"I'm not hungry, darling. You eat," Alisha said that night brushing my hair back. "I think I need to go lay down for a bit and prep for my day tomorrow."

She had to go to the hotel.

I'd seen her sneak only a tiny orange for herself, her brows furrowed as she stared at her phone scrolling through her social media messages.

Before long she disappeared into the bathroom, and I heard the water running for an unusually long time as I ate my food.

My gaze flickered between my plate and the empty pot on the stove, and suddenly, everything clicked into place.

My throat tightened as I realized the gravity of our situation.

We don't have enough food.

And for the first time then I became aware of Alisha as a totally different person.

Not my cool sister.

But as my Mum. Sort of. Not quite. But kind of.

When she emerged, avoiding my eyes, I shook my head at her offer some of my food.

"I'm full," I told her. "I can't finish it."

But Alisha simply shook her head and brushed my hair back. I wanted to cry seeing her like this. I was a watering pot.

I always had been.

"Sis—"

"It's okay, you can eat. I promise I'm not hungry."

"I'm not hungry either."

Alisha laughed lightly tucking my hair behind my ear. "Avani, eat dinner and then read your book, okay? I promise it's all right."

The next morning Alisha got an email from a brand called Ella-Beauty. And Alisha cried. So much.

She held me as she found out and squeezed me so tight.

"Just wait, I promise, I'll work so hard darling," she whispered to me hugging me close to her looking relieved. "We're going to be okay. I promise."

"Do you want to eat dinner tonight?" I asked her. "I can help you make eggs and rice."

She beamed at me. "Sure, why not?"

EVEN THOUGH ALISHA'S CONTRACT AT ELLABEAUTY GOT HER SIX figures according to her, she was waiting for her payments, but in the meantime, Alisha took me to her photoshoots when she could.

"Childcare is expensive," she told me. "So just stay here, I'll be right there the entire time. I promise."

And she was.

I watched them get her ready and I observed from the sidelines with a book in hand the way my sister became a completely different person.

I just wanted to be near Alisha.

Every moment apart filled me with an irrational fear that she too might disappear, like Mum and Dad. So I stayed glued to her side even when she went to shows and other events.

At night, I slept with her sometimes, neither wanting to let go. Her apartment was small so it was either she slept on the living room couch or I slept in her bed.

It felt wrong so we shared our bed together despite being adults. Sort of.

In those quiet moments, I felt both incredibly young and impossibly old.

Alisha's world became a whirlwind of faces and flashing cameras, and I clung to her like a shadow, afraid to let go.

Her face was everywhere—on towering billboards, glossy magazines, and glowing screens.

And after a few weeks of waiting—she finally got paid.

In the meantime, Alisha did work as the receptionist and used her part-time hours to adjust to EllaBeauty's schedule.

It felt strange, seeing my sister's smile beaming down at me from above the busy streets, but I was beginning to realize the more I saw my sister everywhere—the more money she made.

And one day Alisha moved us into a new flat.

It felt enormous compared to our old one, with a bigger bathroom, proper closets, and everything shiny and new.

Alisha gave me my own room—a space just for me.

It felt like a dream and a bit scary all at once.

We filled our new home together, picking out a soft sofa, pretty decorations, and plants that made the place feel alive.

It was surreal. We hadn't had much money, but enough to sustain ourselves.

Now?

Alisha had more money than she knew what to do with and more rolling in with more partnerships and deals.

Alisha let me choose anything I wanted for my room.

I went a bit mad with pink—walls, curtains, pink bedding.

It was like living inside a cotton candy cloud. And my guilty pleasure. Alisha insisted. Books.

Books became my world.

Before, when money was tight, Alisha couldn't buy many.

We'd go to the community center, where I'd dig through crates of donated books like a pirate searching for gold.

Those trips were special—just me and Alisha, hunting for stories.

When Alisha started buying me new books, I was over the moon.

Mum and Dad had always encouraged my reading, even stuff meant for much older kids. Adults. Women.

I missed our talks about books, the way Dad's eyes would light up when I understood a complex idea, or how Mum would explain things with patience and care.

Our new life slowly patched the holes grief had torn in us.

But I saw how Alisha still looked lost. Sometimes hurt.

The person in the magazine wasn't my sister.

My sister at home was the real one.

Weeks after losing Mum and Dad, she started wearing a smile like makeup—perfect for the outside world, but easily washed away at home.

I watched my sister become a chameleon.

In front of cameras, she dazzled, laughed, and charmed everyone.

She looked like the Alisha I remembered from before-the popular girl from secondary school.

But that Alisha was gone now, replaced by someone who wore her smile like armor.

In quiet moments I held onto her tight.

When the cameras turned off, Alisha's shoulders would droop. She juggled her new life and taking care of me, and I worried she might drop something—or herself.

American school was hard.

I didn't fit in, didn't know how to make friends. I did well in classes, but felt like a ghost drifting through the halls.

All I wanted was to go home to Alisha, to our little sanctuary where I didn't have to pretend to be okay.

A year into our new life, Alisha introduced me to Gemma Marchand.

She was like a real-life princess. Blonde, gentle, with a voice like wind chimes. Opal eyes and dazzling. Gemma was a princess. You could not convince me otherwise.

Alisha had met her at some glitzy event.

I remember thinking Gemma looked kind, and hoping she might be a friend for Alisha. Someone to have in our lives.

My sister needed someone to smile with, not just for.

Alisha and Gemma quickly became fast friends, despite Gemma's soft-spoken and shy nature. I liked Gemma a lot.

When Alisha invited her over, I'd peek around corners, curious about this fairy-tale princess who made my sister laugh genuinely again.

Gemma always noticed me, inviting me to join them with a gentle smile that made me feel seen.

Gemma's visits were like surprise parties—sporadic but always exciting.

She'd sweep in with arms full of gifts, clothes and trinkets that made me feel special. I found out Gemma didn't work but she was an heiress and she had money from her family. But Gemma didn't act spoiled.

If she hadn't said anything I couldn't even tell Gemma was… wealthy. In turn, she quietly snuck in things into our house and helped Alisha and me without Alisha really knowing.

If my sister left sometimes late at night? Gemma would come over and she'd order groceries, sometimes she'd bring a nice kettle or something she'd find.

Gemma began to fill in the gaps Alisha couldn't fill all on her own.

Being a Mum and a model were hard jobs.

So I learned to lean on Gemma for everything.

My secrets.
My dreams.
My aspirations.
I talked to Gemma about everything.
And in turn our little family grew a bit more.

AVANI

FIFTEEN YEARS OLD

I was fifteen when I realized I had a *crush* on Matteo 'Teo' DuPont.

Alisha was on her final year with EllaBeauty and the CEO of the company Maxine DuPont's son was Matteo.

Alisha didn't work with him, but Teo was a particular kind of man and I felt flutters I didn't quite understand.

Teo *liked* Alisha. He would flirt shamelessly with Alisha, his eyes dancing with mischief as he showered her with compliments. Alisha would laugh it off focused on her work. I didn't think my sister even saw men.

I had met Teo when I was *maybe* thirteen.

He'd shown up, a gaggle of women fawning over him and I'd been curious about the most stunning man I'd ever seen.

Teo felt like something out of one of Mum's romance novels as I got older and so did my crush on him grow.

He was a *character*; devastatingly handsome, outrageously charming with inky black hair and alien aqua blue eyes, his pupils rimmed in black. Quite frankly, *nobody* in this world compared to Teo DuPont.

He was a dashing hero in my eyes. He swooped in on his horse and I was a princess. And I had the *biggest* crush on him.

Teo was so much taller than anyone in the room, a lean strapping man as Mum would say. Dressed polished. When he entered a room, it was like all the air was suddenly charged with electricity around me.

I forgot how to breathe.

I'd watch, half-hidden behind a book or a corner, studying the way he moved, the cadence of his voice, the effect he had on everyone around him. On me.

Other women noticed Teo.

The gaggle of them always around him. But Teo saved his flirtations for Alisha, and he was unfailingly polite to me.

"So this is your sister," he said to Alisha. "I've heard about you."

He held his hand out to me with an easy grin. *No, I'm a sweaty monster. Don't touch me.* But I took it feeling electric.

I sputtered as I took his hand mumbling something at Alisha's side.

"I try to bring her whenever I can," Alisha was saying as he held my hand with his really nice smile. I blinked a few times a little stunned. He winked.

I may have died that day.

I could not remember a single thing after that.

I tucked myself into Alisha's side for the night aware he was laughing at something she said. They got along well. I got the feeling he rather liked her.

Which…shouldn't have made me jealous.

Because I wanted someone like Teo DuPont to focus on me.

But I was too young.

His "Hello, Avani" never failed to send my heart racing.

But I couldn't speak around him. I was inept.

Bumbling through my conversations with those eyes of his on me.

And then there had been that one time Alisha had been doing the shoot. She had a crowd of people around her and focused on the cameras.

One of the older men had come up to me and offered me a drink.

"Did you want to go out to the back? We have comfy couches and seats?"

Well, that sounded nice. But Alisha would worry.

"I'm sorry, my sister wouldn't be happy." I shook my head at his drink. "I'm all right. No, thank you."

"Come on," he said. He was older, at least college aged. "It'll be fun. I'm sure your sister won't mind." He tugged on my arm.

I took a step back and straight into a wall made of steel.

16

I looked up not remembering a wall where I had been to a stone-faced Teo, eyes a little terrifying as he glanced at the other man. Those aqua eyes of his normally were playful and right now? They were gleaming in the dark lighting at the other man who swallowed nervously.

"Mr. DuPont."

Both of his hands came to my shoulders resting there as he watched him.

"Can I come to?" He asked him, his eyes looked a little crazy. "I have a thing for comfy couches." His fingers tightened on my shoulders pulling me into his chest.

His cologne in my lungs made it hard to think but I had never noticed it until that moment, Teo was a little scary.

His lips tipped up in a grin but this time it didn't look polite.

Not with his canines out. He looked devious.

"Where did you think you'd take her?"

I turned my head to the man who sputtered and made up some excuse as Teo looked downright livid.

"I suggest you pack your thing," he said softly. Over the hum of everything as he pulled me into his arms. "And leave."

His eyes never left the other man who stumbled off looking nervous as another woman frowned at him.

They were talking as I turned to Teo who looked ferocious now.

And hot.

I was dying a little. I was fifteen.

Not completely unaware of men. Especially not when I'd crushed on him forever.

A blonde woman rushed up to Teo and he said something in vicious French before she rushed away to do his bidding.

And then finally he looked at me. With a smile that made him look like the Teo everyone knew.

"Don't drink that, little love," Teo had taken it out of my hand. "I'll stay right here if you don't mind?"

I shook my head speechless and a little unaware of what exactly was happening. I didn't think the other man was being mean to me.

But Teo clearly didn't like him.

He kept his arm around me as he got on his phone, texting, calling, doing his work he said.

He was saying all types of things about car parts to someone named Andrei who he sounded almost playful with.

I got that he was there for Alisha—but for a moment he had been there—for *me*.

Nobody approached me again during the day.

Alisha eventually finished her shoot and sat on the other side of me. "How's it going? Is everything all right?"

I nodded slowly explaining to her about the guy and the drinks and how Teo had been sitting here.

She paled as I spoke and clearly Alisha felt the same way Teo did. She immediately hugged me to her.

"I'm sorry, I didn't see it. I'm glad Teo was here. I told him you'd been coming to my photoshoots and he wanted to drop by…now I got it. Was that the first time that man spoke to you?"

I didn't understand the big deal. I nodded.

"And the last," Teo hung up his phone call looking annoyed and rolling his eyes. "If you need someone to watch her, I can take her to the office I have in the building. Or Andrei's, he has a library she might like."

Alisha bit her lip considering it. "It's just his office?"

"You two can come see it, but it won't be anywhere near these people."

Alisha agreed when we both viewed how private it was.

It was a study tucked away from everything.

Teo explained why he wanted me here from now on and he showed me around.

"The door locks from the inside, the only way to get in is with a code."

He gave it to me and Alisha saying if I wanted to do my homework, it would be more secure.

He gave his secretary directions to get me snacks whenever I came by and Alisha and I marveled a little at him helping us.

While they talked, I wandered around Andrei's study.

It was secluded and private because he liked his personal space.

It was a dream for me and beautiful all emerald and glittering with sapphire detailing. Silver armchairs and throw pillows. Touches of feminine everywhere.

Teo said nobody came in here because Andrei had a temper.

And nobody wanted to touch his things. Andrei was his older brother.

So he let me use it whenever Alisha had to come to do anything, she could drop me off at the study and go about her day. Like…a secure babysitting spot.

As Teo and Alisha talked I felt the full weight of my teenage years, achingly aware of how young and inexperienced I was. I didn't want a secure babysitting room.

But Teo assured me it was the safest place for me to let Alisha do her job.

It wasn't like I could glue myself to Teo.

Even if I would.

In a heartbeat.

Teo represented a world I could only imagine, full of sophisticated parties and easy confidence.

A world where Alisha belonged, but where I felt out of place.

But he protected me and I swear I *loved* Teo DuPont.

Because while part of me reveled in these new, confusing feelings, another part felt guilty for having them at all.

Wasn't I supposed to be focused on my studies?

On making Alisha and Mum proud?

But try as I might, I couldn't quite squash the little thrill I felt whenever Teo was around, nor the way my eyes would seek him out in a crowded room.

It was my first real taste of attraction.

Alisha always laughed off Teo's advances, but I noticed how her eyes would go distant because I found out my sister had a crush on someone else.

Later on I learned his name–*Reed.*

A man.

Sis had a crush.

I overheard her telling Gemma about him, my curiosity piqued by the softness in her voice. By her interest. Because Alisha never showed interest, my sister had focus—drive—and none of it was for a man.

The only person I knew Alisha had a crush on was that guy in a British boy band.

Not…this man.

Reed.

When I asked Gemma about it, she confirmed Alisha's crush but added that my sister wasn't interested in dating.

A knot formed in my stomach.

"Is it because of me?" I blurted out, voicing a fear I hadn't even admitted to myself. "Is she embarrassed—"

Of having a pseudo child to take care of?

"No," Gemma cut me off, her opal eyes fierce. She pulled me into a hug, and to my surprise, I felt tears welling up.

"Not at all. How could anyone be embarrassed by you?"

I melted into Gemma's embrace, realizing how much I'd needed this—not just the hug, but the reassurance.

Gemma held me, rubbing my back soothingly.

"I think your sister is just a little shy," she murmured. "like you when it comes to everyone else."

"But maybe one day she'll be with him?"

Gemma laughed. "I don't think Reed would let anything stop him from what Lara says."

Lara was another friend of Alisha's and she was how Reed and her met. Gemma told me a little about it and told me not to ask Alisha because it might freak her out.

"You'll keep all my secrets, Gem?"

"Darling, they are all my secrets as well as yours. I would never."

"And you pinky promise you won't tell Alisha how I feel?" I felt guilty for keeping things from Alisha but I didn't want to hurt her.

Gemma locked pinkies with me. "I will never tell Alisha about your secrets. Unless it hurts you? And even then I will find a way to help you myself."

AVANI

FIFTEEN YEARS OLD

It was one day when I was reading in the study on one of the couches curled up with a blanket, two people stormed into the room.

Teo said only his family had the code so I ducked behind the couch so they wouldn't see me.

I had gotten taller over the years so I was hoping they wouldn't see me as I ducked.

"Are you fucking kidding me?" A man roared shutting the door.

"Stop freaking out! Nobody saw it!" It sounded like a boy. A younger man. I didn't dare peek. I hid behind my oversized book.

"Fifty thousand people saw it! It was blowing up on the internet before Teo got a hold of it!"

"Nobody will remember it tomorrow."

And then I heard the sound of something slamming. I winced at the sound of a groan.

"You listen to me right now," the older man growled. "Talia and I are done with your bullshit—"

"Surprise, surprise."

"I'm sending you to Cape Verde—"

"What—"

"I am fucking done."

"Andrei—"

"Absolutely not." Andrei growled. "I have *tried*! I have tried for

21

years! Skipping school, drag racing, dropping out, beating up those kids, Thierry! *Get a fucking hold of yourself!*"

Goodness this boy sounded...*adventurous.*

Thierry?

My eyes were wide listening to this unfold.

Whoever Thierry was...he was a bit of troublemaker as Mum would say.

"*But making a sex tape with a woman you don't know, when she was going to blast it to the world—*"

Heavens. I take it back. He's wild. Reckless. Dangerous.

"*She thought I was Teo!*"

Teo? Why would they—Good. Heavens.

Andrei DuPont is Teo's brother. Older brother. Which makes Theirry also his sibling.

"*That doesn't make it any better!*" Andrei roared. "*I'm done, Thierry. I am done trying to fix your fuck-ups. I have given you everything from day one—*"

"*I never asked you to!*"

"*AND THERE IT IS,*" Andrei did a lot of shouting. "*There it fucking is.* Do you wish I left you in Vancouver with *Tasha and her pimp? Is that what you want! Say the fucking word! I will send you back to hell so fucking fast you will never see the light of this place again. I saved you. I got you out when Phillipe didn't care. Tasha was going to sell you at any rate. And this is what you do? Do you have any idea how fucking hard I worked to make sure Maxine didn't know who you were?*"

Thierry was quiet.

"You *just* landed on Maxine's desk. I keep trying to pretend you're Teo! And now she's wondering why her fucking husband's illegitimate child is wandering around Manhattan masquerading as Teo! *Do you understand the position you put me in? Of course not, because you don't think beyond yourself. That's how you've gotten through life—*"

"*I did think—*"

"When?" Andrei roared. "*When the fuck did you think!* When did you think about telling me! *That video got sent to Maxine! I spent years keeping secrets from my mother to protect you!* And now she knows you exist! Do you understand what the fuck that means? I am now at war with my family! Not for Talia, my fucking wife! Out of all fucking things I thought it would be for my *wife. But it's for you! And you don't even care!*"

22

He let out a breath. "You are no longer in high school. You're a drop out as of today. The school granted me a GED for you. Since you barely made it." Andrei's voice was like a serrated knife cutting into me. Into Thierry. "Talia will take you out of the country—"

"Andrei—"

"Not a fucking word!" Andrei shouted and I cringed. "I am done! You are now the newest Talon recruit. And you will obey every single fucking command out of my wife's mouth. And if I so much hear a fucking word come from you about anything—Talia will take care of you. *You* wanted a new life. *Now* you got one. I refuse to sell your soul off to Tasha, so you have my wife instead. Pack your things. You leave with Talia at the end of the week."

Andrei sounded downright horrifying.

Talon recruit?

"Are you fucking serious?"

"Deadly."

"Andrei—"

"I am done. You just pushed my plans for the next three years into three hours! I am fucking done with you! I might've not been the best father in the world—*but I was a hell of a lot better than fucking Phillipe!*"

It was so quiet I didn't breathe. I just held my breath.

But I could feel the suffocating energy in the room since I didn't think either one of them knew I was here.

I didn't even breathe.

Someone took a breath. And then I heard footsteps towards the door and someone else walked out.

Someone was still here.

I sincerely prayed it was not Andrei. Something told me he wouldn't be pleased with finding me here.

I hid deeper into the couch hoping they wouldn't know. But now I was stuck here. *Drat.*

How on Earth did I get myself into this?

As I hid under my book, covering my face my neck prickled a little, a shiver chasing down my spine as I slowly lowered it curious about who was still here.

And a pair of vibrant electric blue eyes stared back at me.

They were clearly DuPont eyes blinking wide eyed and confused at me.

I screamed terrified falling off the couch. "Ahhhhhh!"

"Ahhh!"

"Why are you screaming?" I sputtered.

He jumped back swearing in shock those eyes eerily brighter than Teo's and the pupils rimmed in a black that made them stand out.

"Who the fuck are you?"

I held the book out like a weapon.

He looked confused at the book weapon thing. "What the fuck are you doing here? How did you find this room?"

I took in the taller man with wild black hair and wilder eyes taking me in.

"I was here! Already!"

"Who the fuck. Are. You?"

Except I couldn't speak. I was frozen after scrambling up, chest heaving and terrified.

He looked livid as I saw the understanding dawn in his eyes that I had heard the deeply personal moment.

I didn't know what to say. It had been a bad moment.

That's all it was. Oh, good heavens.

This was horrifying.

And now I was stuck here with this…Thierry.

This has to be him.

He looked closer to my age than the older voice and he looked like a young Teo. Prettier. Sharper features. Inky hair. Leaner.

In a ripped shirt and black jeans that had seen better days.

I held the book to my chest covering it.

"Are you one of Teo's girls? Who sent you?"

He was furious with me and I stumbled back into the shelf of books as he advanced. Scrambling backwards I hit the other wall.

"Wait. Stop running! I won't hurt you."

He seemed to catch himself clearly chasing me around the library. Where I was trapped. With this…wild creature of a boy.

Oh goodness.

I didn't know Teo's family used this room. He said Andrei rarely came by. Clearly he did when Thierry was here.

I was debating how to get out of here. In one piece.

"I'm sorry, I was reading here. Teo said I could use the room. I didn't know you guys would—" I cleared my throat as I almost choked on my words. "I won't say a word."

When I opened my mouth his eyes widened a little, eyebrows

24

shooting up. He frowned a little looking like he was struggling with himself. Slowly, I began inching towards the door.

I could get out. I needed to. I felt my heart racing and I needed to leave this man.

"Wait!" I froze.

His tone softened a little as he watched me curiously. "How did you know about this place…"

"Teo." Small answers. That's how I'd get by.

"You're fucking my brother?" He looked confused. "You look way too young. No fucking way you're legal—"

"*What!*" I was horrified. Offended. *"Do you think just because your brother lent me the library that I would sleep with him?"*

"*No—*"

"Why would you think that—"

"No, I didn't—"

Thierry's brows rose again and a smirk tipped his lips.

"What? Why are you staring at me like that?"

He blinked a little smiling a bit more. "You're angry."

"Indeed. And YOU are a scoundrel." I had heard as much.

"I don't know what the fuck that is, but I bet I am."

He didn't sound the least bit upset.

Well, a scoundrel wouldn't be upset. He'd be delighted.

"It's an…unsavory person. A rogue if you will…" he looked confused. "A bad example."

My eyes darted toward the door wondering how I could get out of the room.

An elegant black brow arched. "That so?"

And then he *moved.*

His long legs eating up the distance quicker than I thought possible until he was in front of the door. *Drat.*

"I'll tell you what, I'll let you out of here on one condition."

"Bloody hell."

His grin grew wider.

"You're a scoundrel."

"Ah," he smiled wickedly, electric blue eyes twinkling now on me the more he looked at me. "That I am. But seeing as you aren't getting out of here, you either give me your name. Or you kiss me. One of two. And I'll letcha go."

What?

"What?" Ohhhh, I despised being English. I sounded like a fish.

His lips tipped up on his wickedly handsome face at my shocked expression. Even if he was a younger version of Teo—just too pretty for my eyes—I didn't want to kiss *him*…

Except I watched him a little aware it was either tell him my name.

Or kiss him.

"My name. Or…why?"

"Because you're cute." He grinned. "If ya kiss me, I'll letcha pass."

Surely it couldn't be that easy. I couldn't just give the man my name. He would know me then.

"Promise…"

"I promise." His smile was all teeth and he didn't take his eyes off me.

But if I told him my name…he would know about Alisha…and he might tell Teo. Or someone else. And I didn't want to be caught with *him*. "Aren't you *already* in trouble?"

His grin never dropped. "I'm having a *blast*."

Even if he didn't look it. I heard that conversation. Drag racing…a pornstar…this man was wild.

Wild.

This man was *dangerous.*

"How old are you?"

"I'll tell you if you kiss me," he raised a brow. "Or your name."

He said it like it was a secret.

"Seventeen or eighteen?"

"Seventeen." He looked impressed. "What are you? Sixteen? How'd you know?"

"Lucky guess," I whispered not lucky at all. He didn't look much older than me. Kiss him. Or…tell him who I was. "And I might be."

I was fifteen but turning sixteen *eventually.*

Did it count? He looked thoroughly devious as I said it.

I didn't think so.

But I'd never kissed a boy before. I'd never even dated.

"You'll let me go…if…"

He looked like a cat that got the canary. Devious man.

He hit the door code unlocking it. "It's all yours."

I hesitantly approaching him. His eyes dropped to the book. "You're not gonna hit me with that…are you?"

"Should I?"

"No. Put the book down." I don't know. I held it at my side.

26

"What if you hurt me?"

"I might be a scoundrel but I would never." He looked almost offended at the thought. "Andrei is going to be back eventually looking for me and I don't think you want to get on his bad side after what you heard."

He was a sly man.

And there it was.

Even if he was pretending to be cool and calm. Collected. He wasn't. He looked almost embarrassed. Ashamed.

It softened his eyes more and his features as I saw…I knew something about him.

"Do you want to kiss me so you *think* you have something over me?"

His smile was back. "No, I want to kiss you because you're pretty. And your accent's sexy when you're all pissed off."

"Goodness. You're quite forward."

"Damn straight." I caught a flash of white as he watched me. "So what'll it be?"

I took a shuddering breath. One.

Another. Another.

Another.

I approached him slowly. I could make it up. I could lie.

Tell him my name was *Amelia* or something ridiculous and leave.

Run. Act like I never saw him. But I wasn't a good liar.

Nor had I ever been kissed. I didn't know if I wanted this rogue to be my first kiss.

The words felt trapped in my throat.

He's leaving the country. What if you never see him again?

Then nobody will know.

"My name's…*Amelia*…"

My inner voice applauded me.

Good effort. Maybe he won't know.

Amelia is a good average name. I could be an Amelia. Did I look like an Amelia? That was a good name. Right?

He blinked. Several times.

A droll expression on his face.

I thought he'd let me go. Let me out. I was terrible at lying and even Alisha teased me about it.

And then he snorted as though I'd said something funny.

"Nice try, but you're a shitty liar," and I caught a flash of his grin, dimples on his cheeks, before he hauled me up to him. And then he stamped his lips over mine.

A noise left me as his mouth moved over mine. Hot. Urgent. Claiming. I gasped at the way he moved, his hands in my hair holding my face as he devoured my mouth.

Good lord, this was *kissing*?

This was...*quite* difficult. How did one breathe? I could see how he'd done porn. I could see it. I could feel it. Oh my word.

I was going to implode.

How was I supposed to breathe through this? Breathe.

One two three. Breathe.

He drew back a little, his eyes a little too bright as he watched me.

"Easy, mon cœur …let me in. I won't bite. Slowly…" and this time when he pressed his mouth over mine, I melted at the contact.

So soft. I wanted to cry a little at it because it unleashed something in me this time. Slower. Softer kisses from him.

Until I was all but trembling in his arms.

It went on for what felt like forever.

I held onto him as his hand threaded through my hair, undoing the pin in it, undoing the locks and running his hand through them. He tugged gently tipping my hair back making a softer noise.

I can see why women lost their minds over him if he kissed like this all the time.

"Tell me your real name," he breathed. "It's not Amelia."

"You promised." I whispered feeling a little out of it.

Was he going to kiss me again? I didn't mind.

You are a scoundrel as well.

I eyed the door. His throat worked and for a moment I wondered if he'd keep me here. And not let me go.

My eyes went wide at that prospect, my heart racing.

He looked like he was struggling with himself.

"I did promise," he murmured with a sigh looking upset with himself. "But see…I don't keep any of my promises."

His eyes held a different weight to them as he said it.

My heart sank a little. At that my eyes watched him feeling something else around him. Something akin to fear as my heart began racing.

"What a good day to start then?"

His lips tipped up higher, the glint in his eyes returning.

Alisha...I think I kissed a dangerous man.

I'm sorry.

And something shifted between us he watched me.

My lower lip wobbled a little as I bit down on it. His eyes immediately softened. He looked away swearing a little.

"I fucked up. Big time, Amelia. This is probably the last you'll ever see me. I have to go now. Why can't I take something like you with me? Someone normal."

What was he talking about?

He looked playfully at me.

"See, you give me those big soft doe eyes, I might do something stupid and give you everything. And then what? I end up in trouble again?" He brushed my hair back and his lips moved across my forehead. "Fuck, you're pretty. You're a model, aren't you? Downstairs. Where the shoot is. Is that why you're hiding?"

"I'm not hiding." What on Earth was he going on about? "I read here."

"I can see that." His eyes went dark at the sight of my book still in my hands. They met mine again. He reached behind him and without looking unlocked the door. "You're free to go. You won't tell me your name?"

I shook my head. *No.*

"So you're not a model."

No.

"But you visit?"

Yes.

"From the UK?"

"Please let me go."

He released me and I should've stumbled back but I saw something on his face. Something I couldn't...I didn't know.

"Good luck on your...adventure." He was leaving the country.

His smirk was back. "You don't come here often, do you?"

Thankfully. No.

He stepped out of the way as I stared back at the door. I handed him my book, historical romance with an adept cover.

"Thank you."

"For what?" His smile was back. "For being your first kiss?"

I gasped as he chuckled. *"Oh come on—"*

"You're a rogue!" I opened the door before dashing out feeling his laughter tickling my neck as I did.

I tore off into the hallway, racing down the stairs of the building seeing his grin as I did from above.

"Tell me your name, Amelia!"

I laughed covering my mouth as I ran away.

I had to find Alisha. I finally did in a room to herself with Gemma out of all people.

"How was the library, darling?" Alisha asked as I rushed to hug her.

"Fine," I squeaked, my fingers brushing over my lips. When we got to the cab I brushed my hair back for my mother's hair pin.

Frantically, I brushed it some more, but it wasn't there.

"What's wrong?" Alisha looked over. "Did something happen?"

I shook my head. "No…"

I lost it? I lost Mum's hairpin.

It was my *favorite*.

Where would I have—a memory of Thierry's hands in my hair floated to the surface. He had his hand tucked behind his back.

He stole my hair pin.

I covered my face. *"He's a pirate!"*

"Who?" Alisha looked confused.

"Nobody."

A shameless pirate.

AVANI

SIXTEEN YEARS OLD

For a while I forgot all about Thierry.

Although, I didn't forgive him for stealing my Mum's hair pin.

But life moved on when Alisha never went back to the DuPont's and decided to pursue her own thing.

She had more money than ever now. Investing it back and doing so many deals.

She was rising up on Instagram as one of the most followed bloggers for the year I turned seventeen.

After Alisha ended her contract for EllaBeauty, she and Gemma collaborated to launch a charity.

They named it the Poppy Project, in homage to Mum and Dad, who had always been dedicated to helping others.

She firmly believed that education was the key to improving the world.

Though she was still widely recognized, her focus shifted.

Thanks to her hard work, she had amassed enough money to support us comfortably, even investing in various ventures with Gemma's guidance.

I learned that Gemma's family was wealthy, though she did not get along with them.

As I turned sixteen, I found myself becoming friends with Gemma as well.

As I neared the end of secondary school, I was growing used to experiencing the perks of Alisha's fame.

While she hesitated to feature me on her social media, I quietly enjoyed the luxuries that came our way.

With Alisha's career flourishing, PR packages flooded our doorstep, each filled with glamorous products that seemed surreal to me.

"It's just free stuff people give you because they think you're beautiful?" I was amazed, tearing open boxes alongside Alisha.

She grinned, her eyes lighting up. "It's amazing. Look at all this shampoo and snacks."

"These boxes are strange. This one has a vacuum that sings when it's done," I joked, delighting in our shared amusement.

Despite Alisha's hectic schedule, she always made time for dinner with me, ensuring we never lacked food.

However, there were times when she forgot to restock groceries, prompting me to use her credit card to pick up essentials.

And I realized it was because of who my sister was and her friends that I hated going to American high school.

High school was a daily exercise in feeling out of place.

The hallways buzzed with chatter about pop culture I didn't understand, filled with inside jokes I wasn't part of.

I felt like a leather-bound classic accidentally shelved in the teen magazine section—technically present, but glaringly out of place.

The classes themselves were a different kind of frustration. Back in England, I'd been challenged, and pushed to think critically.

Here, it felt like I was wading through shallow waters, longing for the intellectual depths I'd known before.

I'd raise my hand, eager to discuss the deeper implications of a history lesson or the subtle themes in a novel, only to be met with blank stares or, worse, eye rolls from my classmates. I didn't fit in.

I hated it.

Lunch was a minefield of social anxieties.

I'd sit alone, nose buried in a book, acutely aware of the laughter and camaraderie at other tables.

Sometimes I'd catch snippets of conversations about parties or dating, topics that felt as foreign to me as if they were speaking another language.

To escape the social challenges, I buried myself in books, racing through classes and taking on more than necessary to hasten my departure.

Alisha, ever supportive, encouraged me to pursue my dreams, mirroring her own ambitious journey.

She took pride in my academic achievements, displaying my exams and papers proudly on the fridge.

During her extended shoots or travels, a babysitter would drop by until I turned sixteen.

By then, having navigated the American school system for several years, I felt independent enough not to need one.

Despite my academic success, I struggled with the lack of rigor in American schools compared to what I was accustomed to in England.

While I breezed through my studies, I found myself disconnected from my peers and the school environment.

I found solace in Alisha's circle of friends.

There was Gemma, with her quiet elegance, and Sonya Amin, whose beauty was captivating.

Another woman was Lara Ford, a burlesque dancer who fascinated me with her confidence and unconventional lifestyle.

Together, they formed an eclectic group whose professional lives seamlessly blended with their personal camaraderie.

Gemma stood out among Alisha's friends as my favorite.

Her quiet demeanor resonated with my own, and she always gave me hugs.

When Alisha was away, Gemma often stayed with me, a comforting presence even in silence, allowing me to simply be in her company.

I found it easy to talk to Gemma, unaware of her wealthy background until her name began appearing in news and internet gossip columns.

But her status as an heiress didn't change how I felt about her; she was still just Alisha's friend to me.

By sixteen, I was on a path to graduate early, preparing for exams at what Americans called AP levels to earn university credits.

This meant I would enter university as a sophomore, a step closer to fulfilling my goal of following Mum's path as an English professor specializing in nineteenth-century romantic literature.

Mum's love for romance had infused our parents' marriage with a depth of emotion that I longed for.

The kind of man my Dad was for her.

The kind she had talked about like he was her entire world. Her home.

Mum and Dad had fallen in love through love.

And together when they'd had me and Alisha, I felt like they'd given so much of that love. I wanted my sister to be happy.

That year, Alisha withdrew more into herself, rarely going out save for Lara's club more as a promoter than anything else. One evening I noticed a change.

A gentleman dropped her off at home one night.

Though I didn't see him, I heard their conversation.

"Sis, who was that?" I asked, peering over my textbooks, trying to sound casual.

Was it Reed?

Alisha's cheeks flushed as she brushed off my question, but I caught the spark in her eyes.

She liked him. It was the first time I'd seen that look in ages.

But when she stepped in, she looked at me and my pajamas that had gotten a little short.

I had shot up in height a little taller than Alisha by three inches. And my body was changing.

Alisha bit down on her lip asking if I would want to go shopping this weekend. I would.

I loved going shopping with her.

The next day she took me to a lingerie store for a fitting as she called it.

"Thirty-four E," the saleswoman announced.

I gaped at Alisha, who simply nodded and began selecting bras.

They were nothing like the practical cotton ones I was used to—these were works of art, adorned with lace, petals, and delicate butterflies.

Alisha described them as corseted, cropped padded bras with thicker straps I'd be comfortable.

I realized I'd inherited more than just Mum's love for books; I was curvier than Alisha was. Taller.

Standing before the mirror in one of Alisha's choices, I felt a mix of awe and discomfort.

"Sis, I don't know about this," I murmured, unable to tear my eyes from my reflection.

The girl staring back at me looked...different. Grown-up.

"Do you not like it because you think it looks bad, or because you're afraid of what others might think?" Alisha asked gently. "Not that anyone will see this save for a boy one day. Some day…"

I giggled at how she wiggled her eyebrows. I never brought anyone home…I didn't even like any boys around me. Alisha knew that. I told her almost everything.

But I pondered her question.

"The girls at school would have a field day if they saw me in this," I admitted.

But part of me, a part I was almost afraid to acknowledge, liked how I looked.

"Darling, you're not wearing these for anyone but yourself," Alisha said, adjusting the straps with care. "It's about comfort, confidence, and yes, feeling beautiful. There's nothing wrong with that."

As Alisha continued to shop, selecting bras, panties, and stockings in various styles, I found myself drawn to certain pieces. A black lace bra made me feel sophisticated.

A soft pink set reminded me of the roses Mum used to grow.

Alisha selected numerous of them with lace and intricate designs.

Some had three-dimensional petals or butterflies-a far cry from the practicality I was used to.

"Shall we get you some fishnets and tights?"

I met my reflection's gaze again, reluctantly acknowledging that Alisha had a point.

Despite feeling vulnerable, there was a certain allure in seeing myself in something that was so pretty and feminine. I felt different.

Better.

Alisha went on to purchase multiple sets of bras and matching panties, along with a variety of tights.

Some were bold in black with intricate patterns, while others were more subdued in dark, solid colors.

She also selected numerous feminine outfits in blush and pink tones, though for school, I opted for what felt safer—a black turtleneck paired with a skirt that, though shorter than I preferred, felt manageable with the new tights and boots.

Alisha affectionately called it my uniform.

As we sat side by side, getting our hair done, I caught glimpses of us in the mirror.

Alisha, effortlessly glamorous, and me—a work in progress, but undeniably changing.

Back at school, my new look didn't go unnoticed.

Boys' eyes lingered a beat too long, their comments ranging from clumsy compliments to things that made my skin crawl.

I hated how their gazes made me feel both visible and invisible at once.

I didn't want their attention, didn't want to date or kiss or do any of the things my classmates whispered about.

Not with the people around me.

Maybe if there was a boy like Teo, someone who was mature and charming and lovely with all that inky black hair…

But there is...

There's Thierry. The pirate.

The rogue. I *remember* him. How could I not?

It had been a year. Andrei had sent him…somewhere with a woman named Talia.

I never told Alisha about my first kiss.

I hadn't kissed anyone since him.

High school boys were weird.

And Thierry was not.

Just a little scary but I liked it.

I did think about him. Sometimes. Often.

I wondered if he was well. Wondered if I should ask Teo if he had an email or phone to contact him. And say what?

Hullo. I'm the girl you kissed. Not to be weird, but are you all right?

As if.

I wasn't anything like my sister.

Cool.

Confident.

Pretty.

But Alisha…

I knew she deserved a lot more than what she gave herself.

Even if the world liked her, my sister kept her wits about her and stayed close to me. We were family.

I was determined to right and make her proud of me.

Alisha was the only thing I had left.

I had missed out on my parents, I never wanted to miss out on my sister.

I would do anything for her.

Anything at all.

PRESENT DAY

CHAPTER 1
THIERRY

"Take the fucking shot, Grim."

Cole Kincade's voice came through my ear-piece.

The cold Minsk air in Belarus was never welcome against my skin as I pressed the rifle to my cheek.

This wasn't my first rodeo.

Not even close.

In the last three years? I had killed so many people. Death was a business where I came from now. And Talia Nash was not an easy teacher.

I dealt in it plenty enough. Dressed in all back, I knew nobody could see me.

If they did, they knew they were dead. My presence meant one of two things—one, they fucked up and they were going to die or two, they were already dead.

I didn't show up for good news or birthdays.

I should've felt at home on the rooftop. I should've been at peace with knowing it was yet another kill.

I felt nothing anymore.

After years of doing this? I hit twenty with a numbing agent across my chest from how many times I had done things that would've made a normal civilian throw up.

A shuddering breath left me as I was looking through my scope from the rooftop of the hotel I was on.

Staring down at the politician on the opposite side of the building. Currently trying to shoot his brother.

I let out an exhale in the twelve degree weather.

I fucking hated Europe in the winter. I hated winter in general. My breath fogged in the frigid air.

I forced my heart rate to slow down as I inhaled and exhaled.

My toes had gone numb an hour ago and now I wouldn't be surprised if Cole had to peel me off the fucking roof himself when I was done.

My target couldn't see me. But I could see him.

In the shadow of midnight I was the grim reaper.

But Cole was my partner on the other side oversight in tech watching cameras, handling surveillance.

He made sure nobody got to me. And in turn I executed everything according to plan.

Or I would. If I could take the shot.

"I swear to God, Grim—"

"I'm *trying—*" I growled. "Target is fighting with his brother—they're too close—"

"Have some fucking confidence," another voice growled. Caleb. Cole's twin brother. The two Aussies were former SAS and solely devoted to tech.

Both of them in my ear meant nothing but a fucking headache for me.

"Shut the fuck up—" I growled.

"Take the fucking shot—"

"You're a fucking pussy—"

I exhaled and turned off the ear piece.

Instead of hearing their voices I heard another in my ear.

In. Out. Breathe.

Breathe.

Breathe.

On your third exhale, take the shot, Thierry.

"I can't," I whispered. "I can't hurt innocents. His brother did nothing wrong."

Her voice appeared in my head. *Alma Nash.*

Current head of Talon. My former mentor. I should've felt something. Anything other than displaced.

My fingers trembled slightly.

I had done this nine thousand times. So why did I feel a calling for something other than this. In the distance, a flash of neon pink went off in another building.

I planted my feet wider. Bracing myself.

Take the shot on your third breath.

Have some confidence. You've done this before.

Several times.

Do not let your thoughts control you.

Breathe.

Take the shot, Reaper.

I exhaled slowly. And on the third exhale—I fired.

"...Hung up on me," Cole was bitching. "That's what he fucking did."

I grinned as I got into the car at his disbelief. My cheeks hurt from the cold and from my laughter. His twin brother, Caleb laughed outright not bothering to hold back either.

"You are distracting as all fuck," I shot back climbing into the SUV as Caleb rolled his blue eyes at me. "I told you I could take the shot I needed *silence—*"

"You could've taken the shot without silence—" Cole sputtered.

"No, I couldn't—"

Yes, I could've. I was good at what I did. *Hence, Reaper One.*

In three years, Talia put me through brutal boot camp. A joke compared to what her father, Malcolm had taught her, but helpful.

I avoided Malcolm Nash like the plague. He didn't like my family because he didn't like his daughter with Andrei.

It didn't take me long to realize why Andrei was so livid.

Nobody knew about him and Talia.

Not Maxine, just me and Teo because Talia was like a Mom to us.

I knew bits and pieces about Andrei's relationship with Talia.

Bits and pieces enough to know—she loved him, he loved her, and her father hated my brother. By default, my entire family.

I had no fucking clue how Talia kept her secrets from him, but it seemed like on paper?

Malcolm trusted Talia enough to believe her. Leave her to her devices.

And I couldn't imagine what she had done to get there.

43

"If you took any longer taking the fucking target out, we'd both be sixty by now." Cole shot back turning around from the passenger side as Caleb, always the driver, took off into the night.

"Shut the fuck up—" I growled feeling irritation.

My headache was back and blossoming behind my eyes. I needed some food and some rest.

Anything to not feel...*whatever* I felt inside of my chest.

"I don't fucking understand how anyone tolerates you in their ear for longer than two minutes. *This* is why Samara tried to murder you in cold blood."

"Twice." Cole smiled as though he was proud for riling up our other team member.

Sitting in the backseat with my rifle I watched Caleb snort.

"Samara would murder anyone in cold blood," Caleb muttered. "She doesn't even need a reason. She'll just do it because she's bored."

"God, I love her bloodthirsty," Cole sighed.

I laughed. "If we tell her you said that she might actually kill you."

"I'd be honored." Cole was smitten. Sort of. I just think he liked her because she was sharp-tongued and lethal.

The entire unit I operated in was broken up into smaller teams.

The other two members of our team weren't out tonight, but that didn't mean anything.

They were handling the other half of the assignment back at the hotel we were in. And the unease was settling into my blood again.

I didn't understand why.

"She get the target yet?" I asked.

Cole started. "Well, if you didn't hang up on me, maybe I would've—"

"She did." Caleb cut in. The older of the two by a solid minute, it showed in his ability to constantly hand Cole his ass on a platter.

The twins were identical, six-feet one, over two hundred some-thing pounds of pure blonde Australia. Save for one thing.

Everything below Cole's neck was completely tatted which how I only knew the difference.

Otherwise?

They were the same person when they needed to be. And Cole might've taken all the personality from Caleb at birth.

I grinned at Cole's expression.

"Why do you two never let me finish?"

"Because you're an idiot." I said it at the same time as Caleb and he shot me a rare grin.

"I am not—"

"Shut up, Cole, it's four in the morning—" Caleb growled. "I'm starting to get a fucking headache from you."

"I'm just saying—" Cole wouldn't shut the fuck up.

I groaned covering my eyes, my cheeks spread in a grin.

I'd met them when I'd joined Talon years ago after Talia had taken me in. Talia was just as scary as she was nice. I'd spent my teenager years running wild and the nine hundred almost-felonies under my belt?

Andrei had gotten fed up and lost it. Talia had offered to train me.

With her family. Natasha, her sister, and their cousin Alma.

In three years? I didn't recognize myself. My first year had been brutal with Talia cutting off sugar and anything bad for me and my ADHD.

I watched the streets pass by as Caleb drove us back.

By the time we got back to the hotel I was tired, but we were flying out tonight. I needed to shower and change and get back to Cape Verde with my team.

Even if I felt that little niggle of something bothering me in the back of my mind.

Even if it was something I couldn't quite put my finger on.

Something I had been feeling for a while as I felt the jostle of the car as I tucked my colder hands into my pocket to feel her.

I just couldn't put my finger on it. The neon pink lights flashed. Butterflies. They couldn't exist here in the cold, so someone turned them into signs. I squeezed around the object in my jacket I carried with me all the time.

I didn't take it out in the car in front of anyone though.

I felt my lips tip up even as I rubbed my chest.

We arrived the hotel adopted our disguises of European college kids and I put a hat on so nobody could even guess I wore contacts to mute out my face.

I always wore brown contacts with the Nash's and this way, nobody knew I was a DuPont, but Talia and her cousin Alma.

I always tucked myself into the shadows so nobody could find me.

"I think that sexy little blonde from earlier is texting me—" Cole stated but got cut off by his brother.

"You mean she's texting who she thinks you are. Remember Alma, doesn't want trouble," Caleb told him eyeing his brother with concern as we walked up casually into the back.

I shook my head at the two of them.

When we'd been younger I had gone through every woman imaginable.

Every. Woman. I. Could. And then something happened to me along the way.

I didn't know what.

I didn't know why.

But everything in my life felt off.

The numbers and letters on the elevator blurred. Nobody texted me because I didn't text.

And even if I felt my limitations weighing on me I was quiet in the elevator as the twins argued about which girl Cole was actually talking to.

They said something about me going with them but I shook my head. Caleb looked at me concerned but Cole dragged him off.

"Be ready to leave!" He shouted. I rolled my eyes walking into my room. The moment I was in the room, my hands drew out something I hadn't been able to throw away ever.

Not once. Not since I got it. For some fucking reason.

I didn't like nice girls. Sweet girls with pretty doe eyes and lush lips. The women I liked were experienced. But I was her first kiss.

I looked down at the pink butterfly hair pin. It looked like it belonged to an older woman when I'd glanced at it.

Not…her. I didn't know her name. Still.

Sure as fuck, wasn't about to start calling her Amelia.

But she was my good luck charm.

I had tucked it into my pocket and kept it that day. It had sat in my bedroom all week before Talia and I left.

Andrei didn't even look at me he was so livid with the war he was in now with his mother. I'd just held onto it the entire time.

Over the years I learned everywhere I carried it, I was safe.

The one time I didn't? I forgot it in my hotel room and I almost got blown up.

Since then, I took *that* pink butterfly clip with me everywhere. I set it on my bedside table aware if I even so much as laid down, she was back.

Sometimes *she* came into my thoughts. Invaded them.

I didn't understand why.

It was stupid. It was just a kiss. Andrei had kicked me out of New York. I shouldn't have thought about her.

But every so often, she snuck into my thoughts. Maybe because she caught me at a bad time because nobody else did.

Maybe because of her sexy voice and insulting me.

The DuPont men definitely had a type.

She reminded me of Talia a little. Giving me attitude. *Lip.* I bit back a grin tucking it into my pocket again.

She was a world away from me now.

And I'd never see her again.

WE MADE IT BACK TO THE TALON COMPOUND WITHIN FORTY-EIGHT hours. Located in Cape Verde, Africa.

Immediately my body sighed at being hit with the sweltering heat.

"Never get used to that heat," he grumbled swearing up a storm. I liked it here. Or I had.

Lately, I didn't like it anywhere.

This wasn't the kind of place civilians showed up in. No.

Not unless they had a death wish.

I didn't know how Malcolm Nash, Talia's father got his start in life, but art security private teams turning into black-ops killers had not been the reality I had been prepared for.

On paper that's what Talon was. Private security. In reality?

It was so much darker.

Once Malcolm had passed control to Talia, the unit had changed a lot, Talia driving a sword through the old guard and revamping the compound to a modern day structure inside an older temple like place.

It was an enormous structure all white stone and fortified. A labyrinth of hallways and bedrooms and split up. On either end were the two towers that oversaw the entire thing.

One belonged to Talia.

The other was empty and sometimes Alma liked to crash there but sometimes she went and kinda did her own thing.

"Carter and the she-devil herself arrived earlier," Caleb muttered to me. "They should be inside."

My grin was quick at the mention of Samara as his she-devil.

Samara wasn't bad per se.

But unlike Talia, Talon was all she had. And she took her job seriously. I didn't have a problem with Samara, but Carter I was partial too.

Bexley Carter was the other half of the IT team, on good terms with Cole and Caleb. The kid was nineteen with way too much potential to be sitting in Cape Verde.

She needed to get out a live a little—even if it felt like she already lived too much.

We barely made it inside before a striking five-eight brunette with her hair pulled into a braid at her back and all black on appeared.

Her outfit and her hair seemed to absorb all the light around her. Caleb muffled his groan into his fist.

"Samara," Cole grinned. Her features were sharp and her dark eyes tip-tilted and feline as she took us in.

"Alma wants you," she motioned to me ignoring him, her voice was low and smooth, with the hint of her English accent.

I wasn't sure where Samara was from but she was definitely mixed.

Nobody here had real identities.

Malcolm had a habit of picking up people who weren't really going to be seen again.

Samara happened to be one of them.

And now, she was Alma's right hand. She spoke for the head most of the time. And Bexley Carter was Alma's little pet. The two girls were closer to her and loyal to a fault.

But I didn't think Samara liked me very much.

I tipped my head to Samara, not because I didn't care to speak to her, my schedule was thrown out of wack, and my headache was back.

Following behind her I watched Cole and Caleb give each other a loaded look as I left.

Those idiots.

48

I always thought while Caleb dreaded Samara, Cole was into the kind of woman who could kill him with a few words.

His eyes lit up whenever he saw her. and right now he was definitely checking out her ass.

I gave him the finger leaving the foyer entirely as we made our way through the hall and I heard a smothered chuckle from them.

"How's Natasha?" I asked her after a moment of silence. Samara didn't want to talk.

Then again, I wasn't her favorite person. I was close to everyone and Samara despised being near anyone save for Alma who she obeyed like God.

"Good."

Got it.

Natasha had been in an accident on one of her assignments.

Her right leg had been injured and she hadn't really recovered fully but I also thought it might've been because of the way Malcolm pushed his girls—she hadn't been able to recover.

She took me up the stairs and into Alma's tower, and motioned for me to head on up without looking at me.

"And Talia?"

"Good."

Got it. End of conversation.

Taking a deep breath I walked up the steps to Alma's space the cooler breeze coming from above letting me know her windows were open.

Inside, the circular room, with white light, billowing white curtains and windows all around—I was momentarily blinded.

Alma was at her perch when I walked in from her seat by the window.

She always liked it there staring at the expanse of sea and the church up ahead in her short white dresses.

I had met Alma years ago when Talia had brought me in as a rowdy teenager and unlike the other Talon operatives who took one look at me and scowled—she had taken me in and been kinder.

She had said I reminded her of her brother who had passed away and she wanted to right by him.

Alma stood to her full five-four and slender self, her black hair flowing around her olive toned body, almond shaped eyes dark and focused on me, long lashes fanning out over her high cheekbones.

She raised an arched brow at me and smiled wide. *Still scary.*

49

I knew Alma had a heart of gold and she was friendly, but Alma was the kind of frightening otherworldly beautiful you had to suspend your reality for. Spooky. Eerie. Downright scary.

The air around her dipped and shifted. Dropping a few temperatures.

But by now I got used to it, her doll-like features highlighted by those dark fathomless eyes.

She was gorgeous in a way Samara wasn't.

But both of them were a little terrifying. Then again, Talia and Natasha were also so I guess that ran in the genes.

"You wanted me?"

She smiled a little. "Sit."

She motioned to her window sill. She often read there and hung out. I didn't know how Alma came to Talon. Only that Talia rescued her like she did the others.

Now Alma was at the top of the pyramid.

"How are you?" She murmured.

Her words had a musical lilt to them and she rolled her r's all the time to my teasing and I figured she might be Latin.

"You don't look so good."

Her eyes watched me carefully.

I resisted the urge to say anything contrary to that. Of course she would know.

"I ask because Talia is not doing good, and I think she needs a break." Alma sat with me and tucked her knees to her chest.

"Not doing good, how?" Now I was worried. Talia was the love of my older brother's life. If anything happened to her? He would burn everything to the ground.

"Not sure…" Alma spoke softly and I heard her out. "Maybe she needs to go see your brother." Alma definitely figured it out when she saw me which wasn't surprising. Talia would tell her about Andrei.

"I can go check on her," I offered. "Andrei would be pissed if anything happened."

She nodded looking out to the sea. "Malcolm will be here in a few days. You need to stay out of his way."

Yikes. That never bode well for anyone.

Not that he was awful. I mean, he was. But nobody could live up to his standards and when he was here?

Alma and I had to pretend to be invisible. Because nobody really knew Alma led the teams. Everyone thought Talia still did.

There were too many secrets across Talon.

And I was one of them.

"If I need you, I'll call." Her eyes met mine searching my face. "You do not look good."

No. I didn't feel good.

But I couldn't put my finger on it.

ONE WEEK LATER, I FELT THE MOMENT SHE WAS IN MY ROOM.

Years of being trained let me know when something was happening. The unease had vanished from days ago, but now it resurfaced.

"Wake up, Thierry. You need to leave."

My eyes opened to Alma in my face.

Dark eyes. Raven hair. Olive skin. Ghostly in the moonlight she looked unreal and frightening in the dark like a wraith appearing.

She had always been a little scary, but tonight more so than ever while jarring me awake.

"You need to take Talia and leave the country. Vamos!"

She was saying something in Spanish I didn't understand.

But then again, I barely spoke proper English with her.

I knew when Alma started speaking Spanish though shit had hit the fan.

Hence, why at three in the morning she was in my room. Talon compound wasn't known for being a place that made noise.

It wasn't known for being the kind of place you freaked out in. No, it was a fortified tower of discretion.

No loud noises. No disruptions.

Years of training kicked in as Alma gripped my face forcing me to focus on her ghostly eerie appearance.

I couldn't deny she was beautiful, but in a way that was a little frightening, with her too sharp features and wild eyes.

"W-what—"

"Malcolm is *dead*. Talia is pregnant. You must take her to Andrei. Tonight. Now."

My brain felt like it was going to explode. *Malcolm was dead? What the fuck? Talia was—Malcolm was supposed to be visiting.*

51

Who killed him?

It was only logical explanation.

"Are you insane?"

Dark, void-like eyes watched me.

When I first met Alma, she made no noise and she was a little terrifying when I got close to her. And it took a lot to scare me.

There was nothing in her eyes.

Like there was no life in them.

Pitch black and I knew anyone who met her in the dark was meeting their worst nightmare. But I loved her as my mentor and the few people in life who knew how to handle me.

The room went frightening arctic.

"Focus. You need to leave tonight—"

"W-why? What?" I was a little dazed. "What do you mean Malcolm is dead? *Who killed him?*"

Alma didn't answer me she just grabbed my face and looked at me with her spooky eyes.

"I told you years ago, if anything happened to threaten your happiness, I will defend it with my life. You are my second chance to do what I couldn't do in my past life. Do not fail me. Take your sister-in-law and leave—tonight. Otherwise, people will die. And one of them will be her."

She didn't need to tell me twice. Alma had told me years ago her loyalty to me was one to Talia, and for her brother who had died years ago.

Alma said I looked just like him and she wanted to right by him.

I nodded dumbly as I leapt up out of bed my head still aching and spinning.

"When am I leaving?"

She tossed me my shirt noticing I was in my briefs.

"Now."

CHAPTER 2
AVANI

"Congrats!"

Alisha rushed at me as I ran to her in my cap and gown, practically lifting me off the ground as she squealed. "Oh my gosh! You did it!"

I'd finally graduated high school.

I grinned ear to ear as she set me down handing me the smashed bright red flowers in her hands.

Alisha's mega-watt smile was infectious.

"I couldn't decide so I just got you all of these," she said as I took the flowers.

"*Sis*," I was struggling to even speak through the sheer joy I felt and the tears in my eyes that blurred my vision. "Love you." She was hugging me tight to her, her own eyes watering.

"Let's get out of here and somewhere nice hm? I got reservations at that lovely chocolate shop you love so much."

I squealed as we headed out past the throngs of parents and their kids celebrating the end of the year.

I had graduated a year ahead of time which was a relief since it meant high school was finally over.

"I cannot wait to eat everything," I said as we got into the cab.

Alisha sighed. "I am starving, when he got to the M's I was so glad our name's didn't start with W, but fear not, darling. I would've waited for you until the end."

I giggled linking my arms with her as we made our way to one of our favorite restaurants themed around chocolate.

"Even if we were the Zapata's?" I teased.

Alisha laughed loudly clapping a hand over her mouth. "Even if we were the Zapata's. But the Zapata's are hungry now."

I giggled into her arms as we went to the restaurant to celebrate.

Alisha had gotten me cake and allowed nothing off limits on the menu. We tried nearly everything.

Coming home with our bellies full and grinning ear to ear.

We passed the guard on the way into the door as he held the door open for Alisha.

I thanked him, an older man with dark eyes and odd skin. Alisha linked her arms in mine as he stared at her and both of us made our way to the elevator.

"Does that doorman ever give you the creeps?" I asked her on the way to our door.

"To be frank, I don't really pay attention," she said. "I feel like everyone stares at me so much I am blind to it."

That made sense.

It was Alisha's job and she had gotten used to pretending like nobody was.

"Aw," Alisha held up her phone. "I texted Gemma about your graduation and she sent this."

It was a photo of flowers she was holding saying she would coming over this weekend to see us.

I grinned. "Gemma's going to outdo you."

"Not possible," Alisha grinned. "But I'd like to see her try."

Gemma did come over a few days later with bouquets of flowers and her weakness—catering.

"Since we have a penchant for burning the house down," Gemma quipped. "I thought some Greek food would be nice?"

Alisha loved Greek food. My Mum would have a conniption if she knew, but Alisha just said it felt better for her.

And if there was anything Gemma brought with her it was always food for us.

"The only thing that would make this better is a six-foot—" Alisha paused looking over at me and I grinned at Gemma.

She was about to say something naughty. She always held back with me. Sometimes I didn't think my sister knew what kind of books I read.

"A good book," Alisha finished. Gemma and I burst into laughter at Alisha trying to stay composed and failing. "You two are awful."

"You're the one who said it," Gemma grinned ear to ear. She sat on our couch looking elegant in her blonde hair and regal bearings only slightly softened by Alisha's decor.

"I'm getting drinks," Alisha looked flustered as she left to the kitchen. "Do you guys want anything in particular?"

"Alcohol!" Gemma and I both shouted.

"Keep dreaming, Avani!" Alisha shouted back and Gemma grinned at me.

"You fight a good fight," Gemma whispered.

I loved having Gemma over. I grew up around her, Alisha and Lara over the years.

When I went to Poppy, Alisha's charity, I spent my days with women or teenagers. But always as Alisha's sister so everyone treated me differently.

"I'm so excited," I told Gemma. "I really cannot wait to start school."

"Do you have any plans this summer?" She asked me taking a bite of her veggies.

"I do," I was excited. "So one of my favorite authors, you know the writer of the House of Midnight and Shadows? She's releasing two new books back to back. One is coming out in two weeks and the other in October. And I wanted to go and try out some new bakeries…" As I talked Gemma grinned wide at my excitement.

"Say," she whispered to me while Alisha got utensils and plates for us. "Would you be open to tutoring a potential student struggling with their English?" What?

I was curious. Gemma knew I tutored some of the kids at Poppy sometimes with their homework.

"I would, when? Is it urgent?"

She smiled. "Not at all. I was just considering it since I believe Teo's younger brother is the one in question and being that your sister is friendly with his family—I thought why not ask you?" Her eyes sparkled a little as she watched me. I was honored. I loved tutoring kids.

"Only if you'd like to, it's not a rush I thought you might enjoy your break for a bit before university but it's something I wanted to ask you. Only if you want to and it doesn't have to be anytime soon," Gemma added.

I did want to take a few days to myself but I let Gemma know a few good dates and times and she texted him.

"Teo has another brother?" I asked hearing Alisha in the kitchen. Did she know?

"He does, but I don't think he's as social as his other siblings," Gemma remarked wryly. "He says he can do in a week in the afternoon..."

I could do that. "And he needs help with English?"

Gemma nodded.

"What's his name?"

"Thierry," she murmured looking at his texts and passing me his number.

I looked down at the contact info.

"His name is Thierry."

I almost choked on my water. "*What?*"

Gemma thumped me on the back. "Oh my gosh, I'm sorry, are you okay?"

"I'm f-fine."

But I was not. Thierry.

There was only a singular Thierry I had met in my life.

"*He what?*"

Gemma's opal eyes blinked at me looking worried as she rubbed my back. "He needs tutoring help. Would it be all right with you? I can completely find someone else but you're closer in age and much more competent than any old fart..." she spoke but I barely heard her.

Thierry?

Thierry DuPont? He needed a *tutor*?

I practically choked out nervously that I would do it, my heart escalating in a nervous drum-beat of anxiety and anticipation at the idea of seeing...him again.

The rogue.

The scoundrel.

"Perfect," Gemma adjusted her blonde hair and smiled wide at me, her eyes sparkling practically. "Now tell me about school...any plans for this summer?"

Apparently just one.

The pirate was back.

56

CHAPTER 3
THIERRY

"Talia, *he's huge...*"

"*He is not. He's normal sized.*"

"...like an extra large normal burrito in this blanket." I grinned down at the baby in my arms. "An *adorable* burrito."

The baby in question was Drew—my nephew. Her and Andrei's son.

As the warm sunlight filtered in through the large kitchen windows of my older brother Andrei's penthouse apartment, Drew's gummy smile lit up his entire face.

He was going to be *enormous.*

I was visiting them today after Talia had settled a little.

Talia rolled her green eyes, brushing back strands of her black hair and sucked her teeth at me as I held my nephew in my arms. She was grabbing some food from the fridge and refueling before she took care of him.

Alexandre Andrei Dupont or 'Drew' for short gurgled in my arms happily so. He was big for a baby. He fit in *my* arms.

At this rate?

He was going to be bigger than his father.

"Don't say that, he's small, but he understands everything. I don't want him to think I don't love him, when I do. Mommy loves you so much, my little pumpkin."

She motioned to Drew who was currently staring at me curiously with wide eyes. At the sound of his mother he turned his head to her and gave her a gummy smile again.

"And he is my baby and I think he's the perfect size for how he is. Aren't you, *sweetie?*"

Drew, who knew his *Maman's* voice chortled and tried grabbing my face again. For the tenth time today.

I grinned at her warming up his bottle as I held him to my chest.

"Do you, little guy? You're probably going to be smarter than your father so that's a relief."

Talia looked away at the mention of Drew's father—Andrei. My oldest brother had turned thirty.

But somehow had lacked the brain cells to know he had to stay close to his pregnant wife when she was giving birth.

As far as I knew?

Talia wasn't talking to Andrei anymore.

At all.

Not after his glorious fuck up *weeks* ago when she'd gone into labor and had Drew early—and Andrei had been out of town.

In another continent.

I had been there with Talia's friend Gemma Marchand.

She had been the one who had been calmer than I had been watching Talia in pain—an experience I would never forget for many reasons.

Thankfully, Teo had been here to smooth it over. For *everyone.*

Including going to fight one hell of an angry Andrei when he did show up stunned and clueless. I just knew my brother was groveling.

Hard.

If I didn't know any better I'd say he was at work juggling my evil step-mother. Again.

And Drew?

Drew was unmistakably Andrei's son.

He had the swath of pitch black hair and the eyes of every DuPont man. A shade of blue not quite bright enough to be true and black rimmed around the edges.

But all of him was subdued with baby fat. He didn't even look like he had knees yet, just dinner rolls for arms and legs.

Adorable.

Even Talia said his eyes were a little eerie but beautiful. It had been part of the reason why she'd fallen for Andrei.

But now? I wasn't dumb enough to mention my brother's name out loud. Not with Talia chopping up some fruit for herself while I cuddled Drew.

A chubby fist reached out and grabbed my lips and he giggled. I grinned down at him.

"Must be nice to be so carefree, hm? Just lay there all day without any responsibilities?"

He gurgled in happiness as I pretended to bite his fingers loving his giggles. He thought everything was funny. Until he didn't. And then he cried and Talia swept in on him with her boobs and everything was calm again. *Easy.*

"All you gotta do is cry and *Maman* is there." The glint in his eyes was back as I grinned down at him. "And you know it too, don't you?"

Of course he did. He was a DuPont. His gummy smile told me all I needed to know as he cooed. Having a nephew was a strange sensation.

Not quite his father but I felt responsible for him.

For his health and wellbeing, making sure he was safe from any harm—and Talia—I had met her as a warrior.

Not as a mother. Not like this. Now?

It was a little surreal as she passed me a bowl of strawberries and chocolate for herself.

I couldn't have sugar. Not with my ADHD.

I would bounce off the walls and careen into New Jersey on sugar.

My other older brother Teo and I both abstained from all things caffeine and sugar.

Otherwise the two of us would just sit down and build a rocket ship at the rate we moved.

"I can think of someone else who's carefree," she eyed me as she passed me the fruit. "Those are for you. Stem-free you big baby."

I grinned. "*Spasibo.*"

I popped one in my mouth as Drew watched me confused.

"Sorry, little guy. All you get is milk. And currently, your *Maman* is recharging."

Talia grinned at me trying to speak Russian with Drew.

I could pick up any language if I wanted to. I was good at memorizing and parroting things back to people. But I lied to Gemma all the time that I couldn't speak English properly.

Talia said something in Russian to me that roughly translated to.

"I'm the size of a cow now."

Talia spoke Russian, some French—thanks to Andrei—and Japanese. I think. She was definitely mixed with every race under the sun.

Her father, Malcolm Nash was a mixture of races, and her late mother was from all over the place.

"You are not the size of a cow."

No. If anything, she looked beautiful with her dark hair in waves, her green eyes brighter on me, and all of her baby weight made her look adorable. Approachable now.

Different than I'd ever seen her but it suited her more.

Drew was a bigger boy. It made sense.

"You look great," I said. "You're still you."

Even as I said it her eyes darkened a little like it upset her.

"Are you upset you gained weight? You had a ninety pound baby —*désolé* Drew, you're still cute—but you are not a *small* baby. It's normal, Talia. Teo and I looked it up."

Drew looked completely unbothered by this. He held out his grabby hands to Talia who looked ready to cry at him.

And I doubted anything could make Andrei stop loving Talia.

They'd been in love longer than I'd known the word.

They were the only thing that kept me calm—like my parents during my tough years.

Her smile was rueful as her eyes shimmered a little. "You two idiots putting your heads together to do pregnancy research is gold."

I shot her a wolfish grin. "We try, sis. We try."

Her sharp eyes turned to me, one elegant brow rising.

"What have you been doing for the last few months besides hiding in that apartment?" She smirked. "You don't think I know you're here avoiding your life?"

Ah. Fuck.

"No," I said keeping my voice light since she knew if I was fucking with her. "I gave birth to him too, I need to see my nephew."

The joke fell flat since let's be real—I hadn't done anything but fuck up.

She burst out laughing. "Oh, you gave birth to him too?"

Drew at the sound of his *Maman* turned his head to aim his smile at her and her eyes softened instantly. And then he did the grabby hands again.

Since becoming a mother I saw a different side to her now. She was so much softer than I knew her and it suited her.

"I was there. I helped."

Sorta. The panic, the helpless sensation of watching Gemma helping Talia. Teo even being more competent than me.

I didn't want to think about it so I switched the subject.

"He still had that new baby smell."

"Speaking of that night," Talia murmured. *Fuck.*

She didn't forget it. Of course, she didn't forget it. Not with her memory. She remembered everything.

My nephew was a few weeks old.

But I didn't forget the night he was born because of one tiny tiny tiny thing.

My disability. In full glory.

"Gemma mentioned she noticed it and I wanted to ask you about it." I bit back a sigh.

I fucking knew someone would notice. It was inevitable even if I avoided everyone.

"Talia—"

"No, I need to say this. I know you're hiding from everyone. You can't hide forever. Have you thought about going back to school? Getting a proper tutor? It's not too late for you."

And just like the years of shame burned in my gut as she said it.

"Resting doesn't count as hiding," I threw in. "Tutors don't work for me."

"They can if you are open-minded and try them out and see if you've changed –"

"*Talia—*"

"You're not fifteen anymore." Her eyes were sharp on me. Green, alluring, and a reminder she had once been deadly. "You can learn again. Especially with not knowing how to fill out paperwork. What happens when you settle down? When you get married?"

I didn't even want to think about ever being with someone.

I didn't even know what kind of a woman would ever manage to do such a thing to me. Even if I had seen Talia and Andrei growing up? Their entire relationship was a black hole of secrets.

I had met her a few years ago after a stunt that got Andrei livid with me.

She'd kicked my ass on until I had gotten so angry and tried to fight back—only to have Andrei step in and brutally kick my ass for even daring it.

You don't ever come at my wife like that.

You come at me first.

Because if she sets you off? You've got bigger problems.

Both of them had whipped me into a shape I didn't recognize over the last few years.

It had been the most emotion I'd seen out of Andrei even when enraged nobody set him off like anything related to Talia.

In the past one errant hair on her head moved and he'd fight the wind if he could. So I didn't know what the fuck happened to them.

"I talked to Gemma about getting you a tutor."

I stopped chewing and looked at Talia straight-faced.

No, she didn't.

"Talia, you didn't." Panic. That's what I felt. I would rather kill two hundred people and go to war on a battlefield than have anyone know what was wrong with me.

"I did." Her gaze was firm. "I can't allow you to slip and fall. I won't. That night was important. And I don't want that to ever happen to you. You need to learn."

It was written all over my face. My stomach turned at the idea of Gemma knowing what was wrong with me.

"Yes, I did," Talia said. "Thierry, you need to move on and do something with your life. School is a great place to start—"

"You talked to Gemma about my—"

"No," she was adamant about this. "I would never tell her about your—"

"Don't even." I covered Drew's ears. "He doesn't know."

Talia rolled her eyes shooting me an exasperated expression. "Thierry. School is good for you. It'll give you an activity. Something to focus your attention on. Besides, Gemma doesn't know and she said she'll check up on you."

Fuck. Just what I needed. My stomach churned and I knew Talia could see it on my face.

"I don't need Gemma Marchand. I can think of a number of activities I would rather do than fu—" I shut my mouth at Talia's glare just as Drew let out an excited noise and then a gurgle.

His eyes met mine as he opened his mouth and closed it again. "Nhhhh."

"What does that mean?" I asked him. I looked up at Talia forcing myself to adopt a lighter tone. "Does he disagree with you as well?"

"I think he's hungry," Talia murmured her eyes warm on him. "Let me drink water and I'll feed him."

"When does Andrei feed him?"

Talia didn't say a word, chugging her water. Got it.

My brother didn't. And it made me wanna choke him out for the way he'd been the last few months.

Since I'd come back with Talia he'd been MIA. She had the best doctors, the best clinics, the best mid-wife and Andrei had been the only thing she hadn't had. I didn't know what happened to them.

I had never seen them like this. I only knew them before.

Back when Andrei and Talia been a team.

Back when nothing could shake them. I didn't know what exactly happened between the two of them.

I didn't even know how to ask.

I felt like I hadn't even seen Andrei since I'd gotten back to New York—Teo was the one who ran around doing damage control for the entire family.

"Gemma means well and so do I." Her eyes met mine. Intelligent green ones that had softened with Drew. "Gemma and I both caught you in the hospital."

The doctor had given me the fucking paperwork and I'd short circuited.

The letters and numbers swam before my eyes. As a Reaper in Talon, I knew how to fight and shoot and take care of anyone. But this?

Words?

Fuck. That. Shit.

"It was one time—"

"You're twenty," Talia's voice was sharp. But soft.

Her eyes darted to Drew and I knew the head of Talon she was required a spine of steel.

It wasn't easy to get to where she was even if her father had given her the spot—she earned it.

And she'd married *my oldest* brother.

On a scale of scary to downright terrifying—Talia was an apex predator in her own right. Part of why she had held her own for years.

And now those eyes were on me.

"You're weak," she murmured. "You need to grow and learn. I taught you enough. So did Alma. But our training doesn't benefit you in this world. If you cannot hold your own." And those words stung. "I think you need something with purpose in your life. Otherwise you're going to lose your mind," she countered picking up some chocolate and coming over to hold Drew. "You need to learn a new set of skills if you're going to make it. And one them, is learning how to read better."

Her eyes met mine as she stood in front of me. "I don't care what your brothers told you or your tutors. Dyslexia isn't anything to be ashamed of—" she said it.

She fucking said it.

"You will fail in this new reality if you do not adapt. And I'm telling you—adapt. When was the last time you did anything that involved not working out or avoiding social interaction?"

Since I left Talon. My throat worked.

Talia was always known for giving it to me straight. She had been raised that way.

Alma was like her too but softer about it.

But neither one of them had given me a second to adjust to the reality of no longer being a Reaper.

One second I was *Reaper One?*

And the next Alma and Natasha had me take Talia back to the city, and that niggle of something akin to relief had blossomed under my skin at not having to live that life anymore.

I don't know why.

It shouldn't have.

I should've felt upset and like I lost something. But after a few years of Talon—I had gotten tired too. Exhaustion seeping into my bones.

Leaving me hollow and aching for something.

Like I was craving something more. Beyond that life. I just didn't know what.

I don't know *why* I felt like that.

I was twenty. I had my entire life ahead of me.

It had ben months since I faced the truth that I wasn't going back to my old life. Not since my entire life had been upended.

Not since Alma's voice rang in my head.

I didn't do right by you in the past. I'm going to do right by you now. I am setting you both free. Leave. Do not come back to Talon. Ever.

Because Alma who hadn't wanted to be the head of Talon knew the darkness we lived in.

And in one full swoop—my team, my life, my everything—was upended. And I wasn't even angry. Shouldn't I have been angry?

I didn't know.

"What's gotten into you? Why are you afraid of your future?"

Talia's eyes were soft on me breaking me out of reverie as she stood in front of me her hands out stretched for her baby.

She'd looked like she'd been standing there a while.

"Drew's had your finger in his mouth for the last ten minutes and you've been so lost in your thoughts?"

I looked down and sure enough, Drew gave me a gummy smile that said 'guilty' with his eyes.

He had the DuPont mischievous look down pat.

Andrei's got his hands full.

But Talia was watching me with an expression that I knew. She was plotting.

"I'm fine."

I didn't mean it. But it was all I could say to her. Being a new Mom was tough on her.

"I am. I think you're just worrying since your Mom instincts are firing off in every direction."

She rolled her eyes again. "I've had Mom instincts about you since I met you."

True. Andrei had introduced her to me and they were both my pseudo parents. Especially since both of my biological parents failed me.

I wasn't *actually* Andrei and Matteo's brother.

Half. Their father, the now deceased Philippe DuPont had an affair with my mother, Tasha Mattison.

Andrei had found out about me when he turned eleven, Phillipe died, and left me in his will.

And suddenly I had one enormous man showing up at my door in Vancouver telling me I was his family—and he'd plucked me out of my shit situation.

My real name on paper was Thierry Theo Mattison.

Phillipe wanted to name me Thierry.

So Tasha had agreed. Too bad the DuPont side hadn't wanted me in their life since I was his illegitimate son.

Until Andrei did.

So I switched between Thierry and Theo on occasion but either way—I never switched to DuPont. Ever.

Nor would I ever.

I wasn't a DuPont.

I would never be fully one.

Not with the way Andrei and Teo knew me. But that was my life —on the outskirts looking into the world. Watching things happen like a snow globe.

Talia's eyes were soft on me now. "I am worried about you. All this home time can't be good for your mental health. What do you even do? Gemma said she can find a good tutor for you—"

Again with the fucking tutor.

I woke up and I worked out. And worked out. And laid there making food and cleaning Andrei's old apartment he'd let me stay in since we'd gotten back.

"I don't need one—"

"Yes, you do. Stop fighting me. Just give in. You are not going to win this battle."

"I'm fine, Talia. I promise. Nothing's wrong and I'm even going to go see Teo today."

"At his office? That never bodes well. He's always in some sort of trouble too. I don't like you two together, it's like a recipe for disaster."

"You fucking love our disasters," I laughed at her expression as I swore in front of Drew. "He doesn't understand."

"He understands." She scoffed as she held her hands out. "He felt everything I felt for the last nine months remember?"

I did.

Talia was five-five, but her pregnancy weight had made her usually sharp stunning features soften a lot more in a way that made her adorable. Dark hair still growing longer by the weeks. Darker green eyes like jade watching me.

"Give me my baby before he chews your entire finger off."

I looked down at Drew quietly eating my fingers, sucking on them hungrily. He was having a blast.

"He's so gummy, I didn't even feel it."

66

As I gently took it out his entire face contorted like he was being deprived of something good, and Talia was on it.

"Ohhhh, I know, sweetie. I know. I'm here. *Maman* has dinner." I grinned at his expressions. "Yes, you just want milk, don't you? Oh, don't worry Maman has milk…yes I do…yes I do…"

I grinned. He clearly understood us because he looked pleased with himself.

"Yeah, you want some?" Her eyes twinkled. "He knows that word."

I shuddered. "I love you, but I can't talk about your tits."

"You're such a clown," she whispered eating some more chocolate. Sometimes I was. "He's only one month old, and the time flew by."

It did. A month ago is when I'd found Talia and Gemma in the penthouse here, after Talia's water broke and she'd been terrified.

I'd been terrified for her. The experience of watching Talia in pain made me never want to have kids of my own. I knew how much her and Andrei struggled to have this baby.

And I never wanted to experience any woman I loved go through that.

"I need to eat some food before I feed him. I didn't think breastfeeding would make me this hungry."

"It burns like eight-hundred calories," I pitched in. "Eat all you want."

She laughed as she held him to her and a smile lit his face again at being close to her.

He looked like the spitting image of Andrei around her.

As she lifted him into her arms I grinned at his size against her.

Talia was full on soothing mode on him as she tucked him into her arms, cuddling his giggling body and grinning down at her baby. A few weeks ago she'd been struggling through her pregnancy and now?

"He's so—"

Talia shot me a look of reproach that could freeze fire.

Full on Maman Bear.

"*Not a word*. He is perfect. He's my baby."

I grinned as she walked into the apartment already adjusting her clothes to feed him.

"Say hi to Teo for me!"

CHAPTER 4
THIERRY

THE SLEEK GROUNDS OF *ROADSTERS* WERE IMMACULATE WITH FOLKS walking around in designer suits, Rolex's, and on Teo's grounds?

It was a landscape of wealth and power and Teo liked his folks pretty.

House rules were you had to be decent enough to get through the front door. Something I had blatantly disregarded in my youth. Now I was grateful for it.

I'd put on some slacks and a black sweater that cost more than people's six month salaries and walked in feeling like an imposter. This wasn't my style. It never had been.

I liked my ripped up tees's, my tattoos out, my jeans. I fucking hated dressing like a cosplayer in my own brother's work place.

But I couldn't make him look bad. Neither one of them.

Not when I'd known the last three years of my life had been filled with things that most people's nightmares didn't hold.

Talon was...bad. Not necessarily.

Many people employed their talents discreetly as a security group attached to Nash Group. Most people didn't realize what it was—until it was too late.

The life was just not for everyone. Hard hours. Long hours. Brutal schedules. Pushing your body to the limit constantly. Some people died constantly.

But the part that always got me was how solitary life was in the shadows. Talia *loved* it.

The structure, the purpose, the missions. Talia had been her father's favorite and she embodied what it meant to be a Talon operative.

She'd been the head of the unit for a reason.

I found Teo at his desk with a deep frown on his face when I walked in. Thank fuck this time he was alone.

Usually, Teo had company.

And it wasn't of any variety I wanted to keep anymore—half naked models and cocaine.

Trouble. Temptation. Same difference.

Seeing me, he smoothed it out as he stood looking a little disheveled into his navy suit.

All six-feet-three inches of him stood to his full height as he took me in impressed. "You cleaned up nice."

"So do you when theirs no hookers," I quipped.

"Ah says the little brother who tore up the city several times—"

"Annnd I got it." I held up a hand as he chuckled. I had been awful.

In the past Teo and I were at each other's throats fighting constantly. I was causing trouble differently than he was. He hadn't always liked me. But year later? When I'd shown up—he'd been better. We both had changed.

Not since we both had outgrown our issues. Or learned to manifest them in different ways.

And then a wicked grin split Teo's lips with the glimmer I saw in Drew's eyes when he smiled.

Talia said all of the DuPont's looked like trouble.

"They're *models*." That was him pretending to be nice. I had walked in on Teo in the past countless times with women all over him.

"Whatever you want to call them."

Tasha Mattison had been a model. Who'd gotten too close to Phillipe. It made my skin crawl thinking I'd been on the same route as my late-father.

"You wanted to show me your new toy?"

His grin turned downright devious as he opened up a closet to his set of keys. He had a key for every car he designed.

At twenty-seven Teo had been *busy*.

As far as I knew, when my brother wasn't on drugs and hookers/models, he didn't sleep.

His ADHD was worse than mine. But it got to a point where Teo needed outlets. He wasn't a fighter.

Not even close. I doubt he'd ever held a gun in his life and Teo struggled with it a lot.

He worked out on occasion with me and he could keep up— but between his schedules and what he liked? It wasn't regular enough.

Not for his issues.

"I have it downstairs."

As we made our way out his secretary looked petrified of him leaving and she ducked down and out of sight.

Everyone else got out of his way. Because my brother while lovable and playful with his family—was still a wild card at work.

And nobody wanted to piss him off.

On the lower levels of *Roadsters*, Teo took me to his workshop where a gleaming beast of car sat.

I blew out a whistle as Teo grinned wider, his canines sharp on his face making him look a little evil.

"You made this?" Aggressive in its design, it had a coupe-like roof sat a sleek black SUV. "It's a sports car?"

"One of the first of it's kind," Teo said like a proud Papa in French. He switched when he was with him.

Its front end was distinct with the Roadster logo of the R in the DuPont family crest. But otherwise?

There was nothing like this out right now.

Teo switched to the proper French as he called it. He despised the Canadian mixture of French that he'd heard out of my mouth when he'd met me years ago.

"Quad exhaust, alloy wheels, looks like it's made out of obsidian and sapphire. And it's got enough in it to go from zero to sixty in 2.3 seconds."

Teo beamed at my expression switching to English. "And I enhanced it with the self-driving feature."

I was floored.

It was a fusion of luxury with enough speed knowing Teo who rattled off the other specs.

Twin-turbo V8 engines. Carbon ceramic brakes.

The predatory lights that gleamed a bright red like a demon. And then I caught the plates.

REAPER.

"Get the fuck outta here." I swore.

He laughed as he handed me the keys.

"All yours. It needs a few tweaks so I'll keep it here for now working on the secondary one," he motioned to another model next to it not quite finished. "But once they're done they'll be two."

"Who's the other one for?"

He shrugged lightly. "I thought it would be nice to have. My friend Kieran borrows it."

"Kieran?"

"O'Hara." He shot me a look. "Chicago Mob."

Ah. I'd never met him but I could only imagine the things Teo did with his buddy to be this close to him. I stayed away from everyone.

"You're close." I took the keys from him.

Teo's grin never faded. "You don't ever come to *De Nuit. You don't know.*"

My brother owned a sex club just for his kind of debauchery.

"I've got discipline, Teo."

"And how's that discipline going?"

Not well.

I hadn't gotten laid in months and since I wasn't seventeen anymore—I wasn't willing to fuck *just* anybody. Or get into trouble for pussy.

Not my style. A lot had happened. I searched my pockets for the butterfly clip in them squeezing my hand around it. Doe eyes in my vision. I blinked them back.

"That's what I thought," he grinned looking devious. I sighed. "One little sex-tape and you're a blushing virgin."

It wasn't *one* little sex-tape.

I'd done full on porn years ago before Andrei had found out, ripped me a new one, gotten his hands on it and erased all of it off the internet—and then shipped me to Talia.

He had been out of his mind with trying to keep me from Maxine.

Now? With her angry with him?

He was a monster to be around.

Snapping at everything in his sight.

Threatening Teo who laughed like a wicked schoolboy at his threats even though I knew Teo was nervous around Andrei too. Something had changed in him over the last few years.

But his voice still echoed in my ears.

I will not have you turning out like our parents.

71

For discipline. Since then I'd completely changed.

But Teo remembered since he'd been impressed at the time at how devious I'd been.

I made Teo look like child's play when my demons came out.

"What's wrong with you?" Teo asked me quietly looking unusually calm for his personality. His eyes searched me. "You don't look right."

Fuck. I didn't need this.

"I'm fine," I huffed out. Everyone was worried about me.

Even Teo looked calm compared to me. The words 'calm' and 'Teo' in the past wouldn't have belonged in the same sentence.

But now?

With Talia back in his life and me? He was waking up to a reality that he hadn't had before.

"You're not acting normal," Teo said. "Not that you were normal to begin with. But Andrei is worried about you too."

I didn't get it.

Why was everyone worried about me?

"He thinks you should go back to school—"

"Even when they don't speak he and Talia have the same brain—"

Teo smirked. "They think exactly the same. They're basically one person in two bodies."

I let out a breath. "She said the same thing to me this morning—"

"That's because they're both worried about you," Teo's eyes pinned me with his stare. "You need to do something or else you'll rot."

Teo murmured his eyes holding a glint in them I knew he had when solving a complex puzzle.

"You have to pick up a book or *something*."

"I don't have to do anything," I watched him with my jaw set. "I don't *need* to do anything. And I can't go back to school even if Gemma Marchand tries to find the best tutor in the world for me."

He sighed as he got into my new car. "You were young in the past. Give it a try. Gemma is good at her job. That's why she's sought after."

A former heiress with a penchant for knowing how to put out fires?

I knew that much.

I didn't want to start this with Teo. Talia wasn't wrong.

With Teo and me in the same room? It was bound to end in one of us in trouble. But it wasn't going to be me.

Teo grinned as he got behind the wheel.

"I don't know why everyone is so concerned—" I got into the other side. "Why do you care so much about me going to school—"

He turned to me then with an expression on his face that said, 'Was I being serious?'

"What do you plan on doing? Making more sex tapes? Maybe you're considering a career doing webcam porn with your dick—" he broke off. "What do you think you're going to do for me or Andrei without your—" he didn't say it.

"I got it." Talia had shaken me up enough.

Teo let out a breath. "Andrei won't be happy if he can't put you to use—because as much as he likes you—"

Andrei was never happy. Not since we came back. Not since my step-mother had decided to try and overthrow him from his throne at head of Durand. A position he built since the moment he found out about me. About Talia and Drew.

"He still has a company to run." And I couldn't be a twenty-year old bum struggling through my words.

It didn't matter how much money I had made in the past.

Andrei and Teo were worlds wealthier and they weren't kidding.

In this new world—even if I became a full-time contract killer, which Andrei vetoed the moment I brought it up—he wanted me to do legit things.

"Andrei wants you to be like us—" Teo stopped himself from saying the world. "Not normal. But just to have your options open. Give it a chance. It might surprise you."

And maybe hell would freeze over.

Either way a tutor couldn't fix me.

Nobody could. I gave it a week before they quit. Just like all the others. Teo started up the car.

"It's June," he said conversationally. "Don't be surprised if we bump into the parade of graduates when we're all over the city."

"Try not to run over the idiots—" I grumbled. Nothing worse than over-eager idiotic kids in caps and gowns completely oblivious to humanity.

"Speaking of kids," Teo said. "How is my nephew?"

"He isn't just yours, you know?"

"Talia and Andrei are in their Cold War phase so Drew only get's her."

"No, Andrei goes to him." Teo murmured his voice so low under the engine. His eyes were dark as he looked left and right. "Drew doesn't let him hold him."

"Drew doesn't…like Andrei?" How was that even possible? I didn't know that. Talia never talked about my brother anymore.

Teo shook his head looking a bit lost unlike his usual confident self. My brother was known for being put together even when he wasn't.

I blamed it on a lifetime of adapting to his family. To our needs versus his own.

"He tries to hold him and he screams and the nanny has to calm Drew down. He won't let Andrei near him."

So Andrei doesn't go home. To his wife and son.

I let out a breath. "Phillipe cursed us."

Teo snorted. "That curse's name is *Maxine*. She's driving Andrei over an edge and on purpose. It doesn't help she knows about you and she has an inkling of the baby. But Andrei is staying away from his family to not distract himself. He's not trying to be a terrible father."

"But he's awfully good at pretending to be one."

My late father's wife wasn't my step-mother. She was a demon hell-bent on wrecking her son's lives if it wasn't for Andrei keeping her at bay.

The woman who was responsible for tearing apart the entire family.

She had been the one who had made Phillipe choose.

Between a model and her.

Phillipe had picked her so she wouldn't take everything he had. When he'd died, his final fuck you had been to leave it all to Andrei.

Philippe had sent Tasha child support every so often and neglected me.

Once Andrei had found out about the payments, and stepped in, he'd kept it a secret from Maxine.

Until she had found out when I'd brought Talia back from Cape Verde.

"She's been angry since she realized Talia was back in Andrei's life."

"Talia has never *left* Andrei's life. Maxine realized how late she was to figuring it out. Because now, all of Andrei's assets go to Drew and Talia. Maybe me and you, but we both know he's going to leave his entire fortune to his son." Teo said. "Too late to save herself or anyone else."

The moment Talia had shown up, Andrei had been on a mission from hell to take his entire family business into his own hands. *Every*. Single. Bit.

Combining everything the DuPont's owned, buying up new projects, and fortifying his wealth into an empire.

A powerhouse for himself, for Talia—for Drew. Where he kept them both safe from everyone else.

Only to Talia she didn't see it that way.

At least, that's what Teo and I thought.

"She'll forgive him," Teo murmured. "I know her. They've been together since they were ten. It's been twenty years. Talia won't stay mad at him forever. She can't."

True. But I knew Talia too.

"No, but she'll stay mad at him long enough to drive him insane."

Teo's face looked unimpressed as he made a noise like '*pfft*'. "*Mon frere,* he was already there."

True.

❧

Gemma Marchand, the blonde former heiress and her too blue eyes stood at my doorstep talking to me about my future.

Because of Talia.

Gemma, being an overachiever had already found me a tutor.

A one singular Avani Malhotra. I had no fucking clue who she was. But she sounded smart. I guess.

"It's just a tutor, Thierry, she doesn't even bite."

"She might, you don't know that—"

"I know Avani, she's wonderful."

I rolled my eyes. "That's her name? Avani? What is that from?" I could've sworn it meant something.

"It's Sanskrit for Goddess of the Earth," she muttered and I snorted.

"You want the Goddess of the Earth tutoring me." I leaned back in my chair in Andrei's living room as Gemma frowned at me with her arms crossed. *Highly unlikely.*

"Thierry, listen to me. Everyone is worried about you and I think Avani is the nicest person in the world—"

"I might eat her alive by the end of the session, Gemma."

And then fire flashed in those eyes as she stood at her full elegant five-eight. "You will not touch her. That is Alisha's little sister and mine."

I blinked as though I was seeing wrong. Gemma. Defending her. She liked this girl.

"Avani," I tested her name out on my tongue. "Do I know her?"

"Highly unlikely," Gemma rolled her eyes. "Look, she said she's willing to meet next week. I have a date and time for you, it'll be Downtown at the library—"

"Fucking fantastic, Gemma did you want to take up a new role as my—"

"Don't you start," Gemma growled showing she was more vicious than I gave her credit for. "I am not your family. I am hers. Not a word against her. You will learn and grow and educate yourself if you plan on existing in this world. Dyslexia is nothing to be ashamed of."

Now she sounded like Talia.

"Avani just graduated high school, she's about to be a college freshman and she's generously allocated time for you. Even though she doesn't have to. She doesn't get paid for it. I simply asked her if she would be willing to help Teo's brother. And she agreed."

Well, I'm sure Avani was a splendid individual.

I didn't say anything. Gemma watched me. "Well?"

It was my turn to spit it out in French. "If I don't go you and Talia and Andrei will gang up on me. So what the fuck is the point?"

She looked smug as she stepped back. "Then my work is done. You'll meet Avani."

"Send me a photo of her so I know what she looks like."

Gemma agreed.

The irony was, hours before, I had been watching the graduates walking past my window.

June brought a whole host of them.

Standing on the edge of the windowsill overlooking the city in

76

the morning as the sun rose—I felt the discomfort in my chest as I stared into a landscape I should've been familiar with.

On one hand, New York was the city of anonymity.

Nobody knew anybody. Nobody had any real friends.

Half of the time nobody really liked anybody either, but New Yorkers were real. Honest to a fault.

They ignored the weirdest shit I could imagine. And most of the time?

Everything in New York was a myth.

Like me. I didn't exist. Not really.

Which left me alone in a crash-pad for the last few months that I'd been back in New York.

After leaving West Africa and the life I had for the last few years.

Now? I was just some average man at twenty who sat at home in the morning with no plans.

And the afternoon. And the evening.

And every single day after that.

I woke up and I did the exact same thing every single day just like I had in Talon—save for hurting anyone. I hadn't done that in a long time.

Maybe I can see why Teo is worried.

I didn't really know how to feel about it.

I stretched, worked out heavy, drank a protein shake—and went about my morning.

This morning however was different.

A wrench in my plans if you will.

And I fucking said yes.

Because why wouldn't I? Talia wasn't wrong. I wasn't adapting to my new life. I wasn't doing anything.

I was turning into still-water.

And any kind of water that sat still for too long—eventually became poison.

Gemma, was a family friend of ours, and Andrei's wife—Talia—in particular took a liking to her.

I didn't know if Gemma knew why or how but Talia did care enough to send Gemma my way.

And she had convinced me to get "help."

Gemma said she would send me a photo of Avani after she got home in the evening. My phone pinged and when it came in I almost I spit my drink out the moment it came in.

Because staring back at me were a pair of doe eyes that had haunted me forever. Chestnut hair. Soft smiles. Lush lips.

Mon. Dieu.

"*Amelia!*"

I almost shot out of my fucking seat.

Fuck. That wasn't her name. But I couldn't call her my little butterfly.

Could I? No. That was weird. That was a mouthful.

Mon cœur had a touch softer ring to it. Plus, she stared back at me next to a woman who had sharper features, but was clearly her sister.

Gemma's text bubble appeared.

This is Avani Malhotra.

"Did she?" I whispered. "Mon cœur …you remember me *too.*"

Because no fucking way she didn't know. She knew my name.

It had taken me three years to learn hers.

And now I wasn't fucking letting go.

I laughed a little at my fucking stroke of luck.

AS I SLIPPED INTO MY HOODIE AND SHOES, I FOUND MYSELF BACK AT my computer staring at the screen of the reason why I had said yes.

Chestnut hair. Pretty dark doe eyes. Soft pink lips and her smile was warm. She looked *edible.*

When I had seen her as a teenager, she was cute. That accent had sunken into my veins and stayed there. Like her hairpin. I fiddled with it while getting ready being careful to not break it. But in all the years I had it—the little butterfly hairpin was strong.

She had an older sister Alisha who was friendly with Matteo and according to Gemma, Alisha hadn't slept with Teo.

Which was…well…not normal since everyone slept with Teo.

That's why she had been there that day.

But Gemma assured me Alisha liked someone else—and Avani was good for me because she was sweeter. Calmer. Relaxed.

Gemma had given me her number and a date and time to meet her. It was June.

In my mind I heard a familiar voice that I heard whenever I was in doubt. I sighed. It had been months since I spoke to Alma. Ever since I left my old life for this one?

I didn't talk to my old life anymore.

Cole and Caleb were breaking the rules if they spoke to me still, but I knew Andrei despised all things related to Malcolm Nash.

I heard Alma's voice in my head. And I wished I could talk to her. Her presence always helped me.

Sometimes life will give you opportunities, my brother always taught me to take them.

I know. But I don't want new. I just want...

I didn't know what I wanted. But I kept hearing that voice in my head but she wasn't anyone I could talk to right now.

She would tell me to stop being such a fucking coward.

And then she'd tell me if I thought Avani was hot—I should just ask her out if I liked her. Because I did.

I heard her thicker Mexican accent in my head. I sighed. "Fine. I can do this."

Besides—I was meeting Amelia.

If anything it might make for a nice distraction.

What's the worst that can happen?

So I got up from my perch, stopped looking at her photos and grabbed my wallet and keys with the car Teo let me borrow while he tweaked the custom beast he'd shown me. And off I went.

To the woman who had haunted me for three years.

CHAPTER 5
AVANI

I DIDN'T MIND NEW YORK.

I'm sure there were worse places in the world and other people had it far worse.

That did not mean it was not *uncomfortable*.

Especially in my pink dress with the puffy sleeves and bodice— when I had put it on this morning I had felt like a princess.

Alisha had gotten it for me and I loved it. Or I would've.

Now? With the creepy men leering at me on the train to the library? I wished I had taken a cab.

But I promised Gemma I would tutor *Thierry. DuPont. Teo's younger brother.*

The pirate who had kissed me years ago. The one who had *ruined* my first kiss. And ruined every man after that with his… ways.

I was now meeting him at the public library Downtown.

The summer sun outside lit up my mood and my hair, Alisha had recently had me get done. It was so nice and warm outside, I could feel the strands tickling my back.

It had been growing up longer and some soft layers had done me justice. I never wore makeup and even less so in the heat.

I didn't ever feel as pretty as Alisha.

Even with my pink dress on? I did. And I wanted to make a good first impression. Well…second impression.

I mean, he had *technically* kissed me on my first one and I had every intention of confronting him. Demanding my hair pin back.

But maybe he didn't remember me. Maybe he didn't know.

Right now I wished no man ever existed on the face of this Earth.

Alisha always said men had spread lies about women dressing to impress them, when in all reality in a world where men did not exist women would be safe enough to wear whatever they wanted.

I did not feel safe right now.

I knew why most men made me uncomfortable. The leering, the cat-calls, the following me around, the inability to take no as a full answer. I understood all that. It was part of why Alisha never went out.

I tugged my dress down. I just…really did not appreciate the creepy men.

But that wasn't just in New York.

They were *everywhere*. Alisha tried to take me on holiday once to Cabo and they were definitely there too. So it wasn't New York.

It didn't make it any better though.

But then again, where I was from in England it wasn't always like this everywhere you went there. In the city? It was different. Men shouted. Cat-called.

And genuinely made me uncomfortable.

I tried not to let it get to me. I was not immune to it though.

I practically raced out at my stop, my heart pounding as I saw him moving.

Thierry would be at the library.

Probably not outside on a hot day.

I was dashing across the street when I thought I saw someone familiar.

In a black hoodie out of all things in the heat, I knew that hair anywhere, deep midnight inky black. I knew that silhouette.

He was a little leaner than I remembered though and for a moment I doubted if it was him.

Teo. Why was he here?

However, when I looked over my shoulder and saw the creepy man I rushed to the familiar face. No. Even if it wasn't Teo I could ask him for help.

"*Teo!*" I was rushing to him and in his arms a second later as he turned over his shoulder to look at me. Any DuPont was better than no DuPont.

"Thank goodness you're here! I thought I was meeting your brother...Please help me. *T-that man is following me. Don't look. Don't make it obvious.*"

I motioned behind me and Teo looked as I huddled into him, my heart was hammering in my ribs.

His arms banded around me holding me to him as he held on.

"*Who?*" His deep voice cut through all my panic for a moment. He sounded different, and something in my chest recognized that voice.

"Grey sweats. Large, baggy, weird looking." I couldn't even look as I held him. I'd hugged Teo before, but he felt off this time, solid, muscled, and...different.

I was a little freaked out, my hands scrunching against the soft material of his hoodie.

"Teo, I took the train here, I s-should've taken a cab—" my accent thickening with anxiety, I stumbled over my words as he rubbed my back.

"No, you're fine." I held on as he all but picked me up, the pink fabric of my dress scrunching against him. "Put your arms around me, I'll take you into the library."

The moment I did, he lifted me up easily into his arms, his cologne stronger and spicier today.

I inhaled his scent as he carried me up the steps and out of sight into the shade.

"Thank you, I'm quite sorry," I apologized as he set me down. "I didn't know what to do—"

"You don't have to apologize."

Not that I remembered how Teo felt but I just knew it didn't feel right.

I took a step back to thank him and then I paused. I *froze*.

This is not Teo.

Blinking twice I took in the man in front of me who had carried me up the steps of the library, who was now watching me with a curious look in his eyes that filled with wonder as I watched him.

He had gotten bigger, almost enormous compared to when I'd last seen him.

Strapping shoulders, he stood taller like his brother, and those electric eyes glittered on me.

His grin was back though. The same one I remembered.

"Good Lord, it's you."

"Not the reaction I was expecting but you're welcome for saving your butt."

For a second my teenage heart had been giddy. I could *die* from knowing Teo had been there to save me.

But then all of the adrenaline rushed out of me and my heart started pounding for a completely different reason.

He had the same inky midnight hair, brighter blue eyes rimmed with that signature black making them a little alien that stood out at me. A playful look entered those eyes. "You've gotten older, Mon cœur."

"You remember me?" I gaped. No way.

"No." He said it with a straight face and for a moment I thought he was being serious until I saw the twinkle in his eyes.

He's still a rogue.

Because facing him now I could clearly see, *he wasn't his brother.*

No. Teo never made me feel like this.

But I was meeting...

Drat. I'd all but mauled him. "You stole my hairpin."

His face went blank. "I have no idea what you're talking about."

"Yes, you do, only you could've taken it."

"Maybe you dropped it."

He looked like a lazy mischievous cat.

"I would never have dropped it, it was my Mum's. And you're a thief."

"That's not very proper of you, Mon cœur ," his smile was sly. "After all, I just saved you from one creepy man. Is that how you thank your hero?"

"You are hardly a hero," I shot back. "You're a pirate! A rogue—"

"A scoundrel—"

"A scoundrel!" I finished at the same time. His smile turned downright devious with those dimples on either side. Oh, I *knew* him. He had my hairpin.

Our neighbor next to Mum's house had a sly cat named Bean who would look you in the eyes when tossing everyone's cups to the ground. With a straight face too.

Except Thierry had never been a house-cat.

If anything, he was much larger, more dangerous, and not the kind of person I wanted to toy with.

Something told me he could do more than knock a few tea cups over.

His eyes were laser-focused on me twinkling a little with amusement? Something else.

"Well," he murmured looking wicked.

I huffed out a breath. This. *Man.*

"Thank you for saving me. Sorry I accosted you. Now that we know you've stolen my hairpin and I have accosted you. We are even."

There was a dangerous glint in his eyes.

He looked like midnight, dark and beautiful in a dangerous way that sent my heart skipping a few beats faster.

One elegant brow rose, his head tilting a little like he was curious. Of me?

"You didn't do anything wrong."

"But I did, I all but—"

"You thought you were *accosting* Teo—" he countered easily. Was he making fun of me?

"That doesn't make it any better."

"Doesn't make it any worse," his lips tipped up. "You're so proper when you're upset." And then he cupped my face with his hands. "It's been forever, Mon cœur. You haven't lost your spirit I see."

"Of course not, why would I?"

I caught the ends of my dress from blowing in the breeze startled by his eyes on me. Alien-blue eyes dropped to my exposed cleavage and back to my eyes again like he caught himself letting me go.

Oh, he's...

"Why are you looking at me like that?"

"You have a smudge of dirt," he wiped somewhere on my cheek. "All gone."

His smile widened a little and for a moment, he looked like a mischievous little boy who had hid cookies in the house after his mother told him not to.

His hair fell over one eye and those eyes shimmered a little despite being in the shade.

"It's not every day a man follows *me* on the train," his voice was amused as he looked behind one of the large roman columns of the building. "He's gone by the way, you're safe now."

"Thank you." How did he know that? He didn't even look.

"Happens to you often?" He tipped his head again curiously at me like he was trying to uncover something.

"Not usually. But I don't usually…look…" I motioned to my dress. "I wanted to make a good first impression—"

"Why? I've already kissed you." A squeak left me at his grin. "Wouldn't this be your second impression?"

My heart was skipping beats now. Faster he raked his eyes down my dress.

"You're not…you're not going to—"

He smirked. "Do you want me to?"

"No." I held out my hands in a staying motion. There would be no more spontaneous kisses. "No."

His grin widened.

"You made a good first impression, *Avani*." He held out his hand. "Nice to meet you…again."

I felt my throat work, my eyes widening on the skeletal tattoos on his hand.

Those hadn't been there before and a part of me clenched at the sight of them.

Something sparked and hissed between us, swallowing the oxygen from my lungs and my eyes met his again realizing I was standing there like a goldfish.

His smile was still in place. Dimples and all.

He was the same boy I met years ago…but different in some ways. The shadows in his eyes more pronounced.

Hesitantly I took his hand.

"Nice to meet you again."It wasn't my imagination, the spark in his eyes was there as the wind blew my dress again and I kept it down with one hand. "Shall we go inside? Gemma says you need English tutoring?"

I was having trouble now keeping my dress down with the breeze. Why did it get so much windier Downtown?

"Having trouble?" He looked absolutely wicked watching my dress.

"No. I'm fine." It was a low growl. I was *not* fine. "Let's just go inside for propriety's sake before I flash all of New York City." Before I lost all sense and sensibility.

"Need a hand?" The deviant was not giving up.

"Oh, please like you'd help?"

"I'd say I helped so far," he looked like he was considering it. "But you know, I realized with me saving you all day and what not, I should just start asking for payment in return."

"Of course you want money." I huffed out a breath. "You're still a pirate."

I turned away keeping my hands on my dress to keep it from blowing around me and flashing my knickers to everyone in sight.

I felt him closing the distance behind me until I could feel his lips at the shell of my ear sending a shiver down my neck.

"You love it, Mon cœur." His hand came around my waist and one of his hands alone was broad enough he held down a side that had fluttered up with the wind. "And maybe I didn't want money."

I didn't even know why I said it. "Well, you're not getting anymore kisses from me, so don't even start—"

"I won't start."

"Very well then."

"I'll just *think* about it."

I turned over my shoulder to see him watching me amused. *"You're a scoundrel."*

"Two saves in one day?" He murmured with his canines flashing. "Careful, Mon cœur , I might stop thinking and actually do something about it."

"Don't you dare, pirate. I will fight you."

For some reason he laughed outright at that.

I pretended his laughter didn't warm something inside of me making my heart skip several beats as we walked inside.

"Come on, we have to go study now."

Whether I liked it or not, I was stuck with him for the summer.

CHAPTER 6
THIERRY

SHE HAD FIRE.

I'd give her that.

I wasn't expecting it with how sweet she always looked.

Those proper British sensibilities as she said with that spark she hid from the world. I fucking knew that much from the moment I interacted with her. She looked like a petit-four in that sweet dress. What were they called?

Sun-dresses. If she showed up in the same thing from now on? It would be the death of me.

I had to remind myself of this when I looked at Avani Malhotra for the first time that she probably wasn't the sensitive sweet girl I met three years ago

No, if anything she was even more quick witted and spirited, my hand feeling it was burning against her skin where I touched her to help her. She was live-wire and if I hadn't been able to get her out of my thoughts before—I definitely wasn't now.

Her photos didn't do her justice.

She was...*beautiful.*

She looked like spring. And she smelled like roses and honey and something spicy. And she was attracted to me.

And as I'd carried her, she fit so perfectly I needed a minute to breathe.

Goddess of the Earth. How fitting.

And a body made for no good thoughts. None at all. Did I flirt with her on purpose? Maybe.

It riled her up and made me laugh. Easily.

Nobody but my family made me feel comfortable enough to be around them. But she did.

The *moment* she landed in my arms, all rational thought had stopped working in my brain for a nanosecond.

I felt those curves of hers molding to my body. Her breasts.

Enormous and lush.

Full and pressing into my chest as she held on. And my focus was on the idiot thinking he could scare her smirking at me.

In Cape Verde, Africa, I would've just shot him—but I was in New York. Adjustments were necessary. Different rules here.

The moment we walked into the public library Downtown I saw every head turn to her—and she was a little oblivious to it.

It was a four story building, with enormous ceilings, roman architecture and soft lighting everywhere.

I was shamelessly watching her ass in that tiny dress.

And imagining how it would fit my hands while I pounded into her. *Shameless.* I liked her. She was pretty.

Soft and sweet and all innocent in a way that drove me over an edge. It was why I'd liked her all those years ago.

Plus, when she talked? Shit drove me crazy. She was a good opponent for me to verbally spare with. And did I know that meant Avani would be absolute fucking fire in bed?

Yuh.

I liked sex. Or I used to. Until it got me into loads of trouble. Now, I hadn't been with anyone in a long time. Long enough to qualify as a monk. And Avani? She wasn't the kind of woman you just fucked and left. She was the kind of woman you didn't touch unless you had every intention of keeping her.

But keeping her meant introducing her to my world. I couldn't do that.

I didn't have any intention of destroying Avani. She was padding across the room quietly, in her white flat sneakers across the floor. With that fluffy pink mini dress, her tanned skin glowing under the lights as she moved—she looked like a *vision*. Fucking floating her way around life. She belonged here. I didn't.

I followed her anyway across the room like a specter, a shadow drawn to light.

Avani navigated her way to the third floor via the elevator and I followed dutifully, aware of her scent around me.

Along with the scent of old books and polished wood—Avani scent was clean as it wafted over to me—she was navigating the place like it was her home.

I ignored the marble columns, the ornate ceilings, the chandeliers above us and the rows and rows and fucking rows of books—for the little lady in front of me.

"Gemma said you were struggling with your English," she said making her way over to the set of the couches in the back of the third floor.

Nobody was here but us.

"Anything in particular you wanted to focus on?"

No. I can't read.

It was like an iron curtain slamming over my thoughts.

And just like that? I stopped thinking about Avani romantically. Or in any way.

I felt my skin start to crawl and itch at the idea of her ever finding out about my dyslexia. My disability. I wasn't stupid.

I just wasn't smart.

Not the brightest tool in the shed when it came to words or numbers. But you ask me to fight or fuck? I was a fucking God.

I was only good at that.

I didn't need anything else.

Until…now. In the normal world. When I had to learn things.

Avani would know I was an idiot.

"You're familiar with this place?" My voice sounded off. Deeper. Rougher than I intended. And it echoed a little so I lowered it. "You come here often?"

She tossed me a small smile over her shoulder. "I am. I come here all the time," she whispered back.

I don't know why I grinned like some fucking idiot. I didn't know why I reacted to her like this. Or the fact that her hairpin did in fact burn a hole in my pocket. I did have it.

She looked so fucking cute accusing me of being a thief.

I was.

Way worse.

Avani sat down on one of the suede grey couches and motioned for me to do the same an expectant look in her eyes.

I sat down next to her trying not to drown in the scene of honey and roses.

All that soft pink all over the couch, her golden skin. She looked like a fucking goddess sitting there all pretty and shit.

And then there was me.

Avani had no idea she was sitting next to…the likes of me.

Death and shadows and all the things in life she should be afraid. She was pure. I wasn't. She was kind. I wasn't. She was light and I was darkness personified pretending like I belonged here with the likes of someone like her.

"Where did you grow up if you don't mind me asking…" she drifted off. Her eyes darted to me and away. "Sorry, I forgot."

Forgot what?

And *then* I remembered why I felt connected to Avani.

Avani had been the only person who had seen Andrei lose it with me and still be…herself with me. Like a person. Not a problem.

Sure, she'd been a little afraid but she'd still kissed me back. And she had been the last person I had interacted with before booted off to Talon. The last bit of kindness and real interaction I'd had.

Of course, she remembered that argument. It was blazed into my head since that day.

I fucking hated Andrei for the longest time until I got to Talon and I realized why he was doing it. Why he wanted me to shape up. Why he pushed so hard. I got it now. It only took me several thousand nights of getting my ass kicked by everyone to get there.

But when I had I rose through their ranks pretty quickly.

Reapers were good fighter and Talia put the Kindcaide brothers on my team so they'd help me with my disability.

"What happen to you?" She murmured, tucking a lock of her hair back behind her ear. "Your brother shipped you off somewhere? You just look different. Did something happen to you?"

I swallowed hard. Oh. Fucking. Shit. I was hoping we'd never get to this. I didn't want to get into this with her. I shook my head struggling with my own emotions because she knew.

She knew what my family knew.

And it was purely some stroke of luck she had been there at the exact same time Andrei and I had burst in.

He had thought we were alone. But Avani…she knew…almost everything. Just enough. Too much.

90

Her eyes were shy on me. "We don't have to talk about it, I just thought…" she trailed off. "Are you in school right now?"

I shook my head again.

Sweet. Jesus.

"I don't go to school."

"Are you homeschooled?"

I opened my mouth and closed it. How did I talk to Avani so she understood

"I'm sorry, I have to ask so I know where you start in terms of reading and comprehension. If I know what year you're in, it'll help me select the books and material. Gemma didn't mention anything out of respect for your privacy but if we're going to work together it might be helpful."

Her eyes went wider as her chest heaved up and down in a way that should've been illegal to be that distracting. "Are you nervous?"

Avani's tits were now in a top five list for all the filthy fantasies I had involving her and me and my raging hard-on.

"Don't be, I wouldn't judge you for anything. Gemma said you struggled with your English. Is it speaking and reading?"

No. Just reading.

"Just reading."

She nodded looking relieved. "Okay, so why don't I get up and grab some books and we can just see where you're at. Is there a particular class you need help with?"

I shook my head. I wasn't sure what to say to her. How did I tell her?

What did I tell her?

Avani, I can't read.

Andrei, my brother, he hired out tutors and they said I was a lost cause.

My brother's wife Talia used to run a unit across the globe that killed people.

I was a part of it.

But I can't write my own name.

How the fuck did that sound?

And then just like that Avani was floating up and around me and I was standing to move with her when she turned to me motioning with her hands I stay.

What the fuck was it about this girl?

"No, please, let me go grab it—it'll only be a second."

91

She wasn't even my type.

And then she was gone. And just like that I felt a little bereft. I didn't want to let her out of my sight.

As my eyes roamed the library and the softer lights up here, Avani returned quickly. And I took in her soft eyes and her smile.

In her hand was a stack of books, maybe a half dozen.

"Okay, let's start small and see what we need to do from here, okay?"

Shit. I looked down at enemy number one. Books. My mouth went dry all of a sudden and a familiar panic was set alight in me. That was my number one enemy—not reading—feeling stupid. Right there.

Avani had all the ammunition she needed to make me a fool. To make fun of me. To laugh. To belittle me. It was right fucking there. I couldn't string together two words without wanting to rip my hair out. It had been the only fucking thing that set me off. Now more than ever.

People always changed when they realized the youngest brother of two billionaire brother's was an idiot. It was the way they spoke to me, their eyes full of disgust and pity, and I didn't know it was dyslexia until Talia came into Andrie's life and she realized what it was.

I didn't need Avani to treat me like I was stupid. Or talk slower. I wasn't an idiot. And I never ever wanted someone to hold it over my head. For a majority of my life people had made me feel stupid.

I didn't want that ever again. She held all the control and power in this situation and that was not ever a road I could go down.

And suddenly this didn't sound like a good idea anymore.

If Andrei's thousands of dollars worth of tutors didn't stick around for me? Why would Avani?

If Avani knew what was wrong with me, she might take advantage of me. She might—she might treat me however she wanted to. Break me. Just like everyone else.

She might not think I'm worth it.

Suddenly, all of her sat down closer to me, the scent of honey and roses drifting over and all my thoughts ceased to exist as she opened up the first book.

"Will you read a passage from this book so I can see where we are at?"

Fuck.

I couldn't do this. I lied to Gemma. I couldn't do this.

Instead, I turned my head to look at Avani ready to tell her that I was sorry for wasting her time but this wasn't working out for me.

And just as I did, I caught those eyes on me, on my chest, my arms, my hands, and then my face. Like I was something worth looking at. Something worth her time.

Her lower lip tugged between her teeth and her breathing a little hitched.

I made my choice then. It didn't matter if she had a body made for sin.

I couldn't do it.

I couldn't be a monster to Avani.

"I'm sorry, I don't think I should do this."

CHAPTER 7
AVANI

"What?" It came out of my mouth. "What do you mean?"

He looked like regal dark prince on his half of the couch, with his inky hair tousled and sculpted features.

He didn't want to read the book or?

"No, I don't think I can do this—" he looked ready to leave. "There's been a mistake. I can't do this. Sorry I wasted your time."

"What?"

He stood like he was going to leave and I stood with him.

"But Gemma—"

"Gemma will live." Standing close to him now I thought he was as tall as Teo. He was not.

He had to be a little taller than Teo.

"But I promised her—"

"So did I, but some promises are meant to be broken." He looked like he was looking for an escape route.

No. Not for me. I always kept my promises. I did.

Thierry couldn't look at me.

"Thierry—Please…tell me what's wrong. Did I do something? Is something the matter?" My t's always hit harder when I was emotional.

"No—I have to go."

"Thierry!" I whispered feeling a sense of frantic despair. *What was happening?*

His long legs carried him swiftly out between the shelves to the direction of the stairs. I couldn't move that fast.

And I moved in between the shelves to get to him my shoulder hitting the side of a shelf. I winced rubbing it as a loud creak came from above me.

I gasped as I looked up. Just in time to see something topple from the shelf. A vase. *Decoration?*

I didn't have time to comprehend it. A noise left me.

I just froze in place, eyes widening as the heavy object plummeted towards me and I heard footfalls in front of me.

A rush of air and blue eyes filled my vision as I saw *Thierry* move towards me his eyes wide. *He came back?*

His large frame appeared so fast I gasped at the impact.

One hand around my waist, the other pulling me flush against him as he shoved me out of the way. I closed my eyes tight a yelp leaving my mouth as I heard the distant impact of the object.

Thierry let out a grunt as he took a few steps with me in his arms.

"Are you all right?" His deeper voice rumbled through his chest. I nodded. Just a tiny bit shaken. *He moved so fast.*

"Yes…yes, I'm fine." I looked into his eyes. "How did you—you moved so—"

"Are you two all right?" A librarian poked her head into the shelves. "I thought I heard something."

I nodded breathless a bit still in his arms. Acutely aware of his heart racing. Or was it mine?

"We're okay." He held me tighter as he said. "She's okay, aren't you?"

His alien blue eyes searched my face filled with concern, something warmer as he brushed my hair back. "She's good."

I nodded frantically unsure of why I felt so flustered.

Then again, I'd been picked up and tossed around by him twice today and this was as close to a man as I had been in years. In ever.

"I'm so sorry," the librarian apologized. "I don't know how it fell over."

All of the logical words in my brain ceased to exist for the second time that day as he held me to him, I saw his throat working.

"You're accident prone," he muttered under his breath. "I leave you alone for two minutes and you've got furniture falling on you."

But those eyes were amused as he looked at me.

My heart was flustered. It was beating out of my chest.

I didn't whether to laugh or be shocked at his teasing. Not after he'd all but quit as a student.

"And who was the one who ran away first? I may be clumsy but I'm no coward."

I don't know where it came from. Perhaps I channeled a bit of Alisha into me. Or some part of me had slipped out. The part I kept close to my chest.

I expected him to be angry. Even insulted. But he looked slightly bemused. His eyes widened a little as the librarian picked up the vase and he looked surprised I'd said something.

I was surprised. The librarian oblivious to our exchange simply picked up her books.

"When did you get—"

"Are you going to stop running and study?"

His throat worked, his beautiful sculpted face on mine blinking a few times. And then a slow wicked smile curved his lips and my logical rational part of my brain shut down at the wicked glint in his eyes and those bloody dimples.

"If I say yes, will you stop putting yourself in dangerous situations?"

"I'll try my best to not attract the attention of creepy men and —" I looked at the librarian who was now putting the vase back. "Ancient Egyptian decor."

His smile was downright wolfish and he considered me then in his arms. This was the closest I had been to a man in forever.

Dimples should be illegal on men that attractive.

"Deal." His eyes raked down my face. "But I'm keeping you away from sharp objects. And people."

I let out a breathless laugh hanging my head, my forehead against his chest as he moved us out of the two shelves.

His shoulders were broad despite being on the leaner side, and the black on black he wore took up space giving him a darker and much more dangerous energy.

Thierry moved easily with me in his arms, and I realized he'd picked me up a few inches off the floor.

A breath left me at how easily he moved back to the couches we'd been in.

Teo was *playful*. His brother on the other hand was not.

Thierry was more intense. Guarded. And if I was being honest…Teo never made me feel like this.

The only thing keeping me hanging by a thread was the thought of him being my student.

My *attractive* student.

Who I was supposed to be tutoring.

I was a sucker for tall, dark, and brooding. And Thierry looked like this pirate king out of this fantasy series I was reading.

The picture of dark fantasy. I still remembered he was a troublemaker but this time, I think I understood he ran away from feeling uncomfortable. It scared him a little. *A lot.*

He set me down on the couch where the books were. He still looked miserable being around it but he was eyeing me now instead.

"I get the feeling if I try to leave you'll somehow get a paper cut from hell."

I shook my head ruefully. "If you just read the page then maybe paper cuts won't be necessary."

"You like reading?" He asked me as we both stood there like he didn't just haul me out of danger. Again.

"I do. I just graduated school. And I want to major in English Literature at University." I motioned to the couch. I had no clue where this part of me was coming from.

I felt a healthy flush coast over my cheeks.

"Congrats." His voice was a low rumble and that deep octave did something to my insides. He sat down next to me and it wasn't my imagination that he was closer now.

"Thank you," my smile came naturally and to my surprise his lips stretched wider that glint in his eyes returning and dimples and canines flashing.

Like a mischievous boy contemplating his next prank.

I was not envisioning myself running my fingers through his hair.

Or the wicked glint in his eyes as he made out with me. Not at all. Never mind that I'd never been kissed. *No.*

I felt a little nervous because I was pretty sure he'd come closer.

His cologne was invading my lungs and it was a little intoxicating. *Breathe, Avani.*

"Shall we get started?"

When I was in high school in my junior year, one of my instructors Mrs. Neary had asked me to tutor a freshman.

He was a young boy with a bit of a knack for deflection.

Kind of like Alisha when I asked her questions she didn't want to answer.

Gemma says he struggles with his English. But his verbals are good.

Is it just his reading?

"Thierry," I began nervously, my fingers clenching and unclenching on my dress. His eyes raked down my body.

Oh my. *Finish the sentence.*

"Can…you read?"

And just like that it was like a steel wall had erupted between us and his smile dropped.

The mask was gone replaced by coldness to him I hadn't expected.

"Of course, I can read." His eyes were a little intense now. A tiny bit frightening. Like a storm cloud behind them.

"Thierry—"

"I can read—"

He was upset.

"It's okay," I looked into his eyes. "It's okay. I've seen this before. I have students like this—are you…illiterate? Dyslexic?"

Somehow I couldn't imagine the youngest DuPont not knowing how to read, but then again, I didn't understand families.

Mine was unique too.

But I remembered that conversation with Andrei. I remembered the things he had done in the past. And I knew this was a sore subject for him. I figured as much.

The tension was running through him, his spine stiff as he looked away from me. I saw a muscle in his jaw ticking and clenching. *"I don't want—"*

"*If* you do struggle," I cut him off my hand landing on his arm, the spot feeling warmer under my palms now and the tiny bit of connection tethered me to him. "It isn't my place to judge you. I would never dream of judging you or anything in your life. It's not my place. If I am going to be your tutor, I should know how to help you. But never judge you. Do you understand?"

"Why?" It was a low growl. "Why would you ever do that? You don't know me?"

I was confused by this. "What?"

"Why would you start off being nice—"

"Why wouldn't I?" I shook my head in confusion. "Being nice is the bare minimum." I said it like it was my truth. "My sister and I, our Mum taught us that—kindness is the bare minimum. You don't need a reason. That's just selfish."

As I said it he looked dubiously at me. Like he didn't believe me or trust me.

"And I keep my promises. I promised Gemma I would help you this Summer in whatever way you need it. Let me."

My eyes implored his own, underneath the dimmer lighting they seemed to glow.

But even still, even breathless by his features my brain logically concluded that this man had been done dirty in the past by others around him.

Possibly even made fun of him.

Even if I couldn't imagine a man like that being made fun of—it explained why he didn't read.

I knew how that felt.

That had been my entire American high school experience. Where I shied away from everyone and everything too afraid of myself and my interactions.

Which was why I preferred interacting with people my sister's age if not older.

I liked maturity in people. And I reckoned after growing up with Alisha, I liked older men too.

I liked him. But I forced myself to focus. I could do this.

"I'm sorry for whatever you've gone through, but judging people isn't my cup of tea I don't know who you've dealt with in the past, but I hope you give me a chance to show you I won't hurt you. I promise."

He didn't say a word just looked at the book like it was an offensive piece of work. Like he was struggling with himself.

"What did they do to you?" I whispered fearing the answer as he looked uneasy.

He shook his head. "Nothing."

"It's not nothing if you look like you're going to be sick," I murmured feeling his unease, his struggle written all over his face.

I felt a surge of protectiveness move through me, for this enormous man who clearly had an issue that the world might have mocked him for.

Maybe his tutors hadn't been kind. Not all teachers were the same.

I had an instructor in high school once pull me aside to tell me she thought, that I thought, I was better than everyone else because I finished all my exams first and really well.

I was astounded and Alisha was personally offended by her assumptions.

But the truth was, some people thought whatever they wanted about you.

Even if you did nothing to warrant it.

"Have people…made fun of you, belittled you in the past?"

I kept my hand on his arm and after a brief second, he nodded. And just like that my heart shattered.

His non-response was enough of a response to tell me they had. Which made me feel for the little boy he had been trying to learn his way in the world.

When the world hadn't been good to him.

Alisha always said I was softer than her but the truth was—I just cared too much about everything because I genuinely thought the world was good. I did.

I thought outside influences made people awful.

"Your brothers, they hired people out to teach you that were mean to you?"

"My brother's didn't know. They just rotated the cast of tutors until—" he broke off looking away. Looking embarassed.

Until they gave up.

"Do you…" I cleared my throat the moment I heard my voice wobble. His head turned to me again. I looked away embarrassed to be crying over a man I just met. "Do you…think you're not teach-able?" I had to whisper it. I just couldn't speak.

I kept seeing a little boy, dark haired and small struggling to make sense of his brain and his life. Struggling in the world.

"Is-is that why you—" I couldn't speak. I wiped my eyes hoping my hair hid my face enough. "I'm sorry."

He was quiet.

"Why are you…crying?"

I sniffled feeling my emotions crest over, one breath was more overwhelming than the next.

"B-because I'm sorry for what you went through." He seemed almost curious as he drew closer to me a little wide eyed as I cast a look at him. "Sorry, I don't usually break down the first time I meet someone. I usually wait until the third or fourth visit to hysterically lose my mind."

His lips twitched. "You don't have to feel bad for me."

"Oh, but I do. Someone should've just been kind to you—"

"They did their best." His smile grew as he watched me with that renewed glint in his eyes while I embarrassing wiped my eyes.

He was so calm about it too. Besides when he was upset, I saw his eyes soften on me now.

Maybe the world hadn't been kind to him or his disability. But I would never do that to him. It wasn't my place.

In that moment I resolved that no matter what or how cute he was—I was do right by Thierry and teach him how to read.

"I would never…ever…shame you for your disability. I understand it took you being very brave today to come out and see me. Thank you for taking the chance and the time to come here. It was really commendable of you. I think you should be proud of yourself —that was the hardest step. Everything after this is easy, I promise." I held out my pinky.

I could do it.

"Now, if you're willing to try and stay, why don't we read it together? Hm? We can do it together?"

The quiet hum of the library surrounded us.

The only two people in this level since it was mid-day on a weekday. I had chosen it on purpose to give us privacy.

Now I was grateful for the silence.

"It's the least I could do for the man who saved me twice in one day." I offered.

It allowed me to focus on him and him to remain calm.

I wiggled my pinky at him. He looked down at it like it was unfamiliar. Those blue eyes of his curious again.

"My sister and I swear by pinky promises. I pinky promise to never hurt you. Do you promise to try with me?"

I'm not one to keep my promises.

But you can start.

And then I as I held my breath I saw him move.

He rolled up a sleeve of his hoodie and my stomach did a flip when I realized he had tattoos. Plenty of them.

One of his hands with the skeletal tattoos up to his fingertips.

And for a heat of a second, just a second, I imagined them on me.

OhGod.

I swallowed hard my eyes darting up to his eyes something in them I didn't recognize. Did he know? No, he couldn't.

He flexed his fingers as he hooked his larger pinky around mine and squeezed, his eyes holding a hint of that amusement again.

"Promise?"

"Promise."

CHAPTER 8
THIERRY

SHE WAS *WONDERFUL*.

The first day she patiently sat with me with a little smile in her adorable pretty face and she pulled out some white computer paper and made a little messy schedule.

Asking me all sorts of questions about my schedule, what made me comfortable, if I liked a genre more than others...and it went on.

I just sat there blinking answering her like it was an interrogation for a jewel thief instead of me being taught by this tiny woman.

She had made a color-coded plan for me and handed it over with her loopy swirly handwriting in it.

"You can put it on your fridge," she smiled. "It's our schedule."

And sure enough every other day she had a little plan, a small backpack with her pack of highlighters, markers, and glitter pens.

Her butterfly post-its notes. And a stack of—

"Those are children's books," I looked at her the following day when I said I'd meet her.

"Yes, they are. I figured we'd start at the beginning for you and strength our foundation before working our way up."

Avani had brought out a stupid book for children maybe under two. And she held it out to me. I knew it was for toddlers when I saw the bright colors and giant pictures.

Ever since she made me do her little pinky promise, I feel like she bewitched me. Because now?

I was obeying her every command.

"Let's pick a book you think looks lovely…do you like this one?" She held up one with a boy holding a blueberry. What the fuck was I supposed to say? No.

I nodded. Her smile was radiant. "Okay, let's start from the top. Do you want to sound out your letters or should we start with the first sentence?"

I blinked a little like I was slow.

I wasn't slow. But she sounded like Talia when she was talking to Drew. I wasn't some baby.

"Thierry?" Her big eyes bat up at me and I noticed she had to move closer for me to read the book with her. "We can read it together, how about that? This way I'm with the entire way?"

Was I breathing a moose? Why was I breathing like that?

My brain was short circuiting.

Get it together. Read the blueberry book!

Avani's long lashes cast shadows on her cheeks as she looked down at the book.

And then her eyes moved to my forearms where I'd rolled up my long sleeves I wore outside to hide my tattoos. I was covered in them.

I had some on my legs and some on my back. But most of them on double sleeves I had.

One crawling up my chest. It hadn't been too painful for me. Just another rite of passage.

Most people in Talon had tattoos save for the head of Talon.

This way they weren't identifiable in any way.

Avani quickly looked away.

I felt like at some point Avani had resolved to seeing me as a student and I willed myself to just see her as a pretty tutor. And nothing more.

I was trying.

And failing spectacularly.

"Right," I leaned in, and inhaled the scent of honey and roses and something spicier. "Yeah, we can read it together."

And so off I went…the first day Avani had been kind to me. I couldn't even form the words. And just like that, I felt her hand move from the book to my hands squeezing tightly as I struggled.

The warmth of her palm seeped into my skin and I felt something in me respond to her in a way it didn't to other women.

"It's okay, you're doing great," she chirped.

Was I?

"Keep going for me."

And my dick heard it loud and clear.

I cleared my throat and she passed me some coconut water.

I rubbed my temples as she turned the page. "Okay, let's try here, but go a little slower for me and let's take a break after this sentence."

I did it. And this one hurt more.

"It's been forever," I muttered rubbing my head.

"Since you read or—"

"Since I did anything that wasn't—" I stopped myself from saying it. I broke off. She didn't know anything about me.

"All right, well, why don't we take a short five minute break and then continue with another sentence today?"

She looked pleased with my nod and then grabbed her phone, quickly texting someone before turning her screen off. "Sorry, my sister worries when I don't message her back."

"Alisha."

She nodded. She mentioned her on the first day.

"What's she like?"

And just like that Avani's eyes lit up with delight. *Oh. She's beautiful.*

"She's the best," she gushed. "She's a social media influencer and funny enough, she worked for your Mum's company."

Avani didn't know I wasn't actually related to Teo. I didn't let her know my real name. Or anything really.

She knew a mirage.

"Did she?"

Avani nodded. "I was visiting that day, Alisha didn't like leaving me alone when she was gone longer hours so I went with her..." she told about an incident where Teo helped her when someone was being creepy.

I thanked fuck my brother had a decent enough moral compass. Especially for saving underage girls from harm.

As she talked I drifted listening to her voice, soothing and eloquent. I could listen to her talk for days. Months. Let her read to me.

Life was quiet when there was nobody to kill.

I was doing it again. Turning into a fucking space cadet because of a soft plushy woman on my lap determined to dig out parts of me I didn't even known existed.

Avani was everything I wasn't. And everything I shouldn't have wanted. Temptation wrapped in a pink dress with a little bow on it. And I wanted.

I fucking wanted this woman.

A sweet small little cupcake trussed up in her tiny little dresses and her lush full tits and makeup free doe eyes batting up at me while she whimpered taking me—*you have a problem.*

I tried to focus on Avani instead of my raging hard-on and the fact that she hadn't used my weakness against me.

I SHOWED UP EVERY OTHER DAY TAKING BREAKS WITH A HEADACHE BY the end of the forty-five minutes Avani allowed with breaks.

Her body pressed into mine not on purpose but just to review things.

The scent of her hair perfume or something in my lungs as I practiced with her.

By the third visit with her, I was grasping it quicker.

"You're doing brilliantly," she said with a wide smile. "At this rate you'll be reading at your age group by the end of the summer."

Which brought me back to reminding me of our differences.

Because I was nowhere near Avani's age.

She just didn't know it.

She thought I was at most nineteen. And I let her.

"At the end of the summer we stop tutoring?" I asked her. I wasn't sure.

She paused looking at me then a little stunned. "I mean…if you need help I'm here. We can work something out, but let's see where we are then, hm?"

And she handled things well too.

I nodded my eyes focusing on the way her eyes sparkled a little when she spoke. Or the way her smile lit up her entire face when aimed at me.

"Let me know when you're okay and we can continue."

As she turned back I felt the back of my neck prickle. I turned my head to find two guys watching us—no, not me—watching Avani. I felt the irritation flare as I turned to her to ask if she knew them, but her eyes were on her phone reading a text from her sister.

When she was teaching me, she pressed into my side to go over things with me.

But now, she moved away automatically.

On the couch, I stretched my arm around until it was right behind her, and I opened my mouth then already figuring out how she worked.

"Avani, I have a question."

Just like that her head looked up and she dropped her phone, clicking it off as she drew closer to me again her knee pressing into my thigh. "Hm?"

I didn't have a fucking question.

"Can you help me with this sentence?"

I pointed to a random one.

She frowned. "Of course, you did so well on that. Did you want to try again?"

No. "Yes."

I cast a glance at the guy who looked away. But they were still there. I internally rolled my eyes.

"Okay, sure," Avani drew even closer into the circle of my arms and I let her get close enough for me to inhale the scent of her hair. *Closer.* "I'll grab this highlighter and we can go over it…"

As she explained I didn't tell her I already understood.

Avani was talking in low tones right up on me, and I turned my head slightly to see the two guys leaving. I smirked. *Idiots.*

"…did you understand it now? Is that better?"

I turned to her finding her eyes on me expectant and bright. A little like Drew's. Like he knew he was small. Like he needed me to be there for him.

I tipped my head. "Better."

By the second week alone, I was warming up to Avani.

She wasn't…using it against me. If anything, she went out of her way to make me comfortable. Out of her way to ensure I understood.

And I had never had that…not without violence.

It was…an adjustment.

But tutoring didn't mean I could just stop the other aspects of my life.

I went to go see Talia and Drew. Andrei wasn't home. *Again.*

As I stepped into the foyer of their penthouse I tried not to let it rankle at me that he wasn't here.

That he was acting like Phillipe.

It baffled me after a lifetime of showing up for his brother's he wouldn't show for his son.

Talia came to greet me with Drew in her arms. "Hey, will you hold him for a bit? The nanny is running late, and he won't let me put him down without crying. And I really need to pee."

"Yeah, yeah I got him." I had his chubby body in my arms all cooing and gurgling at me with a wide smile. "Hey you, you being good for *Maman?*"

He babbled and made noises while Talia ran off to the bathroom. "I'll change into clean clothes too!"

I looked around the spotless apartment with baby items strewn about. I wanted to rip into Andrei. He should be here.

I whispered to the baby in my arms. "Don't take this the wrong way, I love you. But your Papa and me are going to have a talk one of these days."

He didn't understand. No, he just watched me with an adorable expression in those eyes. I sighed and rocked him.

Teo and I were solid babysitters, but even I knew the importance of having Andrei in his life. I had been the consequences of neglectful parenting and an affair.

Tasha had me and went to her parents in Vancouver who didn't really like the idea of me or her.

So she moved out when I was maybe six?

But after that? It was one apartment after another. One missed meal after another.

Did I know what lengths my mother went to protect me?

I did.

But did I know what kind of danger it put me in?

I did.

I wouldn't ever let that happen to Drew.

I heard the door to the apartment opening while Talia was in the bathroom.

And then speaking of the devil, all six-feet two inches of broad shoulders and black suit stepped into the foyer when I went to go see who it was.

"Andrei."

My brother looked like he hadn't slept in days as he stepped in. Out of all of us? I looked the most like a younger Phillipe. But Andrei? He had a mix of his parents that softened his normally hard features.

My brother was like an older version of Teo. Harder eyes. Clenched jaw when he saw me like he didn't expect me.

He looked pissed and stressed and the moment he walked in the temperature in the room dropped by fifty degrees.

I swore internally as in my arms Drew squirmed and my brother's eyes dropped to his baby.

"Shh," I whispered to Drew who was squirming harder. "What's the matter? It's just your Papa." I cuddled Drew to me murmuring as I walked to Andrei.

"You look like shit," I eyed him and his rumpled appearance. His dark chocolate hair combed back but his eyes rimmed red. "What the—fudge happened to you?"

He shook his head. "My mother is an idiot." Ah. Well, that would explain it. Maxine wasn't exactly mother of the year. She'd made mine a living hell until Andrei had helped. And right now my brother was staring at his son.

"Do you want to hold him?" I held out Drew and for some reason Andrei paled.

His eyes locked on his son with wonder and fear and one side of his mouth tipped up at Drew squirming his fists reaching for my face.

The moment Andrei brushed Drew's hair back, his eyes snapped to his father—and he looked almost startled. Spooked. I hadn't ever seen him look like that.

The moment the thought entered my head, I saw Drew's face scrunch up back at me and his mouth turned down.

It was so fast I felt my eyes widen in panic. I knew that face. I fucking knew. *Drew cries every time Andrei tries to hold him.*

"Nonononono," I had him tucked in my arms rocking him. "Shhh, it's okay, it's okay. It's just Papa."

Two things happened then. I saw the way my brother's entire face fell.

Like he *knew* Drew didn't like him.

Like he knew what we all suspected.

Andrei turned away from me giving me his broad back.

Despite not being my height, he was only an inch shorter and the way he carried himself I thought he was seven feet tall.

Right now though, he looked human.

And the second thing, was Drew started screaming. Panicking. I quickly adjusted his body in my arms.

"Shhh, it's okay, it's okay." But he didn't quiet down and the farther I got away from Andrei the more he calmed down.

He doesn't like his father.

And then I realized how bad it was between them.

I held Drew rocking him, walking him away from Andrei but it was too late. He started bawling. Crying his eyes out. The sound making a shiver run down my spine with how loud he got.

I walked him quickly to where Talia was in the penthouse. And it was like she had radar.

She was half dressed in an oversized t-shirt, her hair up as she ran out of the closet. "What happened?"

"Andrei came home and he started—"

At the mention of my brother's name the concern in Talia's face went blank. She quickly took Drew from me and turned away walking away with him quickly leaving me standing there baffled.

What the fuck was happening with these two?

I went back to the foyer to say something to Andrei, anything at all. But he wasn't there. His keys and jacket that he'd hung up were gone.

"There is no fucking way he left again."

I looked around the foyer and sure enough, his shoes were gone too. I sighed. *He left.* He just left.

I let out a frustrated breath and stormed back to find Talia feeding Drew, thankfully covering him with her shirt but I knew, his chubby little toes were wiggling now that he was happy with *Maman*.

"How long—" I broke off.

How did I ask her?

"Do you know he does that?"

I wasn't sure if I meant Drew crying or Talia dealing with my brother's vanishing act. I saw him for two seconds in two months and he left. He didn't give a shit.

He was turning into Phillipe. *Why?*

Was there something in our fucked up DNA that did that?

I looked at Talia and I saw her eyes on Drew. She didn't even look up at me her entire expression blank. *Why?*

I ran a hand through my hair.

"What the fuck is happening in this house?"

Talia shrugged lightly and rubbed Drew's hair back under her shirt. "I need to feed him. He's my priority."

Not Andrei.

I let out a breath. *What the fuck happened to those two?*

I first met Talia a few years after Andrei took me in. He hadn't introduced us until later.

But I had seen the way Andrei was obsessed with her.

"Gemma said she found you a nice tutor," Talia said quietly like her husband of fucking years didn't just leave the house after he made his baby cry.

"She did." I was a little disoriented but she was deflecting. Because she didn't want to talk about it.

"What's he like? Is he good to you?"

He? Did Gemma not…*of course the secretive heiress wouldn't tell Talia or anyone.*

Gemma had a habit of not saying a word to people. She kept her secrets close to her chest. A trait shared by the entire Marchand clan.

"I'm surprised you hadn't complained to me." She didn't look at me once but she smiled.

I was processing what was happening to my family. The happiness I once saw with Andrei and Talia.

"It's different than what I'm used to."

"Not like Alma—"

"No, but…it's not bad."

"Maybe you needed a different style of teaching. This isn't combat or warfare. You can't just kill your tutor if you don't like them."

No. But I couldn't fuck her either.

Because I liked Avani. I liked her chestnut hair, her soft soul-filled eyes. Her warmth. Her laughter.

Being with Avani let me know that in this aspect of my life? I didn't need the drill sergeant yelling at me.

111

But maybe I needed her. I needed someone who helped me in ways good for me. Intellectually I recognized that.

I wasn't attracted to Alma.

She was attractive but a little terrifying for me. And I sure as fuck wasn't attracted to Talia—Andrei's wife was gorgeous but strictly Andrei's. Teo never dated.

Adjusting to my attraction to Avani as it grew was different for me.

"Thierry," Talia's voice cut me out of my spell.

"Sorry, I was distracted." I shook my head. "I'm sorry about everything. Let me know if you need him—me. Sorry. Me."

She was quiet. I had seen Talia through a lot of things.

A few months when we left Cape Verde when she had been three if not four months pregnant with Drew, I thought I had seen her shaken up.

Crying over her father. And of course, when she'd arrived to Drew, she'd been happier. So I thought.

My brother? Was a completely different man.

I let out a breath. "Do you want me to beat him up for you?"

As soon as I said it—she went quiet. Talia had a nervous habit of refocusing her attention on other things when she was stressed.

I was her current focus. Because Andrei had fucked up. Big time.

"I'm fine." But she sounded far from it. "Just keep me updated on how it goes, I can't wait to see how you progress. Don't do anything Teo would do."

As in, don't fuck my tutor.

The girl I'd been dreaming about for years. Or her hairpin in my pocket.

CHAPTER 9
AVANI

*Syrena knew she was on a dangerous path. The old
Pirate King Damon was known for his wicked
ways but she found herself unable to resist
temptation.*

MY EYES WERE GLUED TO THE PAGE, SIPPING MY COFFEE WITHOUT
taking them off. I wasn't missing a single detail.

"*It's happening!!!*" I squeaked. "Hurry Syrena, I hate slow burn
romance." I kept reading.

*When she made it to the hull, she knew she was in
his lair. His realm. And nothing was going to
stop her from striking up a deal with him.
Her virginity for her sister's life.*

Good. *Heavens.* I *knew* she would do this.

On the inside I was squealing because I knew there would be
smut. Pages upon pages upon pages of filth for me to read.

I practically giggling and wiggling my toes.

"I waited a whole year for this!"

*As she approached the mist from the night curled
around her lending an almost ethereal aura to*

113

the ship. Damon was known for having the most
impressive, largest ship in the land.
"How will I find where he is?" She muttered under
her breath wishing grand adventures came with
a better map than the one she had. "Do I just say
his name and he appears like a genie?"
A dark voice came from behind her. "He can."
Oh no.

Oh yay!
"Avani!" Alisha's voice cut through my story.
Oh no.
I groaned hanging my head and closing the book.
I waited *three* books for Syrena to finally find Damon.
And my sister was standing in the way of me and possible demon pirate king smut with a mermaid who had just gotten her legs.
The world was cruel to me.
"It was just getting good."
Alisha called me into her room. I loved my sister, but sometimes she had the worst timing.
She was puttering about her bedroom.
"Have you seen where I put that white dress? I have a photoshoot today and I can't find it—" she broke off walking in and out of her closet.
Uh-oh.
I looked at the pile of clothes on her bed. I did know which white dress she was talking about.
Because I may have borrowed it to wear when I was seeing Thierry.
Not that I was spending a little extra time on my outfits.
Or wearing a little more perfume. Completely being professional of course. I told myself it was the *proper* thing to do when going out in public. That was all.
Nothing to make a big deal out of it since I did not fantasize about Thierry DuPont in my bed, taking me like that dark pirate king took the Syrena the mermaid—*oh dear Lord.*
I stepped into Alisha's bedroom as she muttered about her memory.

While my bedroom had been pink all over—Alisha's was more subtle.

Alisha's bedroom was a woman's dream with cream and lush pink and vibrant colors here and there.

Her vanity done in a classic way with lightbulbs around the frame. The lighting overhead romantic and soft.

My sister was in her bra and panties rummaging through all her clothes trying to find all the items she needed.

"Umm," I went over to one of her chairs and sat down while Alisha stepped out slipping on a pink dress. "Don't be upset."

She stopped like she hit a wall. "Please tell me you didn't borrow it."

I bit my lip hard enough to leave marks.

"Avani," she put her hands on her hip. "I literally purchase half a store for you, and yet you steal the clothes in my closet—"

"I didn't steal it, I just—"

"Temporarily relocated it?" Alisha leveled a look at me. "Where is it?"

"In the hamper." I squeaked it out feeling like a mouse.

Alisha sighed her mock frown in place not quite hiding her amusement. "Darling, why don't you just tell me and I'll buy you one just like it."

But I liked hers because it felt like if I wore her clothes I felt more confident in them. Her clothes felt like armor.

I wanted to feel confident around Thierry.

And I didn't always. Maybe if I wore hers I wouldn't turn into a mess or a puddle of goo whenever he leaned in closer to read something or tapped my hand to get my attention.

He was adorable when he wanted to be.

I was acutely aware of how nervous I felt to be around him and sometimes he drew so much closer to me than I knew what to do with.

I knew we were just studying. It was just close proximity due to studying—that was it.

Not like his cologne made me dizzy or something due to the ventilation in the library or the way he pouted a little when he didn't understand something.

That's all it was.

I didn't have a crush on him.

I didn't imagine his skeletal tattooed hand on my body, wrapping around my throat.

Not with how those fingers would feel against my skin, how his grip would tighten enough, or him pressing me into the couch and taking me right there.

Propriety be damned.

Or the way he might growl my name in frustration or pleasure.

I didn't imagine him making out with me, over me, his body on mine—*finally*—I covered my face a little behind Alisha's pile of clothing and her blankets.

Because I completely and totally wasn't imagining him right now, taking me, right there covering my mouth growling sheer violence in my ear for retribution if I so much as squeaked.

I was about as red as strawberry now.

"I'm sorry, I'll let you know."

Her eyes softened. "It's all right, just let me know. I'll find something else to wear."

Alisha's closet was treasure trove of things. I always stole things from her.

Even if she did buy me things, it made me feel good to hoard all her objects. I wanted to keep my sister close to me. If anything happened to her?

I couldn't even imagine what I would do without her. I didn't want to.

"Can I help you pick something out?"

I hesitantly asked and she shouted I could. I followed her into the giant walk in closet she had and went through outfits until we found a few she could use.

"Do you have tutoring today with your student?"

"I do." I handed her a few pieces of jewelry. "Are you excited about your shoot?"

Alisha chewed her lip. "Not really. I'm not feeling it. I kind of want to do nothing. The housekeeper should be in tonight. I'm sure our fearsome doormen will give her a hard time."

I wanted to laugh at her joke but I saw how exhausted she looked in her eyes. "Why are you taking on so many jobs when you don't want to?"

Alisha was rummaging through her shoes. "No reason. Just wanna keep busy."

Her voice was light but I heard something in her tone I didn't like.

Instantly I felt a twinge of guilt.

Why was she deflecting? Thierry had done it initially but somewhere in our sessions I'd like to think he'd given in.

"It keeps me occupied," Alisha said breezily. "I guess like your tutoring."

She looked at me then a little breathless from finding the shoes she wanted. "Did you want to go to brunch this week?"

I did. But I got the feeling Alisha wasn't meeting my eyes because she only did jobs she didn't like when we needed money.

More money. Because of me. And suddenly all of my residual frustration faded, evaporating in smoke until I felt nothing but guilt at even thinking ill of her. She was always doing the best she could. I shouldn't have done that.

If Alisha was doing videos and features and a bunch of other things, we needed it…the money, the free items, the brands working with her for the next four years while she supported me.

Not because she wanted it. But because of her sense of duty.

I'm starting school soon.

I swallowed, my throat working hard as I nodded with a smile I didn't feel. "I'd love to."

Her eyes went bright. "Still reading about your pirate king and fairy prince?"

I ducked my head at her laughter. Alisha might've not read fantasy but she still knew about the hot supernatural men I loved.

I COULDN'T FOCUS THAT SESSION WITH THIERRY.

Not when my mind kept spinning between guilt about Alisha and awareness of him sitting so close, his cologne making my head a little dizzy and weak.

I knew about his life enough to know it wasn't pretty. Not by his brother's rage or words. I knew some of his struggles or where he had been.

But he didn't know mine.

I couldn't just tell him either.

Not about Alisha. Not about us. In my mind Alisha had always been ironically, a private bubble in my life.

117

When I went home and I closed the door the outside world stopped existing. It was just the two of us.

Sister movie nights and stolen dresses and sleeping next to her whenever I got too scared.

I was attached to her and our little world after losing Mum and Dad.

I had never really let anyone in or had decent friends in secondary school.

But today the weight of my life felt a little heavier at the thought of Alisha running around the city trying to make our ends meet.

Whenever I suggested we make eggs and rice, Alisha shook her head now and said we can have nicer things. Better things. She'd gained weight over the years and she was healthier.

But money was a big factor behind it.

Rather than being focused on the next sentence in the book, my mind was running through ways to tell Alisha I didn't have to go to the university I picked if it was too expensive.

I could go to a normal city college, instead of Astor University.

I could easily not go either. I could go to school online...

The last thing I wanted was for my sister to struggle more.

My vision blurred at the memory of Alisha's struggles and my throat tightened.

"Avani," his voice was deep and he dipped his head so fast in front of me then his eyes curious. "What's the matter?"

I couldn't focus properly and I kept blinking back my emotions as I spoke, using my hair to block out his body so he wouldn't see me losing it. I looked away, my gaze on the carpet

"Allergies," I whispered rubbing my eyes so he wouldn't see me break. I felt so stupid. "It's all right, let's just focus on—"

"Avani." His voice was firm.

"It's fine. Just some family stuff."

He paused and I didn't look at him. I felt his eyes on me. I always did and I felt inadequate.

Because a man like him wouldn't like someone like me. I didn't think Thierry was much older than me. Maybe nineteen.

"Alisha is all right?"

I nodded. I looked at his book and realized we hadn't even moved a page. I felt bad.

Now I was taking up his time with my grief.

Gosh, was there anyone I didn't hold back?

I wanted to scream. I sniffled then and turned the page.

At the same time his hand moved to take mine. The contact was electric for me as he gripped my shaking hands.

"*Avani.*"

His voice was low but deep and I swore he was even closer than he'd been in a long time.

"I'm sorry," I whimpered. "I don't want to hold you back."

I didn't know Thierry for long and I was already breaking down a little.

"Hold me back?" Those fingers gripped my hands. "Avani, what's wrong?" I turned and nearly jumped back to find him right there.

A centimeter away from me and his other arm had wrapped around me.

Those electric blue eyes widened in alarm, the black rings making them look even more striking as he searched my face.

He said something rapidly in French before switching to English.

Gemma had tried to teach me French growing up. Safe to say, I didn't get.

"What's the matter?" He wiped my eyes making a noise I didn't expect to come from him. "Did something happen to Alisha?"

At the concern in his eyes, his thumb wiping my face, and his soft whisper as he drew me closer, something in me, what little resolve I had—shattered. When was the last time anyone did this?

A broken noise left me, and next thing I knew he was drawing me into his arms, hauling me on his lap. Months, if not years of pent-up emotions I only cried about in the shower or in bed and never in front of Alisha, poured out of me.

Thierry murmured something I didn't catch as I muffled my cries into his shirt.

His hand rubbing my back as I broke down. It felt like it went on forever.

I couldn't stop and every single time I thought I would?

I just imagined Alisha and her eggs over rice and us not having anymore food.

I couldn't stop.

"I-I'm sorry," I croaked.

"Shh," he rubbed my back and out of all people Thierry was not the person I expected to comfort me. "It's okay. Tell me what happened, *Mon cœur.*"

I didn't know what that word meant but it spilled out of me before I could even stop it.

Here, in his arms, I couldn't help myself from saying it.

"My parents passed away years ago. In an automobile accident. It was a drunk driver. They were visiting home, in England."

I laid there in the crook of his neck as I realized he'd tugged me onto his lap, one hand bracing my head to him keeping me tight to him.

And *nothing* had felt better.

"Alisha, she took care of me from the beginning. Sacrificed everything for me." I brokenly stumbled through the eggs story.

Alisha and her crying. I couldn't stop. I wiped my eyes over and over hiccuping as I said it.

"When she worked for your Mum the next day, everything changed for my family."

I was acutely aware that he was a DuPont, but somehow I didn't think anything I said would go anywhere.

"Everything changed for us. Alisha worked so hard and she was gone a lot but I knew she was trying to support us..." I told him about this morning. And I felt him wiping my eyes with me.

All the boundaries between us were gone in that moment and any worry I had about propriety melted away.

He made a soft noise. "*Mon cœur* , your sister isn't unhappy with you." He cupped my face then and I was a little stunned as he lifted my face to look into his eyes. "Not at all. If she didn't want to she wouldn't. She does everything for you because she loves you. She wants to. There's nothing you have to feel bad for—"

"But school—"

His expression was one of complete understanding as he urged me to look at him tipping my head up. "When I met my brother's I thought I was a burden to them. I acted out a lot. I thought they were giving me charity. Giving me shit. And I thought it was all about me."

His eyes met mine with warmth and a glint in them I recognized.

Despite his dyslexia he was highly intelligent and I saw it then.

He wiped my cheeks, softening as he watched me.

"It is not about you. Alisha is a lot like my older brother Andrei.

They're older siblings. Responsibility is their thing. I can tell you Andrei would never trade a day of work or anything to not provide for us." He brushed my hair back as my chest thumped a little from the contact. He held my face in both his hands.

"Alisha does what she does out of love. Don't ever think you're a burden or you're holding people back. You aren't. Hell, you're teaching me how to *read*."

He shook his head like he couldn't believe I didn't believe it.

"You're not anyone's burden. I promise you that." He held his pinky out and I hesitantly took it.

"H-how do you know that?"

He smiled softly, one dimple popping. "Lucky guess."

But I could tell that wasn't it. Not at all.

I licked my lips then feeling how dry they were and his eyes dropped to the movement. I stilled.

Sometimes when I was with him I would see another side to him. A side that I didn't really see all the time unless he knew I was in danger. But I liked it. I liked him.

It was a darkening of his eyes, his eyelids drawing lower and the way his Adam's apple bobbed—I could feel it in the air, the space between us feeling thicker as I did it again.

He looked like he was struggling with himself as he murmured.

"I've met a lot of people in my life. I've done a lot of things, and been to a lot of places. And I can tell you one thing. You are more profound than you realize. More impactful than you give yourself credit for. I don't even think you understand the impact you make in people's lives day in and day out. But I bet you do," he held my face as he said the words his eyes meeting mine.

Who was this man?

Gone, was the student I taught things to.

In his place was this…intellectual. He may not have been able to read but in that moment I recognized he didn't have to, to be this man.

His mere presence crowded my lungs and my thoughts then as I saw his lips move.

"You should never be upset," he whispered. "I hate seeing you upset."

My throat worked as he spoke. Like I was entranced with him, watching him with his eloquence and I almost couldn't fathom the duality of him.

"You're very eloquent for a man who doesn't read."

He smirked. "And audio books don't exist, Mon cœur ?" He raised a brow. "I didn't take you for a snob."

I was instantly embarrassed. "No, not at all. I just thought—"

"My interest in books applied to learning in general?"

"Yes. That's exactly why."

"You think you need to be able to read to learn everything in the world?" His voice was soft as though he were considering my next words.

"No, but a good majority of it is nice to have." I rushed to continue. "My grandparents were from Calcutta. They made sure my Mum got her education. They said a woman being able to read and write held more power for her, so she wouldn't end up with a man who took advantage of her. In their culture, it's common girls don't go to school past nine. Not as of recently, but there's still places that believe women should not be educated. It's quite important to me to maintain my education."

His eyes softened. "That's why you're so passionate about it."

I nodded eagerly. "My parents taught at Astor U. It's second in the country for being the best school."

"Why the second?"

"Well, I believe Kingsley U their competitor has a rather stronger sports department or something—Wait, we're talking about you!" I turned on him. "I didn't mean to imply you couldn't learn. I just thought your aversion to books applied to all things book related."

He was teasing me. He had to be. His smile widened, dimples and all. "I like to learn. I just don't learn like this. I have audiobooks. I read a lot."

"You do?" I was all ears.

He looked almost embarrassed. "It's all non-fiction—" Poo. "But it's just developmental stuff, philosophy, not fiction."

"Fiction is incredible," I nodded eagerly. "You're missing out."

"Oh yeah," he leaned closer. "What do you read?"

Oh. No.

Immediately no. Immediately no. The siren in my mind as all things Avani shut down and hung a 'closed for the day' sign at the thought of Thierry ever discovering what I read.

"I know you read," he smirked. "I can see the books on your phone when you swipe to text your sister."

I gasped. "That is most rude—"

"Yuh," he said like 'Duh' making a silly face. "What is it? I can't tell by the covers." That's the point. Who would ever think I was reading smut if the cover had a giant feather on it? Maybe I was reading about the anatomy of dust.

"I read non-fiction too." I said lying through my teeth.

"Like what?" Drat.

"Oh you know…" I looked around discreetly. "The same things. Self-help. Things that are um—" I cleared my throat. "Intellectually stimulating." I mean, it was definitely stimulating. But not intellectually.

"Like what?" Oh, he was a persistent devil.

I ducked my head. "Oh, I'm just finishing this book about…the sea." And pirates. And steamy mermaid scenes.

"The sea." He didn't sound like he believed me. "You like self-help stuff?"

"I do."

"So you've read Terry Morris?"

Who? "I have."

"And you like his work?"

"Fabulous."

He was quiet. I quietly turned a little and he was biting back laughter. "And you thought he was great?"

"I did."

His grin was wide. "Terry Morris is a musician who died in nineteen forty-five."

Drat! "I knew that." I turned away as he chuckled. "I was simply testing you."

I felt his shoulders shaking as he tugged me closer his voice dropping to a whisper. "You're still a terrible liar, Mon cœur."

"What does that word mean?" I dared to ask feeling the heat crest my cheeks. I despised non-fiction. But I didn't know what Mon cœur meant and he called me that all the time.

"It means, you're a terrible liar." He grinned against my cheek. "What do you read? Is it romance?"

This. Pirate!

I gasped clapping my head over my mouth as a triumphant expression crossed his eyes.

"Aha! It is romance. That's why you won't tell me."

A healthy flush lit his cheeks up.

"Is it historical romance? Knowing you, you would like that stuff since you talk like a seventeenth century queen..." He trailed off watching me as I turned away offended.

"Is it?" He asked again.

"I do not talk like a seventeen-century—oh, let me out." I tried squirming off his lap but his easy-going laid back demeanor was gone, and his arms felt like bands of steel around me now.

"Not so fast," he looked like he was utterly delighted. "What is it? What kind of romance? Is it filthy stuff?" His eyes went wide as he mock gasped and I ducked my head.

"*No.*"

He laughed outright covering his mouth. "Mon cœur , I'm going to start giving you lessons in lying from now on. You say that No, like you didn't steal all the treats and hide them."

I was beet red.

Beet. Red.

"You're incorrigible."

"Perhaps," he whispered, dropping his voice again. He gently turned my head. "It's pretty fucking filthy isn't it?"

At my expression his eyes went even wider. "Damn. Never took you for the type—"

"I do not—"

"To be a horny—"

I gasped and thwacked his arm as he laughed lightly. "You are a terrible, horrible, scoundrel of a man—"

"Oh no, please help, she's beating me up—" Thierry fell back into the couch filled with silent laughter that shook his shoulders and I felt nothing but heat and embarrassment as I rolled up the children's book and pounced on him now.

I took him down to the couch lightly batting him with the children's book. "You should be ashamed of yourself—"

His mouth opened in a wide grin as he kept his laughter silent.

"Stop teasing me about my romance novels," I hissed. Thank goodness nobody was up here.

"So you admit," he stopped laughing. "You read them?"

My jaw dropped as he burst into laughter again looking like a tickled baby. "I'm leaving you!" I hissed and I made a move to get up.

Or I would've had he not chosen that moment to stop laughing, and move quicker than I thought possible. I knew he was powerful and quick. I didn't know how much until now.

His hand shot out, lightening fast, hauling me down onto him and into the side of the enormous couch. Pressing me into it before I could yelp, his body a rock solid stable force against mine. His nose immediately pressed into mine.

"No," he said calmly, like he hadn't just yanked me and pinned me to the couch. "Stay. Let's talk about this like adults."

The air left my lungs, I lost my train of thought for a moment. Electric blue eyes rimmed with that black around the pupils watched me.

Every move of his lips brushed against mine, the scent of his cologne in my lungs as I inhaled.

The tip of his nose pressed into me and I didn't move a little wide eyed at his reaction.

How he managed to take me from emotional to intellectual to losing control—I didn't know. I just knew I was here. Trapped. A little helpless. A lot breathless.

"Like intellectuals," he said like I wasn't pinned half under this rogue.

"Are you moving your head closer so you can kiss me every time you speak?" I whispered trying to sound offended and failing because how could a woman not. It wasn't every day I was accosted. Not by this man at least.

My lips didn't brush against his so I knew he was trying to kiss me over and over. And I was amused. I was fighting my laughter.

Those electric blues turned wicked, flecks of lighter blue in them, the black rings made him even more striking like this.

"Am I?" Scoundrel.

"I can't believe I thought highly of you."

He looked delighted. "You did now hm?" His hm was pressing his lips to mine.

"You're a devious man."

"I've been told."

I heard a noise and I gasped trying to move but it was impossible with how tight he held me. We were lying on the bloody couches for Christs sake.

"Someone might catch us."

"Who? Who?" His lips did that thing again where they stamped on mine. "Who might catch us?"

"Are you really sneaking in kisses right now with every *Who* that comes out of your mouth?" He was. A menace. His smile was wide. Canines. Dimples. Electric blue. Wild. *Dangerous.*

"That depends. Do you like it?" He grinned wider looking downright devious. "You insult me if you think that's a kiss."

His eyes glittered dangerously on me. "It's not my fault your lips are too close to mine. If I didn't know any better I'd say you liked kissing me."

I would've gasped had it not been the truth right now.

Because he was a playful dangerous thing that held onto me now. Teasing me. Toying with me in a way that made my heart squeal with delight.

"You are going to get us in trouble."

"You are the woman who jumped me." He pretended to faint, leaving my face for a second "*Accosted*, by the Brit!"

A reluctant giggle left my mouth at his antics. "Why are you like this?"

His head snapped back up and he pressed his nose against mine again. "So, is it erotica? What kind of romance?"

My jaw dropped. "You're not letting go are you?"

"Of course not," he looked like I was the one who didn't understand. Electric blue eyes flashed at me. "I wanna know. I wanna download the audiobook."

"*No.*" The horror. I imagined Thierry reading or even listening to half of the smut I did read and I was *horrified.*

He must never know the filth I consume.

"*It is erotica.*" I caught his grin, wicked and canines flashing with this eyes of his. "*Oh, Mon cœur —*"

"*Stop talking—*"

"*Make me.*" His nose was on mine again pressing. "*Who's gonna make me?*"

Every *who* pressed his lips into mine.

"You know what, Mon cœur ? I think on my way out, I'll just announce to the *entire* library that little Avani likes her—" he raised his voice as he said it and I didn't think twice. I yanked his collar and slammed my lips into his.

The moment my mouth touched his it was electric.

I felt a noise leave me as I pressed further into him, until every inch of him molded to me.

His mouth moved over mine as a sigh left him, hot and hungry, his tongue tangling with mine.

A softer noise left me as he did and I held him closer until I gasped pulling myself apart. It felt like a feat.

"There." I managed breathless. "Are you happy now? Are you going to keep your mouth shut."

His smile was devious.

I'm a slut for dimples.

"And for your information, it's not erotica. It's romance. Some of its dark. Some of it's not. *And it is an art!*" I whispered furiously.

An angry voice cut through the air.

"Excuse me, you two! What do you think this is?"

I gasped and shot up at the sight of a librarian frowning at both of us. A sinking fear shot through me and my heart dropped to my stomach. "This isn't your house where you can come and hang out."

"I am so sorry!" I started feeling the shame and embarrassment boiling over me. I looked down at Thierry ready to haul him up and leave here.

"Ahh," Thierry clutched his eyes. *"It's still there."*

What? What on Earth was he? I looked at her and then at him. "Darling, what's wrong?"

"It's still in my eye." *What on Earth was he talking about?*

He shot me a look. I was confused. Until he rolled his eyes.

Ohhh. Right.

"Let me see," I leaned over him as I pretended to open his pretty eyes for what, a twig? A branch? "Eyelash?"

He nodded. Right. And I was Jane Austen in disguise.

I blew on his eye a little for show as I apologized to the librarian. "So sorry, he's like six-five, and I can't reach." I turned back to blow on his eye as he rubbed it.

I caught a smirk on his face as I had to lean over him more.

Devious. Scoundrel.

But he's trying to get you two out of trouble.

"Sorry, we'll just be out of here once I make sure he's not blind." I apologized breathless to the librarian who looked less angry now as Thierry slowly sat up with me. I brushed his hair back.

He blinked rapidly, putting on a show. "Thank you." His voice was polite, professional as he smiled at her. "Sorry about that, she's tiny like a bean. So she had to reach over and—" he motioned to his eyes.

She looked like she didn't believe us so I grabbed our books. "We'll be on our way now. Isn't that right?" I motioned for him to follow me as I stood. Both of us politely nodded to her as she frowned at us.

We rushed down the stairs and I didn't look at him until we burst through the sunlight doors, Thierry hot on my heels. The moment we got outside, we took one look at each other and burst into laughter.

"An eyelash!" I thwacked him with a book. "Out of all things."

"It worked!" He shouted back looking delighted. I couldn't stop laughing.

"You're mad! I can't believe you! That was my favorite library—" I broke off covering my mouth to hide my smiles.

"You can find a new favorite," he shrugged lightly still grinning ear to ear. "Plus, it cheered you up to get kicked out."

"No, it didn't! I was only smiling because I kissed you and then you pretended—" I broke off at what I just said. His grin never faded and I had to duck my head I was so embarrassed. "I was right about you being a rogue. I bet you did it to get out class today."

"You looked like you needed it." Electric blue eyes were soft and filled with amusement as he watched me. "A break." He motioned out into the sunlight steps, the street. "I needed a break too."

I shook my head ruefully at this man.

"You realize what this means right?" He eyed the library.

I did.

"We can't study there again."

"Oh no," he didn't look sorry at all. "Where shall we go?"

"Is that your mock impression of me?"

"No, that's my mock impression of me doing a mock impression of you," he laughed outright at me grabbing his book to smack him. "Easy, we can go to my place."

"What?" I squawked. "Why?"

"Are you quitting on me?" He asked teasing but I caught a hint of something else there.

"No," I shook my head, looking away now embarrassed. "Not at all. It's just…you trust me in your home?"

He snorted like that was funny. "Avani, I'm only concerned with you eating all the red-velvet cupcakes in my fridge."

I gasped motioning to thwack him again and he held his hands up like he was guilty. "Easy, there is no cupcakes in my fridge."

I lowered the book.

"Why do you always get me so worked up?"

His grin was back. Wicked. Wild. A little like him. But I liked that smile. It was turning into favorite thing in the world now.

"Because you look hot when you're pissed."

I take it back. He was a scoundrel. *"You are truly—"*

"A scoundrel." He mocked in a deeper British voice, his height looming over mine. Inky hair messed up in the wind and grin in place he looked devastating.

"A scoundrel." We both finished. I huffed out a breath and shook my head. Truly. This man. I was tempted to throw a book at him.

Or kiss him.

I didn't know which one.

One moment, I was crying in his lap, the next we were getting kicked out of the bloody library.

"Now what?" I asked him motioning around us.

"I'm hungry." He said his eyes twinkling and never leaving mine. "Let's go get some food."

CHAPTER 10
THIERRY

"Mon cœur, you keep staring at me like that over your pizza and I might think you wanna kiss me again."

"Oh, shove it, pirate." She scowled angrily taking a bite of her pizza. She frowned adding in more red pepper flakes.

I snorted. "You want some pizza with those red pepper flakes?" It was covering every inch of the slice. "You're so vicious underneath all that fuzz."

"I like my food spicy," she whispered over the hum of the fridge we sat next to. "I am not vicious. I simply don't eat next to a pirate who insists on making fun of me the entire time."

"I'm not making fun of you—"

"No, pray tell what are you doing then?"

"I'm teasing. There's a difference."

She frowned chewing her bite and covering her mouth all proper and shit as she asked me. "And what's that?"

Well. For one thing. She'd love me teasing her. And for another, I'd never make fun enough of her. I would tease her until she kissed me again.

I'd found us a tiny pizzeria that was a hole in the wall because I needed something solid. They did sandwiches and I got myself one with extra meats, and Avani a few slices with a few toppings.

That she then drowned in red pepper flakes. The spice made her cheeks flush and her lips pouter than usual. Avani liked spice, liter-

130

ally and figuratively. I was thinking a little about her love of sex. And all things sexy.

She sat across from me, chestnut hair pushed back, doe eyes batting at me innocently as she ate her food.

Instead of answering her question I took a bite of my sandwich as she ate her slice.

"You're incorrigible," she muttered.

That I was. She wiped her hands with some napkins. "Do you always eat..." she motioned to my sandwich. "Healthy?"

I grinned covering my mouth now as I chewed my bite. "I wouldn't say it's healthy."

"Compared to mine it is." She sipped her lemonade and I drank my water to wash down the dry bread. I needed fuel. But I didn't eat junk, sugar or soda. I told her that and watched her eyes bug out.

"You don't eat sugar? Or dessert?"

"No."

"Cupcakes?"

I smirked. "No."

She sat back looking stumped. "And to think I kissed you—a man who commits blasphemy on a daily basis."

My face hurt from laughing so much with her. "I kissed you first."

"Don't remind me," she looked down at my food.

I grinned down at her expression. "Do you want some Mon cœur?"

It was turkey and enough veggies on it to qualify as a salad between two slices of whole wheat. Not the 'healthiest' but compared to Avani's pizza, it was questionable.

She frowned. "No, I have pizza. It would be rude."

"*You* beat me up with a children's book."

"*You* started it."

If I laughed any harder today my cheeks were going to go numb. "Here just take a bite." I held it up at an angle with both hands.

She looked hesitantly.

"Mon cœur , if you don't take a bite I'm telling the man up front about your literotica—" she moved so fast her mouth coming down over it to take a bite.

Except as she did, and moved back brushing her hair back and chewing with an angry little furrow in her brow—I kinda lost my shit because she looked cute as fuck. My entire body noticed.

"How is it?" I tentatively asked as she finished and took a sip of lemonade.

"Delicious, I wasn't expecting that much lettuce to be so good," she admitted. I felt my lips quirk. "Say, what does moon kur mean? You call me that and now I feel as though I should know?"

Two could play at this game. Mon cœur was my heart. Probably just a slip of the tongue. Not a big deal.

But I can't tell her that.

I cleared my throat to compose myself. "What romance novel are you reading now?"

Her eyes went wide. "Excuse me, I need to use the restroom." She rolled her eyes a little and stood up, the pink dress she had on today had hiked up a little and did I shamelessly watch her walk away with a little giggle.

I grinned leaning back but my thoughts were wild.

How did I tell her?

I wasn't a student. I wasn't a real DuPont.

I'm a former assassin who got laid off, who is skilled in two things. Fighting and fucking.

And of those two skills—I want to do one with you—I'll let you take a wild guess as to which one.

I day dream about you every single fucking day since I met you. Unhealthily so. And as a man who sticks to his diet and his discipline I put you right under sugar.

Because if you got any sweeter?

I wouldn't be able to resist you.

The end.

Yeah.

That would go over real well.

Idiot.

Just as she did go to the restroom, the bell on the door dinged a little and I saw two guys walk in. Latin, dressed in oversized clothing, and if I wasn't mistaken one of them was carrying. Judging by his jacket? I'd bet on it.

Immediately my instincts were on edge. I wore my ball cap inside the restaurant in public, but they walked in and one of them went to the back to use the bathroom.

But there was a mens room and woman's room.

I relaxed a little. Not like he'd there when she—Avani chose that moment to step out then wiping her hands and tossing the paper towel in the trash as he walked by her. She didn't look up, instead her eyes found mine and she smiled a little at me.

Like she was relieved to see me.

And then he said something to her.

I didn't catch it. I couldn't hear it over the blood rushing in my ears, but I saw *her* head turn to him confused and disgusted.

Absolutely. Fucking. Not.

I was up and moving faster than I thought fucking possible for me, food completely forgotten, red fury in my vision as I caught up to her just as the guy walked into the mens bathroom. I operated on pure rage.

Every predatory instinct in me alight.

"What did he say to you?" I rounded on a wide-eyed Avani.

"I don't know it was in Spanish," she shook her head looking off, but something in me wanted to slam in there and kill him. "But he made this noise with his mouth, like a sucking noise, I don't know it's disgusting."

Her eyes met mine then, worry in them cutting through my rage. "Come here," she pulled me with her smaller hands over to our table. "Come on, let's go. Let's pack up."

"Why?"

Her eyes were alarmed at my face. "Just let's go. Okay? I'm not comfortable here and I don't feel safe. We can go somewhere else."

Like where? But Avani was already packing up her pizza rapidly and my food.

She moved quietly and quickly like she had experience in this and before I knew it she was taking my hand. We were leaving just as the other man was coming out.

"Why did you—"

"We'll talk after I promise," she was moving across the bustling streets of the city, holding my hand making our way to the nearest park. "Come on."

When we got across the street, she motioned to a park bench and pushed me gently to sit.

She set out food down and stood between my legs taking my face in her hands, I could feel the blood still rushing.

The need to fight him for disrespecting her or even thinking he could? Ran rampant through me.

"Hey, hey, what happened?" She murmured over my face. "Where'd you go just now? You don't look like you."

I blinked as the scent of honey and roses, chestnut hair and soft eyes cleared into my vision.

"I left because I was worried about you more than me, I saw this look in your eyes. I know what you're capable of, I don't doubt for a second you'd rather kill him," she spoke softly but I was the one startled now at her understanding.

The calm in which she spoke told me she knew.

She fucking saw it on my face.

"I've dealt with harassment before, I believe Alisha says it's the sad truth of being a woman. Had there been no men, she said she might actually feel safer most of the time." Avani's smile was soft but humorless. "I don't like escalating the situation, or putting you in danger—"

"I wouldn't have been in danger—" If she needed me I was Death. I could do it. I was a fucking former Reaper for fucks sake.

"I don't care," she spoke over me. "I don't want to see anything happening to you. Especially not because of me."

"You don't want me to fight for you?"

She shook her head, the wind whipping the chestnut locks around. "It isn't worth it—"

"It is!" *How could she say that?*

"No," she held my face tighter, as though her smaller hands could contain my violence. "It isn't. Not over them. Not over small things. It never is worth it. It's a lose-lose situation—"

"Not if I kill him—" it spit out of my lungs.

She huffed a breath out not batting an eyelash. "Then Andrei sends you back to where?"

As she said it, it hit me like a gunshot.

That's why she's protecting me. Because she knows me. She knows.

She wasn't kidding. She did know I was a wilder child. To put it lightly. She was trying to save me from myself.

"Take a deeper breath," she murmured. "It's okay. It's just words. I didn't even understand any of it. I don't care. Besides," she motioned to our food. "We haven't finished dinner."

She held my face tighter. And tighter.

Her voice came through soft and hesitant, her eyes lighting up with something I recognized. Heat.

"Want me to distract you?"

I was all ears now. I brushed my nose against hers. She was so close. So close. All warm and honey and soft. Pink in my field of vision now than anything else.

"Want a kiss?"

Just like that all of my anger shattered like glass and I felt her words sink into a softer part of me. "*Maybe.*"

Her smile was bright as she stamped her lips over mine.

CHAPTER 11
AVANI

TODAY I WAS POPPY WITH GEMMA.

Over the summer I decided to spend some time at Alisha's charity and while she held meetings in the building with Gemma, I was downstairs with the kids packaging boxes.

Putting away books. Busying myself when my phone buzzed.

Thierry.

He was the only person who messaged me besides my sister. And just the thought of him sent my butterflies roaming through my stomach.

It was a photo of his new book with a page folded in.

I knew if I responded he'd call.

So I don't know why I tempted it. I reacted to the message and he called instantly. And my heart skipped several beats at that.

Ever since he'd comforted on his lap two weeks ago? I'd felt my heart lose it when he was around.

I still taught him and he was graduating to early middle school level books easily, albeit simpler ones—he was in my every waking thought.

"Do you like your book so far?"

I could hear his grin as he said. "I do. This must be why American kids have overactive imaginations. A magical tree house that transports me to any destination in the world?"

"Perks of growing up in America, you be transported to anywhere in the world. By a rocket ship, a magic school bus—"

"A treehouse or a dragon scale, Mon cœur."

My cheeks would hurt with how hard I was smiling.

I walked past some of the volunteers to Alisha's downstairs space. "Hang on, I have to get comfortable for this conversation."

"Where are you?"

"At Alisha's project, Poppy? It's a little away from Midtown?"

"My apartment's not too far from there."

"Oh." *Oh? Why don't you just make a fool of yourself!* "Must be nice."

He chuckled. "Are you doing anything with your sister?"

I was. "Yes. Alisha likes this chocolate shop and Gemma has been talking about this Greek place she wants to us to. My sister can cook but simple things."

"Andrei can cook but Teo can't. You should see him with—"

"Avani!"

My sister beamed at me from the doorway of the office I was in, in her red outfit and hair half up, half down. She looked polished in her business casual outfit.

At the sight of my phone to my ear, she pouted. "I'm sorry, are you in the middle of something? Someone brought cinnamon rolls. I thought you might like some. Gemma's been meaning to get us chai so I thought we'd take a break."

I loved cinnamon rolls. With chai.

"Ohh, save me one. No, two. Are they the big ones from Butterscotch?"

Alisha grinned, eyes sparkling on me. "I'll save you three, so you don't eat my arm, you tubby bunny."

Alisha laughed. "Gemma and I made sure we picked out the large ones."

This was so *embarrassing. Is this what families did?*

Oh Gosh. Could Thierry hear this?

I covered the speaker so Thierry would not hear her. Or I tried hiding my phone. "I would never—"

"Save it, red coat!" She giggled as she left. "Come upstairs when you're finished I'll close the door."

"I'm not a red coat!"

"Whatever!"

I put the phone to my ear again. *"Sorry,"* I was a little breathless. "We have—"

"Cinnamon rolls." There was a smile in his voice. I could hear it. "Mon cœur , you and your sweet tooth."

I winced. "Please tell me you didn't hear the rest of that."

"I did not," he said with a flat voice that sounded awfully like he did. I knew that voice. "What's a red coat?"

I groaned covering my eyes. "No. We are not doing this."

I could feel him there watching me with those eyes of his. Alien-blue but the most beautiful. Thierry was like midnight and sin wrapped in a dark package. And for a tiny tiny *tiny* moment he was mine.

"She has chai and I will accept any fate should there be good chai." His laughter made my cheeks hurt now. "I should go. Are you going to be all right teleporting with your magic school bus?"

"It's a tree-house, red coat."

My laughter echoed off the walls of Poppy, my cheeks hurting from the pressure. "I'm hanging up now."

"Nonono, wait, Mon cœur."

I was breathless. How could I say no to that?

"Yes?"

"We're still good for tomorrow?"

I had tutoring with him. "Yes. Did you need more time or did something—"

"No. I was just…" he trailed off sounding off. "No. I'm fine."

But he didn't sound fine. He sounded like he had something to say and I didn't know what it was as I turned to exit the room. "Okay, well…I'll see you tomorrow?"

I grabbed the door handle and yanked it. Only for it to not move. I didn't hear Thierry as I tugged again.

"Tomorrow."

I thought he'd hang up and so I yanked again.

"Alisha! Did you lock the door?"

That wasn't like my sister at all. I yanked harder.

"Lish! This isn't funny! Let me out!" I tugged and pulled, before banging on the door. "I swear to *everything* Lish, if you've locked me in here—"

And then the light plunged out. I stopped breathing. The only glow was of my phone. I looked down to call Alisha when I saw— oh, Gosh. *He hadn't hung up.*

"Hello…" I whispered tentatively.

"Are you all right? What just happened?" His voice was hard. His tone completely different than before.

"I think the door's locked, I need to call my sister," I know I sounded like I was going to cry but I couldn't help it.

"Keep me on this call, while you do. Text her instead and keep me on the phone," his voice was full of command that even I couldn't disobey.

I didn't understand why though. "Why?"

"Because if she doesn't remember you, I'm going to come over and get you out."

It was said with such force that I truly believed he would drive over to Poppy just to help me.

I wanted to tell him that wasn't necessary but I was too creeped out.

My heart sputtered as I texted Alisha.

"The powers out, Thierry."

And then just like that the door burst open and I felt a shriek leave me until I heard.

"*Avani!*"

I recognized Alisha's voice anywhere.

I was in her arms a moment later, her scent all over me in the darkness. "Oh Gosh! I thought you left me here!"

"*No! Are you mad? Never.* Someone tripped the breaker. I'm so sorry, I ran to you as fast as I could. I was upstairs, Gemma is figuring it out and I came to you."

She was running her hands all over me and making sure I was fine. I saw her bright eyes taking me in the dark.

"Are you okay? I'm so sorry!" She held me to her. "I didn't know that stupid door locked. Gemma keeps it propped open. I'm sorry!"

She sounded devastated like she had committed an offense that wasn't forgivable. But it was Alisha. I could forgive her for anything. But right now? My heart was pounding and racing as I held her back.

I clutched my phoned tightly, aware Thierry could hear everything. And then the lights flickered on.

Alisha let out a sigh. "I really have to fire the idiot who decided to flip a random breaker." She sighed, pushing my hair back. "Let's go upstairs, hm?"

I nodded clutching my phone to my side.

"Let me grab my backpack."

Alisha waited outside the door as I went to pick up my phone and I saw Thierry had hung up. Instead I saw a message.

A photo of a gif that said 'tomorrow.'

And I felt relief and something akin to disappointment course through me that he'd hung up.

For a moment I wanted an excuse to tell Alisha about him. About the boy who wanted to come and save me.

Instead I got another image from him.

He texted in photos and gifs because it was easier for him. Or he called.

This one was of a magic school bus.

I felt a reluctant smile tugging at my lips all while his voice was in my head.

Because if she doesn't remember you I'm going to come over and get you out.

"THIS IS YOUR BROTHER'S APARTMENT," I BLINKED WANDERING around the warm gold and sapphire themed penthouse.

It was like an *enormous* hotel suite.

"Andrei used to live here when he lived alone. All of the fancier touches is from his wife, Talia. She made it livable. Otherwise my brother would live in a box. But Talia said she was inspired by her favorite room over at the Primrose Hotel? I don't know if you know it, one of her friends actually runs it. They're friendly with the Nash family and so she modeled it after that suite…"

As I walked around with him, Thierry explained Talia was the nicer of the two and I remembered her name, but I did remember Andrei.

"Your brother is not kind to you?" I murmured casting a glance at his taller form over my shoulder. An embarrassed look entered his eyes.

"It's not that he's not nice, he's just…complicated. He's had all this pressure on his shoulders, and he's always had it, but I made it worse."

I remembered. When I met him. Andrei said he had been at war.

"What did Andrei mean when he said…what he did…" I felt it leave my mouth unable to stop and Thierry's face went blank. All the warmth vanished out of his face like a door slamming shut on me.

On me.

I remembered Andrei saying Thierry would go train with Talia.

A recruit. For Talon. Thierry never spoke of what he was or what he did. I just knew...when I saw him again after all these years —he looked *darker*. Different. The shadows in his eyes, the way he spaced out sometimes, the darkness he wore on his skin. The skeleton tattoos. I got the scythe on his wrist once. He had plenty of them.

Not that I'd ever seen him shirtless but I imagined it ran further up.

Thierry ran his hand through his inky hair. "Nothing. Just family stuff."

Immediately, I felt the curtain drawn between us. Things he couldn't talk about. I tried not to feel a little hurt by him, but considering he'd kissed me? It stung just enough.

I turned away so he wouldn't see my expression, but I felt his eyes on me.

"Mon cœur."

"No, it's all right. I understand. We should go and review your next book."

Thankfully, I adjusted my skirt as I brushed my hair around my face hoping he wouldn't press the issue. He didn't.

He adjusted the lights, and I walked through the high ceilings and lavish looking space a little awed by the amount of gleaming appliances, gold hardware, and stone that caught the crystal lights inside.

"It's very pretty," I whispered changing the subject, padding around when I got to the living area straight out of a magazine.

Ivory rugs, curved comfy sofas in white and blue, abstract art, and softer touches that told me a woman had lived here. Throws, lot of pillows, and books on coffee tables.

"That's how I know your brother had a wife," I pointed to the pillows desperate to fill my emotions with something other than... this. "No man believes in ninety-three pillows for his couch."

I felt Thierry's masculine chuckle behind me, so close as I turned to find myself right in his arms.

His inky hair was pushed back but that little bit kept falling over one electric blue eye. "So what do you say, Mon cœur ? Do you wan to study in here or on the island? Either way I made sure to get you snacks and junk if you'd like."

He said it like he had imagined me here and my comfort. It made my heart ratchet up a few beats. It looked like the earlier tension was forgotten. Which I was grateful for.

I blinked up at him and then looked around the place. "I am hungry…"

He tugged my elbow gently. "Kitchen it is, probably easier to focus too."

And so I ended up in his kitchen doing our library routine.

Except it was a slight bit more distracting now.

Part of me was still pondering about why he kept his secrets.

The other part became aware of him when he rolled his sleeves up and then finally gave up and took his hoodie off to reveal a ripped band tee underneath.

And I had to…look away and breathe a little.

Because if I thought he was dashing and handsome before…I would clutch my pearls if I could.

Muscles roped his biceps and forearms, but he was covered in double sleeves of tattoos. The skeletal tattoos on one hand.

Just enough for me to be more aware of him. Sure, he made us snacks and tea, but time here was an illusion.

Unlike the library, here in Andrei's place there was no clear delineation of time. And for some reason Thierry seemed more irresistible. More intimate. More real.

More…mine.

He moved around the kitchen with lethal beauty, all midnight and grace lined by his casual clothes. For a man and a family with money he didn't dress like it. Here, he was just Thierry.

Comfortable, talkative, and more willing to try something new. Even as I felt a little daunted by the access of wealth he had.

It was a little triggering to be reminded of what he had and I didn't have regardless of how much money Alisha made.

Then again, we always lived within our means. I fiddled with my tea cup as he practiced his lines. He was getting better.

I wondered one day, when he wouldn't need me at all, if he might still want to spend time with me.

I'd kissed him sure. And he had kissed me that day at the library, but…we hadn't talked about…anything. I wasn't sure where to start or what to say.

"I rather like this," I murmured absently trying to distract myself. I wasn't sure how long it had been but I had finished some of my snacks. "But since we don't have a library I'll bring books from home."

"Oh," his mouth quirked. "I don't know why I forgot…" he stood motioning for me to follow him.

We walked down a carpeted hallway, his footsteps quiet than mine, as we wandered through the place entering another study.

"He's got ninety of them around the city because he likes to be alone, but this is Andrei's personal library."

He motioned to the cozier room I was in. I peered my head inside to the emerald space that was a little different.

"Oh, this is gorgeous," I breathed out. Wooden panels lining the walls and the white bookshelves everywhere. Plush seats. Soft pillows. Art pieces. Decorated similarly to the rest of the apartment, I marveled at all the bookshelves, artwork, but mostly—

"She reads romance novels!" I rushed to the shelves on one side where there was an entire bookshelf dedicated to them. "Talia has great taste!" I was immediately checking them out, my earlier nerves forgotten.

"She has the original House of Shadows and Midnight! Ohmigosh!" I squealed feeling myself bouncing almost. Ohhhhh. This was perfect.

"Do you know they released six thousand of these? I can't believe she has a copy." I ran my fingers through the smooth cover. "I caught onto the series a little later but this is insane. I love this cover so much—" I broke off darting around all the shelves now. "This is the only romance shelf."

"Yeah, Andrei split it with Talia saying he needed his non-fiction or else he'd lose it, but I didn't think he minded much."

I didn't even feel Thierry come up behind me as he drew my attention to the photos dispersed on the shelf.

One in particular caught my eye of two kids, one looking like a younger Thierry with lighter hair and sparkling eyes, and a dark haired woman grinning holding up an award.

"That's Andrei and Talia," his voice was softer here. "They met when they were eleven in school, and my brother and her hit it off as friends. Pretty sure they've been dating for a majority of their life." An odd look entered his eyes as he said it. "She's twenty-nine now, and he's turning thirty. They just had their first kid."

I blinked. "This is your elder brother." I looked down at a young Andrei grinning ear to ear. "Hard to imagine him now."

Thierry nodded pointing to another frame. "And this is Teo."

And then he showed me a photo of Matteo probably a pre-teen scowling, looking like a drowned cat, and Talia and Andrei laughing in the photo. "I think they pranked him or something. Talia and Teo got along well. And since she became Andrei's wife, even better."

There was a soft quality in him when he showed me photos of his family frozen in time. It was endearingly vulnerable, but I understood these were private pieces of his life. A life without words.

"Andrei likes to keep things private, so he puts them in his study where he says he thinks the best."

"They look happier here," I whispered almost feeling like it was a secret. Since I got the feeling the way he said it, they might not be anymore.

But there was one thing I did notice as I put the book back on the shelf.

"There are no photos of you."

None of him at all. Just his family. And I don't know why it made my heart ache.

And *just* like that the wall was back. I remembered something about Andrei saying he had picked up Thierry from a woman named Tasha.

How Maxine DuPont had found out. It was a little confusing for me.

Unraveling him. His mystery. His identity.

"I didn't like photos," he murmured not looking at me. Instead he turned to the book I put back. "You can take that copy if you'd like. Talia and Andrei don't live here anymore. It's my crash pad. So none of it is mine or hers technically. With Drew she doesn't read anymore."

"Oh no," I was a little jarred as my chest ached watching him retreat into himself for the second time. "I couldn't. It's not mine."

"Talia won't mind," he murmured.

"No, I shouldn't." I shook my head feeling unease ripple through me. Why didn't he want to tell me? Was he afraid I would judge him?

144

After all that I knew. He turned to me a little more and I turned away not wanting him to see my expression.

Every single time I asked him anything personal he seemed to draw back a little.

Even if I had kissed him, there seemed to be walls between us I couldn't fathom.

One minute he was playful, teasing, endearing, and the next he became someone else completely.

Even if I had known bits and pieces, there were chunks of him left in the dark I couldn't seem to reach.

I didn't know how I felt about that.

I was navigating this too.

"Mon cœur—"

"No, it's okay—"

"Don't be upset. I don't like talking about my family."

"Why?" I dared to peek over my shoulder and I would've jumped back at how close he was. I didn't hear him move.

"Same way you're tight lipped about your *Didi*. It's my bubble." And just like that my anger soothed. His bubble. His privacy. "I don't like to mention it. Not used to it. Nobody ever gets near us and you're the first person I've brought over here. I'm getting…used to this."

His eyes were electric, but honest and soft as he watched me and I turned in his arms. It was like the world Alisha and I had.

"You want to protect your peace from the world?" I asked him.

"I do," he murmured.

"But I let you in about Alisha." I looked up at him.

"This is me letting you in about my family," he brushed my hair back. "And right now, this is as comfortable as I am. This is new for me too."

He let out a breath and I caught how vulnerable he looked right then. The dangerous edge to him gone, replaced by the softer look in his eyes.

The black rims of his eyes softened completely as they dropped to my lips.

"I asked because I would want to see photos of you. As a kid, as a teenager…" I trailed off feeling my throat work.

"I don't have any photos of me," his face blanked out again.

I don't know why, but I just knew, something was deeply wrong.

Because…Alisha and I took photos all the time.

She put them on our fridge along with my report cards and essays and other trinkets.

If she found something she liked, magazine cutouts. Our fridge was a collage of life that belonged together.

Alisha's sexier cooler self with me dressed as an oversized rabbit one year and all our memories. Even Gemma and Lara were on the collage.

We had photos on the walls sure, but…

"What about memories?" I blinked up at him unsure of why I felt this overwhelming urge to cry for him. Again.

Especially after my heart broke the first time learning he didn't know how to read properly. Another part of him hidden away from the world. Another part of me kept in the shadows.

He shook his head and I was rapidly blinking back my emotions as I glance at the photo of Teo, Andrei and Talia wrapped around each other. What about Thierry?

Where did he belong?

Where did he fit into his family?

Maybe he can fit into mine.

The thought drifted into my head like smoke. And it stayed there.

"Well, then…" I swallowed feeling my emotions threatening to choke me. "I guess we'll just have to take plenty of photos together then."

He made a noise and I turned back to him trying to smile but failing over how much of a watering pot I was.

"Lots of them. I have a camera at home and I'll bring it next time—"

"Mon cœur—"

"No, no arguments—" I wiped my eyes a little and felt his arms around me. "I'm bringing the camera next time. On our future dates where you eat way too many vegetables a person should be eating."

He was quiet for a long moment.

And every single time we did anything after that. I would cover his fridge and his walls with memories.

I cried harder as he hugged me to him, and I felt his lips all over my cheek whispering things I didn't understand.

"You should know I'm a solid C- in French," I croaked through my tears.

His chuckled filled my ears as he kept going.

CHAPTER 12
THIERRY

I HAVE MEMORIES.

She *wanted* to make memories with me.

Avani had a decently expensive polaroid camera that printed large enough photos in real time and she began bringing it in a little backpack everywhere we went.

Everything we did. The museums, the art galleries, the restaurants, and all of our dates.

She took photos of it.

And she collected them neatly into a little folder she had.

Every time we were at Andrei's after one of our dates—she put another photo up.

She even got me magnets of spooky things. Pumpkins. Spiders. Vampire fangs.

"It fits your darker aesthetic," she shrugged at me looking at my fridge—Andrei's fridge—now covered in photos. "I love it. It's spooky and dark, but cute—like you."

Nobody had ever called me spooky and cute.

My schedule from her now tacked on there proudly, my accomplishments from my beginner reading levels to now.

It was a little jarring seeing all of it displayed so proudly.

Avani beamed as she tacked on photos of food we ate together. She brought out a sharpie and decorated them labeling them.

Avani and Thierry's Day Out

Pizza Night

Eww, vegetables

Spooky Aesthetic

Thierry and Avani's Home

SHE'D DO CUTE HEARTS AND SHIT AND I REALIZED WHY MY BROTHER let Talia reign free over his home.

Now I fucking got why Andrei was obsessed with Talia and had been for almost two decades.

Having a woman in your life like this was different.

The first time I met Talia I didn't know my brother could love any woman like that. I had been a rowdy teenager and she'd been over for dinner.

That night I learned some of my brother's secrets.

And I learned who she was.

Avani reminded me of Talia a little. The way she put up funny dog photos too in between.

I grinned at the sight of her turning my fridge into a collage.

"I also got some lights we could string up to put our photos on…" she trailed off at my expression. "But I need your help, I can't reach."

And so there I was dutifully stringing up photos of us and our adventures together around the city in my brother's apartment all the while watching Avani find the perfect spot to put them in.

I didn't tell Avani I had no intention of staying here, and that I had nothing permanent to take with me.

I never had.

I had never had more than a suitcase.

I didn't have baby photos. I didn't have too many good memories.

Just memories of Andrei bringing me to a place like New York and keeping me at his side. Discreetly.

Always a secret in some way shape or form. It was different with Avani.

I hadn't…cemented anything with Avani.

Hadn't taken her even if I wanted her. She didn't know the truth. And it would never be fair of me to do that to her.

I didn't have the heart to tell her about my reality. Even if she had heard some things?

It didn't mean she knew everything.

And the words stayed choked up in my throat as I helped her put all our photos up.

I wanted to kiss her again. Mess with her a little. Tease her.

None of it came out though as she beamed up at her work and I looked up at my photos. Pictures of me. Pictures of her. Of us.

Together.

"This is how you make sure everyone know's I belong to you," I tried to tease her but my voice was too gruff for my own liking. "This is you marking your territory, hm?"

Avani's doe eyes widened on me, lips parting a tiny bit as she blinked up. "Oh."

I felt my lips tip up as she recovered quickly. "You're just saying that because you want kisses."

"Maybe—"

That I did.

But I meant it.

I belonged to her. I knew I did for a while now. I'd do whatever she wanted, whatever she said—happily.

"And that depends," I felt my mood shift. "Are you offering?"

"That depends if someone else is going to admit they want kisses."

I cuddled her tighter.

"You know maybe this is why my tutors failed—"

"Because you didn't get kisses—"

"I was going to say because they didn't care, but now that you mention it—"

"Don't you dare—"

"Maybe kisses would've helped—"

I laughed at her turning pink.

"Come here, mon coeur."

"No, you're a scoundrel—"

"I'm your scoundrel."

"This may true—did you just bite me?"

"That depends. Is there kisses for me? Or has the kisses bank run out?"

"I would never run out for you—"

"Then I've come to collect with interest."

She turned beet red and I laughed harder at her squirming as I lunged for her hauling her into my arms easily.

"Don't fight me, mon coeur. I like you too much to let you go."

"THIS IS EXCITING," SHE BEAMED AT ME ONE AFTERNOON. "YOU'RE graduating to middle school level which is insane considering we started not too long ago. You're doing great."

I grinned at her expression. I was doing better.

We talked about all the books and I found out Avani was teaching me to read with some of her favorite books growing up.

"I haven't ever done this well with my other tutors." I didn't know why I said it out loud but the moment I did her brows rose.

"Really?" her eyes were surprised. "Were they terrible? I'm not doing anything out of the ordinary."

On the contrary, she was.

"You gave up your summer to teach me and you don't think that means anything?"

She ducked her head with an embarrassed smile. "I do other things too." Her shy smile made me grin. "I spend time with my sister too."

That I knew. Both of the girls had a heart of gold.

I'd seen her Instagram—both of the sisters were stunning, but Avani did something different for me than her sister whose features were sharper.

Avani was soft with pastel pink all around her. I could practically see the butterflies floating around her head. Woodland animals all around her outside.

And then there was me—the dark God who fucked her in her field of flowers not giving a shit about who was watching.

I might've called her mon coeur, but she was more than that. She was sunshine and light. Brighter than I was.

Avani's smiles, her personality, everything about her was real.

In a world where I was hiding in plain sight constantly, invisible, and un-noticed, I was next to a beacon that drew in life. And I wanted some of that for me too.

I couldn't explain my pull to her.

Maybe because she saw me like some fool who couldn't string his sentences together and she didn't judge me. I struggled a lot when we read together.

But Avani was calm. She pressed kisses into my cheek. Sometimes she sat on my lap and read to me. Snuggles and kisses. That's what I'd been reduced down to as a man. Nothing more, nothing less.

Helping me sound out the words.

Letters. Shapes. Pictures.

"You're doing wonderfully, Thierry."

"You're not just saying that, mon coeur, you can tell me if I'm dumb—"

"You're not dumb," she held my cheek with her hand and kissed me steadily. Quietly. Until I melted into her body. "Shh, it's okay. I promise you're not dumb. Come here, let me kiss you again."

"Mon coeur—"

"This is my interest."

I laughed lightly into her kisses as she smoothed my hair back. Messy and unruly, Avani tamed it with her fingers before she stopped and asked me to read the lines again and again.

She didn't laugh or tease me and just encouraged me gently sounding things out and helping me.

Probably because she saw me at my worst, my underbelly soft and squishy around her gentle touch for her to pet me and tell me I was doing a great job.

I felt tame around her.

Part of me becoming someone I didn't recognize.

"I don't know what it is," I murmured not looking at her and focusing on the books in front of us. "But it's working."

"Indeed," she sounded warm. "You're now reading at seventh grade level in five weeks. It just shows you had the ability all along, with a bit of practice and persistence you did it. It means you have this knowledge, you just needed to hone it."

I had. I made significant progress. But thanks to her.

"You did it," I turned to her. "And you don't even get anything for this."

She looked adorably perplexed. "What do you mean?"

I fucking hoped to everything my face was neutral. "You teaching me. Gemma said you didn't ask for anything. Why?"

"I didn't want anything."

A tendril of her hair fell and curled around her breasts.

She wore soft colors all summer long and this particular shade made her skin glow again.

My eyes flickered back up to her face.

She turned red and looked like she was fighting a smile. And didn't that make me grin more.

"I did teach you, but you're also a good student and receptive to feedback."

"Spoken like a true professor." Avani wanted to go to college and get her Phd. I felt nothing but admiration for her.

Talia taught me to be a better warrior.

Alma taught me to be a better man.

Avani was teaching me life skills and how to read so I wouldn't drown as a civilian again.

She was a future professor. And me? I didn't have a future.

Yet *another* reason why I didn't even consider asking her out. Doing anything with her.

I'd been tempted to kiss her the first time I had seen her. But I wasn't that kid anymore.

Even if I wanted to kiss her? I knew better.

She bit her lip her smile growing as she looked away embarrassed "Not yet. Soon-to-be."

My cheeks hurt from smiling so fucking much about her.

"Besides," she said looking smug. "You always had the potential to learn. You just needed a firm hand. Who knows, maybe you'll end up in university and brag about it to me." She mock deepened her voice trying to mock me. "*Look, Avani I did it.*"

My grin was wide at her impression of me.

This fucking girl is adorable.

"Maybe, but I owe it to you." I gave her credit where it was due. And then I dared to ask because it was the end of July and she'd be going to school in a month. "Is this…are you going to be tutoring when you're in school?"

Because if she said no, we didn't have much time together and I didn't know why my chest clenched at that.

But if she said yes, she'd have to juggle me and my stupid ass along with her courses.

Something I would never make her choose between me or her schoolwork.

I wasn't a complete monster.

Avani looked down at the books, wringing her hands together making her breasts squeeze tighter and I had to look away or else it would enter my top three fantasies of her. All pink and pretty and flushed all over for me.

"Well, I'd like to adjust to the semester first," she whispered. Like it was a secret. "If you still want—"

"I want—" I broke off. Holy. Shit. I almost said it.

Breathe, motherfucker.

Avani paused. And I dared to look at her to find her eyes on me quickly darting away. "If you want to, we can continue when my semester starts but after I get my schedule?"

Be cool. Be cool. Be cool.

I nodded clearing my throat. "Sounds good."

AVANI FOUND ME A MYTHOLOGY BOOK TO READ TO GROW MY knowledge of everything I had so far.

She was starting school in two weeks.

So this would be one of our last weeks as she got settled and got ready to go to school.

Time was flying by with her. Being around Avani I felt less like myself and more like someone else.

A different man I didn't recognize. Talia checked up on me from time to time but I didn't have the heart to tell anyone. I didn't know how to voice it.

What could I have said?

I'm falling for my English tutor?

No. I couldn't have fucking said that...could I?

"Did you like the new myths book I got you?" She asked. "It's from my own library at home and I think it reads rather well."

"I do. I'm almost done with it too."

"Who's your favorite?" she asked me conversationally writing something down on her pink post-it notes. "I bet it's Bacchus."

Debauchery? *No. All Teo.* I had a personal favorite as I looked down at my notes.

Now my books were covered in her handwriting. In mine. With hers. Her script and loops next to my flat garbage handwriting.

Easy answer. "Hades. Hands down."

Her brows rose a little looking amused and surprised. "Not Ares or Zeus?" For some reason she looked down at her hands with a grin.

I shook my head. "Those two were dickheads. I'd pick Hades any day. He's just doing his job. He's misunderstood. Everyone sees him as the bad guy but he's the only one doing anything relatively worthwhile. Plus, he's faithful to his wife. Something Andrei taught me was the bare minimum after Phillipe's bullshit."

I froze. Did I let on too much? Shit, it just slipped out.

Lucky for me Avani didn't catch on. She chuckled looking warmly at me with something in her eyes I didn't recognize.

"He is rather misunderstood when you put it like that."

I turned to her then with a grin. "What about you?"

Her eyes held a glint of something I couldn't put my finger on and I saw her move her hand over her myth book.

"I haven't finished reading the book either." She shook her head looking a little shy. "But I would say Athena."

That was surprising. I would've at least picked her for Artemis.

"Strong and resilient." I guess, I got it.

"Pretty sure she almost ate her father," she quipped.

"I thought he ate her?" I teased.

She squirmed. "Eww."

"She's also the goddess of wisdom." And Avani wanted to be a professor. Made sense.

"That she is," Avani whispered looking at the book. "I got this book at the beginning of the Summer. I thought it had the best retellings of the myths. More accurate. So I'm not surprised, or at least I shouldn't be you like Hades."

Her smile grew as she looked down at the book. "He is indeed faithful. And a woman likes a good husband. What's the phrase? Happy wife, happy life."

Andrei needed to learn that phrase.

For the rest of the session Avani quickly focused on getting out the rest of the chapter.

When we finished I opened my mouth to offer her a ride home. But she had declined me weeks ago.

I don't know why I dared to now.

"Can I give you a ride home?"

And to my surprise she chewed her lip and considered it.

"I was going to pick up some things for Alisha. If it was up to my sister we would have eggs over rice and mochi donuts all the time." Her expression made smile. "Maybe some other time?"

My heart didn't like that. "Where is it?" I tried to keep it casual. "I can drop you off."

Desperate, much?

She squirmed again. "Um…it's a bakery. *Butterscotch's.* I think it's named after their dog. They do really good sandwiches and cookies, but I'm going to go there before I head home." Her eyes drifted up shy almost. "It's a little bit away from here—"

"Where is it?"

She told me the address. It was about a twenty minute drive. But it got me twenty minutes with her.

"I can drop you off at the bakery and then head home? It's not too far from Andrei—my apartment." I corrected myself feeling a pang of something else. I'd kissed her sure. But I hadn't…we hadn't…talked about anything else. "It's our last session before you start shopping for college, it's the least I could do." I put a hand to my heart and offered her a smile.

She chewed her lip looking a little shy, a faint blush on her cheeks telling me she was thinking about it. "Okay."

I grinned wide then turning away to pack up my books.

"I parked in the next block, do you want me to bring the car around or do you wanna walk with me?"

"I'll walk with you," she murmured. And together I finally fucking finally stepped outside with Avani.

After weeks and weeks of tutoring with her, cooped up in the dark, stepping out into the sunlight with her felt good. I felt like I was with her.

I didn't realize how dim the library was until we did.

"What kind of car do you drive?" She asked me quietly.

"It's a Roadster. Teo got it for me." And then I realized my plates on the car were custom. Avani wouldn't know what they meant but it wasn't ideal. *Shit.* What did I do? "It's Teo's car. I have to bring the car back to him in a few weeks to tweak it."

Smooth.

She smiled at me with that same trusting smile, as I moved to the sidewalk side of the street.

I'm an idiot for lying to this girl.

And that's what's holding me back.

Because I had to lie to Avani about fucking everything in my life? I knew I couldn't do anything beyond this with her.

I reminded myself that as I saw how absolutely fucking delectable she looked in lilac.

A fucking mini *dress* hugging her tight ass and breasts.

As she walked they jiggled a little and it took every single fucking thing in me to not throw her against the wall and fuck her, sucking on them.

I had problems.

As we walked I caught a wolf-whistle and Avani's smile dropped from her lips, a different look entering her eyes, like she was sick to her stomach.

Both of us turned to find two guys eyeing her and I realized I'd been walking a polite two feet away from her.

No chance of that anymore.

Nothing would happen to her ever on my watch.

Instantly I was on her, wrapping my arm around her shoulder shooting them a look as they *instantly* stopped.

Fucking idiots.

Her weight pressed into my body as she stumbled a little. I caught her deftly, hauling her back against me for the first time in a long time.

"Breathe, I'm right here," my voice felt off. "I won't let anything to you."

I felt how tense she was and I tucked her closer to me.

The fact that idiots like that made that shiver run down her body make me want to tell Cole to hunt them down just so I could torment them a little.

The wave of possessiveness that hit me was only something I reserved for my family, for the people close to me and my circle.

Avani—she was profoundly more important that.

Not just because she was a source of light amidst the darkness I was. But because something in her soothed me.

The idea of anything threatening that part of her had to be eliminated.

No questions asked. When it came to her? I'd pull the trigger every time against any threat against her.

"Thank you. I do hate that," her shoulders relaxed a little as she let out a breath.

I felt a reluctant smile curve my lips as I matched my steps to her smaller ones. "I can't imagine a woman who likes it."

Her curious eyes turned to mine. "I take it you're not one of those men who thinks women deserve it or are asking for it?"

"*What?*" At my expression she smiled. "*Avani.* That's asinine that men say shit like that. God, if Andrei's wife, Talia? Or Alma? Shit. Natasha? Avani, my sister-in-law would kill people for saying that. Let alone *thinking* it."

Both of the girls, Talia and her sister Natasha would torture a man alive for even touching a woman like that.

Alma was just as bloodthirsty.

But she was quiet about it.

In my memories there was never an instance where Andrei, Teo, and I said something so fucked up. For all of Teo's antics, women flocked to him either way.

I grinned drown at her expression as we approached the garage.

"That's rather modern of you," she said her eyes looking a little dubious at the garage. "You parked here?"

It looked a little creepy to say the least. I swallowed. "If you want, you can wait outside I'll go grab the car. That's what I would've said but then—" I looked behind where we had left the creeps. "I figured why venture into a sunlight path with two men leering at you when you can venture down into a dark basement with a man you kinda know?"

I shrugged at my attempt at humor.

Because the garage looked beat up and run down and that's exactly why I chose it.

I parked in the lowest level in the dark. I was armed and my knives were in the trunk.

Not that Avani's sweet self *needed* to know she was right next to the most dangerous thing in the city.

Sometimes I forgot I used to murder people.

All the time.

When I was with her? I forgot who I was entirely.

I watched her look at me and then the basement and then to my surprise—she motioned for me to lead the way.

I grinned offering her my arm that she took. "To Butterscotch."

Avani giggled a little. But as we walked further it got darker and darker and I saw her biting her lip.

"Thierry—"

"Can you do me a favor?"

Her eyes met mine as she stopped walking. My heart was beating a little faster now. Much faster than it had been earlier.

"Let me…it doesn't get any brighter and there's broken pipes and—" Shit. I sounded like I was insane. "Look, I'm not crazy. But the car's parked in the basement level and it's a little scary. If you want, I can carry you." I held out my arms with what I hoped was an innocent expression.

Me. The picture of innocence.

Besides, I had seen the way men leered at her.

The last person she was in danger from was me.

Even though I was one of the more dangerous things in the city right now. If Avani even knew half of what I had done? She'd be terrified of me. She could never find out what I was.

But right now Avani was terrified for a different reason.

I won't hurt you, mon cœur. I would die before I did.

Avani looked completely out of place in the darkness as I took a step closer to her. And closer. Until she was in my arms.

"What do you say, *mon cœur* ?"

Do you want to walk into the dark with me?

Her eyes looked up at me as she nodded. A wave of something unfamiliar and foreign shook through me then.

It rocked through my system as I bent to lift her up easily into my arms with one arm.

She squealed a little, the sound echoing in the cavernous garage with my laughter.

"You don't weigh a thing—"

"I weigh enough—" she protested breaking off as I laughed harder.

"Close your eyes," I murmured holding her closer, feeling her entire body press up against mine.

My inner demons loved that she trusted me, loved that she leaned on me, her eyes closing giving me a chance to look at her

159

slightly chubbier cheeks, those long lashes, right before she nuzzled in and tucked her head into the crook of my neck.

Oh fuck me. I melted a little.

That was the thing about Avani, something about her personality and demeanor thawed out parts of me I didn't know I could.

Me. I had spent my entire life among whores, prostitutes, models, assassins, darkness and everything under the sun that didn't belong in the light of day sometimes.

Avani was a breath of fresh air.

And I knew it.

"This is far," she whispered like someone was listening to us. I bit back a grin.

"I like my privacy."

"Clearly." But her fingers gripped me tighter.

"You trust me, mon cœur ?"

She nodded, her head bumping my chin and I felt it tugging somewhere in my chest again. My dick meanwhile had a mind of its own imagining me taking her in my car for another reason.

I used the other hand to hit the elevator button holding her close to me. "Almost there."

"Did you park in the Underworld?"

How apt.

I grinned ear to ear as I walked with her down the long hallway.

"Just close enough to it," I murmured brushing my lips at her temple.

She trusts me.

And I will never do anything to break her trust.

When we got to the car I hit the keys, her eyes were still closed and she didn't see the plates.

I cuddled her to the passenger side and opened her door, helping her in. Once she was in, she opened her eyes as I fit her seatbelt in. My eyes met hers.

"It's dark down here."

"I'll turn on the lights."

And she was a centimeter away from my face. A fucking millimeter to the point where I could kiss her. Time froze. I saw her dark eyes watching me a little wide-eyed.

"It's really dark," she whispered.

Right. Because she was scared. And I was being an idiot. I quickly went to my side and the car turned on and Avani gasped.

"It's *red* everywhere."

I grinned. The outside had sapphire tones. But the interior was blood red. Decked out in the finest materials Teo could get. This car was his pet project.

I also thought it was a little apology to me for being a dick to me years ago, but I didn't want to assume.

"It's beautiful," she whispered. "This is Teo's car?"

I nodded even though it wasn't.

"He has great taste."

I grinned as I turned it on dimming the lights a bit and driving us to her cafe. Avani was marveling at it asking me questions I knew by heart. I knew my car.

She ran her fingertips over. "It's really beautiful."

I grinned hiding my sigh.

From Avani, it was more so her admiration for nice things. And of course she thought the little scythe Teo hung from the mirror was adorable too.

We got to the cafe and I parked a block away.

As she got out I went to follow and her eyes went wide. "You're coming with me?"

I nodded. "I was gonna pick up some stuff."

Liar. You just wanna be next to her.

I did. Shamelessly.

Who the fuck cared?

Avani smiled. "I don't know if they have things that fit your dietary needs."

"I guess we'll find out."

Stepping into the lush little bakery, I realized she was right once I looked at the cases that had sandwiches, croissants, sugar. Sugar. And more sugar. *Fuck.*

At this time the bakery was more empty save for a few stragglers.

I can't have shit here.

I caught Avani eyeing me with a little knowing smile and a twinkle in her eyes. "They have sugar free stuff in the fridge?"

She motioned to the fridge that did have some health food in it. So off I went grabbing a handful of sandwiches and some chia pudding.

Avani was placing her order at the counter when I came up next to her setting down my two sandwiches and pudding waiting for my turn to pay.

"And you guys are together?"

Avani didn't hesitate. "Yes, you can ring him up as well."

Wait, a second—No.

"Mon cœur —"

"Your total is…"

I didn't even blink and Avani had tapped her damn phone on the pinpad and she paid for my fucking dinner. I gaped.

Damn. Technology.

"*Avani.*"

She shot me an impish smile over her shoulder. "All good."

I gaped as she handed me a bag for my food and moved on to the waiting area to get all her stuff. One of the women behind the counter handed Avani a cupcake as she laughed at something she said.

I had gotten *handled.*

"Avani, I have money—" I dropped my voice drawing her closer to me feeling the way my skin prickled and heated everywhere she touched it. "You didn't have to do that."

"I wanted too—"

"I have the money, I would've paid for you too—"

She smiled up at me, those knowing eyes of hers on mine. Every part of me felt heated the moment they landed on me.

Having Avani felt like a privilege and I didn't even understand why.

"That doesn't mean I can't do something nice for you." Avani whispered back. "It's the least I could do for you driving me."

This fucking woman.

"Avani, I drove you because you've tutored me all these months, it's the least I could do." I resisted the urge to growl and bring her closer to me.

She clapped a hand over her mouth as she laughed, her face turning redder as she did. "Look at us, we keep trying to out-nice each other."

I grinned feeling every ounce of her laughter settle into somewhere into my chest that had been previously iced out.

"Let me out-nice *you.* I'm driving you home, woman."

Her eyes wide and surprised peeked up at me with a shy smile. She held out her pinky to my surprise and I gripped it with a fierce expression.

162

Her laughter was musical as we waited for her and Alisha's dinner. I didn't let her damn pinky go, moving her closer to me as she stood in between my legs waiting.

At some point one of the guys who'd come in began staring at her and while I hesitated to touch her hair or put my arm around her before, I didn't anymore.

I moved so fast wrapping my arm around her waist and drawing her closer to me eyeing him.

Everywhere she went she attracted attention. Every single time. Did she not see it?

She was on her phone and she looked up at me. "Everything okay?"

I tipped my head to her noticing the way she wet her lips. I was tempted I was. I drew closer and closer feeling the scent of her consuming me. She was the only thing I knew was real in the world in that moment.

She squinted up at me teasingly. "Sometimes I swear we're the same height but then I forget."

"Hm?" I raised a brow feeling like she was going to say something—

"And then I remember you're shorter than me."

I grinned unable to resist now tugging her into my arms, feeling my mouth open in a playful bite to her ear.

She squealed a little giggling and turning into me. Until my mouth was a fraction away from hers. In public. With Avani. The weight her pin in my pocket felt heavier now with her near me. Like she was my talisman too.

Who I wanted to kiss. Right now. I looked down at those lips. At her eyes batting up at me.

Fuck.

"So," I breathed a little remembering we were in public. She was waiting for her food. I was…me. "How's the view from up there?"

Her grin lit up mine and she laughed until she covered her mouth and leaned into my chest to hide it.

I breathed out a sigh, resting my chin against her head as we waited for her food.

And she fit perfectly.

She felt like heaven against me and the warmth that filled my chest shouldn't have felt so right.

It did. For once, I understood why Andrei had been so in love with Talia that he'd been a completely different man.

There was something blossoming in me that I couldn't explain.

I didn't know what to call it.

Her hairpin was in my pocket.

I denied stealing it sure, but I had the damn thing. In one piece. I curled my hand around it as I held her in my other arm.

And for a moment—just for a moment—I imagined what life would feel like if I stopped hiding, if I stopped being a secret, and if I stepped into the light.

With her.

CHAPTER 13
AVANI

I couldn't stop thinking about Thierry.

Not *once*. He was midnight and sin and things I could only dream of.

But I couldn't *stop* dreaming about him.

The flutter of butterflies were going to drive me over the edge as I felt heat and frustration licking at my skin. Feeling his touch everywhere on me. His electric blue's focused on me. Nobody had eyes like that.

The kind that haunted me all the time.

Aching for a man was a new sensation for me. Even in my past I didn't want a man like this.

I liked him. No. I *lusted* after him.

The romance novels did no justice, no amount of K-POP music could drown out my thoughts about him. *I want him so bad I don't even know what to do.*

"Avani?" I snapped out of my thoughts to my sister's voice calling me, her head poked out of her closet again. "Did you hear what I said?"

No, I was too busy lusting after my...student?

When I was younger, I used to watch Mum get ready for work. Or anything.

I was going to go to school soon and I was soaking up all the time I could with Alisha.

I hadn't seen Thierry in a week.

165

I just needed some breathing room, but I also had to pack up my bags, and find some clothing, some decorations, and bedding for my new dorm room.

Sure, it was right there in the city. But it was special for me. It was a big deal.

I was leaving Alisha and giving her privacy and growing up. I was scared but I was looking forward to it.

How could I not?

Maybe now Alisha will live a little...

I was watching Alisha was getting dressed to go to Teasers with Gemma and meet up with their good friend, Lara Ford.

Teasers was a burlesque club owned by Lara that Alisha loved. For two reasons.

The first of which was, her girlfriends were all cool and she loved them.

The second?

Reed worked there. Kind of. He *owned* the security team and therefore on occasion stopped by. By some stroke of luck, he was always there when Alisha was there.

Gemma had told me Reed was the CEO of his own company.

He must've been successful to have all that time on his hands.

And so currently my sister was in her closet, rummaging around searching for the perfect outfit.

I grinned behind the covers as she frowned over a black and red top with enough cuts and peeks to look like nothing on her. My sister's wardrobe was risqué.

I was laying there watching her, pretty certain I was getting my period since I had dull cramps and wanted anything with chocolate in it in my body.

It felt like my cramps were just ramping up.

Which meant I got to lay on her bed while she plucked out her clothes from the closet.

"*Didi*," I started. "Do you think about dating anyone?"

I had to ask.

But I saw Alisha stop like she hit a wall. Half dressed in her bra and a mini skirt, Alisha always looked so pretty and put together.

My sister didn't take after my Mum or my Dad. He'd been a blonde, my Mum had brown hair and dark eyes like me.

Alisha had come out with raven hair and my father's hazel eyes.

Her features were sharper than mine and I always thought Alisha was so much prettier than me.

And right now those eyes of hers were dissecting her outfit.

"Oh, darling I don't really think about dating," Alisha started, looking a little flustered.

Instead of looking at me she turned away and began fidgeting with her options.

"Forget about me, what about you? Are you doing anything over the Summer besides going the library? It's been weeks of this library, I'm beginning to think you don't like being at home."

I was glad Alisha wasn't turned to look at me.

I knew she was deflecting.

A lot of people in my life did it to protect me from their answers. I understood that now.

And I was doing something at the library. I just wanted *him* to do *me*. I covered my face.

Thierry was severely dyslexic. But over the weeks he had been improving. It made my heart almost explode when he read through a few sentences and smiled over at me.

I did it, Mon cœur.

You did. And I resisted the urge to not squeeze him with all the emotions he brought up in me.

Thierry hadn't had anyone really focus or try to help him without consequences. And I was trying to be the best possible person for him.

"I'm just tutoring a Canadian exchange student," that's what came out. Technically, he was Canadian. And my student "It's just the summer."

Perhaps. Maybe longer. I didn't know what the school semester would bring.

"Oh? That's marvelous, dear." Alisha's husky voice broke me out of my reverie. She slid into a tighter black top with mesh. *It looked good but—*

"Looks a bit off with the skirt…" she tore it off and tried another top on. "Is she nice? Do you think you've made a new friend?"

I don't know why I didn't tell Alisha it was a boy.

Maybe because I didn't want my sister—who had sacrificed so much for me—to think that I was spending my summer's running around town with a boy.

167

Or maybe because I felt a little bit protective of Thierry.

Alisha wasn't necessarily close to Teo, and with Thierry's disability I felt the need to not speak about it.

I felt like it was kind to him since I didn't want Alisha to say a word to anyone. So I kept him tucked away in a bit of my heart that I didn't want to show the world.

"I did. She's wonderful. A bit different than I am—" Completely. And I may have kissed him. Of my own accord. I didn't know what we were. But I did. "But still a good friend."

"That's exciting you've made a new friend. Are you two hanging out at the library?" Alisha finally tore off her mini-skirt and went for a black dress that clung to her smaller curves.

"Sometimes."

Alisha finally stepped out of the closet and this time?

"Waaaah! You look incredible." Her smile was infectious as she squealed.

"You think so?"

I did. The best part about having a sister like Alisha was, she was my best friend.

But that didn't mean I told Alisha everything. Some things were also mine.

Alisha twirled a little in it and I grinned. Reed was going to *love* it.

At five-three Alisha was less top heavy and more hippy than I was. She looked glorious in a little black dress and some chunky heels she loved.

She glammed up her eyes a bit and before I knew it she was sparkling as she stepped out.

Alisha would assume it was a girl.

"Say, Didi." I started. "How come you've never dated Teo DuPont?"

Alisha who had finished applying her lip gloss paused and turned to look over her shoulder. "What's got you so curious about my dating life, darling?"

I assumed an expression of innocence. "I'm just curious if you know what his family is like."

She thought about it. "Well, I know he's got an older brother. Andrei. Gemma is friendly with them. You might have better luck asking her."

I did text Gemma about meeting Thierry and it going off without a hitch. I didn't however tell her anything in detail.

"But what's this?" She came over and sat on the edge of her bed, her hand immediately coming up to brush my hair back and I curled into her on instinct. "Is something the matter with you? You should be out tonight, to the movies, somewhere fun, don't tell me you're staying home—"

"Curled up with my new book?" I grinned at her expression. It wasn't that Alisha didn't like to Reed, she just was more a visual person.

Having opted out of university for her social media career.

She threaded her fingers through my hair.

"Are you all right with me going out? You know if you need me to text me or call and I will come right home?"

"I do." She always did. I didn't make it a habit but every so often when I needed anything Alisha was there even if she couldn't physically be there.

My love for Alisha was different now that I'd gotten older.

I didn't just love her—I couldn't imagine a world without her. She'd been my rock and my home, holding it together for my sake and hers. I just wanted to see her happy too.

Her smile still didn't reach her eyes and I had never seen her talk about any man like Reed.

"I guess I was just curious," I watched her expression. "Is Reed going to be there tonight?"

And just like Thierry, my sister's eyes changed, looking away a little uneasy. "Darling, it doesn't matter—"

"It's okay," I said sitting up a little on my elbow. "I know about him. And it's okay if you like him."

But Alisha's smile dipped a little and if I wasn't mistaken, my sister looked a little afraid. Just enough for me to know I had pushed her a little too far.

"But it's also okay if you wanna spend time with me," I teased lightly. "After all I am your favorite person."

Alisha's smile returned as she turned back to me a little her eyes delighted. "You are."

She bent to kiss my forehead and I felt the stick of gloss and her perfume. *Nobody* smelled like Alisha.

She smelled so good. I stole her perfume growing up until she'd gotten me my very own and mixed with my hair oils and scents, it smelled different on me.

"Be good," she murmured. "I won't be too late."

But privately I wished Reed would just ask her out.

I flopped back into Alisha's bed inhaling the scent of her cardamom and spice perfume.

When the door to the apartment shut my phone pinged and I picked it up expecting it to be an automated text or alert.

It wasn't.

It was Thierry.

He sent me a photo of his new study material. A children's book. *Mike and the Magic Crayon.*

The smile that split my lips was wide.

I giggled texting him back.

hard at work on a Friday night, I see.

CHAPTER 14
THIERRY

"I didn't take you for the type to pick that book."

I felt my lips split into a wide grin I couldn't control at the first words out of her mouth.

"Better than the one about the kid having a bad day *all day*."

Avani's laughter was musical and soft. And my entire body calmed down listening to it.

"It's not a bad book."

"He has a shit day the entire story."

"*Aha! So you've read it.*"

I grinned wider. "I *may* have *peeked*."

Avani had a sense of humor.

"Glad to see you're doing better. I'm very proud of you."

I didn't know what to do with that. It was different from any training I had ever gotten. Praise was given, sure, but praise for something so mundane from her?

It was unfathomable for me.

She was temptation.

My only temptation nowadays. My eyes drifted to her hairpin sitting on my dresser.

Despite my life being shrouded in shadows somehow this little bookworm had gotten under all my defenses and she was staying there.

Now I knew why people didn't give into temptation. Because once I did once? I couldn't stop.

Mostly because I had spent most of the day thinking about her. Every single day. Like she was my new drug of choice and I hadn't even *had* her.

And it was easy. I was addicted. To her smiles. To her olive skin. To her lush full body. *Fuuuuck.*

I was raised to be a fighter. A warrior. The DuPont crest was the lion and the motto? *Take by force.* We were a family of former fighters now parading around in suits and ties pretending to be civil.

I started my morning off with Kyokushin training followed by boxing for a bit and then doing Andrei's salmon ladder he had in the basement. Andrei had issues to say the least.

After the De Nuit moment, Teo called me asking if I fucked with Kieran who was telling him about his tattoos. We got a good laugh out of it.

But with Avani? I'd never tell a soul.

Even if I imagined taking her on my lap and sliding my hands into her shirt. Even if I knew she was

Just slowly. Sound it out.

There you go. That's wonderful. You did great.

And she was in my thoughts now. Temptation.

Besides, I hated texting.

"Thank you," the words felt foreign on my lips.

Her laughter was low as I heard her shifting. A soft rustle.

"Surprised you're not out tonight," I don't know why I said it. "How's shopping for college going?"

Out of all the conversations I expected to have? This was not the one. But I found Avani surprised me.

"Should I be?" I knew she didn't do it on purpose, but every so often her voice got this huskier quality to it. "It's lovely actually. Although, Alisha seems to be way more excited at spending quadruple the amount of money we need. But then again, she doesn't hold back when it comes to shopping."

I laughed easily at that. "Talia, my brother Andrei's wife is like that. But lately…"

"Lately?" She whispered. "Is she okay?"

I let out a breath. I was not imagining Avani in my ears whispering things to me I had no business thinking about it. *None at all. None I could have.*

I forced myself to focus.

"She's good. She just had a baby. My nephew Drew. And she's occupied to say the least."

"I can imagine," her voice was low and she sounded like she was shifting and getting comfortable in bed.

Discipline was my entire world now. After my youth spent tearing up the streets? I thrived on it.

And Avani was temptation I could never give into.

I never expected her to make my cheeks hurt from smiling.

"So no plans tonight? You plan on partying into the dawn?"

Her laughter came again and this time I couldn't stop myself.

"In my dreams." She sighed. "I just wanted to read for the rest of tonight. Although cupcakes sound really nice. Who knows? Maybe college boys are into nineteenth century literature and red velvet?"

I heard nothing but college boys. Avani's age group. Yet again something I was not. Maybe I was just torturing myself with Avani. That had to be it.

I was a masochist with a penchant for torturing myself with the woman I couldn't have.

The idea of Avani at a college party was unthinkable. But imagining her at one had me imagining the guys there.

The ones who'd grab her by the hips and—*oh, I would kill him.* And then I quickly shook that thought out of my head.

I didn't know her well. I didn't know her at all.

No. I had no right to feel this way.

"Doubtful." I heard my own voice. "Apparently they're all into lip fillers and unattainable standards."

She laughed, the sound infectious as I felt my lips stretch at still being able to make her do that. "What about you? No late night festivities for you to partake in?"

Not anymore. Only Avani talked like that.

Little did she know, I never left the damn house anymore.

I don't know what possessed me to call her but it was Friday night and I was at home reading. Out of all things.

We didn't meet on weekends since she wanted to read and lay there in her bed and be a potato as she called it.

Except I didn't think Avani looked like a potato in bed.

I thought Avani looked edible with her lush soft body in her no doubt pink sheets and her soft skin—I needed to relax. *Relax.* I practiced my breathing.

I could hear Alma laughing in my head as I said. "I don't live my life too much anymore. Figured I'd stay in bed with this crayon book."

Avani giggled. "I am curled up in bed too. It's too cozy to go outside. I don't know how my sister does it…"

So technically…*we were in bed…together.*

I sighed unable to hold it back.

No wonder she sounded all soft and…sweet. I tried to dispel the image of Avani in bed. But I couldn't.

"So no wild parties for you," I choked out dropping the damn book onto the side of my navy comforter.

I stared up at the ceiling and the vaulted fancier lights Andrei had in here.

She sighed dramatically. "None for me. Although my sister just left for this club she really likes with her girlfriends."

Avani rarely talked about her older sister but when she did her voice held a note of affection.

"Did you know Alisha was friends with Teo, your brother? I always forget to ask you since we just talk about your schooling…"

"I did. I went to see him today," I made conversation with Avani.

"That sounds really nice."

"It was." For Avani, the mundane was nice.

After a lifetime of jumping off cliffs and wild adventures, her nice was my nice.

"Did you have a good day with him?" Avani was genuinely interested. I smiled wider.

Conversations with Avani were *fluff*. I fucking ate that shit up. Made me feel all warm and shit. I loved it.

Like I had been deprived of it with the life I had. Constantly shifting houses until Andrei came along thrusting me into a world I had no business being in.

Talia then taking me for discipline in a place I had no business being in.

I had a lot of women in my past who wanted a piece of me. Of the DuPont name. Of anything but…me.

Women I used and threw away. My life was synonymous with being a whore. But now? Not so much. I couldn't remember the last time I'd gotten laid.

Even with Teo owning a sex club.

De Nuit was a good playground but not something I saw myself in. It was a good way to lose control—and I didn't do that anymore.

I wouldn't even say it was good. But yeah. "I did."

"What did you do?" Mundane conversations with Avani were initially a bit weird. "Besides not have any caffeine or sugar."

When Avani discovered having ADHD meant an aversion to sugar and conventional methods of using up my excess energy—she'd lost it a little.

Because Avani loved sugary treats.

Her favorite cafe was a place called *Butterscotch's*. And she'd learned the first time she'd brought treats that I wasn't susceptible to them.

I laughed outright. "It helps—"

"Right," even her sarcasm was light. "I was going to get pizza tonight and watch a movie…" she trailed off about her plans.

After an hour of us shooting shit like Avani was my friend or something, Avani made a smaller noise. One of distress.

"You okay?" I sat up in bed. "Did something happen?"

"I am," she whispered. "I have cramps, one second…" I heard her getting up. "I need to grab a few things, sorry."

"Period cramps?" I murmured. "Don't apologize." What the fuck did I do? I wasn't there for her.

Alma had them. Talon had women in it. I wasn't a stranger to women's cycles. But Avani didn't know that.

Avani's voice was lowered and in pain. "Just need medicine, it's my fault. I lost track of the time." She made another noise as I heard her shuffling around.

I didn't know what to do. I didn't want to be weird and ask her where she lived. After a moment she came back on the line.

"If it's all right with you I think I'm gonna turn in for the night." *Why wouldn't it be?* "It's all good. Do you need anything?"

"No," but she didn't sound convincing. "Just took some medicine, and grabbed an entire candy bar." She let out a weak noise that was supposed to be a laugh I guessed.

"Avani," I heard my own voice. "Alisha is out. Do you need anything?"

I didn't like this girl being in pain. Even if it wasn't anyone's fault.

"Mhm," she whispered. "I think I'm going to go for tonight. I need to lay down and I can't focus."

Okay. "Okay." NOT OKAY.

But my brain and my body were screaming. I knew where she

lived. I did. I dropped her off that day in front of that apartment complex.

"Avani—" I broke off. What the fuck did I even say? Let me come over and cuddle you? Let me help you? Let me be there? What the fuck did I say?

I couldn't do that.

"Avani. I—I—" I was struggling now. Fuck.

I just wanna go over and snuggle with this girl.

I didn't even understand who I was.

"Yes?"

I laid back in bed. My entire body and brain at war with itself. I swallowed hard around my emotions.

Did I go? Did I do it? My body was screaming.

And then something swam into my thoughts.

Andrei wasn't there for Talia. He let her down.

And I wasn't Andrei.

And then the words left me.

"Let me come over, *Mon cœur.*"

It was out of my mouth.

It escaped like a feather in the wind. And I couldn't stop it. I didn't want to. All my fight was gone.

She was mine. And she needed me.

That was the end of that.

I wasn't Andrei.

She was silent for a beat.

"I don't want Alisha to know…"

Right. I closed my eyes. Because Talia and Andrei had no fucking clue my Summer tutor was a girl.

"I can sneak out."

Another beat passed.

"Okay."

I let out a breath.

And leapt out of bed.

CHAPTER 15
AVANI

HE WAS COMING OVER TO MY APARTMENT.

Well, to Alisha's but same thing—*and I was on my period.*

So I knew he wasn't coming to sleep with me. But I had never slept with a man. Let alone, kissed one.

This was completely out of my territory.

My heart was racing. Pounding. Adding to my cramps already and then some.

I just knew Alisha was out at Teasers tonight, and I didn't want her knowing I had a boy over. A man. Into our home.

But he was a DuPont. She'd be fine with that…er. No.

She wouldn't.

Alisha hadn't dated anyone in the time I knew her. Maybe one or two odd dates, but it hadn't worked out.

My sister was stuck to her girlfriends.

And right now a boy was coming over.

Oh my God a boy is coming over to my home.

Maybe I made a mistake.

I must've made a mistake.

I must've made a mistake.

Oh Gosh, what do I do?

I wondered if he lived far or how long it would take? What if I told him this was a mistake? I was spiraling. And my cramps despite the medicine were still aching.

I looked at the chocolate bar I nabbed from the kitchen feeling zero appetite.

What if Alisha came back early and caught him? What if she was upset with me? What if she didn't love me anymore if she found out?

Oh God.

"I made a mistake," I whispered. But my fingers felt frozen trying to text Thierry to not come. I couldn't do it and I didn't understand why. Oh Gosh. "I'm about to sneak *a boy* into my home."

Not just any boy. A tall, dark dashing prince who was coming over for my period cramps.

Only twenty minutes later. I didn't have to worry.

Too late now.

I heard the doorbell go off and I quickly peeked. His tall form was on the other side. I wiped my sweaty palms and I rushed to get it like I was sneaking in a fugitive.

I opened the door and his expectant smile fell as he took me in. "Mon cœur."

I knew what he saw. Ratty hair. Dark pajamas. And me bloated like a potato watching him wincing a little.

He moved so quickly, his arms gingerly around me as he shut and bolted the door. "Mon cœur , which way is your room?"

I pointed down the hallway.

"Is it okay if I—" he reached out to me.

For some reason, he looked off as well. He looked haggard, his inky hair a mess, eyes a little wild as he took me in, sleeves rolled up to his elbows revealing more of the skeletal tattoos.

I forgot sometimes how beautiful he was and all my thoughts stopped working as he leaned in and I nodded. *Be still, my heart. Just be still.*

And just like that I was in his arms.

He set me gently on my bed when he got there, eyes taking in the pink with a small smile.

"Let me make sure the door's locked, *Mon cœur ,* I'll be right back."

I felt like I was in a strange dream as he tore off his hoodie and I caught the flash of his abs, all of those tattoos I had seen for weeks peeking out of his sleeves, his muscles.

My mouth watered a little as heat bloomed on my face watching him quickly tear it off.

And then he went and rushed back out the door. "Gotta close your door."

I sat up in bed and I caught my reflection in my own pink vanity at the shock on my face.

"Dear Lord, a man is in my bedroom," I whispered to myself. *"A man."*

He rushed back, his eyes on me like if he missed out for a second something would happen to me. "Are you all right, Mon cœur ? Should I get you something?"

I was dreaming.

I was having a very strange dream.

But if I woke up from this dream it would be too cruel.

He motioned to the bed, his throat working like he was nervous. He was nervous? I was dying.

And then I winced as I cramped again and rolled over to my side with a noise. "Mmm."

I held my heating blanket to my stomach feeling the bed dip as he swore softly. Was he getting in with me? My heart was racing. I was going to die. *Oh my. Lord.*

And then he got into bed with me.

Wrapping his arms around me like I belonged there and I fought the urge to cry as his lips pressed into my temple, as if he belonged here. With *me*.

"I'm sorry," he whispered, his breath tickled my skin.

"You did nothing wrong." But my voice was weak.

"I kept you on the phone." His voice was tinged with something else. "I should've been here."

"Should've been?"

"I don't like knowing you were here in pain." He made a softer noise nuzzling into me like he was comfortable.

There was something in his tone I didn't recognize.

How could he say that? Why did he sound like that?

My head was spinning with the implications of what he was saying.

"*I* stayed on the phone." He snuggled into me until it felt like he was a part of me and my heart raced. Not my boyfriend. Not my friend. Not quite my student. "I missed you this week."

I confessed it like I shouldn't have.

He was quiet for a second, but I felt his breath stirring the hair on my neck as he laid there. On. Top. Of. Me.

"Missed you too, *Mon cœur.*"

I was going to implode from my emotions. This was real. *This* was happening.

"Are you nervous about starting school?"

"A little," I whispered. "I mostly just feel guilty...what if I'm making the wrong choices, Thierry. I don't know what I'm doing sometimes."

"I don't know what I'm doing any of the time."

I bit back a laugh and failed as he chuckled behind me.

"Do you want some food? My sister-in-law could eat a whole pizza when she's going through this. She says she doesn't hate herself she's just hungry."

"That does sound nice. Pizza sounds so good right now. With—"

"Red pepper flakes. On it." His lips brushed over my ear making me snuggle against him. "I'll get one and you can tell me how bad you feel after a few slices."

"Who made you?" I grumbled. "How did you turn out like this?"

His laughter filled the room.

"I grew up around my brothers," he said simply. "Andrei used to take care of Talia. All the time. We used to get jealous of how much attention he paid her." There was a hint of something else in his voice as he said it. "Teo and I learned from the best. Lately, they've been a little off with their son, but for the most part, they've been together for a long time?"

On cue my stomach growled in agreement. His dark chuckle was soft against my skin as he brushed my hair back.

"Please put jalapeños on the pizza. And chicken. And mushrooms."

"Half-jalapeno," he muttered sounding amused. "Does Alisha also eat as spicy as you do?"

"She's worse, she thinks habanero is a candy."

Behind me he shuddered and I giggled into the covers. At the thought of Alisha, in my mind I imagined Alisha *and* Mum fainting.

Because this was my first time breaking the unspoken rules and sneaking a boy into my apartment.

Alisha would die if she saw him, but right now? Alisha didn't matter. Since he was...here. Taking care of me.

After a moment he was back under my covers. "It'll be here soon. Thirty minutes tops."

I felt a little smile curve my lips as he cuddled in.

"What's Andrei like?" I asked to distract myself from my fluttering heart. Besides being angry at him, he couldn't have been angry all the time.

"Strict as fuck."

I laughed low at that. "He doesn't sound like that. He sounds wonderful."

Thierry wrapped his arm around me pulling me flush against him. "He can be. Sometimes…sometimes he's just a dick."

I gasped turning around a little until I was facing him and the intimacy of having him smiling while laying on my pillows was one I wasn't prepared for.

His eerily bright eyes were now dimmed down, soft in the light of the bedroom.

We had crossed the line between what we were so long ago but I didn't know what we were now.

"You've got a lot of books in here, Mon cœur ," he grinned at me. "I didn't know you were this much of a bookworm."

I couldn't have turned even more red. "I like reading."

He laughed a little amused. "I'd say you more than like it. You never told me how much." His eyes drifted around my room. "This makes the library pale in comparison."

"Oh, stop it," I batted him chest lightly. "Tell me about your brothers. You rarely talk about your family and you know about mine. Just introduce me to your bubble."

"Well, Andrei is a father now," his eyes softened on me. "And Teo is a handful. Always has been. You should see the two of them in a fight. It's actually funny."

"I can't imagine Teo fighting." I admitted. "Alisha says he's wonderful to be around."

"Most of the time. But Teo doesn't do any of the fighting. Andrei does all the growling and then Teo laughs in his face and it sets him off more."

A laugh burst from me at the image and Thierry grinned his eyes softening as he took me in.

"Your family sounds amusing."

"They can be," something dark was in his eyes as he watched

me. His hand reached up to brush my hair back. "Alisha left you alone?"

"I'm an adult," I whispered feeling my heart putter about. "I am completely of age to take care of myself. Alisha needs to go out and cut loose sometimes with her girlfriends."

"Hm," he made a noise watching me and for a moment the air between us shifted, changed and it felt different when his eyes moved over my lips.

The moment his lips brushed over mine, my entire body sighed, absolutely sighed.

His lips stamped on mine then harder and I was hyper-aware of this man. Hyper. Aware. I felt everything.

The way my fingers tugged on his hoodie drawing him closer to me, the way he held my face with one hand and then rolled me onto my back so he was over me.

I felt a soft noise leave me at the pressure of him.

"Shh, I have you, Mon cœur."

I was on drugs with how he kissed me.

Slowly at first, and then I followed his lead, feeling clumsy but eager. I wanted him.

Dizzying pleasure coursed through me, my entire being sighing in his arms as his tongue tasted mine.

For a moment—I forgot every damn thing. *Everything.*

It lasted forever. Thierry kissed me the way he did everything else. All consuming. *Intense.* Passionate.

It made every dream I had of him pale in imitation because his mouth on mine felt like bliss.

No more pretending, no more hiding—I felt wanted.

And just like that the racing stopped. It calmed down. The longer he kissed me the more softer noises left me.

I gripped his shoulders as I felt my body clenching somewhere deep for him.

My cramps faded into the back of my mind as he pulled back a little.

"Mon cœur , no, shhh." He brushed his lips over mine once, twice whispering that I was a good girl and I had to breathe.

His voice was dark sin, decadent and everything I had wanted in my life. "I know, but you have to breathe."

I shook my head slowly. I was drowsy now. Like I could fall asleep in an instant. I felt so…warm. Content.

More warm than I'd ever been.

"Why did you…why did you come…"

"You needed me."

And just like that my heart, expanded contracted painfully aware of him in my bed now. His eyes met mine. I was Avani. Not Alisha's little sister.

When I was with Thierry I felt like…me. And like I was good enough. To be liked by this boy.

"I needed you and you ran over here…"

He tipped his head brushing his lips over mine watching me with soft wonder in his eyes.

"There is nothing I wouldn't do for you."

"Why?" I shook my head. "All I've done is tutor you."

His grin was back but this time there was something that softened it.

"You have all the control and power in this relationship," my heart sputtered as he said the words. "And yet you never use it against me. My brother said loving someone and losing them is not the hardest thing you can do. It's loving someone, trusting them with your soul, and them doing everything they know will break you."

His eyes held mine as he spoke. "You knew my weaknesses, you took them on and made me better for it. There is not enough thank you's for that. Let me take care of you, *mon coeur.*"

I swallowed unable to speak around what I felt. For this man. This wild beautiful man who came back into my life like a whirlwind and trusted me with his life. His bubble. And the ache that blossomed in me grew for him.

He was mine. I would never hurt him.

He believed love was dangerous, I believed love was safety. He believed love was weaponized, I believed love was unconditional.

Our spaces were different. Our homes were different.

But I loved him.

"I love you." It came out so much easier now like this. I felt my eyes watering a little. "I know Andrei took you from a woman…" as I said it his eyes held mine with a different emotion. Grief. And that made me cry. "I know it was probably your Mum. She wasn't nice to you, was she? And then you were an outsider with your family here…" I swallowed around the grief I felt now for him. "I know you're hurting sometimes. But I would never use your hurt against

183

you. Love is healing. Nurturing. Kind. I wanted you to have to the things I had." I blinked my eyes rapidly as he held my face tighter now coming closer. "I am so s-s-sorry for your hurt. I do want to take it away sometimes."

I couldn't stop crying now wiping my eyes as he smiled softer. "I would never hurt you. I promise to love you." I held out my pinky.

He took it and kissed me at the same time, pressing his mouth over mine. "You love me."

"I love you," I nodded. "I *do*."

"I love you, too." It sounded awkward, off, and a little uneasy coming out of his mouth almost like he was trying it out for the first time. And I didn't take it personally. I mouthed it again.

He repeated it.

"Like we practiced," I whispered into his lips. "One more time. I love you."

"I love you, too" he said it more confident.

I felt our lips tip up together as I said it again. And he repeated it. Until his smile grew, dimples and all. I felt warmth blossoming somewhere deep in my chest for him. For this man who tried his freaking best every step of the way.

I did love him so much. I wanted Alisha to meet him.

"That's easier now," he murmured.

"We can practice all you want," I said softly.

Maybe one day I could yell at Andrei for Thierry's sake.

"Wanna practice now while we wait for the pizza?" He rubbed his lips against mine. I grinned into his kisses.

"I feel like you want to practice something else now."

His dimple was back. "Don't tempt me, mon coeur."

"I love you."

"I love you, too."

This time he said it easily.

CHAPTER 16
THIERRY

"I love you, mon coeur."

That felt nice.

She giggled in my arms. "I love you too."

"Even if they forgot the red pepper flakes?"

"*Yes*. Even if they forgot the red pepper flakes."

Because her love wasn't conditional. It didn't come with asterisk's, with caveats, and with weaponized words.

Avani's love was all-consuming and soft.

Like the wings of a butterfly that caused a hurricane in me.

Avani's love was life-giving.

Avani was and always would be the epicenter of me.

I *loved* her.

We stayed up talking, Avani cuddled into my chest while she talked to me about Alisha and her friends. Showing me photos.

At one point the pizza came and she wandered up with me to show me her fridge.

Padding adorably in her bunny slippers she looked up at me telling me about the apartment. Little things that made her happy. I passed by stacks and stacks of books.

And I noted the differences between my place with my family and all of our houses and apartments, and this place. This is not just an apartment, this was a *home*.

The furniture was bright, the lamps warm, photos everywhere, throws Avani said were from her grandmothers. And more books. Lots of them.

The kitchen was the only part of the house that didn't look too used, but Avani said they both rarely cooked.

I kept her hairpin tucked into one side of my hoodie, but I stole some of the photos of her from the fridge while she wasn't looking.

Avani had made Andrei's apartment a home for me with these personal touches she brought from her world.

When we went back to her room, it took two slices of pizza and her talking for Avani to fall asleep in my arms in the middle of mumbling out a sentence.

I grinned ear to ear cuddling her close on her bed as I set the box down.

Leaning back against her headboard I felt the unfamiliar sensations of having a woman in my life. For once.

I'd never had a girlfriend. I had fucked women. Lord knows, that's all I had done. Even when I'd met Avani initially years ago as a teenager, I'd seen it as a challenge. A cute girl in my brother's library?

I was all over her.

But then…she'd stuck by me. I gently took out her hair pin.

It was shaped like an old pin with combs on one side and a butterfly on the other. Avani said it belonged to her mother. I should give it back at some point. Maybe. One day.

Not today.

After my time in Talon? I had killed enough people to know serious relationships were not something we considered. I didn't know how Talia did it with Andrei other than neither one of them talking about it.

It was her memory that had me hustling my ass over to Avani.

Or my mother needing a man and him not being there? Of Phillipe abandoning her and her taking it on me eventually.

Of not wanting to be like the men in my family, in my life.

All of it converged into one emotion—*one* need. To get to Avani.

It didn't matter what I wanted or thought.

I refused to be Phillipe. Andrei. Anyone who failed me.

She believed love was kind. I believed love wasn't real.

Initially. Until she kept coming back. And then I had to believe something existed.

She needed me. I heard it in her voice. I couldn't say no.

She was temptation in a tiny package of a woman.

She was everything I wasn't, everything I shouldn't have wanted, and *everything* I craved with my entire fucking soul.

AT SOME POINT WHILE AVANI SLEPT I HAD HER E-READER IN HAND flipping through it taking notes on what mon coeur was reading. So I could download these damn audiobooks.

And it was *filthy*. I was taking mental notes of these titles.

The Werewolves Lover
Tangled Up In You
Tainted Love
The Devil's Princess
Who named these books?

I scrolled until I found House of Midnight and Shadow. I kept meaning to look into these books and I didn't know why I kept forgetting.

"There's seven books?" I whispered in shock. But they were popular. Supernatural erotica meets mystery and suspense? I bookmarked it. As I did, the doorbell rang in the apartment.

I froze.

Avani didn't stir in my arms.

Frowning, I turned my head. Alisha wouldn't knock. Even if she was drunk, she had her keys. Avani knew not to open the door for anybody. She told me so.

I slowly untangled myself and thankfully, the lights had been turned off by me earlier.

I wish I'd brought my gun up from my car.

I had left my gun not knowing what to expect at Avani's but I knew for a fact she didn't expect me to have a gun.

I darted into Alisha's kitchen and grabbed the largest knife I could from the butcher block and went to the door.

I peeked through and saw the…doorman in the building. He was a little creepy and old but I blamed it on his general disposition. Now? His eyes bothered the fuck out of me.

I opened the door a crack and peered out. Sallow dark eyes and sickly skin met my vision as he looked stunned I had opened the door. "Sir. Excuse me, I thought Miss Malhotra might be home."

Which one? Had he seen Alisha leave?

He'd been on shift when I came here.

The hairs on the back of my neck stood up around this mother-fucker. And I didn't even know why. I trusted my instincts though.

Something about this guy was off.

"Can I help you?"

I aimed my best face at him to intimidate him. Hardening my jaw and my eyes focused on him. Five-ten. Overweight.

A little sick. *Civilian.*

"Miss M-malhotra had a letter she dropped."

I didn't even look at it. I stayed tracking his movements.

Why was he nervous?

One hand of mine, held the door and the other one held the knife behind my back. *Fuck.*

Bracing the door with my foot, I didn't take my eyes off the doorman as I switched the knife into my other hand to take the letter.

"I'm sorry," he drew his hand back. "I can only give the mail to authorized users. Is Miss Avani available to pick up her letter?" I resisted the urge to roll my eyes at this quack. I didn't like the sound of her name in his mouth. Or why he was here late at night instead of leaving the letter at the front desk.

Or why he was even waiting around for her to begin with.

I didn't like this motherfucker one bit.

"I'm her husband," I said to him with a straight face. "That makes me family. I can take the letter since according to your lease papers, I'm blood. Sooo—" I held out my hand in a gimme motion.

He blinked looking surprised as he slowly turned it over to me. I didn't even know why I said it. It just came out naturally. Adapting to the moment.

"Thanks, man." I took it out of his hands. I didn't dare even look at it. "I'll be sure she gets it."

"Her h-husband."

"Yup. She's my wife. I got this," I winked at him pasting on a grin I didn't feel and shut the door in his face. Or I tried to.

He looked past me into the apartment but I didn't care for him to see anything so I blocked it with my body. "Anything else?"

"No, sir." He almost looked disappointed as he looked at me again.

Something was off about his eyes.

He expected Avani to answer the door. He's on shift tonight.

He saw Alisha leave.

It didn't take an idiot of figure it out. I saw the way men hounded Avani. I knew by the look in his eyes he was weak. I'd have to sneak over here more often if Alisha left her alone whenever he was here. I didn't mind.

I tipped my head to bid him off and closed the door on him.

I set Avani's letter down and the knife.

I'd ask her about it later filing the information away in my head.

Alisha had been gone an hour. Avani mentioned she stayed out but always came back before eleven.

I'd stay until I heard Alisha coming back and then I'd sneak out the fire escape.

When I went back to the bedroom, Avani was still fast asleep. And my body calmed down as I crawled into bed with her.

I made a mental note to let her know whenever Alisha was gone to call me so I could come over.

I didn't trust Avani being alone. Or Alisha at this rate.

When Alisha did come back, I heard her.

Alisha was not subtle. The keys. Her heels. Walking towards Avani's room.

I got out of the bed and hid in my girl's closet.

And sure enough the first thing Alisha did was whisper. "Avani?"

Some part of me wanted to stay with Avani and let Alisha see me. Let her know I existed in her sister's life.

The other part of me, the part that had been a secret? Hid.

Because I wouldn't do anything without Avani knowing. One day maybe, we could introduce each other to our respective families.

For now, I liked her too much to let her into the clusterfuck of my family.

"Darling, are you sleeping?"

She was. My girl was passed out but through her closet doors I got a glimpse of Alisha in the flesh. She was pretty in a striking way, dark hair, different build than Avani, more hippy.

When she saw Avani was asleep she closed the door and left us alone.

I let out a breath as I waited a few more minutes. And then I went over to my girl laying there.

189

I didn't think twice. Pressing my lips to her temple I whispered. *"Call me again when you need me, Mon cœur."*

I never told Avani it meant my heart. I never would.

∼

"HEY ORACLE."

I was home. I snuck out the fire escape and climbed down it. My car was in their garage and I drove away feeling the late night chill in my bones.

Oracle was an AI program embedded into my car. In all my technology. Every member of Talon had it on them.

Back when I worked for Talon, Bexley Carter had installed an AI into our phones.

It had taken Carter a year to finesse it into submission and now? It was intelligent and capable of emotions which was unheard of.

"Yes, Grim."

Alma's voice was the baseline for Oracle. It came through clearly. And it was the only time I could hear her.

I sighed unable to believe I was asking her this. "Can I get a list of period products for women?"

"Certainly, sir."

She began listing them off and I ordered a few I thought related to Avani.

"Address, sir?"

"Send them to the residence listed in address book."

"Certainly, sir. Will there be anything else tonight?"

I paused.

"Look up Alisha Malhotra on Instagram. Beauty influencer."

"Certainly, sir. Searching for Alisha Malhotra now. Username is…"

And then Oracle pulled up a whole thing on Alisha and I let her list it off while I got to know Avani's world a bit better.

"Also, download these audiobooks…" I rattled off a few.

"Which part, sir? There seems to be a seven part series in the works."

I thought back to Avani's e-reader. "All of them."

"Certainly, sir. While I know you're not partial to explicit material may I add this rating…is noted as having graphic and explicit content listed as a warning. Will that be all right?"

190

"Yes."

"Certainly sir."

And when I got home, I laid in bed again finding the myths book open to the page I left it at. I had almost finished it.

Almost.

I flipped to the book realizing this book was from Avani's personal collection and in the back there was a list of questions.

Now it made sense. She'd plucked it out from her stack.

Hades. You?

Athena.

But it wasn't Athena.

In loopy handwriting I read it slowly.

Persephone.

I fucking knew it.

CHAPTER 17
AVANI

"Oh, what do you think of this? You'd look so good in pink."

Alisha held up a cute silk mini dress.

I nodded absently, my mind too busy daydreaming about Thierry and his hot kisses.

My sister's voice dampened most of the heat I felt despite the ghost of his touch lingering, the warmth of his body against mine, and my heart raced at the thought of his arms around me again.

He had slipped out of my room and Alisha hadn't said a word figuring I was on my period at the sight of pizza.

She didn't even ask about the weird topping choices.

Part of me wanted him to come back.

Part of me wanted to tell Alisha about this new boy in my life.

Another part of me knew better.

Because Alisha did everything for me. I didn't want her to be disappointed by me.

I didn't want Alisha to think that I was messing around with some boy and knowing him and his tattoos and his…everything—I didn't know if my sister wold think I was…being silly.

I loved Alisha. I did. But I was acutely also aware she didn't live her life. And it made me feel guilty in turn for living mine because who was I to have happiness when she couldn't? She was my whole world.

I didn't want to say a word to her yet.

Instead, I eyed the shopping cart in front of me filled to the brim with items as a laugh bubbled up in my throat.

"*Didi*, it's too much. We should get some stuff later."

"Nonsense, you're going away to university, it should be a big deal, darling. I'll just get everything. It'll be wonderful."

I bit my lip as Alisha dumped a few more items into the cart.

Goodness, at this rate I need an entirely new dorm.

I wasn't thrilled at the idea of sharing a room with someone. For the price the university charged I would've thought I could have my own space.

"Didi, I just want to wear my usual uniform," I looked at the growing clothes.

"But what if you go on a date?" Alisha countered. "I want you to feel pretty for normal things to, not just class."

She said it matter-of-factly and I knew it was useless to argue. I let out a breath and Alisha grinned at me tossing her raven hair over her shoulder.

My sister's normally bright hazel eyes held a glint to them as she wandered over to the artwork section of the store.

Alisha was losing her mind with college shopping.

I thought she was trying to make the space comfortable for me but I saw a hint of guilt, the tension in her face as she picked the perfect items for me.

"Didi," I kept my voice low as I watched her. "I know you want to make everything perfect, but you know I'll still come home all the time to see you."

Alisha's face was turned away and she whipped it to me surprised. Like she hadn't been expecting me to say that. There was nobody else in this section of the store thankfully right now, and I saw Alisha's eyes soften.

"I know," she kept her voice just as low. "But it's your first time away from home. And it should be comfortable for you. Even if you don't take everything—"

"Why don't I take simple things? And once I'm more comfortable? I can take more." That had been my plan.

I had heard of too many horror stories on the internet of college roommates and I certainly hoped mine wasn't.

But to be safe, I didn't want to take too much initially.

I wanted to get comfortable. Not too comfortable. I had plans to graduate university as early as high school. Three years and then move on. Not be a burden to Alisha.

I didn't want to hold her back anymore.

I had always spent time around older women, all of Alisha's friends were more mature than their age, and in turn, I had picked up their traits as well.

Which brought us to another Saturday morning filled with shopping for my dorm.

I laughed at Alisha's pout at a painting.

"Didi, those are just pink lips."

"I know, pucker up."

I burst out laughing so loud I had to cover my mouth or else face stares from other customers. Shooting my sister a lock of mock reproach only made her giggle.

"Oh come on, it'll be lovely. If you don't get it, I'll get it for youuuuuuu." I grinned wide.

"I'm going to fight you by the end of day."

Alisha wrinkled her nose. "Just yesterday you were the size of my arm and now you want to fight me?"

"Didi, I *am* bigger than you…"

"I know, don't remind me."

I grinned as we finished hauling back our bags into the apartment complex.

As we walked in, I noticed the doormen changing shifts.

Alisha paid no mind as I saw the creepy doorman from the other day watching her. My sister wasn't oblivious to stares. But it was her entire job.

Maybe Alisha was right. People did just stare at her because they knew she did social media. Even as I thought about it, an uneasy sensation settled in my gut.

"I cannot wait for you first day in school," Alisha said in the hallway as we waited for the elevator. "When did you say it was again?"

I told her the date as the doormen switched.

"Oh goodness that's my birthday!"

I know. And I felt so bad. It was just dumb luck, but I had to set up my space and the timing couldn't have been worse.

"I feel so bad," I told her as we stepped into the elevator manuvering our bags in. "I don't want to miss your birthday."

She flushed a little from the weight of her shopping trip.

"Nonsense, it's your first day at university, you should be with people your age living your life…" as Alisha talked I felt a pang of guilt. Alisha didn't get to live her too life too much.

Not really. Privately I wondered if she'd be celebrating her birthday with Lara or Gemma.

I hoped so.

"But still." I murmured. "Promise me we'll hang out after I get settled?"

"No, Avani," Alisha said deadpan unlocking the door with a struggle. "I will not be hanging out with my favorite and only sister." I giggled as my phone buzzed.

I knew exactly who it was. I knew. It could only be him.

I didn't check it until Alisha went to wash up and make some lunch for us so we had the energy to try on our new haul.

When I did my heart skipped a beat.

It was a photo of a pile of books and the text under was a green check mark. He didn't text at all.

He only sent photos. And I knew if I responded, he would call.

With Alisha? I couldn't pick up.

I hadn't told her I was tutoring a boy. She thought I was spending my days with a new friend my age. I was.

I didn't want Alisha to think I was dating him or lying to her for no reason. I just didn't want Alisha to think I was out secretly living my life when I wasn't.

Gemma who juggled her own life hadn't said a word to Alisha but I also reckoned most of the reason why Gemma didn't say anything was because how big she was in privacy.

Gemma kept a lot to herself and she kept all my secrets.

She wouldn't ever mention anything about Thierry.

I used the audio button and quickly whispered. "I'll call you later."

He put a thumbs up on the audio in seconds.

I smiled. My heart doing that erratic little flutter it did and yet it calmed down around him more now. Especially since I loved him. I did. And I wanted to tell Alisha about him.

I just didn't know how to approach it.

Sooooo, Didi, remember that boy I was tutoring? I mean, Canadian Exchange Student?

Turns out, he's actually a man I've been dating and I met him when I was fifteen and we may have kissed multiples times—Oh. Gosh. A disaster.

Except I don't want to hide Thierry.

I rushed back outside to find Alisha setting out plates.

"What are you making?"

"I wanted to have scrambled eggs with onions over rice? Call it cravings but I remember Mum used to make this all the time whenever we cried to her."

I remembered that. "I thought you didn't like it?"

"Not true," Alisha looked over her shoulder. "I love it. But every time I eat it I get super emotional and I'd rather not sometimes."

Just like that my throat tightened. Because it was our…we-don't-have-much-money meal and even if we had money now, Alisha didn't want to be reminded of those moments. I got that.

I felt like I had caused those moments.

And just like that any inclination of sharing my happiness with Alisha faded.

Not out of spite. But what right did I have to share something like this when I knew—I bloody well knew—Alisha wasn't dating anyone because of me.

"I'll get tomatoes and start chopping." And together Alisha and I made dinner.

"You haven't been eating much," she murmured as she cracked the eggs into a separate bowl to whisk. "Is everything okay?"

"I promise, Didi. I'm fine." I smiled in what I hoped was reassuring stirring in the tomatoes. "How are you?"

My sister's eyes didn't look at me as she whisked the eggs.

"Not too bad. I think I'm going to do some photoshoots this summer to have content for the next few months. I don't know when I started despising making content daily, but I really cannot keep up with it anymore. I don't want to. I want to try something different."

Alisha's job as a social media influencer had changed a lot over the last few years.

An influencer had a different shelf life than a normal job.

Whereas a doctor could be a doctor forever, Alisha's niche would have to change if she wanted to survive—or so she said.

"What do you think you'll do?" I tried asking as I helped her season the eggs.

"I don't know," Alisha murmured. "I've had this idea about designing my own clothing line, remember?" I did.

I knew Alisha still had her moments. She needed Mum and Dad sometimes. And then there was her crush—Reed.

I didn't dare ask about him.

Not when I couldn't talk about Thierry.

And how much I liked him. How I wanted to kiss him and I held all my words back trapped in my throat.

I listened to Alisha as I plated up our food and grabbed the obligatory veggies we mandated we have since if left unchaperoned Alisha's fridge would have coconut water and donuts in it.

"By the way, I wonder if the management here has a prerequisite to hire ominous doormen..."

Alisha laughed loudly her cheeks red. "Darling, they have to be scary to keep the hooligans and criminals out. I don't know I rarely even look at them."

Right. That's all it was.

ALISHA WAS EMOTIONAL DROPPING ME OFF TO MY DORM.

I held onto her.

"I'm right here, just a few minutes away," I whispered breaking down in her arms.

My roommate had left her clothes here and left. I thanked the universe she wasn't here.

Everything on her side was pretty much a mess.

As moving day had approached, Alisha's anxiety manifested in a thousand tiny ways.

Her hands, usually steady as she applied her flawless makeup, now trembled as she brought in my singular suitcase. I didn't pack much.

It helped Alisha lived right there.

Alisha looked around my new dorm room with an uneasy expression in her eyes.

Alisha pressed her keys into my hand, her fingers lingering.

"Come home anytime, okay? *No matter what. If you need me, I'm right there.*"

"*Didi*, I'll call every day," I promised.

Alisha smiled, a real smile this time, even as tears glistened in her eyes. "Every other day is fine, darling."

I was terrified of what lay ahead-of making new friends, of challenging classes, of being on my own.

Being without my *Didi*.

"Your birthday's coming up," I said. "Do you have something planned?"

I pulled back from Alisha to look at her smile and a faint blush on her cheeks. "Oh, I'm sure Lara has *something* planned."

I beamed. "When I get settled we can have brunch?"

"Of course." She pulled me into her arms again. "Anything you want. I'm here."

I CAREFULLY ARRANGED EVERYTHING IN MY ROOM KEEPING IT organized.

I hadn't brought too many books opting to leave everything with Alisha.

The one personal thing I had was a photo of my family. Alisha in my father's arms his arms around her and Mum holding me kissing my cheek.

Both of us had been grinning ear to ear into the camera.

I tried not to get emotional at being away from Alisha.

But she needed to live her life as well. I was doing this for both of us. I needed to do this even if it felt like I had left a vital part of my life behind.

The unease stirred in my gut but I attributed it to first day jitters.

I showered and tidied up my side of the room before crawling into bed exhausted. It was lumpy, uncomfortable, and I despised it already.

No, think positive. Just think positive. This is the university life. It's supposed to be different.

And even then in my thoughts, Thierry's eyes were in my vision. I exhaled hard closing my eyes so I wouldn't see anyone. I hadn't seen him since he'd left me that night. Snuggling me so close, I hadn't ever slept that hard in anyone's arms.

"If only he was here…" I whispered. But that wasn't possible. He wasn't.

I didn't remember falling asleep.

But at two am, I felt myself jolted out of sleep with the sound of loud music blasting. It was so loud it not only woke me up, a splitting headache formed behind my eyes.

I blinked completely confused.

Was that my…roommate…really blasting music this late?

"Excuse me?" I rubbed my eyes. She poked her head out the shower. Her skin was darker than mine and her hair dark brown against her scalp.

"Oh, did I wake you up? Sorry, I had a late night, and this song is my new thing."

What? Her tone was more amused than apologetic as though waking people up this late was normal for her? Was she raised by wolves?

No, wolves are considerate creatures.

"It's two in the morning," I managed to whisper. "Why are you blasting music?"

"Don't be so uptight," she said with a smirk. "It's college, Queen of England, not high school."

Her dismissive attitude sent a wave of fury into my spine. It made my blood boil. I was not about to deal with a mean girl in university.

"It's two in the morning," I said with more emphasis. "I'm not being uptight, I'm asking for decency."

I summoned all of Alisha into my spine then. "I'm asking you to stop." Because nobody got angrier than a threatened Alisha, my sister snapped from sweet older sibling to a wildcat in seconds.

And then her eyes shifted as she swore, grabbing her phone out from the sink and turning it off.

"There, are you happy?" She turned away from me without waiting for a response. "Jesus Christ, what an uptight bitch."

The silence felt jarring to me but on top of that, I was disgusted with her uncalled for insult.

Wave after wave of emotion went through as I was fully awake now. I didn't understand why she was being rude but on top of that?

She had woken me up. I felt a hot prickling like heat descend into my body and the wave of hurt hit me there too.

It was my first night too.

She had her back to me and I left the bathroom feeling a storm of emotions rolling through me. One burning hotter than the other.

Was I wrong for confronting her? No.

Because I needed sleep too.

Alisha and Gemma would never have done this to me even if they came home late they tiptoed around my room.

I went back to my bed laying there the bright light of the bathroom we shared jarring to my eyes and safe to say—sleep was going to be elusive now.

I went to grab my phone unsure of what to do.

What did I do?

Alisha said I could go back to her. Whenever.

But I couldn't. I just left. How pathetic would I look going back to my sister tonight?

My fingers moved over the chat I had with Thierry. But he didn't text. Not even now. My fingers typed out a message over and over before deleting it.

I felt the hot burst of tears in my eyes. I didn't know what to do.

"Hey Ma!"

Dear Lord. That girl was now on the phone with her mother out the shower?

"My first day isn't so bad." She lowered her voice. Or so she thought. "My roommate is so annoying."

I heard her say something else and then she started giggling and the headache behind my eyes bloomed louder.

I wanted to scream.

Was she serious?

I don't know what possessed me to want to confront her. I didn't though. I didn't even move. I didn't know what to do.

I closed my eyes and my phone buzzed in my hand.

I opened my eyes to look at the chat I had open with Thierry.

His message had appeared.

What's wrong?

I saw the bubbles. I wasn't asleep. Are you okay?

Do you need me?

I sat up slowly in bed, my headache throbbing.

Was he...was he texting me?

He *never* texted. I took a deep breath and texted him back with trembling fingers.

> First day. Nightmare roommate.

> No. I'll be okay.

I held my breath.

I saw the bubbles appearing letting me know he was typing.

> What's happening?

> What did she do?

> Nothing. Woke up to blasting music at 2am in the shower. Asked her to stop. She cursed at me.

His response came so fast.

> Is she still doing it? Stay on the phone with me.

> Yes. She is. Why?

I stopped breathing. *What? What did he—*

My phone buzzed. He was calling me.

"Hello?" My voice was a whisper.

"Record her. Anything she does, record it, now, Mon cœur."

My hands shook as I stayed on the call with him but went to the voice notes feature.

I didn't think to argue as my fingers trembled. With shaking hands I put the phone back to my ear.

"Don't say anything, Mon cœur. Just text me your response, okay?" My heart was racing a little.

> Okay.

"If she does anything to you at all? Report it. I'm coming to get you right now."

"What?" And then I remembered what he said. *Right. I have to text him.*

"Right now. I'm not leaving you there. Especially if she cursed you out. She's insane. It's the first night. Are you fucking kidding me?"

He said something in French I didn't understand.

No. Thierry. It's my first night I can do this.

"I know you can do it. I'm saying you don't *have* to."

My fingers trembled as I typed because the urge to go to him was ovewelhming. He wasn't Alisha. I didn't feel too guilty. But Alisha had dropped me off and she expected me in school.

"Stay with me tonight. We can figure it out tomorrow." Gosh, that was the most tempting thing he had ever said.

Was he being serious?

"I'm being serious, I am. I don't like the idea of you being bullied. I can't imagine your sister would either."

Low blow using Lish like that.

"I have to, Mon cœur. Otherwise you won't do it."

I felt the reluctant smile curve my lips even if I felt exhausted. It was late. I don't know why I was reluctant. The phone was still recording her but my mind was on Thierry.

Alisha dropped me off…I feel bad.

His response was instant.

"Alisha might feel worse if she knew her baby sister wasn't getting sleep because of her dog shit roommate—" he swore as he said it. "Is that her playing music in the background?"

I wiped my eyes now hearing her playing music again and cackling on the phone with her mother. No doubt she got her manners from her.

"Y-yes."

"Pack your things, *Mon cœur* —"

"No." I needed to just deal with it tonight. "Just give it a day…I'll just…" I forgot he told me to text him. "Just…"

He let out a breath.

"Avani."

I knew when he used my name he was serious.

"Let me bring you to my place."

"I'm too tired…" I whispered back laying on my pillow feeling my eyes leaking. "I'm exhausted."

"I know, little love. But let me…"

"I just wanna stay here. I just packed. Just moved. I'm tired." I didn't want to stay here but I was extremely bone-deep exhausted and I wanted to cry.

I didn't know why I didn't say yes.

"Stay with me?" I was so exhausted the words were mumbled.

He let out a breath. "Fine. *One* night. You get one night. I'm coming to get you tomorrow. Do you understand?" There was an edge to his voice I didn't ever think I'd hear from him.

Not at me but I could tell it upset him. The unease grew in my stomach. Tears threatening to spill out earlier now escaped from my eyes.

"I don't want to be a burden," I sniffled.

"You're not a burden, Mon cœur. I will stay with you." I heard him mutter he was coming to get me tomorrow though.

I just laid there until I passed out nodding to him even if I knew he couldn't see me. I just knew the last thing I felt before was guilt.

CHAPTER 18
THIERRY

I REGRETTED WAITING UNTIL THE NEXT DAY.

I shouldn't have invited her over to Andrei's place. It was my secret. My hideaway.

Now I was inviting this girl over to it?

It was against everything I believed in and if Andrei knew? He'd lose his mind.

But I'd faced down death several times in my life to know this wasn't like me. And yet?

The moment I heard that little noise in her, the distress in her voice, part of me wanted to run over all the other logical and rational thoughts in my brain to go and get her.

Because in the last few months I'd known her? I'd given her the most vulnerable parts of me. She had no clue.

She had no idea who I was, my backstory, what I did for a living —and she gave me her kindness without expecting anything in return.

It made me want to be good to her. Return that kindness back to her ten-fold.

She was everything I wasn't. Pure, uncorrupt, un-tainted by the world—and everything I shouldn't want. But I wanted.

I did. Since I left her bed I had been a man on the verge of drought.

Her body against mine, her laughter, those eyes—haunted me. She was softness, sweet things and sunshine and hopes and dreams

I didn't have.

This entire time I toed my lines in the sand carefully enough to note, it didn't matter if she was of age to tell me she wanted me—I could never be with her.

When I woke her up at my place, it would be buried deep inside of her until she gasped my name and moaned until she came all around me.

My darkest fantasies played out in vivid detail in my head.

Making her cry out my name over and over until she admitted it was only me who touched her and wanted her.

I blamed it on the House of Midnight and Shadow.

I had no clue why Damon the Demon Pirate King who had started out as this purple eyed asshole turned into a character I was rooting for.

I was on the third book now and I blamed Avani for me listening to these six hundred page audiobooks.

I was one book away from the book where Damon finally got his lady love Syrena, the mermaid who'd saved his life years ago back. Or Syrena got him. I didn't know.

And I was waiting to chug through book three to fucking get to it. Because this motherfucker Damon was filthy.

I couldn't fucking process Avani reading supernatural fantasy porn.

But on the other hand, when I considered it?

Given how sweet and shy she was sometimes unless you got her riled up? It made sense.

And that was another reason why I held back.

I could tell kissing her, she wasn't experienced, her soft hesitancy, her eager hands—Avani had never been with anyone.

I couldn't take advantage of that.

I was depraved for wanting her. I knew that much. But I couldn't take advantage of her. Not her.

Never her.

The only thing I wanted more than to love her—was to make sure I could repay Avani for the goodness she brought into my life.

She called me. Not her sister.

Which meant deep down? I had to analyze Avani trusted me, wanted me, and I was her safe place. Several times.

Every single time.

I'd be damned if I fucked that up for her.

The need to make sure she was okay, she was safe in a world like mine—overrode any common sense and sensibility I could have. To shield her from the darkness the world had in store for anything like her.

Now, at ten in the morning I hadn't slept a wink and I needed to go to her room to get her. I was on edge already, sleep-deprived and in a shit mood ready to snap at anything that came at me.

When I walked up the steps into the building, her door was already open.

I found her in there in dark jeans and a darker sweater, her hair down around her.

It was the first time, I noted, I had seen Avani in anything other than color. In black.

What happened to my pink princess?

Where did she go?

She looked darker and different and not in a way I liked.

Her roommate wasn't there but *my* girl—she was on the verge of tears when she saw her, dark shadows under eyes rimmed red.

I had her in my arms a second later the image of her imbedded into my retinas.

I held her tightly on pure instinct. To comfort. Her quiet tears chipped away at the carefully constructed layers of my mask. "I just wanted to be an adult."

"You're an adult, mon coeur, shitty roommates are a part of the package bundle deal."

A reluctant laugh escaped her sounding weak.

"Ready?" She nodded into my neck, her head bumping my chin as I cuddled her to me. "You packed your things?"

She didn't have much but she'd left her sheets and bed on there.

I felt the rage inside of my chest brewing only tempered by her weight in my arms.

I closed my eyes inhaling her scent into my lungs. It smelled like old socks in here and the scent of Avani was so low I was worried.

"Come on." I held her with one arm taking her duffle bag.

I couldn't kill her roommate. I mean…I could. I could if I wanted to. *Breathe. We don't kill innocents.*

But I could focus on only what I could control. Which was her. Right now. With me.

I got into my car with her and drove her out of there.

Avani cried quietly in the car and each quiet sniffle broke me down little by little.

I didn't like when Avani cried, because she was soft-hearted and I knew everything affected her differently than me. While on one hand I was grateful my partner was my perfect foil, on the other hand I recognized how much she hurt.

When we got to the apartment she barely looked around at anything. I took in her slumped shoulders. Her expression.

She couldn't look me in my eyes.

"Avani."

She wiped her eyes, the gesture itself so innocent, small and defeated that I knew how bad she must've felt. I knew her.

She was in my arms a second later sobbing into my chest. I moved us to the couch lifting her into my arms easily.

"I wanted to take you from there last night so you wouldn't spiral, Mon cœur. You're tired. You haven't slept all night have you?"

She shook her head. "Lish…she left me there…I didn't want to bother her." Avani's words were punctuated with hiccups.

Each little tiny noise tugged at my heart somewhere deep.

"And I didn't want to disappoint her. I feel terrible." She broke down again in my arms. "I'm a watering pot."

I fought a smile tucking her head under mine fighting a grin as I brushed her soft hair back.

"No, Mon cœur. Breathe for me. One more time…there you go…one more…good girl. Tell me what happened with your room-mate last night. Did you record it like I told you to?"

She nodded.

Good, I'd listen to that audio and see what the fuck was going on.

She quietly told me everything that happened hiccuping every so often. I told her to breathe in and out deeply until she calmed down.

"Let me see the recording on your phone."

Avani took her phone out from her pocket of her jeans and handed it to me opening it up. I sent myself the recording before brushing her back tossing both of our phones to the couch.

"You did nothing wrong. Asking for someone to be quiet when living with them is the bare minimum."

She nodded believing me. "I wanted to make Alisha proud though."

"You can make your sister proud *without* sacrificing your own needs."

She shook her head at that looking stunned at me for some reason. "No, I can't. It's all Alisha has ever done for me. She puts her needs second—"

I held up my hand quieting her. "She's your guardian. It's her job. It's not *your* job to suffer in silence because you feel like you owe her something. Alisha wouldn't want you to suffer for her. It was the first thing Andrei taught me. He just wanted me to do right by me, not to pay him back. I have money now," I motioned to the apartment.

"I keep the lights on here. Andrei doesn't want a penny nor does he want to see me suffer. The entire point of him taking me in, from Tasha was to do right by me. Same with Alisha."

The words flowed out of me as my truth.

My reality. And it was easier to tell her now for some reason.

"My Mom Tasha wasn't a bad person." I felt myself struggling to admit it to her eyes. "She was nineteen when she was modeling in New York. Poor girl from Vancouver without much money. She met my father, Phillipe DuPont and had this affair. Nine months later? I turned up. Except Tasha had been at the beginning of her career. If she thought Phillipe would leave his established family and wife and kids? She was wrong."

I saw Avani's eyes widen as I said the words I knew as my truth.

"Tasha came back to Vancouver and her parents hadn't supported her being a model, let alone having a teenage pregnancy. When she reached out to Phillipe, he sent her a lump sum of cash and cut ties with her."

And she never recovered.

"My mom struggled a lot. She was a kid having a kid. Eventually…" I trialed off. Tasha had found what some young women found was easier money. I skipped the horror for Avani's sake. "She was a prostitute. When I was eight, Andrei came and found me while her pimp was in the house. He thinks she was trying to sell me off."

Avani's eyes went so wide, her shaking hands clamped over her mouth and I held her close to me not because I was emotional—but because her weight felt grounding in that moment.

"Andrei took me that day. I showed up in this dirty oversized t-shirt and I smelled weird and he even admitted if I hadn't been the spitting image of Teo he would've even doubted it—don't cry, mon coeur."

Too late, Avani was already sobbing quietly.

"K-keep going."

I smiled a little not because it was funny but because out of everyone I knew, she had the biggest heart. And she was currently mine. The fact that she broke down over me years later shouldn't have surprised me.

She brushed my hair back lightly as I talked.

"Andrei cleaned me up. He got me clothes. Kept me in his house secretly aware that Maxine, his biological mother would be livid. He's eighteen at this point doing all this."

Avani blinked. "That's even younger than Alisha."

He *had* been young.

But he'd always been…more mature. More stable.

More serious. The only time he warmed up was around Talia. I met her a few years later for some reason.

He kept her to himself for a majority of the time but he figured she'd be a good influence on me.

I told Avani how they'd been my pseudo-parents in a way raising me.

I held her hand gently as she sniffled watching me with wide eyes.

"Talia and Andrei, they took care of me growing up, most of the time after Andrei took me in." I admitted honestly. "For a while I didn't understand it. I had never had siblings and all of a sudden I had two. I thought I was a charity case initially. And then Teo and I didn't get along when we met since he was always the baby, and now all of a sudden I existed. Neither one of them told Maxine."

And then I had begun lashing out.

"I think a combination of failed tutors, failing school, not being good at things like my brother's led me to losing my mind a little." I was honest with her for fucking once. "I was on drug for a while, cutting class, tearing up everything I could get my hands into—I got into trouble with girls." I wasn't proud of that and Avani stiffened a little as I rubbed her hand. "I wasn't…a good person when you met me a few years ago. I was awful actually. But now, I feel like I understand why Andrei was so hard on me. It makes sense now. It's part of why I can see where Alisha is coming from."

And also because I didn't want to talk about Talon with Avani. I couldn't go there.

I didn't want to. Andrei and my family were a safer bubble.

Plus, the weight of not sleeping properly combined with the lack of my morning routine, my entire schedule being shaken up was getting to me. If I kept talking? I would spill more than I wanted to and I couldn't do that.

"I wasn't a charity case. They genuinely gave a shit what I didn't bring to the table. Sure, Teo and I fought sometimes," I grinned at the memories of us beating each other up until Andrei and Talia yanked us apart eventually.

"In all the years I've known them? Anything they did for me was as their youngest brother. Not only have they expected me to suffer in silence and not give anything to me. She's your older sister, she would never expect you to go through that last night and not reach out to her."

But I was glad she reached out to me.

She wiped her eyes. "That's insanity," she whispered. "I can't believe that happened to you."

"It's all right, sometimes I barely remember it." But if she saw it written on my face she didn't press. She just wrapped her arms around me. Sometimes I did remember it and hated myself for it.

Not quite a DuPont. Not quite me.

Somewhere in the middle, in the darkness, straddling two worlds that didn't quite fit.

She was quiet for long moments holding me. A light yawn escaped her. "That's why you don't have memories."

I closed my eyes feeling her voice sink into my skin. "I'd rather not have them. All of my memories are painful." Until now. "Until you."

She drew back a little.

"Until I met you," I murmured. "I love my family, I do. But I have never felt like I belonged with my family. Not quite them. Not quite myself. But when I'm with you…I feel like…" I chose my words carefully. "I feel like everything makes sense. It feels like peace. Like it doesn't matter who I am. It doesn't matter where I came from—"

"Of course not—"

"You are the one place I don't have to be anything but who I am."

She just wanted me. She made that very clear. And that was enough.

"Come here, Mon cœur." I held her to me again fighting every urge in my body. "Let's get some rest I'm burning out fast."

I pulled her down on the couch with me feeling it taking over already, the fog descending as she snuggled into my side.

"Do you have a blanket? What if we get cold?"

My eyes drifted around the living room, to the ottomans. I reached over us stretching as she giggled lightly while I shoved one of the ottoman lids open.

"Thank fuck, Talia thinks of these things. Better?"

"Hmmm," Avani sighed. "And we'll figure it out tomorrow?"

I yawned. "Once we wake up."

We were both out like a light, her weight on me the most comforting thing I had in a long time.

CHAPTER 19
AVANI

I woke up to someone.

Thierry.

My body recognized it stoking something in me, bolts of lust blossoming in my core, making my legs clench together.

Except I couldn't.

And my eyes shot open, blearily blinking to in the sight of inky back hair on my chest.

The morning and last night came rushing back over me.

I was…in Thierry's apartment. My roommate was a bitch. And I was sleeping on his enormous plush couch. With *him.*

Thierry was asleep on top of me, somehow we'd moved during the day, to his head resting on me.

I didn't whether to laugh or die of embarrassment. This was new. But he looked so content from here I didn't have the heart to wake him up.

He was right there. Lips grazing over my skin as he stirred a little more. He muttered something as his lips moved.

Ohgodsthisisintense.

I ran my fingers through his hair hesitantly tugging lightly. He didn't move an inch.

I'd wanted him for so long it felt overwhelming to have him now. *"Thierry."*

My voice was a desperate whimper as I arched into him.

"Please—" I didn't even know what I was asking for.

Deep down, I just knew I wanted to be his for so long it felt like second nature to ask.

To beg. I would do *anything*.

And then he woke up, eyes startled wide on me. His mouth opening and closing like he wasn't aware.

His throat worked, Adam's apple bobbing. "A-avani...I just—I almost—I could've—" I could see how wide his eyes got, his hoarse voice filling the space between us. *"I almost took advantage of you."*

"It's okay...it's okay, I promise. I wanted it."

I don't know why I said it. But his reaction was electric.

If possible Thierry's eyes grew comically large.

He swore a little and moved off me so fast leaving me to scramble up. "Thierry—"

He scrambled back holding his hand out to me. *"Nononono*, I didn't—I shouldn't." He looked away like he was horrified. "I thought I was dreaming. I would never—"

That cut through me. It sank into my skin like talons clawing their way into my chest.

Was he...did he want someone else?

Was I just—A cold fear gripped me.

My heart skipped at those words.

Which meant...he knew it was me?

Or...the idea he was doing it to me while imaging someone hurt so much more than I thought it would.

"With me..." The wavering in my tone would have betrayed my vulnerability and hurt to *anyone*.

His head whipped to me, an intensity blazing in his eyes. *"There is no one else."*

The wave of relief filled me. More than it should have.

"Then...why..." My heart was pounding out of my chest. *"Why?" Why did he stop? Why did he look like that?*

"Because..." he looked like he was struggling with himself right now unable to look at me. He shook his head. "You're staying here because you're supposed to be safe—"

"I'm safe with you."

"No, you're not." It was a growl that left him and when his eyes met mine, they became dark pools, and a look entered it of nothing but dark hunger and even to my own inexperience, I knew he knew it was me.

"I *can't*—"

But he was the only man I *wanted*.

My lips fell open darting to his. I felt it quiver as I looked at him. "I don't understand."

He looked absolutely ruined as he looked away from me closing his eyes. "I—I can't—I can't do this with you."

A sharp stabbing pain began in my lungs at the sound of that.

"Why?" It was a whisper.

I *liked* Thierry. I liked him from the day I met him. And over the course of the summer that like had grown and grown. In the recent weeks?

Him taking me to the bakery, showing up to Alisha's respecting my wishes, simply his presence had filled me with more comfort than I could explain.

I trusted him.

"I don't wanna take advantage of you."

"But I want to be taken advantage of."

Now that was a response neither one of us had been ready for, his eyes landed on me wide and dark.

"I didn't want you to stop. I want…you. Do you want me?"

"Avani," his dark eyes reflected back his own emotions. "You don't know what you're saying." He shook his head in disbelief. "You won't know what you're asking for. What I am."

"I do," I reached for him then unable to stop myself. And he didn't stop me, but I felt him tensing, his shoulders stiffening, his entire being closing itself off to me.

"*I see you.* I *know* you. I know who you are. You're the man who saved me from that creep the first moment I met you. And then again. And again. And *every single time* you showed up, I knew you were brave and open-minded and *kind*. You have showed up for me over and over again. *You've been there for me through so much and last night—*"

"*I'm trying to help you—*" he couldn't look at me as he said it though and I grabbed his black hoodie forcing him to look at me.

"You did." My eyes met his and they widened at whatever he saw in me, pupils dilating and focused on me. "You've always done right by me. *I want you.*"

His chest rose and fell, his breathing hitched as his hands curled and flexed. He shook his head. "I can't."

I felt my heart ache. Shatter. I didn't understand it but the shards of pain were almost too much as I drew back feeling my vision blur.

Stupid girl.

I turned away from him. "I don't understand you," I whispered. "You want me but you won't have me. What do you want then?"

He was silent.

"I'm sorry," his voice was gruff.

"Me too," I stood on shaky legs. And I felt him move.

"Where are you going?"

Where I belonged. Not here. "To my space. I don't belong here."

I hid from the world all the time and right now I was forgetting myself and I wanted to curl into myself and cry a little. A lot. Even with a horrific roommate—I was going to make it.

I wrapped my arms around myself. The pain in my chest ached so bad I didn't know what to do. I didn't want to cry around him though.

"Avani—"

"I'm fine," I was just…I just needed some space right now. He'd rejected me after I laid my heart bare. "I think I need to go home."

"To Alisha?"

I nodded lying to him without ever looking at him, the curtain of my hair blocking my eyes and my face from him, I stood walking to his foyer putting on my shoes quickly.

"Avani—wait…no, please." I felt him grabbing at me. "No, let me take you."

"No," I pushed him off not looking at him. His hands were everywhere then. "Let me go. You promised…"

"*Mon cœur —*"

I turned away from him as tears blurred my vision.

My heart shattering with each step as I walked away from him.

I only let myself cry once I was in the cab feeling every inch of pain I knew I had done to myself.

Why would he ever want me?

I wasn't Alisha.

I was just Avani. And even after everything, after all he said—I wasn't enough.

CHAPTER 20
AVANI

THIS IS WHY ALISHA DIDN'T WANT TO BE WITH A MAN.

They hurt too much.

I got home to my new dorm bleary eyed and uncomfortable like I spent the last forty-eight hours under water.

Thankfully, by some miracle—my roommate wasn't in my room. And my items were still where I left them.

I stumbled into my room and cried into my pillow. Collapsing into my bed I inhaled the scent of home that was fading day by day.

Heartbreak, even my first one was brutal.

It was awful.

My mind kept replaying every single moment with Thierry wondering where I mis-read anything. His lips. His touch.

Everything. The memory of his mouth on me, and the horror in his eyes—it was too much.

I missed Alisha so much. I just wanted my sister.

I wondered what she was up to.

She was no doubt celebrating her birthday still with Gemma and Lara at Teaser's while I was supposed to meeting new people in university.

Not being rejected by a boy.

I cried harder realizing this might one reason why Alisha never let a man near her life.

Because this sensation was too painful to ever go through twice.

Eventually I moved through the motions of my shower, to clean up, to realize my stomach was rumbling.

I didn't remember the last time I'd eaten but now I could eat a horse.

I didn't even know where anything was. I needed to find the cafeteria, the study hall. So much I had to do.

Even as my heart ached.

A dozen different emotions ran through my heart, and all of them more painful than the last.

I blew out a breath into my mirror to examine my blotchy cheeks and red-rimmed eyes and wet hair. "I have to clean up. I have to do this."

Because this was my…opportunity. To be better. To be an adult. To have experiences. And I would have them.

I put on clean clothes and stepped out on campus to find the cafeteria first.

⌇

IT WAS THE SHRILL NOTES OF MY ROOMMATES ANNOYING MUSIC THAT woke me up.

I groaned a little burying my face deeper into my pillow wishing I didn't have a she-devil as my neighbor.

But at least it wasn't three in the morning but a solid six am.

Not bad.

I yawned waking up resolving to ignore her and go on with my day. It worked out for me because I had orientation now at eight so I could hurry and get to breakfast prior to that.

I could start the day right.

I laid there processing the last few hours of my life.

Now with a fuller belly and having cleaned up? I felt like the hours that passed?

Took me farther and farther away from what happened with Thierry. Erasing him from my skin. My sweater from his place in a hamper to wash later.

I tried not to think about his eyes being unable to look at me. Or the way it ached as I left his place.

It wasn't all consuming even if I teared up about it? It didn't feel like the sharp pain it had been. It was now a manageable ache.

The weak chai combined with a stale bagel and cream cheese did nothing for my stomach as I rushed to the orientation hall.

I heard the cacophony of noises spilling out from the large auditorium filling up with students.

I adjusted my uniform of my black mini skirt and stockings and my black turtleneck before I stepped inside—suddenly I was self-conscious.

This was a huge step in the right direction for me.

I should've been excited. And I was a little cross with Thierry for taking some of that away from me.

I slid into a section of the auditorium towards the middle if not back trying not to broadcast that I felt awkward, had no clue what I was doing, and that I just wanted to be left alone.

I don't want to be hurt today anymore.

A flash of vibrant violent pink caught my eye when I saw a taller girl with pink hair beaming at me from my right.

An edgy goth outfit complete with ripped jeans and combat boots, her shirt a little torn up stood there watching me with wide green eyes.

"*Sup*, is this seat taken?" She motioned to the one in front of me, her New York accent was thick.

"Not at all," I gave her a friendly smile.

"Sweet." She turned her head. "Aye, Queen Rosie. Your throne awaits."

A slender model-like woman with raven hair at her shoulders, and bright dark eyes grinned like she'd stepped off the runaway in Milan with her sleek black outfit.

She clicked her way over to us and I stared wide-eyed as she slapped the pink haired girls arm.

"Stop shouting, idiot. Everyone already knows you exist with that hair," she smiled as she said it to her friend.

Marissa shot her a smirk. "Yeah, and now they know to stay the fuck away too." She looked smug. "Look, Rosie, I made a friend."

She motioned to me and suddenly the dark haired woman eyed me with wide eyes.

"Oh, I'm so sorry Marissa accosted you," she apologized with a horrified expression slapping Marissa's arm again and Marissa winced.

"Whaaat," she protested, her pink hair swishing down to her back in the high pony-tail. "I did not."

The raven haired woman shot me an apologetic smile. "Marissa is obnoxious. We can go sit somewhere else if you'd like your space."

"Am not," Marissa grinned flashing her white teeth. "She loves me, she does."

"I'm Rosalie," the dark haired model held her hand out and I took it. "And this demon spawn is Marissa. But we call her Mari—"

"Because my full name sounds like a pornstars," Marissa cut her off motioning for them to sit in front of me. "It's Marissa. I'm not even making this shit up. My parents were probably hippies although they deny it."

I giggled at their interaction feeling warmth blossom at finding new people. "I'm Avani. Are you two freshman as well?"

"Dude, that accent is hot. You could totally be a porn star instead of me." Marissa looked impressed and her expressions made me laugh as Rosalie growled.

"What Marissa meant to say was, nice to meet you Avani," she shot Marissa a look. "Don't scare her. We just met her."

"And she should be warned because with that accent half the freshman class is gonna devour her." Marissa's brown eyes shot to me. "And yes, we are freshman. Sorta. Rosalie over here, took a gap year to model."

"Yes, Avani," she mock rolled her eyes. "We are freshman. Both of us." She slapped Marissa for the third time.

"You can keep it up, I'm into that shit." She winked at me. And I grinned feeling my cheeks hurt.

"Are you two roommates?" I asked gently curious about their dynamic.

Rosalie nodded looking droll. "Unfortunately, luckily we've been friends prior to this. We went to the same high school and now I'm stuck with this demon for life."

"Dude, this college is so fucking expensive, I'm going to take a page out of your fucking book and go into modeling too."

Marissa would be a stunning model, with her eyes and hair.

Rosalie scowled. "You hate modeling."

"True, but I figured feet pics wouldn't hurt anyone."

I almost choked on my laughter then.

At my expression Rosalie shook her head. "Avani, don't listen to Marissa. She's a terrible influence. She's got sarcastic poetry geek down."

I glanced over at Marissa. "You're an English Major?"

Marissa nodded with a smirk. "You?"

"Me too." Someone like me. "What are you studying?"

"I wanna get into the Russian writers. Way more raw than the garbage American writers."

I grew even more excited now. "I'm studying nineteen century romanticism."

"Ohhhh, that's sweet," Marissa said. "You have to check out Professor Lumiere then. She's the best advisor you can have. Or Professor Singh but they're both solid."

"How do you know so much?" I had done research but they seemed to be more informed.

"I pay attention," Marissa winked. "To everything. And I've spent the last two days talking to everyone in the campus. Trust me. I've got the list down to who to avoid and who to absolutely fuck."

Rosalie snorted. "You'll have to excuse her Avani, Marissa isn't exactly subtle." No, she was not. But it felt refreshing. Like I had met my versions of Gemma and Lara. It felt good.

Even if the bagel I had earlier didn't sit well in my stomach thanks to my pseudo-heartbreak. I still wanted to make friends.

Marissa turned to me. "Are you doing anything this weekend? Levine and I were gonna go see a movie and then get a whole cake."

Rosalie threw a pen at her friend who ducked. "You are getting the whole cake. I have to maintain this size."

"No, I don't have any plans, besides sleeping and reading to be honest."

Marissa looked disappointed. "Come out with us, it'll be fun. Besides you look like a lost middle schooler and I'll be fucked if you get picked up by the douche canoe twat-waffle jocks."

She motioned her head to the other corner of the orientation hall.

Where I saw my roommate making out with some guy.

"Gross."

"Indeed," Rosalie echoed. "I don't know, Caroline is dating the captain of the Gray Wolves hockey team, Oliver Hart. You know? The sworn enemies of Astor U?"

I did. Astor U had a notorious feud with Kingston Prep.

They were about a few city blocks away from each other. But you would think we existed in different countries.

"Astor's Dark Knights have a match this weekend," Marissa looked gleeful. "Out for Oliver Hart's blood."

Rosalie explained her friend Caroline who was a junior had been dating Oliver.

The two of them had been going strong, but unfortunately Oliver was the captain of a team my school hated.

The entire thing was silly to me.

"Caroline should date whoever she wants," I added.

Marissa rolled her eyes. "I would." She looked at me. "I'm here on scholarship and I'm about to do webcam shows to pay for my books."

Rosalie and I laughed so loudly people stared at us.

"As long as I get time to study my script," Rosalie said. "I don't care what you do with your feet."

"Oh, look there's Ben!" Marissa shot up. *Yo Benjamin! Bring that ass over here boy."*

I winced at her yelling as Rosalie growled at her to stop. But a cute blonde boy who had just walked in with his friends looked over at us. At Marissa waving, he grinned wider.

Dressed in a band t-shirt he looked a little nerdy and taller than all of us. Not as tall as Thierry though.

"Stop screaming, pornstar," Ben chuckled at her.

"Ben went to high school with us as well," Rosalie explained with a grin at Marissa. "They're friends." Ben had a few friends with him as well as he sat down near Marissa.

"What is wrong with you?" He tossed her a brown paper bag. "I can't even get two steps into the room without feeling like I'm in a music video."

He looked over at me and then at Marissa.

"You've already started corrupting new people?"

He was cute, all golden curls and easy smiles and bright blue eyes. As his eyes met mine again, I tossed him a polite smile. I felt… nothing. Not spark. Nothing.

Not my type.

Turns out I only liked the dark and dashing princes of darkness with a penchant for breaking my heart.

And at the thought of Thierry again my smile slipped just a little bit more. *Does fighting mean we break up?*

Were we together?

I kissed him and told him I loved him.

221

Being in a relationship is hard.

"Ben, this is Avani, she's new here too…"

His eyes turned to me with a smile. "Hey, I'm Ben." He held out his hand. I took it.

No electricity.

Nothing.

He wasn't Thierry.

As Ben moved to sit next to me I caught Marissa eyeing Rosalie with a grin and a wink.

And then both of them turned to me with a knowing smile. I turned violently pink ducking my head as orientation started. Ben turned to me with an easy smile I didn't feel attracted to.

"So Avani…you from around here?"

"Yes, I think the orientation is starting," I motioned to the front. "I should pay attention."

Not to a boy.

Now I understood why Alisha never let anyone in.

CHAPTER 21
THIERRY

I WASN'T FINE.

I wasn't remotely good.

She'd been out of my life for a few *days* and I was losing my shit.

Staring at my fucking butterfly hairpin for hours. Tossing it around in my hands. I memorized every groove, every ridge, every bit of it. It was starting to wear and tear. *Should've gotten her more.*

Sleep remained elusive after she'd left because I just wanted to run after her and apologize. Tell her I wanted her. I needed her.

That soft spun lush body, chestnut hair, and dark eyes under me while I fucked into what was mine.

I was wide awake for hours, my entire schedule of discipline, working out, thrown to fucking shambles.

Every single fucking second wasted with thoughts of her and how she'd wanted me to ruin her.

Wanted me to corrupt her.

I wanted to grab her and keep her in my apartment, tie her up to my bed, and fuck her whispering my feelings into her lips while sinking so deep we both saw stars.

Keep her there forever. Brand myself into her skin and stay there until she didn't know where I started and she ended.

That husky soft accent crying my name, and I'd swallow every single fucking ragged scream with my mouth.

But I couldn't do that.

Because I wasn't a monster. I wasn't my father.

223

Couldn't allow Avani to consume my thoughts when I needed to go and switch cars with Teo.

I'd picked up Avani in his and she'd been so out of it she didn't even notice.

The entire drive to Roadsters I had her and our morning in my mind and how I fucking wished I was another man.

Someone like her.

Someone who could read at her fucking level.

Someone not me.

I stepped into the building taking off my cap, aware that I looked a little out of it. I was thinking about Avani to the point where I didn't even realize I was standing in front of Teo's door.

His secretary stood. "Sir, he's got a visitor."

"Yeah, I know all about it."

I didn't give a shit. Like I hadn't walked in on Teo fucking women before in then.

He didn't even pause the last time just tossed me a set of keys and went right back to making out with her.

Safe to say, out of the three of us—he was the new animal.

But it wasn't a hooker.

No.

My vision went red at the sight of Teo, wearing a grin and pinned to the floor to ceiling windows by a taller man in a suit. His tattoos peeking out on his neck and wrist.

"*Reed* Whittaker," he growled. "I'm not interested in Alisha. As beautiful as she—" My brother was goading him? Shit.

I drew out my gun with the silencer on moving quietly. The other man was so invested in Teo, he didn't even see me.

"Watch your fucking mouth."

I felt the rage rising in me, my sheer need from not having Avani adding fuel to the fire. Who the fuck was this motherfucker?

Idiot.

I moved, on him in another second.

"Or you can watch yours."

I turned my safety off and I fucking knew this idiot heard it.

Get your hands off my brother before I tie you to the back of my fucking car and drag you through the streets you motherfucker.

"He's friendly," Teo said with a grin as he watched me.

He knew me. He knew how bloodthirsty I was on the inside.

He knew I was going to kill this son of a bitch as I shoved the gun into the back of his neck he stiffened. Good.

I felt blood thirsty. First, lost Avani. *And now this?*

"You should pick your friends better, *Teo*."

I pressed my gun into that motherfucker who slowly released Teo and turned. I got a glimpse of stormy bright grey eyes, and muscling chiseled features that looked stunned at me.

Teo was grinning at me letting me know he might be on something.

"You have a twin?"

Who the fuck was this motherfucker? I took him in.

Solid. My height. Stormy eyes. Built like a fighter. He took me in as well like he knew who I was. *Impossible.*

Teo's grin widened.

"*Non*," Teo said. He motioned for me to lower my gun and I did reluctantly. I was still ready to kill this man.

"Not a twin," Teo said as I took in the newcomer. "He's family."

I appreciated Teo saying the words he knew meant the world to me. But not in front of this man.

Reluctantly, I backed off and moved to the couches on the other end of the room.

I didn't want to say anything else. Didn't need him to know who I was. I knew I looked like hell after the night and day and I had.

I couldn't get the image of Avani crying out of my mind. Her in my lap.

And now this fucking moron wanted to get in my day.

"I have nothing to do with your Alisha. I'm happy she is happy, though you are not what I expected." Teo shrugged lightly.

Hang on. *Alisha? Your Alisha? Who the fuck...*

"However, if she is being threatened, we can always offer our assistance."

Teo motioned to me and I was aware I looked less than fucking thrilled since there was no fucking way there was another Alisha in the world.

"I got it," the man said looking livid.

"Then why did you come here?" Teo looked calmer now. He leaned against his desk. "If you have no need for my assistance, and you knew before you walked in that I have never dated Alisha, what was your motivation?"

Alisha. Malhotra. This man, tattoos and temper was dating

Avani's sister? Was he here to goad Teo? Why the fuck was this happening to me?

I eyed the guy up and down. He wasn't comfortable in his suit.

"If I wanted Alisha, I would have her," Teo said to the man. "I enjoy flirting with her, like all women. But I would not defile someone so lovely."

That was the fucking truth.

Teo could eat Alisha alive. Part of why I kept Avani away from me and I hadn't pushed her. But Teo?

I grinned at my brother who looked downright devious.

"You can borrow our assistance, for Alisha."

I bit back a sigh. So much for staying away from Avani.

"No need." The other man straightened his suit, tossed me a cool glance over and to my gun before storming out.

I looked over at Teo who looked amused. The door had barely closed as he said. "Alisha Malhotra's new boyfriend, Reed Whittaker."

I noted it mentally.

"Why's he here?"

Teo rolled his eyes looking bored despite being attacked a second ago. "Sounds like she's got an overzealous fan sending her love letters and he's…"

"Protective."

"Annoying," Teo finished with a yawn. I grinned shaking my head. If there was a fire Teo would find it boring.

I blamed it on our insane family.

"Your car's finished. Sort of. I think I have a new attachment coming in a few weeks so I'll make some changes then."

"He say anything else?" I asked casually since Teo was getting the keys to my car.

He shook his head. "No, his idiot friend called me at three in the morning or something. I'm not a moron to make enemies out of the Titans."

"The Titans?" Why did that so familiar?

Teo explained Reed Whittaker was the CEO of a private security firm and that Alisha was dating him. Well. *Shit.* We walked down out of his office down to the garage.

"He came because he thought you were sending Alisha love letters?" I smirked even though I knew full well I'd do the same for Avani. That man was dating her older sister.

Hm, I'd have to keep an eye on that.

Teo laughed looking devious as he sighed. "Even if I did want Alisha, I'm not a complete idiot."

Teo switched to French so nobody could understand him.

"Both of those sisters are too sweet for me."

I knew. That's why I loved the younger one. She was my heart and I hurt her. I didn't want to fuck her. I mean—I did—but I didn't want to do it with lies.

I wanted to tell Avani everything about myself.

Everything.

And then what?

Wait for her to reject me?

I felt like I was trapped in an impossible situation. The frustration bubbling over until it felt trapped in my body.

"Both of them?" I casually murmured. Nobody knew Avani was tutoring me and fucking Gemma kept her secrets.

"Oui, she's in school. The baby of the family. Adorably pretty— reminds me of cake." His grin was wicked as he winked. *"If she was older maybe it would be a different story."*

I resisted the urge to go full Reed Whittaker and tackle my brother for saying that about my girl.

The surge of possessiveness was so dark and unfamiliar I didn't even understand why. The last time I'd gone after Teo was because he broke a toy of mine.

And we'd been rumbling on the floor for a bit until Andrei swore and found us tearing us apart.

Right now? I wanted to rip into Teo for even dreaming about going near Avani with anything he liked.

Especially now that I knew her sister had a psycho-fan after her. Besides, was Avani safe alone?

I had told her to call me when Alisha left so she wouldn't be left alone what with the weird doorman and all.

But now she was in school. Did that mean she was safer?

I mean, I could go check on Avani.

Make sure she was safe.

Maybe even from a distance?

I heard Alma in my head. *Like a stalker, pendejo?*

No. Like her protector.

Yeah. I could do it.

I could watch over Avani.

She wouldn't even know. It would be fine.

~

I WAS WALKING ON CAMPUS TO HER DORM BUILDING.

The drive here had been nothing but a blur.

I didn't remember how I even got here parking my car in the lot with the throngs of students flowing in and out of modern buildings.

My heart was throbbing a little in my chest at the idea of doing this to her but if it meant she was all right I would do anything for that girl. Even if she hated me now.

I did want her. I just didn't know how to let her in. Or why I hesitated.

It wasn't like I was a part of Talon anymore. Why had I held back? Because I had to be honest? Or because I had to be vulnerable?

And if Avani could be open with me? Couldn't I let her in?

I could if I tried, right?

How the fuck did I even start?

I'd thrown on a hoodie and some sweats to blend into the college population along with a pair of glasses and baseball cap. I even borrowed one of my books from home on Andrei's shelf to make it real.

Everyone always saw what they wanted to. And right now—I was hidden in plain sight. A secret.

I told myself I was coming to check on Avani and make sure she was safe and nobody was stalking her.

I lowered my ball cap a bit as people passed me. Like this? I doubt I even looked like me fully.

I heard the sound of feminine laughter and a gaggle of students coming out the library.

My heart began to pound a little in my chest as I looked over. I don't know why—but I knew when she was there.

I *knew* her. I wasn't wrong because behind the gaggle of people emerging was Avani—sweet beautiful soft Avani—a wide grin splitting her lips, the wind in her hair. She was laughing.

And a part of me ached at seeing her like this.

This was her world, the sunlight streaming into her hair setting her apart and making her glow from within as she laughed again.

My own lips tipped up at the sound.

I used to swallow those laughs whole and tuck that warmth into the deepest coldest recesses of my chest. I stood apart from everyone—the shadow.

The Grim Reaper. Darkness compared to her light. Her softness.

We'd never work. I was stupid to even let her in. I was being an idiot.

I was going to corrupt her. And I needed to stay the fuck away.

I went to follow the crowd when I stopped. My blood ran a little colder than usual at the sight of a taller man, wrapping an arm around Avani's shoulders.

And just like that jealousy, hot and familiar twisted my gut again.

Get your hands off my girl.

College kid. I could take him.

He leaned into her and she laughed again as a woman with hot pink hair looked over at them.

She had another guy on her right. What the fuck? Was this some sort of date?

She tells me she wants me—and then she fucking moves on that quick?

And just like that my anger turned into something else for her. A rational part of me knew I had no fucking right to feel anything let alone betrayal. I'd been the one to push her away.

I did this to her. I ruined our relationship. And yet, I couldn't stop myself as Avani broke off and the guy followed her keeping his arm around her and she laughed at something he said.

Like he's actually that funny? Please. I'm funnier. I can make her laugh.

At some point Avani broke off and walked into another building waving goodbye to him with a wide grin on her face.

"Be good, Ben!"

"You too, little lady!" He winked at her, watching her walk away and I couldn't fucking resist coming up right behind him as he turned—too focused on my girl's ass to see me coming. She did have a nice ass.

And it was mine.

I shoulder checked him, pretending it was an accident as he dropped his books.

"Hey! What the fuck—"

I didn't even apologize following after Avani. *Where the fuck was she going?*

Entering into the building, I followed her discreetly behind her to a long hallway and she headed up a back exit towards the parking lot. And then across the street to the back of the dorms.

I didn't know she could even go this route. Was she going back to her dorm? Why was she taking this route? This was a back route. It was more dangerous.

I kept a safe distance between her feeling irritation flow through me.

First at her already moving on and now putting her life in danger.

Irritation coursed through my veins at her, at her smiling at another man, at her telling me she wanted me and then moving on to the first college frat boy she could find?

I felt a growl building in my throat as two college guys walked past her while she was on her phone and I sped up closing the distance between us making sure I was right behind her eyeing them down.

I took off the damn Superman glasses and my muscles coiled as I approached her.

She was too focused on her phone to look up until I was right there as the two guys walked by her not looking at her anymore.

I waited until they walked right by before I was on her.

Careful, Mon cœur.

Before she could scream at me being so close and drop her phone.

I caught it with my free hand, the hand holding the stupid book wrapping around her waist as I brought her flush into my chest.

"Don't scream, *Mon cœur.*" I licked the shell of her ear feeling her still, her mouth opening in shock as I gripped her tight to me. "It's just me."

It wasn't just my heart racing anymore in my chest, but my cock hardening, responding to every squirm of her body against mine like it had the night before.

I inhaled the scent of her perfume going insane by the second. Her chest was heaving as she let out a broken noise.

I was a disciplined man. Controlled tight. And now?

All of my control was unraveling.

I took her earlobe into my mouth as she whimpered standing there clutching my arm and trembling.

I wrapped both of my arms around her tighter than before.

"What did you think, Mon cœur? I would let you fucking go after I felt how *much* you wanted me?"

I was insane. I had been suppressing and maintaining control and discipline for so long. For so fucking long. I had finally snapped.

My walls crumbling at the thought of losing Avani to anybody.

"You've haunted every single fucking dream I have had since the day I met you. Do you have idea what that's like? Having you in my arms, falling asleep with you knowing I *can't* have you? I tried to stay away from you, I did. And now I'm done fighting it. I can't stand seeing you with anyone else. Not when I know you're mine."

I let out a ragged breath as the confession spilled from me.

I pressed my lips to the space behind her ear feeling her shiver.

"I need you like my next breath. Tell me you don't want this, tell me you don't think of me still. I saw you wrapped around that motherfucker. Is that what you want now?"

I huffed out air as I gave myself over to her. Surrendering completely and whole.

Dropping my head further over her shoulder, I felt her stiffen in my arms. I went to look at her and I froze. *"Mon cœur?"*

"Are you mad?"

Well. Shit.

"Are you absolutely out of your mind?"

I fucked up.

Again.

CHAPTER 22
AVANI

ALISHA HAD ALWAYS SAID I WAS SOFTER OF THE TWO OF US.

I was. Sort of.

I noticed when I did get angry though? It spilled out of my lips like fire.

"Are you mad?" I felt his arms around me tighter than steel. *"Are you absolutely insane? To come to campus and follow me because of what!"*

I shoved at his arms and it was like pushing a wall. Of iron. I couldn't get out.

"Let. Me. Go."

"Don't run from me, *mon coeur—*"

"I have no intention of running! I have every intention of giving you a piece of my mind!"

I was so angry with him. I whirled on him the moment he hesitantly let me go. We were standing in the middle of a walkway for anyone else to come by and overhear and I didn't give a bloody time.

I stared into those electric-blues rimmed in red and looking exhausted as he watched me.

For a nanosecond my heart ached for him.

Because I knew him.

And when I looked at him, I saw the eight year old instead of the twenty year old man he'd become.

I saw the seventeen year old who kissed me all those years ago.

I saw him looking a little lost and afraid. Worried.

He had come to campus. And while it dimmed my anger a little I was still frustrated.

I had done orientation and spent the next day with my new friends who were a blast.

Ben was friendly to everyone and easy to get along with, but I felt nothing for him. And then later Alisha had asked me to go to brunch with her.

Today I'd spent my day on campus with my new friends.

The *last* person I had expected was him.

"You are only here because you're jealous!" I snapped back. "Not because you actually gave a damn—"

"Of course I give a damn—"

"Then why did you push me away!"

I was breathing harder.

"You pushed me away! After I tried! I promised you I would never hurt you. And yet you hurt me—"

"I'm sorry, mon coeur—"

"No, I let you in. I slept with you," I lowered my voice. "I trusted you. And you can't even tell me why you won't…" I was a little embarrassed.

I realized I was actually angry with him for one apparent glaring reason.

"Are you angry with me for not taking you, or are you angry with me for not telling you why?" He said it. Those eyes watched me knowingly. Of course, he knew. He bloody well would!

"Both." I couldn't believe I said it. I thought if I ever saw him again I might cry, but instead I crossed my arms over my chest watching him warily. "Why did you follow me?"

"I wanted to make sure you were safe."

How is a woman supposed to be angry now?

"I'm sorry, Mon cœur. I came to make sure you were okay. I promise. I saw you and I lost it—"

"Why?" I demanded. "Why would you lose it—" He had been following me. "Did you see me with Ben?"

His entire face turned dark, his jaw tightening up a muscle ticking in it as I said his name.

"Are you jealous of him?"

His eyes took on a different edge. "You moved on from me? That fast?"

233

I didn't even hesitate, I dropped my backpack, unzipped it, and took out the folder I had with my orientation documents and thwacked him with it.

"*Are you mad!*" Whack. "*Why are you such a nincompoop! I have been dating you! All summer!*" Whack. Whack. Whack. I rolled up my folder in my hands for better leverage refusing to be cowed by his wide-eyed shock. "You are out of your mind. Stop following me. I can't believe this! Moving on from your—Ugh! And *you're* supposed to be the sensible one!" I growled at his bemused expression as he stood there a little stunned his hands up as I whacked him one last time. "*I'm leaving now! Go home.*"

I shoved my folder back ready to turn when he grabbed me.

"I'm sorry," he said quickly, moving quicker than I gave him credit for. "I'm sorry. I didn't know why—I saw his arm around you—"

"Ben is friendly—"

His frown was back. "He knows exactly what he's doing—"

"*Which is?*"

"Flirting, mon coeur—"

I couldn't believe this. "He isn't my type. Besides, I barely got through my day without thinking about you all the time, why on Earth would I move on with someone so quickly? *Who does that?*"

He looked a little sullen as I said it. I huffed out a breath. "I can't believe you thought I would." And now I felt hurt. I closed my eyes for a second breathing in and out as others walked by us glancing at Thierry holding me.

I couldn't think with his cologne in my lungs. Dark and spicy. A little wild.

I felt my head spin when his lips brushed over mine.

"Open for me, Mon cœur." I made a low noise as he stamped his mouth on mine again and again and my tongue tangled with his.

I whimpered as he sucked on my tongue and parts of my body responded, my thighs clenching on his lap as he cuddled me close to him.

Hot and commanding and desperate in his attempts to get closer and closer to me until I was molded to his body.

Hungry little noises leaving me for him. He groaned, fisting his hand in my hair as he licked my lips like an animal. My insides squeezed down at that sensation alone.

I was dizzy from the sensations and his taste alone, as he gripped my face, my neck, like he couldn't keep his hands off me.

And in return, my fingers that had gripped his shoulders now tangled in his inky hair, tugging him closer to me.

"Thierry—" I gasped.

"Let me take you home," he panted. "Back to my place. Let me take care of you, mon coeur."

"No," I don't know why it came out. "No. You cannot come back here when I move on—"

"*I'm not—*"

"Yes, you are." I was surprised by the sound of my own voice. "*I begged you. I asked you. I gave you a chance—*"

Confusion, fear, and something else stirred under my skin as he whispered it.

"I don't want you to hurt me again! I promised you, I wouldn't do that to you!"

He let out a breath as I felt his lips on my cheek. "I won't I promise—" the hoarse confession against my skin broke me.

And I looked at him to find him looking as devastated as I felt.

"*Why did you hurt me?*"

But the last thing I expected came out of his mouth.

"*I didn't wanna take advantage of you—*"

"I ~~already~~ told you," I ~~whispered~~ hissed at him. "*I wanted you! It's not taking advantage if I consent to you! For gods sake I desire to have a choice. I deserve it. Does my choice mean nothing to you?*"

"*Of course it does—*"

"Then let me make my choice!" I huffed out a breath. "Is that why you ~~you~~ pushed me away? *You felt guilty? You felt like you were taking advantage—*"

"Partly." He looked almost embarrassed.

I wiped my eyes now fully watching him.

"You cannot come here and kiss me because you felt bad I made a friend—*Ben is just a friend*—but you *reacted* that way because you saw me with him. And I don't want you to be hot and cold and switch at the drop of a hat. That isn't okay." I shook my head feeling the turmoil running through me. "*What do you want from me?*"

He blinked like nobody had ever asked him that question before. Like *I* surprised *him.*

"Because I don't like this," I whispered feeling how much it ached. "I liked when we were together. When we were honest with each other. I want you to be honest with me. You're not being fair, you didn't even consider telling *me*. *Making me your partner.* You *can't* push me away on a whim and then decided to take me back when you feel angry—"

"I'm sorry," his lips swooped in to kiss me again quickly. "I'm sorry, Mon cœur, I promise I won't. I just can't let you go. Hurting you—that was *never* what I wanted. Give me a chance to fix it, please." He whispered something against my lips.

"W-hat does that mean?" I whispered.

"It means I swear on my life I would die before I let harm come to you. I will do anything to protect you. Even if it means from myself," his eyes met mine. "I do love you too."

Something was in his eyes as he held my face in his hands and my heart threatened to jump out of my throat as he said the words.

"I love you. I haven't even *had* you and I love you. Some part of my soul knows you the way you know me. And I didn't think I was good enough for you."

"*Why?*" I searched those blues. "Why would you ever think that?"

At his silence I knew. *I bloody knew.*

"*Because you can't read?*"

"*You're an English major. You're eloquent—*"

"*So are you!*"

"*You're clever and funny—*"

"*So are you!*" I held his face now. "*Goodness!* You cannot seriously believe that me being able to string two sentences together takes away from the fact that I like you? I don't care what you have or what you don't have. I know you! I have seen you! *I understand you!* I do not need a bloody book to tell me if you are intelligent or not!"

"I went to school with men and boys who read and let me tell you, the art of being able to read does not make anyone *intelligent*. If anything, the more bookworms I meet, the more convinced I am we all have a superiority complex and I have no inclination of being with a man who routinely makes me feel less than because he learned *one* big word that week."

He blinked a little surprised at me.

"That's the *most* you've ever said."

I felt a reluctant smile curve my lips. "Well, I feel rather passionate when I am upset. And I cannot believe you thought your age or your background would ever make me see any less of you. How could you? You didn't have faith in me?"

He shook his head in disbelief. "I didn't feel like I deserve you."

He covered my mouth as he fought a grin.

"I'm prepared for another scolding, Mon cœur. But I mean it. I was afraid. I still am. There's a lot I haven't said to you. You deserve great things, Mon cœur. I never want to be the reason why you don't get them."

I frowned as he said it. What was he talking about?

His eyes were boyish with innocence as he looked down at me. "Do you still want me even though I'm fucked up?"

I pulled his hand from my mouth feeling my emotions swell, crest and bubble over.

"I do not think you're fucked up. At all. Of course I want you. I do. But you cannot do that ever again. You have to tell me the truth. When it happens. When you think like that. If I am going to be your partner I want to be your equal. You have to let me in, Thierry. You cannot push me away to protect me. It only hurts me."

And he didn't want to hurt me.

I didn't even notice how the sun had began dipping around us but the rays hit his eyes and half of his face making them glow.

My heart was thumping louder as I watched me.

And to my surprise, his pinky appeared in front of me.

"I promise to tell you the truth. You're my equal. *Always*. Will you give me another chance?"

I stared down at it feeling my heart pounding louder and louder.

I took it and stamped my lips over his.

CHAPTER 23
THIERRY

I HAVE A FUCKING GIRLFRIEND.

I felt the stupid smile curving my lips as Avani's dark eyes drew back a little to watch me.

I dipped in unable to resist her lips, soft and lush like the rest of her siting on my lap now making out with me in a fucking picnic area on campus. She smelled like fucking heaven. Tasted like honey. I wanted to kiss her forever. I always had.

The first time I saw her, her sweet face and those doe eyes, I knew *then* I wanted to kiss her.

Now?

It was a raging storm in me to get my lips on Avani and get her home to me. For good.

My fingers squeezed her curves tighter to me.

Being around Avani I lost track of who I was and all my thoughts became mush—she was temptation personified for me.

Now, once faced with the reality that I had to admit to her something I knew?

I realized now might not be the best time given the conversation we just had.

"I don't want to stress you out right now. I promise I will tell you later. It's getting late and I know you probably have nine different things to do."

She looked a little skeptical but we were working on her trusting me again after my fuck up.

"All right, but you promise?"

I took her pinky. *I promise. Always.*

"I'm walking you back to your room," I murmured. "And then I'm coming to get you when you're free tomorrow. Hm?"

I brushed her chestnut locks back hating how red her eyes and cheeks were. The scent of her honey and rose perfume drifted over me then.

The twilight emphasized the warmth of her expression making her look like a sun-kissed fairy on my lap.

"Roommate still giving you trouble?"

She shook her head, tendrils of her hair flowing around her, as she rubbed her eyes looking almost sleepy. I felt a pang of unease at seeing her like that.

"Not sure what her major is but she's always busy. Or I see her around campus making out with different guys which is a relief because at least it keeps her in their bed and not mine."

I felt my lips stretch into a wide grin. Only she made me laugh like that so easily. Regardless of the relationship I had with my family—I hid around everyone. Save for her.

"Come on." I picked her up in my arms, my heart feeling lighter and fuller. "I'll carry you back."

She squealed a little as I adjusted her and handed her the phone and book to hold. "What is this?"

I shrugged. "Stole it from Andrei's library."

She giggled as I cuddled her close.

I could get used to this.

I WENT HOME AND SLEPT LIKE A ROCK.

In my dreams I felt Avani in my bed with me and I was tempted to let her stay here.

Maybe even once the warehouse was done being renovated I could move in and have her stay with me. We could be together.

Once I stopped fighting her and I let her in? I realized the entire reason for fighting her was stupid.

I wasn't Talon.

I wasn't anybody.

I was just Thierry Mattison with Avani.

It didn't matter who I had been. And even though I loved her, to be fair, she said it first and it had felt easy for me to say it back to her.

The day after I told her I did? Avani went to her room and I went back to my place promising to come see her this week. I felt… different.

Because the promise of being hers? The possibility of moving into a different territory? It was all too much.

My entire life I had been someone's secret. My mother's, Phillipe's, Andrei's—but to not be Avani's secret anymore?

To introduce her to Andrei one day, to Talia? As my girlfriend?

Elated was an understatement.

I heard Reed Whittaker is a problem.

Alma's voice was in my head again. Effervescent and beautiful, lush with her baby pinks on. Her smile on me.

"Maybe," I muttered into the air. "But I don't care about him. Mon cœur won't take let him take me away from her. I have faith in us."

I had spent nearly three months getting to know Avani. I knew her like nothing else. I had faith in us.

I hadn't slept with her to know she was wonderful.

And the way I knew?

It was *simple*.

The only true way to know if someone in this world was good or not, was to see how they treated people that could do nothing for them.

The kindness, the soft spoken words, the sheer warmth Avani had given me—outside of my money, my looks, my body, my identity, and my brain?

Avani Malhotra was worth her weight in gold. I knew her soul inside and out and I knew her from her smiles, to her soft looks, and the way she held firm to me to encourage me to keep going in my education. Nobody had done that for me.

Tasha, my mom, had thought I wasn't that bright.

Andrei had hired tutor after tutor and medicated me and deep down I wondered if he felt guilt or why he took me in when I wasn't as smart as him and Teo.

Talia had done him a favor and tried to get me some discipline and I had become a good soldier.

And while Alma was my mentor?

Now that I was no longer Talon—I had no value.

No use.

But Avani?

She was the one person in the entire world who accepted me as I was.

In nothing I brought to the table.

Because to Avani the only thing that mattered was who I was on the inside.

When had that ever been the primary factor for anyone?

I knew a hidden gem when I saw one.

I met up with her in the evening picking her up from her dorm room where I waited outside her door.

I didn't want to burst into her room since Avani and I had talked about her psycho roommate. As she slipped out I heard the loud music from here.

What a bitch.

Avani's eyes widened on me and then she was in my arms a second later hugging me to her. "You can hear that."

"I can. Come stay with me at Andrei's if you need to." Avani hadn't really moved in. And I didn't mind having her sleep with me in my space. I cuddled her to me. "You can stay tonight if you need to."

She shook her head looking uneasy, a shiver went through her as I rubbed her back making me draw her in closer to me until she was tucked under my chin. Where she belonged. "I have class tomorrow in the afternoon."

My hand skimmed down the curve of her spine, down to her hips as I held her and then back up, my lips pressing against her shoulders. It felt so good to touch her.

"Even better," I murmured over the music not liking her staying here in this claustrophobic brown boring space.

It was sucking the life of her and I could see it.

"Come on, Mon cœur. Pack your things."

She smiled up at me with shy eyes dancing with amusement.

"No more kicking me out?"

I kissed her steadily unable to stop seeing those soft lips pout at me. She was my fucking undoing.

"I wouldn't dream of it. If there's anything in there you want you can grab, otherwise, I have extra stuff in my place. I'll buy whatever you're missing."

She looked embarrassed. "I have clothes."

My lips tipped up automatically not thinking twice about what I said. "You won't need much." And my smile turned downright dangerous at her blush. "Come with me, Mon cœur. Stay with me. I'll take care of you. I promise, remember?"

She shot me a look full of something as her breathing hitched.

For a moment she didn't say anything and then finally she pouted giving up.

Delicate lines of her throat worked as she said. "Do you have a spare toothbrush?"

I grinned feeling my chest expanding, feeling the darkness in my heart shrink as her smile grew.

She felt like the sun.

Warm and full of light and spring. In the wake her warmth, I felt something new blossom in my chest and it felt oddly like hope.

"I'll have you back by eleven."

"Deal."

"THIS IS SO TASTY," SHE TWIRLED HER FORK IN HER PASTA. "I CANNOT believe you have a personal chef."

"Andrei has one," I corrected. "He still maintains the place. And it makes him feel less guilty for not being here."

"Does your brother spoil you in some ways to not feel guilty?" She asked curious.

"Sometimes," I nodded. Sometimes he avoided everyone to not feel anything. Like his family. I didn't know what had gotten into my brother. I didn't know how to ask.

I wanted to talk to him.

But Andrei wasn't the kind of person you had heart-to-hearts with.

Avani sitting in my kitchen island in one of my t-shirts eating dinner with me had not been something I had planned for.

But the moment she'd switched into my clothes and put her hair up, she looked like she belonged her.

I felt the overwhelming urge to keep her here forever.

"I can't remember the last time I ate, and the university cafeteria is sorely lacking. Why is everything either dry or wet and nothing in-between?"

I pulled her stool closer to me needing her against me even if we ate. "You can take whatever you want from me, stay here as much as you need and go to school—"

"But what about the commute?"

"I'll drop you off." I grinned at her frown at me. "It's not a problem. I don't have a job since I retired from my previous one. I've got money and time now."

I promised Avani I would be honest with her.

I promised her I'd tell her the truth.

Somehow breaking it to her that I was an assassin or former one was not the thing I needed to do over dinner.

Even if the weight of my past pressed down like iron into my lungs I knew I had to say something.

But not everything.

Not when I hadn't told her about her sister yet either.

At the rate I was going I'd have more lies than truths if I kept this up.

"What did you do?" She asked innocently enough eating her linguini. "I never thought to ask. For Talon, right? What is that?"

Avani had good memory.

Decent enough to remember things like this. Somehow she had assumed that my name was DuPont when I told her about

"I worked in private security," that was half of the truth. I worked for Nash Group technically on paper. It was something.

"Talia's family runs Nash Group. They have a building in Midtown." It was actually right around the Titan's Midtown office. "They work in art security and theft and they're *comfortable*. She took me under her wing for a private security company they have I was with them until a few months ago? Talia, she just had my nephew, Drew. And I was readjusting to being back in the States when I met you."

Avani sipped her water before she asked. "Andrei let Talia train you for a private security company job instead? Like a trade?" Sure. Death was a business that paid well enough.

And because I wasn't a DuPont, at the time, nobody had given a shit. Malcolm Nash, Talia's late father and Andrei hadn't gotten along.

It explained why every time Malcolm's name had come up, Andrei looked like he'd rather swallow nails.

"That's insane," she marveled munching on a piece of garlic

bread. "Did you *want* to do it? When I saw you again you looked changed."

I smiled at her curiosity. "Not really. But the only thing wilder than working security jobs, was me." I grinned wider at her expression. "I wasn't a good kid. Or a good teenager. I got into a lot of trouble. I did everything I shouldn't have."

Come clean to her. Tell her a little bit. She doesn't have to know everything, but she deserves to know the truth.

She does. That is what I was at the end of the day. Not a DuPont. A Mattison. Always.

The darkness that had followed me my entire life. I didn't have Avani's upbringing. Golden. Full of smiles.

Even when she'd talked about her parents in the past there was warmth in her voice.

Something tugged low in my gut at the sensations of telling Avani the truth.

She might've been the one woman I did tell the truth to. The only one I let in.

I didn't know how I knew. But the word 'brother' drifted into my head then.

He closed the distance in the house dressed in designer clothes and he'd picked me up instantly.

I don't remember anything that happened.

I just remember waking up on a plane and then in his penthouse to him looking absolutely distraught.

As I told Avani she cuddled up to me listening horror etched into her features.

I told her about the first time I met Teo and how his jaw had dropped which brought a reluctant smile to her face.

He'd been stunned because we did look similar enough. But he'd been upset.

Teo had been the baby of everyone's eyes and now there was a new child.

I told Avani about Andrei and then his wife and how she'd become a part of my life.

"It was good for me, Mon cœur. It was what I needed. It made me stronger."

She nodded. "But it also hurt the entire time."

And there it was. The part of me that paused with all the quiet ways this woman challenged me. Was that what it was?

Is that why I never felt at ease with it?

"I don't think eleven year old boys need to learn how to be strong. Sometimes they just need to be loved."

I never thought about life like that.

I was regimented and disciplined to a point I could minute by minute map out my day. Until her.

Avani was everything I wasn't.

Soft where I was made of iron.

Gentle where I was trained to kill. And warm where I had a heart made of ice.

Darkness and decay had been my companions for so long feeling Avani smile at me like that? I felt my soul thaw out a bit more day by day with her.

The killer instincts in me calming down.

I *liked* this girl.

No. I *loved* her. Her smile thawed my world like sunlight on ice and I didn't want to lose her ever.

"You are the only one I don't have to pretend around." I felt it slip out like a confession. "When I'm with you, I forget everything. Who I am. What I've done. All the things I'm not proud of that make me who I am. When I'm with you, I feel normal, like a normal man, a normal person. And nothing else matters anymore. I didn't know I could want those things until you."

Her eyes softened. "I promise I won't tell a soul what you told me today," she held my face closer to her. "But I will say this. Who you were, where you came from, does not matter in the grand scheme of things. You are not measured by your past, Thierry," she whispered.

"I'm sorry about your past. I can't make that go away. But I promise you I will never do anything to hurt you. I hate that your entire life you've had to hide, and you've been kept a secret. I won't do that to you. If it's all right with you, I'd love for you to meet my sister."

As she said I remembered I had to tell Avani about her sister.

"I think Alisha would love you," she whispered. "I know I do. And I want you to be a part of my family too. I'd like you to be mine. I've been so nervous because I've been dealing with my own emotions. But I also know…you like to keep me to yourself and I feel the same. But maybe…maybe one day you might consider meeting Alisha…she'd love you too."

I nodded swallowing hard as I felt the emotions filling my chest. I wanted her to meet Talia.

"Let me choose you. All of you. Every part of you. And all your secrets and your past and the things you aren't proud of. I'm proud of all of you. You've come so far in the time I have known you. I choose every bit of that man. Past, present, and future. If you'll have me."

"Have you?" I thought my jaw was going to drop. "Mon cœur, I'm *never* letting you go."

She giggled. "Yay."

CHAPTER 24
THIERRY

HAPPINESS AND DATING WERE NOT TWO WORDS IN MY VOCABULARY.

But with Avani?

It was.

We did everything we could while she focused on school.

When she came home to me, to Andrei's apartment now, she curled into the couch and did her homework looking adorable as she used her books and phone.

My heart swelled every single time I saw her getting comfortable and adjusting to my space now.

She'd been through a lot over the last few days and I was determined to make her life easier.

Now my apartment saw a little more life and color with her in it.

Then I noticed her working off an older laptop. And because I was her boyfriend technically, it became my job to make her life easier.

I realized she probably needed a new laptop. Knowing Avani she wouldn't ask.

So I discreetly bought one for her and one day I asked her if she wanted to 'borrow it.'

Because knowing my heart, she wouldn't accept it from me without feeling indebted.

Her eyes wandered over it. "It looks so new."

I bit back a grin. "Nah, this old thing?"

It was the latest laptop out on the market with all the right specs according to Teo who'd sent one over for me the moment I asked him about it. So technically I didn't buy it.

Right?

"Oh, really?" She blinked down at the shiny silver sleek screens. "It's wonderful, are you sure you won't need it?"

I shook my head and handed it to her gently. "Not at all. Take it, Mon cœur." And she quietly tapped away on it muttering about how it was pristine while I played house with her.

I grinned as she typed away her essays and papers for a few hours while I made us dinner.

Bringing them over to her and watching her work diligently over her shoulder.

"Tea?" I offered her a cup and then set down some snacks for her. I was turning into a fucking house wife and it was so nice.

Because of Avani, now the house had sugary snacks and food. So she got a cupcake every so often and hot tea. And me sitting over her shoulder watching her quietly. It didn't take me too long to start moving around. I didn't even notice it.

She laughed whenever I began. "I'm sorry, I am neglecting you in your own home."

"No, it's all right, Mon cœur. I wouldn't ask you to put your—" before I finished she closed her laptop and reached for me. "Sorry, I was organizing all my assignments out for the term. It's much easier this way..." As Avani explained it to me she moved my head into her lap and raked her nails through my hair.

I groaned as her laughter filled the living room.

Tamed by head scratches. This is the best.

No wonder Andrei can't let Talia go.

On the weekends I took Mon cœurout to art exhibitions, interactive shows full of sculptures and paintings. Did I enjoy it?

I could give two shits. But Avani liked it and I liked what she liked. Period.

We went to a food festival where I choked down bites of stuff Avani loved, and she insisted I try one bit of everything. Sticking to the cleaner options while my girl downed a bunch of weird stuff. Avani liked her food spicy.

Good thing, I could handle it.

Sometimes. Sometimes, Avani put ghost pepper in her mouth

and said it tasted like candy and it was in those moments I knew why Mon cœur was my lady.

Because she scared me a little eating scorpion peppers and ghost peppers with that nice little smile on her face.

"It's kinda cute how vicious you are," I murmured while she tried hot sauce on her taquitos. She drowned them and then added some fresh chili paste. I swallowed a little in unease.

"Mon cœur , while I enjoy kissing you…" I trailed off staring at the medley.

She burst into laughter at my expression. "Not a fan of sugar and spice?"

I dropped my voice at the look in her eyes. "Only when it's from you."

Her eyes went wide as she licked her lips and I shook my head. "Absolutely not, Mon cœur , I can smell how hot that is and my eyes are crying."

I wiped them for show and she laughed utterly tickled. I took Avani out whenever I got a chance actually living my life with her.

Sure, it was with a ball cap and a hoodie on to cover my tattoos, but we'd curl up all the time together through whatever the other picked.

I found out Avani despised horror movies while I got a good laugh out of them. Until Avani landed in my lap cuddling tight to me.

But the darkness in the theater allowed me to drop my guard and be her man.

Not a protector for a tiny bit.

Between her classes that I rushed to drop her off to, her sleeping in my bed every other night or whenever she could, and us juggling the new relationship we were in—we both decided to enjoy it and get used to it.

Before I told Talia, before she told Alisha.

Especially since I did sit her down and tell her about her sister's overzealous fan.

She had been nervous but thanked me for telling her.

"She's all right, Mon cœur ," I murmured. "She's seeing someone too."

When I told Avani about Reed, her eyes went wide. She explained everything to about her sister and Reed and what she knew.

I listened intently taking in as much information as I could not knowing why the back of my neck prickled a little.

Not just about Alisha's weird fans, but about Reed Whittaker.

I needed to contact the Kindcaide twins and ask them about Reed Whittaker at some point.

Something about him was off. I couldn't put my finger on it.

Avani had sat there a little bemused. "Why wouldn't Alisha tell me she was with him? I've been rooting for them for months!"

I didn't know, but I knew Reed Whittaker ran a private security company. Which meant he was the head of something similar to Talon.

I didn't know what he dealt with but if he was anything like Alma or Talia? He was ruthless.

And he was seeing my girl's sister.

I needed to tread carefully and I didn't know why.

"Maybe it's good we aren't saying anything either," I shrugged lightly keeping my mask up. "Let's me enjoy you and not face interrogations."

She smiled. "Alisha would never interrogate you." No, but I pulled a gun on her man. A fact I couldn't tell Avani.

Or that he'd tried to attack Teo. No, I just let Avani know he was in Roadsters when I'd gone to see my brother and I wanted to make sure she was solid.

Right.

Another lie after I swore to tell her the truth. But what was I going to say?

I bet solid cash Reed Whittaker kills people for a living?

I wasn't calling the kettle black, but I mean—I do too. So I'm not one to judge.

But I bet money I am infinitely more dangerous than Reed fucking Whittaker.

Not to her. Never to her. I needed to distract her to not worry about her sister, I didn't like that little frown she wore.

"What are you reading, Mon cœur?"

She squeaked grabbing her phone that was open to a page, nearly dropping off the stool as I caught her quickly.

"Just some homework."

I pressed my lips together to not smile, hiding my face in her hair to breathe and hide the way my chest expanded from her hiding her romance novels from me.

Avani didn't know that I knew what she liked. What she read. What she was into.

The only reason I hadn't snapped was because currently my hand and my dick were best friends.

"You don't have to hide your books from me, Mon cœur ," I murmured bringing her closer. "I won't judge you, you know? Science fiction, hm?"

"Mhm." It was a squeak.

I grinned into her hair wide.

Avani was a terrible liar.

But now that I was closer to her I bit back a laugh because the scent of her made me respond like pavlov's dog, and just like that— I was harder than steel.

I held onto her nuzzling into her neck feeling her reaching for me.

Breathe. Do not destroy your princess. Do not hurt her.

Every thought of her, doing *anything* to that soft body that had started sleeping next to me every single night, cuddling her cold toes into my legs?

Made me lose my ever loving mind.

Every morning I woke up for my workouts and showers even before she did.

I took a shower downstairs in the gym so Avani wouldn't hear me fucking groaning as I came. I was losing my mind for my girlfriend.

But she doesn't know all my secrets.

And it fucking kills me not to tell her.

I wanted to be honest with her.

I also knew her favorite author just released another book this year. And I knew she was looking forward to reading it.

"Avani…" I whispered. "Let's just get some rest."

I just didn't know how to tell my girlfriend now I knew what she read and I thought it was *hot*.

I almost fell off my damn treadmill when he got to fucking her. Several times. Several chapters later?

I was convinced my girlfriend was hornier than I was. Which wasn't helping my dick that was getting excited even now just thinking about her.

Pulling back I looked into her wide eyes blinking at me.

"What's the matter? Your cheeks are so red…" she pressed the back of her hand to my face and I could feel how warm it was.

I was probably redder than I had ever been trying to hold back and not tear into my innocent girlfriend.

I cleared my throat. "I'm good, Mon cœur. Just gotta go run or something."

"Right now?" She tilted her head curiously. "You don't look so good. Are you getting sick?"

And then she was all over me, her hands pressing to my neck and my chest trying to see if I was burning hot or not and I caught her hands deftly.

"No, Avani," I was running on a thin leash. If I slept with her and she found out I was psycho serial-killer this would not go over well. Avani would never forgive me.

That leash was thinner now. If she kept touching me, I was going to snap. And the last thing I needed was to eat her up tonight.

But you could eat her.

And stop when?

When would I stop?

The truth was I wasn't going to stop until I was buried balls deep in her, with her sexy little accent moaning my name over and over.

Noooo. No, I can't have sex like this.

And then her mouth was over mine asking me. "…do you feel hot?"

I did. *Very.* I stamped my lips over hers unable to restrain myself anymore. I fucking loved kissing her.

"I do," I panted. "Very. But we can't. You have class tomorrow. We can't, Mon cœur."

"Why not?" She whispered knowing exactly what I meant. "*Why not now?*"

I groaned. *God save me from curious bookworms.*

"You've never—" I whispered. "I know."

She pulled back a little her cheeks turning bright red.

I knew. I knew enough to know Avani didn't even have an ounce of experience.

"And a quick fuck is not what I want for you. I don't wanna ruin *anything* for you, Avani. Do you understand?"

She kissed she back harder. "It wouldn't be ruining anything if it was with you." And then she reached for my shirt.

Danger.

Absolute.

Fucking.

Danger.

And then she went and said things like. "Please, let's just—"

"No." I closed my eyes shaking my head. "No, Avani. We can't."

Thing that took my resolve and launched a javelin into it crumbling it into pieces. I don't even know how the fuck I stayed strong.

Words I had never said. She was eager, practically begging for me to take her, but I meant what I said—I didn't want to hurt her. That was the last thing I had ever wanted.

Plus, I knew her kinks.

And I was into *all* of them. I didn't want her to hurt though. I swear, I didn't.

"Make no mistake, Mon cœur." I held her face in my hands as I dipped until my lips grazed her ear. "When I *finally* take you, there will no quick fucks for you. I intend to keep you in my bed for days. I never want to hurt you. Not once. I plan on taking my time. Hours. Days. And when I do finally get you, you will know just who I am and how far I am willing to go to *keep* you there. In my bed. On my cock. Screaming my name. Nod if you understand me."

I felt her head bump mine as she did, trembling a little.

Enough for me to know the impact my words had on her.

"You can do that now," she whispered. I grinned wider feeling the laughter in my throat despite my dick being hard as iron.

And nothing felt better.

She was hunger that never abated.

A longing I felt with no relief. Not yet at least.

My new temptation was now living with me and driving me insane—and I had no intention of letting her go.

For anyone.

CHAPTER 25
AVANI

"You good, Avani?"

Marissa looked over at me in the cafeteria as we grabbed sushi and some juices.

My tangled thoughts now interrupted I focused on Marissa's green eyes.

Her violent pink hair was up in a messy bun with tendrils all around her.

"I am—"

"You guys—Are they freaking serious—"

Before I could answer Rosalie came up behind her, looking put together in a tweed mini dress, her purse held in the crook of her arm.

"I freaking *hate* how everything has like ninety grams of carbs —" Rosalie interrupted her. "*Ninety*! What ever happened to protein? Is everyone allergic to a healthy diet? How am I supposed to fit into my clothes if I keep eating like a buffalo?"

"I think they stuck that label on upside down, Levine."

I laughed at their exchange checking out using my meal card. College lunches were not designed to be affordable.

I had absently gotten a few items and it was paltry to even think about. Living off coffee and leftovers until I got to my second home, Thierry's apartment.

The two of them bickered leaving me in my thoughts as I checked out and waited for them, my smile feeling pasted on with the thoughts like a whirlpool in my head.

My head had been *swirling* all throughout class.

Alisha was dating Reed and now she was getting threatening notes from fans. It sounded like something out of a movie.

Thierry had wanted to come check on me and make sure I was all right. I was.

I didn't have anyone pining to kidnap me.

But something nagged at me.

When I'd gone to brunch with Alisha after university started, she hadn't said anything to me.

Was she trying to protect me? Was that why Reed was involved in her life?

I was still acclimating to the university life. But that didn't mean I shouldn't have known?

At least Thierry is honest with me.

It had been Thierry out of all people who had told me. I couldn't stop thinking about him.

My friends had no idea I was staying with him and avoiding the dorms unless I had to.

Thankfully by some miracle my mean girl roommate was nowhere to be found which I thanked the campus gods for.

And my thoughts were on him.

It hadn't stopped being about him as I'd raced out of the house today with his laughter in my ears, my backpack on his shoulder as the two of us made our way to campus where he'd dropped me off.

Make no mistake, Mon cœur.

There will be no quick fucks for you.

I never want to hurt you.

When I do finally get you, you will know just who I am and how far I am willing to go to keep you there.

In my bed. On my cock. Screaming my name.

In my daydreaming I almost bumped into someone and gasped out of their way.

I wanted to scream.

And it wasn't just his words. It was the sheer devotion behind the, the conviction—not fleeting, or empty, but full of promise. I was aware he was a good man. I was.

But sometimes I wondered if he was holding back with me or why he was.

255

I wondered if the age difference combined with the fact that he knew I didn't have experience was one factor.

He had become my escape. Something I wanted.

Over the last few weeks our relationship had changed even more so with Thierry.

Was Reed Alisha's escape?

Reed had been her crush for years. Reed was the man who she wanted and now with her being threatened, naturally he'd step in for her.

Marissa and Rosalie faded into the background as I processed my life now.

Within a matter of weeks I had gone from being sheltered with Alisha, to dating a man she had no clue of—which didn't really make me any different from her.

I picked at my sushi while walking with the girls to our next class.

"Are you guys excited for Professor Singh? I've heard on reviews she's the best professor for our major," Marissa asked. "Avani, Rosie's taking the class to fit in with the normal people so she doesn't come across as a stuck up queen."

Rosalie rolled her eyes. "If you must know Avani, I wanted to try something new."

We walked to the building today and I could've sworn as I crossed the street I saw a familiar blacked out car pulling into a parking garage.

No, he couldn't be here.

I was imagining it. I was always seeing things. Seeing him now.

The girls and I stepped into the building and I was right back in the thick of it.

Another day, another class—and I'd go home to my boyfriend.

Who I wanted.

Who wanted me.

CHAPTER 26
THIERRY

"So what's new with you?"

Talia looked genuinely curious and pleased with me as I spent time with baby Drew.

He'd gotten a lot chubbier in the last few weeks but he still gave me those gummy smiles that lit up my face and his.

The truth was everything was new. And nothing at all.

My world had shifted, and I didn't know how to tell Talia that a certain college freshman was the one person I had been falling for?

"Not much," I started and she leveled a look at me.

Right. I can't lie to this woman.

I just didn't feel comfortable telling her right now. It wasn't that I wanted to keep Avani a secret from Talia.

But, Talia wasn't in the best of places right now. Nobody brought up Andrei.

Drew took one of my skeleton tattooed fingers in his mouth gnawing on my finger.

"He's hungry again."

"I know," she murmured her eyes instantly soft on him. "He's always hungry. He's a newborn. Teo said he's coming over to bring him new toys if you stick around you might catch him."

While I was torn between the desire to see my brother, and the urge to go find Avani—Mon cœur was in class. Which meant familial obligations won out.

Thirty minutes later my older brother ambled in holding an enormous stuffed plushie and some gummy toys looking ridiculous.

Talia made a delighted noise. "Oh my God, look Drew, is that Wally? That's your favorite whale plushie look."

"That plush is bigger than Drew," I snorted as my nephews eyes widened on it his chubby fists grabbing for it. Teo's smile went wide at the sight of Drew.

I got the feeling Drew did to us what we needed.

It was healing the family to see Talia become a mother.

Despite Andrei being absent, I spent time with her enough to know being a Mom had changed her.

Deep down I recognized the three of us lacked things Andrei and Talia tried to give us. More so our pseudo-parents than siblings.

"He'll grow into it," Teo said grinning at Drew who was being bottle-fed by his Mama.

It was odd thinking about us as the picture of domestic bliss.

My brother, the billionaire playboy, my sister-in-law, the former head of a technically terrorist organization and black ops unit, and me—her former killer.

Bonding over Wally the Whale and our adorable nephew.

I wish Avani was here.

The thought appeared like smoke screen in my mind and I realized with alarming clarity that I did want Avani here.

I wanted her with me all the time. Everywhere I went. I wanted her by my side.

Me. Who'd never been with a woman until now—wanted my girlfriend everywhere.

Teo's eyes flickered to me like he could read my thoughts. His eyes were knowing and he always knew *everything*, he just said nothing about it.

My phone went off discreetly the screen lighting up.

It was a heart.

I felt my lips stretch wide as I looked down at a photo of sad looking sushi and a question mark next to it.

> Questionable finds. I don't even think this is tuna. It tastes like bell pepper.

Miss you.

I grinned down at the sushi picture.

Let me know when your class is over and I can
make us dinner.

You mean your personal chef will make us dinner

I am your personal chef * *

This is true.

How's your day been?

I thought our professor would be here but she had
an emergency so she called out.

Instead, we're all reading and hanging out in class.

The finest education for 100k a year

I wish I'd known college was easy my ass
would've been there a long time ago

Maybe it would've helped me read

...says the guy texting me now fluently

I paused. My hands hovering over my keypad. I just slowly realized what I'd done.

I'm texting her.

I'm reading what she's sending me.

Something exploded in my chest.

And in that moment the noises of Talia cooing to my nephew
faded into the background. All I could see was my girl texting me.

Me texting her *back.*

My chest expanding and contracting painfully as I realized what
she'd done for me.

Everything else vanished to nothing.

Something akin to gratitude and something more primal made
it harder for me to breathe and string together words.

She taught me how to read properly.

Something others gave up on figuring I had my brother's money
or that being a DuPont didn't mean I needed to know anything.

259

I didn't tell Avani but for a long time I felt like the stupid brother.

The one who couldn't comprehend things. The one relegated to being a soldier.

Now, I was dating a girl who wanted to get her PhD in English and become a professor, and she had been the one to sit with me all summer long and teach me how to read.

And because she'd changed my life in ways I didn't even realize I wanted to show up for her in every way shape and form.

Darling?

Sorry, Mon cœur

I love you

I loved her.
I did.

Love you too 🤍

As she typed I saw the shadow pass to my left and I caught the fruit flying at me in mid-air, whipping my had to a grinning Teo.

I squeezed the orange reflexively and tossed it back to him.

Teo caught it and dropped it back into Talia's fruit bowl.

Talia was gone and Teo was the only one in the room. How had I missed that?

"Who is she?" His eyes were twinkling on me in a way that made my grit my teeth.

Avani did know him or of him at least.

She spoke highly of him, but she also didn't know my brother. She knew one of his many chameleon personalities.

I tucked my phone away. "It's nothing. It's just a meme."

"Hm," he smirked. "You've been busy. You don't show up for me anymore. You come to see Talia. I heard you had a tutor this summer and they didn't end up dead." And then my brother's grin stretched wide. "Which brings me to the point. *Who is she?*"

Oh shit. Leave it to Teo to figure that out. My brother wasn't as stupid as he pretended to be. Everyone overlooked the charming billionaire playboy vibes he gave off. Nobody realized how whiplash intelligent he was.

My scowl was permanent now. "Nobody."

And if possible, Teo's grin widened. "Nobody makes you smile like...that? You know Jace traces you but maybe I should have him spy on you now?"

I shot him a look. "Jace doesn't time to spy on me. He's too busy running around with your demands."

Jace Lawrence was an IT hacker, Teo had on his team. Competent and highly intelligent, Jace did Teo's bidding and Teo in turn kept his identity quiet. Our family knew about him. And that was it.

My brother looked like it was Christmas at my expression.

"No, I'm not—"

"Yes, you are—"

"*No.*"

Teo's eyes sparkled as he looked me over. "You seem adjusted to reality now. Is she taking care of you?"

It hadn't been long. Maybe a solid few months. Not even a year yet.

I watched him eyeing me still looking amused. "Fuck off."

He rolled his eyes with a smirk. "The least you can do is admit you've gotten *adjusted* with a girl."

"I don't wanna talk about it."

My growl would've made most men nervous. Most men were not my brother. That was the thing with siblings and *no* boundaries.

"I am adjusting. It takes time."

His eyes softened on me, the teasing glint fading to something closer to understanding.

It was odd sitting across from him and looking into a reflected version of me. Not quite DuPont.

Not quite there yet. The only person I really belonged around was Avani. And even I knew that.

The feeling of being an outsider, of hiding, it never really faded.

Teo was a little cruel to everyone around him but his family.

"*Do I...know her?*" His sly smirk was downright devious as he watched me. "Is she connected to our family?"

Yes. And. Yes.

I would not be telling Teo about Avani.

"I will shoot you."

And Teo being Teo laughed outright. "I do know her! Ohhhhh." As he made a noise I threw something at him as Talia came back.

"Okay, Drew's asleep, what did I miss? No, you two are not throwing my scented pears. Give that back!" Talia's smile dropped the moment she saw me throw it and it hit Teo's chest—almost—he caught it and threw it back. "No, I love that pear. It's part of a collection. Both of you. Thierry, give it back."

I grinned holding the pear. "You used to be taller than me once," I laughed at her expression. "Now you're tiny."

"I'm not a giraffe like you," she held her hand out. "Give it. I collected those in Morocco."

"Do you mean stole it?" Teo grinned motioning for me to throw it back to him.

I chuckled at Talia's mutinous expression.

I tossed it back to Teo and Talia growled crossing her arms over her chest at both of us.

"You two cannot be serious right now."

We both chuckled down at her as she turned redder by the second. Teo grinned holding it up. "Did you want it back, sis? I still remember you and Andrei doing this to me when we were kids—"

"You were a little shit—"

"*I was not—*" Teo made a pfft noise and tossed it back to me and I laughed at Talia's whimper.

"My pear—Teo, you were terrible—Thierry give it back—"

"Who's gonna make us?" Teo joked. "You know once, you were this leader and scary woman. And now you're like a little bear—"

"I am not a bear!" Talia turned mottled red. "You take that back." She grabbed a large spoon from the island and held it up to beat Teo with and I grinned.

Talia would love Avani. They were similar as a whole.

Talia was good-natured about this stuff and I had every intention of giving her the damn pear back right then.

"You don't wanna ask that question." The deeper voice cut through the kitchen and all of us froze.

I stilled holding the golden pear candle thing. Teo looked like he was going to vomit. Talia stiffened as her eyes went comically wide.

Teo and I were the only two that turned our heads to find Andrei stepping into the kitchen.

The frigid air blasted into the kitchen despite it just being Fall right now.

There was a familiar clink of keys as Andrei set his things down and stepped into the kitchen in a signature black suit. His eyes landed on Teo. Who grimaced. Instantly. I fought a laugh at the two of them as I saw Talia's throat work.

Andrei's eyes skated over to me and instantly I handed Talia her scented candle.

Sure, I might've been Talon once—but nothing inspired fear in anyone than Andrei. He didn't smile. He didn't say a word. He rarely went off on me anymore but his presence turned the room to ice.

He reminded me a little of Alma, but between the two of them—she was scarier.

Talia set her pear down fidgeting with her robe and hair as Andrei turned to Teo. "Are you fucking kidding me right now?"

His sculpted features turned to granite.

"Missy Delacroix's daughter is publishing another article about you in the society papers…" and he was off.

Teo looked ready to fall asleep as he bit back a yawn from this angle. Ever the provocateur, Teo was ready to drive Andrei crazy.

Talia caught my eye making a subtle motion that we needed to leave while Andrei lost his shit on Teo. An escape.

I didn't wanna leave my brother but Andrei was going off about how some oil baron's daughter claimed Teo got his daughter pregnant.

Teo made a noise of disbelief sounded irritated now. *"I didn't get her pregnant—"*

"How do you know that—"

"Because I'm not an idiot."

Only Teo handled Andrei so casually. Talia and I shot each other a glance completely and shamelessly nosy now.

"Even if I did sleep with her, you think I'd ever let that happen?"

"Did you?" Andrei looked furious as the temperature dipped to frigid.

"I mean—" Teo broke off sliding us a glance that told me he was going to fuck with Andrei. But one look at Andrei and he decided against it. "She's not pregnant."

"How do you know that!"

"Because last I checked you can't get pregnant from swallowing."

Fucking Christ. Teo.

I coughed into my hand to stop my laughter from bubbling out, and Talia made a strangled noise like she was dying.

Both of us turned away from them our shoulders shaking as she shot me a look.

She pointed to the door and we both took a step to leave the kitchen.

"Not so fast."

We both froze. Andrei's voice was iron.

"Thierry. A word."

Oh. Fuck. Me.

Talia gave me a hesitant smile as she shrugged a little and left, her face hidden by her raven hair now. She looked almost...lost. Sad. I had never seen her look like that.

And I didn't know why...Avani's voice was in my head.

I would never use your hurt against you.

Love is healing. Nurturing. Kind.

And something in me snapped. She would never use my hurt against me. Talia had a baby. Teo and I came over to make her life easier. Every single time we did, Andrei wasn't home or he left, and he didn't make an effort anymore.

Why? Was it different now?

Talia's life hadn't been easy. And now he was the one thing making it harder. I snapped then.

I turned on him the moment she shut the door.

"You wanna tell me what the fuck is going on?" I said it first. He blinked surprised. Teo's eyes went wide on me. "*You ignored her the entire time—*"

"*My marriage is none of your business—*" Andrei looked ready for blood. Too bad I was too.

"It is when you keep hurting her, you can't even speak to her! The first thing you did is yell at your brother—"

Andrei's eyes were livid. "You don't come into my home and tell me how I live—"

"Thierry. Andrei—" Teo stood up fully now. But Andrei's eyes flashed in anger at me as Teo got between us when Andrei took a step forward.

I couldn't stop myself feeling the rage in me at my brother turning into—"*You're acting like Phillipe.*"

At that all the fury in Andrei's face faded.

"You act like him. This is what he would do. He did it to me.

You're doing it to, Drew." It burned in my throat since I did love Andrei. But he was a piece of shit.

Teo didn't move standing between us focused on the pear from earlier.

His throat worked a little as he didn't look at either one of us.

"I don't have anything to say to you," I looked straight at Andrei. "Since I came back, all you've done is act like our father. I get it, Maxine this and that, it might be my fault, but it also isn't. It's not my fault your father slept with Tasha. It isn't. I'm just a fucking casualty of two idiots. But since you had Drew, you've been a scumbag. And I told myself you know what? Once he gets Durand and everything in his pockets he'll be fine. It'll be fine."

I took a breath at the way Andrei's face paled. The color drained from his face as he looked at me.

"But all you've done is shit on your family, ignore us, and then the moment you think you can you walk in here and treat us like shit. When was the last time you spoke to Talia? *You didn't even greet her.*"

His expression changed at the mention of her name again. He'd just given her candle back. He still loved her. He did.

I saw it all over his face. They'd been together for almost eighteen years now. I knew that much. But this was getting a little ridiculous even for me.

"I don't want to talk to you, I don't care about what you have to say."

I looked at him head on. I knew why it poured out of me. Because in mind I wasn't alone. I felt Avani at my back, her hands pressing into my body warm sunlight flowing through me.

Her unconditional acceptance of me. Never using my weakness against me.

"I need to go now. But I think you need to start fixing your now home before throwing stones in ours."

I walked away feeling my blood boil, my stomach turning at his haunted expression.

Teo looked at me a little stunned and I just left. I couldn't do it.

I have been spending so much time with my girl, that I forgot sometimes I was with my family.

Andrei had tried his best with me. He had. He had been eighteen years old. He didn't know how to raise an eight year old.

265

But it wasn't until Avani, but I realized how much I hated my dynamic with my family.

I couldn't be vulnerable, I was always a problem, it always came with conditions, it always required me to be some form of perfect for the DuPont standard.

I had it known how to read, and the best tutors in the world that he had hired. We're only using him for his money, not to actually teach me.

As I stepped outside into the sunlight of the day, I realize how much I missed her and I just wanted to be back with her.

It wasn't just about learning *how* to read with her, it was about the fact that her patience showed me strength.

Her belief in my weaknesses showed me that I wouldn't fail.

Avani showed me love shouldn't be withheld on conditions. Criteria. Love was she loved me at my ten percent the same she did at my ninety.

And she taught me my family had a boatload of trauma to work through.

She supported me, I saw a different sibling dynamic with her and her sister, I saw that family could be different. I saw more in her apartment than I had with my family.

And I knew that all around I was evolving as a person, and I didn't want to continue to feel like that.

I wanted to go home and look at our memories on my fridge.

I had memories now.

And I deserved better. And I was eternally grateful to Andrei. I was. But that didn't mean that I was the same kid that he rescued.

I got into my car unable to formulate words. I texted Avani even if she was in class. I sent her a gif of a cartoon character pointing to their lips.

She would know.

It took her a few minutes as I drove but when I parked the car at her campus, she texted me back.

> My class ended early.
>
> Do you want to meet up for kisses?

YES.

No, mon coeur, I'm going to find a fish in the Downtown Seafood market to make out with instead.

Her name's Harriet.

Make sure Harriet's prettier than me.

I'm sure you're going to love how she smells .

I grinned.

Impossible. Where are you now?

Baton Hall.

I can wait for you by the campus coffee shop.

The sign broke so now instead of A Steamy Dream it's just Steamy. LOL.

Nothing dreamy about it.

Half of the lights are shut down in the cafe and people think it's aesthetic.

And there's no soap in any of the buildings.

I might have the black plague.

I laughed harder.

That's what happens when you pay one hundred grand to go to a school.

Really, mon coeur, you expect working signs and soap in your bathroom?

Pssssshh.

The plague huh? Sounds hot.

Don't make me laugh so hard.

I can hear your sarcasm in my ear and people think I'm insane now.

Indeed.

I fear I'm contagious.

I'm trying to find a place to bleach myself
right now.

> I'm parked in the B parking lot. Should I come
> to you?

> I can bleach your hands for you

> with you

> at the same time

No, I don't mind the walk.

You naughty scoundrel.

> Call me naughty again

> I'm into that shit

> I can be your schoolboy and you can be my tutor.

> Can I get extra credit?

You are incorrigible.

Why are you like this?

> But it's cold.

Yes Thierry, the mere breeze will knock over my
delicate frame.

Whatever shall I do?

> Exactly.

> Let me come get you. Forget the plague.

> I need that extra credit, Miss. Please.

I swear to god, I'm walking there right now. Don't
move.

I look insane laughing like this.

> Hurry, before I make out with Harriet.

268

Oh, I'm definitely walking slower now.

No extra credit for you

I have the black plague now, mon coeur

I'm dead. You did this to me.

CHAPTER 27
AVANI

ALISHA WANTED ME TO MEET REED.

My sister was *dating* him. I guessed as much but when she asked me to meet him one evening—I was stunned.

My previous home, smelled like vanilla chai and cardamom when I stepped in. The moment I was in her arms again, I was enveloped by the scents, Alisha's perfume, spicier than mine, and I felt nothing but nerves.

This was a huge step for her and it sent my heart bubbling with excitement for when I could introduce her to Thierry.

Maybe the four of us could have dinner together one day.

Her living room was creme toned with pops of color everywhere and the sight of it almost made me emotional. Almost.

Because when Reed appeared I lost my train of thought.

"I'm Reed. It's good to finally meet you." He smiled warmly as he approached, pressing a quick kiss to my sister's hair.

"I ordered dinner already. Alisha said you like Japanese food, so I got some takoyaki and a handful of other things I thought were remotely Japanese. Is that all right?" His eyes were twinkling as he took me in.

I couldn't even laugh at the way my sister sputtered at his easy smile. I looked at my sister, and her expression was still dumbfounded.

"Yes, you're—*that's* lovely."

He grinned and winked at her as the doorbell rang again.

"I'll get that, Angel." My sister's jaw dropped as he walked away. I bit my cheek to keep from laughing.

"That's him?"

I was leaping over to Alisha's side staring at Reed's arm and back. "Oh my God, look at his tattoos. I can see our governess crying." She'd been a tiny bit strict with us since Mum wanted us to be proper growing up. Papa was always the one getting into trouble with us.

She laughed a little holding me tight to her gripping my hand looking a tiny bit nervous. "Wait until you get to know him." But my sister looked happier than I'd seen her as she watched him.

Oh, she likes him a lot.

Reed came back and brought a mountain of food over.

"I can't cook," he shook his head at me. "I can't even pretend to cook."

Alisha smiled as she grabbed plates and helped him and before long we were seated on the couch with Reed's focus on me.

"How's school going?" Reed started, passing me sushi and a few other items that were delicious.

Alisha ate quietly while Reed and I talked.

I noticed throughout the dinner his focus was on me with him handing Alisha items every so often. He was trying not to be weird about it as he sometimes flickered over to make sure she was all right, but the more I interacted with him, I saw why Alisha liked him.

Reed was really intense with his eyes and his grin, but also really sweet underneath. I understood he had a hard time expressing himself though and he opted to ask me questions to get to know me.

Once he realized I liked reading, his eyes glittered with amusement.

"Did Lish buy you the entire library in here?" He motioned around the odd stacks and piles.

I blushed squirming a little. "I do like reading. I recently started a new series…" And I told Reed about something harmless. Something young adult because I was not going to admit my smut filled life to my sister's boyfriend who seemed genuinely sweet.

I grew animated though talking about it, building the plot and losing myself with him.

His grin grew and he reminded me a little of Thierry. But Reed was a little intense.

They were the same height with tattoos and I realized my sister and I had a type.

But Reed was different.

There was something about him that I couldn't quite place.

Unlike Thierry who teased and laughed easily, Reed seemed to hold himself back.

A little more serious. He was older than my sister for sure, and Alisha was quieter but relaxed around him.

Reed owned his own company, he was more public than Thierry so I thought maybe—it influenced how he behaved with people.

I didn't know if he had siblings or not, but that might've played a part.

Thierry as the youngest brother was more playful. Even silly with me most of the time.

But Reed was great for my sister.

"…And then the hunters they're on book five but I just found out the author has all these plot twists…" I chatted happily feeling comfortable around him. My sister trusted him and so did I.

Reed smiled at me listening and asking questions.

"And what's the mark for?" He asked me about the hunter's each having marks of this fantasy series.

I explained and I saw Alisha smiling at us wider.

Oddly enough, even though I just met Reed—I saw why Alisha loved him. I could see it in her eyes.

They'd been together not too long but she loved him.

Thierry would like the two of them.

"But the marks can only be put on the hunters not humans?" Reed frowned. "But then how did the girl get the mark?"

"She's half hunter," I emphasized loving how he got into it. "She's a mortal and her father is the enemy and he gave her half of his powers—"

"Oh that's fucked up—" Reed agreed his frown in place. "And then she broke into the church to get her cat back—who was a werewolf."

"Close. A were-*bear*."

"A were-bear—"

"Not to be confused with werewolves. They aren't the same species—"

"Of course not." Reed blinked and slowly grinned at the word were-bear. "I really have to suspend my reality for this."

I grinned wider at his expression. "It beats reality sometimes. Sorry."

"You never have to apologize to me for being excited about something," he said warmly. "Mochi?"

And then Reed passed me the entire tray as Alisha gently got up excusing herself.

Reed who had been giving me his undivided attention during dinner, his eyes darted to her retreating into the hall.

Alisha's hand rubbed over her chest a little as she did and I saw Reed's eyes shift darkening just a bit.

"My sister likes you," I whispered unsure of why I felt the need to. Like it was a secret. "A lot."

I saw why she had a crush on him. Even when they sat together, they practically were in sync.

His grin was back on me, his eyes lighting up with genuine interest now. "You think so?"

I nodded eagerly. "She's never dated someone like you. You're different than anyone in her life. And she's had a crush on you forever."

If possible, Reed looked delighted and devious. "That so?"

"Mhm." I bit into a mochi. "Lish never goes out with anyone. And you're the first man here in our home."

"Damn straight." Reed practically preened. I grinned at his humor.

Reed was friendly and I wondered if he would like to see photos of Alisha and me I had on my phone.

I knew she had an entire fridge covered in them, but now I wanted to show Reed a little bit of our world.

"Would you…like to see photos of me and Didi growing up?"

"Fuck yeah."

Reed's face looked triumphantly as he nodded a little and I dared to come a bit closer to his polite distance as I opened up my phone careful to keep my photos of Thierry and me away.

I wasn't ready to tell Reed about my boyfriend just yet. It didn't matter that we had been dating for a longer time than he and Alisha.

I didn't know how to tell Reed about Thierry.

Not yet.

Instead I opened up the album I had of Alisha's photos with me as the couch dipped with Reed looking at them.

"Damn, send me that," he said to a photo of Alisha and me hugging our parents. I swiped to another photo of Alisha and my dad. "That one too."

His eyes were softer and then I got to her high school modeling photos and they changed completely with admiration as I flipped through those photos as she turned twenty. Into her twenties.

"It's crazy how she started so young."

I agreed. It had been something I admired in my sister.

"Mhm, Mum wasn't happy but our father always encouraged Alisha…"

I told him all about our childhood and high school for Alisha where she found fashion magazines over books and she'd been gone.

She pursued her dreams and landed smaller jobs. I flipped to a photo of her at seventeen posing for a jean brand.

My sister was short at five-three but her legs made her long taller. Her landing deals had been pure luck sometimes as a beauty influencer.

"You know, when Alisha and I were struggling a bit a few years ago, we lived off PR," I admitted. "But then Alisha made more money and things got better. My sister looks happier with you."

I pointed to a photo of her grinning ear to ear with me in her arms, Gemma behind us holding a spatula about to swat something on the counter.

"Happier?" Reed looked curious at the photo occasionally hitting the heart button.

Had I said too much?

I had a bad habit sometimes of doing that when I felt comfortable about Alisha.

I told Thierry almost everything about her, and he'd just smiled and rubbed my hair as I did. Reed, looked curious.

"Mhm, after Mum and Dad passed, she told you?" Reed nodded. "Alisha got her deal after that with the beauty company she worked with and they didn't get to see it. It was her biggest deal and she thought it would make them proud. But before that we struggled a lot. I hope you'll take care of my sister because she's been through a lot and she just wanted to make Mum and Dad proud. And me."

Reed's eyes were softer on me like he was taking me in now with those intelligence greys. "Alisha takes care of you and your education?"

I ducked my head feeling slightly embarrassed and unsure why. Maybe I felt like under Reed's gaze I was aware of who I was too.

"I plan on graduating early so she doesn't have to for very long, but yes. She does."

A point that always made my heart feel heavier.

"You go to Astor Downtown?"

I nodded. He looked like he was thinking about something deeply then.

Reed was quiet for a bit and I felt like the walls were closing in on me then as I sat there until Reed motioned to the phone. "What's that?"

He looked devious as he looked at a photo of my sister at a Christmas party trying on accessories Gemma had gotten us.

I grinned down at it. "That's *Didi*, two years ago at a Christmas party."

"Send me that." Reed grinned, looking at the photo liking it.

"Are you two going to team up against me?" I heard Alisha behind us as she leaned in and gasped at the photo. Oh no. "When did you take that photo!"

I knew this. I quickly moved away from her. "*Didi*, you said I could take photos that night."

"When did I put a mustache on? *Why is there an enormous mustache on my face?*"

"You were two drinks in, and I thought it would be funny."I explained, looking at the photo where she still looked attractive for the giant mustache. "You're still really cute."

"*I look like the Monopoly man.*"

I put my phone behind my back. "At least he didn't see the one with the monocle and top hat!"

And just like that Alisha's eyes widened as my phone buzzed a little. I looked down, taking it out from behind my back and alarmed I looked at Reed with a wince.

When we had been sitting down Reed had selected the photos he wanted. When I got up to hide my phone, my thumb accidentally sent him the album. *Drat.*

"*Oops.*"

Reed looked like he was holding back his glee as I looked at Alisha.

"Uh-oh. Don't be mad. You know when Reed asked me to send him your photo?" She covered her face with both hands looking distraught. "I accidentally shared the entire album."

Her mouth fell open as she looked at me stunned and I got the feeling I messed up pretty badly.

"Wonderful, Reed. You can now witness all of my humiliating moments in full pixelated resolution. I left something in the restroom. Excuse me."

And Alisha was whipping around back to the restroom.

Oh no. I messed up.

"*Didi—*"

"*Angel—*" Reed stood quickly holding a hand out to me from running after her like I did more damage than good and I felt my eyes water at upsetting her which didn't happen often.

"I'll be back!" She called out.

He let out a breath and looked at me with a reassuringly smile, his eyes going wide at my tears.

"I'm sorry, kid. I'll go take care of it—"

"I'm sorry, I messed up—"

"You did nothing wrong." He was quick and adamant about it and then he reached out and hugged me quickly. "Let me go get your sister, stay here, don't leave and have some mochi. It'll be fine."

But my appetite was soured at the idea of hurting her.

I felt terrible. My phone dinged in my hand.

mon coeur, it's late. Do you need a ride?

No, I'm still with my sister. I think I upset her over dinner with Reed.

Alisha's boyfriend is really sweet.

He's friendly and he got us Takoyaki. But I messed up. I think I said something wrong to my sister.

Thierry knew I was meeting them today.

He'd dropped me off and let me know to call him when I was done so he could come and get me.

I typed in what had happened.

He called me. I quickly picked up quietly wiping my eyes. A soft sob left me as he crooned into my ear.

"Nooo, Mon cœur. Don't cry. It's fine, I promise, it's fine. You did nothing wrong."

"B-but-but I did," I broke down a little. "Alisha went to the back and Reed went with her and told me to stay here—"

"I would do the same for you, Mon cœur. Don't cry, it's okay." He calmed me down urging me to take breaths. "This is your first time meeting Reed, you were nervous. I'm sure you did nothing wrong."

"But-but-but, I feel stupid."

"You're not stupid," I swore I heard him chuckle a little. "Little love, just breathe with me."

I did sniffling as he worked me through and asked me how dinner went. "It was good. Reed asked me about the Shadowbane Series and I told him about it. You know, the one with the were-bear cat…"

I heard a low laugh. "And what else?"

He distracted me on the phone while I told him about my day and rewinded until I got to when he dropped me off at school. As he kept me busy I calmed down more and more.

"You did nothing wrong, Mon cœur ," he murmured as I finished. "You couldn't. Trust me. It'll be fine."

I sniffled wiping my eyes as I heard voices in the hall.

"I think I heard Lish and Reed coming, I'll go now."

"Love you."

"Love you, too." My head snapped up as Alisha looked at me with wet eyes. "*Didi.*"

"Oh, *darling, you're* all right."

As Alisha closed the distance between us and hugged me I apologized over and over. Reed put his arm around both of us and held us closer.

"Come here, kid. Your sister thinks we should have a Halloween party."

Distracted by his sudden announcement, I blinked a little up at him.

Uhh. I couldn't even speak at that idea.

"It's all right." Alisha teased. "Reed volunteered to be one of those fairies from that fantasy series you like so much."

"*Which one?*" I blinked. There were so many options but I already could imagine it.

"Ladies, what kind of fairy are we talking about?" Reed asked. "Shit, it's late for you." He turned to me. "You don't have to go tonight. You're welcome to sleep here. It's more your space than mine."

Oh. But I stayed with Thierry and I didn't think meeting Reed was the right time to bring up my boyfriend.

Not when Alisha was happier like this.

I would wait for the right time. Meeting Reed now, I felt more confident I could tell Alisha about Thierry. Especially since she had her boyfriend. I didn't feel too guilty…

I looked down at my phone where I saw a text from Thierry unopened.

I was going home to my life.

But it was tempting to spend more time with the two of them. Especially since whatever Reed had said had calmed Alisha too.

"I have class tomorrow, but…It's super early. Otherwise, I would stay."

Alisha looked worried about me. "You can't go back alone this late. I'll take you."

Reed stepped in. "I can call someone. My guys are solid."

I didn't have it in me to argue with the two very determined adults watching me now with worry. And less than twenty minutes later a gorgeous brunette appeared.

Instead of her dropping me off at Thierry's she was dropping me off on campus. Which was fine. It was so late I could stay in my dorm room.

Even if constantly changing sleep spaces was uncomfortable. It was just one night.

The brunette that appeared had bangs and doll-like features, her tip-tilted luminous emerald eyes on me. *This woman is prettier than anything I have ever seen in real life.*

"I was in the area," she said with a thick Latin accent. I was instantly daunted by this woman being Reed's coworker because she looked like one of those femme fatale's out of movies.

"I'll be taking you home, si?" And then she turned those eyes on me.

"Please drive *Paloma* reasonably." Reed muttered before turning to Alisha with a softer smile. Both of them turned that smile on me and for a moment my heart and stomach flipped.

Because I saw Mum and Dad in them. Just a little different. Reed didn't have hazel eyes and I looked more like Mum than Alisha did, but she was my parent.

I turned to the woman who introduced herself as Selena.

Like the Mexican singer?

She was gorgeous as we walked down to her car and when I saw it was utterly sure Selena was too cool to work for Titan.

"This is your car?"

"Her name is *Paloma*." She nodded as she motioned for me to get in.

"She's beautiful."

Selena was wonderful and we talked on the way to school, the entire ride I took in her manicured red nails, the letterman jacket in her backseat, a ball cap. Selena was *cool.*

And she was like Reed asking me questions and getting to know me with an easy smile on her face.

"You work with Reed?"

"Si," she nodded with that soft smile on her face. Under the neon lights of the city as it passed by, it made her eyes glow like Thierry's. *I should text him so he doesn't worry.*

Selena dropped me off right in front of the building and I got out after taking her number down.

"If you need anything, let me know." She smiled and I realized Alisha must be doing fine if everyone around Reed was so wonderful.

I walked back to my dorm room texting Thierry.

> Reed's coworker Selena dropped me back at my dorm. I'll sleep here tonight and come over tomorrow?

Part of me says no but I know you need your sleep. Are you safe?

> Just got to my room and the she-devil is playing music again. On second thought I may never sleep.

> Want me to come get you?

THE OFFER WAS TEMPTING BUT I SIGHED RESIGNING MYSELF TO MY fate.

No. If he did, it would be super late and I did have class in the morning.

Rosalie and Marissa were counting on me to show up at the minimum otherwise I was sure the girls would send a team after me.

> No, it's ok. Love you, gonna head to bed. Sort of.

> Love you, Mon cœur

The moment I entered though, my roommate was in the shower blaring music like always. I sighed.

Another day another nightmare.

I walked into the bathroom where she was. I knocked on the door feeling something rolling through me. "Can you turn the noise down?"

She pretended to ignore me. I huffed out a breath.

Even though, I was seventeen and my roommate was almost twenty, she behaved like a child. "Excuse me!" I knocked again. "I need you to turn the music down. I need to get some sleep tonight, I have class early tomorrow morning."

She opened her shoulder curtain. "Can you not come in here and—"

"You're going to turn the music down, or I will report you to the RA for the vile, racist comments you made towards me the other night. And if you so much as try to say something to me—do not think for a second I will not go and report it. Quiet hour started at ten."

Thierry had been livid when he replayed the audio back.

He said he had sent the audio to someone who worked for his brother in IT.

A man named Jace had sent a clearer version of the audio back to Thierry who now had it.

She looked at me with a smirk. *"Who the fuck is going to believe you? I didn't say anything—"*

"Yes! You did! And I suggest you turn the bloody music down or I will call the RA—"

"What the fuck is wrong with you—" she turned off the shower and grabbed her towel before turning off her music. She approached me with her towel around her. "Why are you stuck-up Indian bitches always so fucking annoying. Bad enough you take up all my space. You're such a fucking—"

"I suggest you do not finish your sentence, Christina."

An English accent cut through the air and we both turned to the door.

That I had accidentally left open.

A woman with long blonde hair stuck her head in through the door.

Her bright blue eyes took in my roommate who had just insulted me. I knew racism existed especially with my sister being a model. She had rude comments thrown at her all the time.

Being pretty didn't stop people from thinking you were less than them for your skin color alone.

"My name's Sloane. I live down the hall and I'm the RA. I suggest you do not repeat what you just said. I was walking by to see what the fuss was about."

She looked downright livid as she stepped into the room in her blue nightie looking out of place in our room.

She was much taller than Rosalie, but she looked like a princess completely out of place in a college dorm.

I blinked a little at the icy-blonde now staring down my roommate, Christina. The dinner with Reed and Alisha felt like it was days ago instead of a few hours.

"You've been here all of a few weeks and we've received six complaints about you. Put your clothes on and meet us downstairs in the common area." Sloane said to her before turning to me. "I'm so sorry about that. I completely understand if you don't feel here tonight. I can arrange it so you can stay somewhere else instead of—" A disgusted expression crossed Sloane's face as she looked at Christina who looked shameless despite being caught red-handed.

"I can call someone," I said quickly. I didn't want to stay here a second longer. "I have friends."

I did. Rosalie and Marissa lived not too far. I could walk to them.

She nodded. "It's dark outside, if you don't mind, I can get someone to walk you."

"I'll be all right, it's a short distance away." I eyed Christina one last time grabbing my duffle bag. It was kind of surreal having a bag packed because your roommate was a racist idiot.

I blew out a breath feeling how sick I felt in my body, the way my stomach rolled, my body heated—and I just wanted to get out of there. I would never understand people like her.

And as much as I wanted Thierry—thankfully I had a support system outside of him too.

I called Marissa on the way out and told her what happened. And I heard Rosalie shriek on the phone.

"Stay put," Marissa practically shouted. "Queen Levine and I are coming to get you."

"At least put pants on," Rosalie shouted at her back. "You're going to flash all of campus—"

"Relax, I put a QR code my car so these horny motherfuckers could send me money—"

"Idiot. Sorry Avani, we are rushing over to you. Do not leave the dorm alone."

I laughed quietly waiting for them out in the hallway by the door.

It was endlessly late. I had class tomorrow. I missed my boyfriend. And my roommate turned out to be a racist cunt.

All in all, university was turning out to be eventful.

Not perfect, but eventful.

CHAPTER 28
AVANI

THE NEXT DAY THE LAST THING I EXPECTED WAS FOR REED TO SHOW up to campus.

The autumn breeze rustled through the trees making me wince a little.

It got colder in the city quickly, as scattered golden and deep red leaves flew by Marissa and me who yelped grabbing onto her scarf.

I giggled stepping out of the building when I saw him.

Reed stood across the building, his hands in his pocket with his black bomber jacket looking handsome, his windswept hair and features drawing the attention of women everywhere.

The sunlight catching his eyes as he focused them on me and smiled.

"Whoa, who's that?" Marissa looked at him wide-eyed.

"My sister's boyfriend," I murmured. I was delighted to see him again after the previous night. He'd been nothing but wonderful to me. I looked at Marissa who was eyeing Reed. "I'll catch up with you later."

"I'd like to catch up with him later," she muttered and I grinned ear to ear walking up to Reed. I felt my breath coming in puffs as I closed the distance to him.

"*Reed*! Is everything all right?"

"Yeah, I was wondering if you were free. I'd like to talk to you."

"Of course," and he asked me about my classes as we walked to the nearby coffee shop.

The place was sprawling wide and the couches were overflowing but Reed and I found a space there after he ordered coffee for both of us.

"What did you want to talk about?" I asked him knowing he might've not come here for small talk. I got the feeling it wasn't good and my anxiety was thriving like a wildfire in my stomach.

"I heard—I know your sister pays your tuition. Your books. You live in the dorms out of your own accord."

I nodded. Was he here to tell me she wouldn't be anymore?

Is that what Alisha had said to him?

Was he going to take her away...I never considered the possibility in that moment that if Reed was in Alisha's life—I couldn't be.

And that ached. Reed kept going.

"I have a proposition. I paid your tuition in full. If you need books, I created a way for you to pull money from me."

What?

It felt like I slammed into an invisible wall at his words.

What did he just say?

He slid a card over to me and I looked down at it. *Why was it black?*

He continued looking almost embarrassed.

"That's mine. But you're welcome to use it for emergencies and whenever you need *anything* at all. I also got the go-ahead to move you into a place by yourself. So you can focus on school and not your shit roommate."

If my jaw could have dropped on the floor? It would've. It would've completely shattered as my heart dropped to my stomach. *What on Earth did he just say?*

"In exchange, I'll have an operative shadow you on occasion if I need to."

A what?

"No questions asked from you. I'd like to take the weight off your sister's shoulders, so she doesn't have to worry about you. I can take care of all of it. Both of you."

He isn't real.

Reed cannot be a real person. Did he just say what I think he said?

I had a hard time comprehending the words coming out of his

mouth. Unable to formulate a single thought other than he would take care of us. And he wasn't finished.

"And more importantly, I'd like to take care of you. I understand without parents both of you haven't had it easy. A lot of that weight falls on Alisha, I want to take some of it off her. I'm not trying to replace her."

Alisha better marry this man.

I felt the emotions rising and cresting over with their intensity. If he had punched me it would've ached less.

I just saw him watching me with a soft uneasy expression. Like this man was worried about upsetting me.

Despite his intense presence he was in love with my sister.

He cared about her so much he was taking care of me?

Not only that but he was…he was trying to be there for both of us?

What did I say? What did I do?

He already paid my insurance. The black looking credit card on the table staring back at me with…it had my name on it. Reed was giving me access to his money. Without questions or anything?

I looked back at him stumped and at a loss.

My vision blurred. "I have to pay you back."

He smiled a little as I said it not looking surprised at all by that statement.

"I thought you might say that, which is why I have two acceptable forms of payment."

I nodded, eagerly wiping my eyes as his softened on me even more. Reed's entire expression mellowed out.

"One, you have lunch with me once a month so I can make sure you're alive and well and away from your sister so I can get to know you. I intend on being in her life longer than she realizes and even if I can't—I'd like to still be there for you. And the second form of payment is you tell me first when shit happens to you. Not Alisha."

His smile was soft with the shock written on my face.

I knew he knew he surprised me.

What did he mean? Not tell Alisha? The more Reed talked the more I spiraled aware of what he was offering. Security. The ability to get my degree. Reed was the CEO of his own private security company. Thierry said he was wealthy and he made enough money to support me and my sister.

And the more he talked? The more it sank in what he was offering me.

Freedom.

"Not because I want to keep secrets from her, but because everything can be resolved at my level. You can tell her, but I'm asking you to let me fix it first. Anything. Leaky ceiling. Taxi rides. Tickets to a concert in Dublin. Just give me a heads up if you ever do. I don't want Alisha waking up at three am panicking when I can send a SWAT team to get you, does that make sense? I would rather be able to know both of you are good, then— *oomph*."

I threw myself at him. Wrapping my arms around him and holding him close, the scent of sea and spice filling my lungs as I inhaled him in.

His word shit me like tidal waves, each one more powerful and present than the last washing away my anxiety, my calm, my mind was reeling now. I was processing the magnitude of what he was saying as it filled my head. Paid tuition. A card. A place to live. Security.

Alisha's freedom.

My freedom.

Alisha's money wasn't stable and she was spending so much of it on me. Because I chose to stay in the city.

It was shock, wonder, fear, apprehension, and love. So much love for him. He wasn't real.

He couldn't be real.

But he was.

"Where did you come from? *Yes, I accept your terms.*"

I lowered my voice aware people were watching us.

"I know you're in love with Lish, but this is a lot too for me."

And Reed nodded looking like he was holding back his emotions. I got that a man like Reed might not show his true colors very often, but when he did, I saw the interior.

He pretended to be hard on the outside like he did when I was watching him, but the moment you were let into his world—he was the kindest man ever.

His heart of gold hidden underneath his intense icy exterior.

"I can't wait to tell her," I said. His smile dipped a little. "I can tell her…can't I?"

Reed shook his head. "I don't want you ever telling your sister about our arrangement."

What? Why would he do something so monumental and keep it a secret?

"If your sister likes me back—I want her to like me for me. Not anything else. You can't tell her about our little deal—"

"But what about when she asks about my tuition—"

"You have a scholarship."

"And the books and everything else?"

How was I supposed to do that? I was already keeping so many secrets from Alisha? One of them was picking me up from class later. I wondered if I could tell Reed about Thierry. Maybe we could break it to Alisha together.

"She only knows what you're willing to tell her. Alisha didn't go to college. Neither did I, so I'm not judging, but until I looked into everything about yo—*college* I didn't know either. Tell your sister about class. She had your tuition on autopay, that's been replaced with my account. She'll never know if you don't say a word."

"You want me to keep this a secret?"

Another secret? So many secrets churned in my stomach now I didn't like the idea of not telling Alisha. If she knew? She would flip out but no doubt she loved Reed enough.

"I don't want her to worry about you any more than she already does."

But this was already killing me.

"This is already killing me."

"But you want to take it."

I felt almost embarrassed as I nodded.

"I shouldn't feel like this though. It's not proper."

"True, but if you keep a secret at the expense of not hurting someone it isn't so bad is it?" His eyes leveled with me and for a moment I saw something underneath the softness. I got that Reed might've been a solid negotiator in whatever he did in his job because he could convince me anything.

He had thought about everything and the sheer relief of not living with my roommate, not having to deal with anything?

It still rubbed me the wrong way as he said if he kept a secret at the expense of not hurting someone, it isn't so bad—because I agreed. I was doing that to not hurt Lish. I didn't want to hurt her in any way.

But I thought Reed felt the same.

"Is that what you do for Lish?"

His face was unreadable.

"I would do anything for your sister. And that umbrella of care extends to you. So what do you say, deal?"

I looked down at the card. It had my name on it.

Which meant Reed knew—or hoped—I would take it.

He was handing me everything I could've asked for peace and security and the future. It was right there. I could use it for anything I needed. He trusted me. Because he loved Alisha.

I watched him sip his coffee knowing as relaxed as he looked? He knew what I was going to say.

"Deal."

"AND NOW...I HAVE THIS NEW PLACE AND HE TEXTS ME ALL THE TIME!"

My voice bubbled with excitement at Thierry's grin as he sat across from me in my brand new furnished little alumni apartment.

To my surprise when I'd arrived, Reed had movers going in and out and all my items had been packed and taken from my room to the new apartment.

"He doesn't do anything in half measures," I told Thierry who'd been surprised. His taller frame had stood in the center of the cozier space looking comically large as his dark eyes had scanned every corner.

He checked the windows and locks and every single nook and cranny while I'd walked around in wonder.

At my new space.

When he was done I'd ended up squealing in his arms with his laughter in my ears as he picked me up.

"My own place!" And then I'd told him about it as we unpacked and Thierry helped me with everything.

He'd gotten us pizza and I'd devoured half of it as he watched amused.

"He said he can install a security system and even a doorbell with a camera so nobody does anything weird," I added. "And we're doing lunch once a month. When he can. But he's been texting me in the meantime checking in on me."

"That's great, mon cœur."

His eyes were soft on me as he listened to me tell him about

Selena, something in his guarded expression letting me know he wanted to tell me something.

"She's so pretty, she's got these bangs, and these eyes…" and then I told him about Reed and I was talking so much I felt out of breath.

He grinned at me wolfing down more pizza. He took my plate out of my hands at one point.

"Breathe," he urged me. "Drink this water before you choke on that slice."

I quickly drank and he laughed low at my enthusiasm as he took a bite of his. He rarely ate poorly but with me he struck a balance and indulged every so often.

"I don't have class tomorrow so I can unpack and we can decorate and—Why do you look like that?" I stopped noticing the shift in his expression.

He looked a little uneasy. A mix of emotions swirled in the depths of his alien blue eyes still. He looked carefully neutral. "Are you going to be staying here?"

Oh.

I didn't think about his space.

"I mean…" I looked around suddenly aware of the weight of his gaze. "It's my new home but that doesn't mean I won't be with you? Is that what you mean?"

His face was unreadable to me, carefully neutral, but I knew him. I knew him from the tension in his jaw, and he nodded a little bit.

"Did you think if I moved here I wouldn't be with you?" A knot formed in my stomach as the guilt of making him think I wouldn't be with him filled me. "Is that what you're thinking?"

He didn't say anything as he took in the space with me.

"Thierry."

His head turned to me. And I saw it in his eyes. Thierry liked me staying with him—he needed it. I needed him too.

Didn't he know that Reed taking over in so many ways wasn't diminishing his influence? Thierry had taught me so much living with him.

I wouldn't just leave him because of Reed.

Part of me knew I needed to soothe him.

"I'll still stay with you," I murmured. "Of course I'll come back to you. I always would. Reed doing anything doesn't mean I don't spend time with you. This is just better than my roommate."

A myriad of emotions went through his face, watching me with a curious expression. He tipped his head.

"I'll help you get your stuff together tonight."

Even if his offer was simple, I felt like something was wrong.

He wasn't upset at my new beginnings, was he worried about something else? I just didn't push him into answering tonight as he ate quietly and moved to help me with my new place.

I looked around. I felt like I had barely started university and now my first semester was two months away from being over.

I watched Thierry smile as he took out my photos.

Maybe nothing was wrong and maybe he was just as new to the experience as I was.

"Hey," I called out to him while he was moving my stuff. He turned his head and I tapped my lips. His smile was instant and he walked over to kiss me. "Better?"

"Mhm. Way better than Harriet the Fish."

Our laughter mingled as he kissed me again.

CHAPTER 29
THIERRY/AVANI

SOMETHING WAS WRONG.

I wasn't upset with Avani moving into her new apartment.

Or her new found freedoms.

I stood in my kitchen stirring the soup I was making and grilled cheese sandwiches with some chicken on the side for us. My mind feeling irritated at the thought of Reed Whittaker.

I was more concerned with Reed Whittaker's involvement in her life. His sudden involvement. And the fucking operative he may have had shadowing her which meant I had to work overtime to make sure nobody caught me.

It would take one simple search to realize—I wasn't on paper. I didn't exist anywhere. Not as Thierry Mattison at least.

Reed was moving fast—*too* fast.

Which meant he either loved Alisha to pieces or he had alternate motives. My money was on the latter.

Knowing Reed Whittaker, knowing Talia, who had been in the same position—he liked controlling his situations. To a fault.

Because I knew exactly why my heart had agreed to him. She was independent despite being inexperienced in life. She wanted to learn and grow and continue to thrive. He was giving her security for good.

It wasn't about the money.

It was about influence.

And it had more to do with who I had been in my past and the fucking gun I held to his head for threatening my brother than anything else.

I didn't tell Avani for fear of causing strain in my relationship with her.

And now? I felt like…I was losing Mon cœur.

Which was *stupid*.

I couldn't lose her rationally—that's what I told myself. mon coeur mine. She was mine. I didn't know she needed her tuition handled. I could've done that. I didn't know he'd just hand her his credit card. Doubtful she even used it since I secretly got her whatever she wanted, but she'd taken it.

I knew exactly why she had—*Alisha*.

If there was one leverage that would make my girl make the choices she did—it was Alisha.

It was always about Alisha.

And that was something I didn't have.

Reed had come into his life on his white horse and proposed a deal.

He taken care of her—and in turn Alisha would be at ease.

I fucking knew my heart would take that route.

Because she did everything to put her sister at ease.

Didn't call her when her roommate sucked, no Reed had found out on his own—and now?

He used the leverage I didn't have.

So how did I get through to my heart?

And why the fuck was I so upset? She was in my apartment. Showering right now and cleaning up. She fell asleep in my arms, in my bed, she existed with me. Because she did belong here. Not under Reed's eyes.

I wouldn't have cared. I shouldn't have cared.

But I couldn't fucking explain it.

"Darling! Have you seen the extra towels I have for my hair? I just washed it!"

"Coming!"

I dropped the kitchen towel from shoulder as I rushed to bring her towels.

She was standing in the bathroom on the rug barefoot with a tiny towel wrapped around her body and all of a fucking sudden my brain stopped working. Everything in me began to short-circuit as she blinked up at me.

"Darling, did you get the towel? It was too high for me."

All the blood rushed from my body down to my cock as I handed her the extra towel and she shot a look of gratitude as she wrapped her hair up, while the towel around her tits strained tight. *Fuck. Me. She's gorgeous.*

A dripping wet Avani in my place? Under my roof? Looking like a wet dream?

My desire for Avani was intense, all-consuming like an inferno that could never be quenched.

Besides loving her emotionally and respecting the shit out of her intelligence? Combined with her body?

It was a recipe for disaster.

Because I wanted her so fucking bad, it physically hurt being around her.

I promised I wouldn't take her like some cheap quick fuck.

And since then, between her schedule and need for rest? Going back and forth from campus to my place? Avani hadn't exactly been throwing herself at me.

No. My girl was a virgin.

And I wasn't about to corrupt her with the likes of me. At least not yet. When would I take her? Now? Later? When? I wanted Avani like my next fucking breath as she misted her face with her skincare bottles.

She had a row of them lined up all next to my stuff. Fancy shapes and colors and scents. She went through her little routine like I wasn't standing there all hungry for her.

The explosion of feminine hygiene products in my shower, combined with her fluffy house slippers, and her scent all over me?

I was a powder keg waiting to be set off.

"Darling, that smells really good, did you make that chicken you made last time?"

Well, Andrei's chef made it. I just reheated but I nodded unable to form words. Let alone think around Avani.

I was like my entire brain just stopped working.

Swallowing hard I watched her blinking up at me like a mermaid out of the shower, the steam still in the air, the scent of roses clung to her, droplets of water on her shoulders, her cheeks bright from the mist she used.

"Are you all right?"

I nodded. "Fine." She flushed a deep pink as she smiled almost embarrassed. She motioned to the door. "Should we?"

Right. Because I hadn't seen her naked.

I was trying to do right by her. Key word—*trying*.

Because doing the right thing meant watching your beautiful girlfriend pad around your apartment with nothing but a towel on knowing full well—she had the sexiest curved figure I had ever seen. But she trusted me, completely, and that innocence alone made me want to protect her.

I didn't trust my voice right now. Or my body.

She had no fucking clue the effect she had on me. This woman brought me to my knees with that soft smile. She had from day one and after weeks and weeks of resisting I had given into her.

I was...tamed by her.

Stepping out of her way I held the door open turning to the side but it didn't fucking matter, Avani, for all the romance she read? Was inexperienced. And I wasn't about to shove my dick on her.

I wasn't a completely monster.

Avani

OUT OF ALL THE PLACES I STAYED, THIERRY'S WAS MY FAVORITE.

It smelled nice here, his apartment was upscale without being outlandish.

It was warm with cream and gold accents, soft carpeting, a few plants here and there with warmer lamps that somehow fit in.

The towels were heavenly and soft and I groaned rubbing my hair acutely aware this was the first time Thierry had been in the same room with me after I showered.

And he'd never...he never pushed. He never did anything remotely...weird or uncomfortable.

Was it messed up that it only made me want him more?

Because I wanted him. I didn't even understand what he did to my body. I just knew it was him and it drove me crazy.

The warm glow of the lights combined with knowing he was right there was going to be the death of me.

"Everything good?" I asked him aware I needed to rub myself down with my towel since I was still wet all over, but another part of me turned to find him leaning against the door watching me.

Ever since I'd told him about Reed and my new apartment he'd been a little off.

I wondered if that other part of him thought our relationship was fleeting and that I would leave him the moment I had Reed. But the truth was, not worrying Alisha or ever being a thorn in her side was all I cared about.

I didn't understand how he felt.

He pushed off the door frame and my eyes took this man in. My man. He was mine. He would always be mine.

Each step he took towards me I felt the electric charge between us. One. Another. Another.

The air between us growing thicker until the towel almost dropped from my hand and I clutched the one around me tighter.

He stopped a few centimeters away from me and I craned my head up to look at him. I could feel his heat. Midnight. Electric blue eyes on me. Burning bright with something I couldn't name in that moment, I was too far gone.

"Are you…will you…" I was almost embarrassed to ask him.

Take me.

Take me now.

I wanted to scream and beg but I held back.

I wanted him so bad.

I couldn't finish because I didn't even know what I was asking for. Didn't know how to start or where to start. He brushed my hair back from my face as he took me in.

"Mon cœur , we have dinner." He brushed his lips over mine when I knew—I knew—I could feel him and his desires. The disappointment crashed over me.

I blinked a little confused by the intensity radiating off him them.

Why did he hold back so much?

Did he still think I was some child and he didn't want to take advantage of me?

I tried not to frown as he drew back and left the room his hands trembling at his sides.

I didn't understand why he fought it—I was his. I always was his. I was old enough to give consent goddamnit.

I wanted him so bad I might die from it. That was the only

logical solution I could imagine. *Can a person die from sexual frustration?*

I don't care about our age difference.

I flopped back on the bed.

Out of all things I despised about romance novels—I was currently living in my worst nightmare of one.

"I hate slow burn romance," I whispered up to the ceiling. "I hate it."

CHAPTER 30
THIERRY

I WAS IN MY APARTMENT WHEN I GOT THE CALL FROM THE UNKNOWN number.

My stomach dipped a little as I answered knowing it could only be from one source.

My thumb hovered over the answer button. My heart was in class. I'd dropped her and her lunch off for the day.

I shouldn't pick up.

Not after I spent a night restless, tossing and turning to Avani's sleeping form next to me. I don't know how she slept through it, but she'd been so tired lately.

She was taking four classes when she didn't have to take the extra one, and running around with me.

I knew it was a lot for her and I didn't want to add to her stressors.

I huffed out a breath and answered.

"Good evening, this is Tom Womack's office. This is Andrew speaking, how may I help you?" It was morning. And I sure as fuck had no idea who those people were.

"Hey, Grim," the South-African accent on the other side was not what I was expecting. "Guess where we are?"

And just like that I realized why the back of my neck prickled.

"Don't tell me, Carter," I muttered keeping my voice down.

Don't tell me. Period.

Bexley Carter's voice was waaaay too excited for the time of night. Through the speaker I heard Bexley singing. *"We're in New York, bitch!"*

Fucking Fantastic. I bit back a groan as she continued.

"We have a bit of a problem," she chirped. "Someone stole from Alma so we're invading the enemy territory." And just like that my heart dropped.

"What?" *Who would be dumb enough?*

Bexley rattled off what happened. Apparently, some jewel thief stole something from Alma. What the fucking fuck?

After Malcolm died, Alma and Natasha had been left in Cape Verde to do damage control. Across the board. The old guard had been completely eliminated, any old Talon agents,

"Alma's pissed. Natasha's running the show. And so Samara and I came to New York to kill this bitch Lucy and drag her back to hell with us."

Shit. Shit. Shit.

The headache that hadn't been back since Cape Verde was back. I let out a breath. "Where are you now?"

"We're staying at this fancy place called the Primrose? Samara thought it would be good and Alma likes their brunch menu. You should come see it—"

"Carter. Where is Alma?" There was only one person that mattered. Because right now this fucking phone call was getting on my ever loving nerves. My patient was wearing thinner by the second.

She was quiet and when she spoke her voice lost its chirping quality and instead just made my blood run colder.

"Ummm…Alma's pretty pissed. She's doing her own thing right now and I'm on intel gathering. So far I've got a list of potentials the jewel thief was working for.

I sighed feeling my head throbbing and I pinched the bridge of my nose. Thank fuck, mon cœur wasn't here for this.

A blast from my past was not welcome at all.

"Why did you let me know?"

"Well, I thought you'd be happy to see me." She sounded way too eager and the back of my neck prickled at the lie. "I mean, aren't you?"

No. It wasn't that I wasn't happy to see her. Had she been here on some tourist shit—maybe. But she wasn't.

No.

If Talon was in town?

Someone was going to die.

Several somebodies. They already operated around the city, and I had the cards every so often.

I knew Natasha was working and so was a few other operatives doing their own thing.

But no one had come close to touching my heart or me. As long as they stayed away from my family? I didn't give a shit.

"That's not the truth."

She puffed out a raspberry. "Okay, fine. You and your family know the lady who stole from us."

A suspicion niggle began forming in the back of my neck.

Please don't be anyone related to my heart.

"Who?" I asked keeping my voice deceptively nuetral.

"Your brother Andrei he knows Lucas Devereaux right?"

Oh. Thank. Fuck.

Lucas Devereaux, the real estate magnet. I didn't know him too well, but he knew of me thanks to Matteo. A cold dread began settling into my stomach.

"Right."

"His sister stole from us," she squeaked. "Blonde, curvy, dangerous. She walked right into the hotel where Alma was staying and took something from her."

I noted Bexley never mentioned what it was. Not yet. But I'd get it out of her.

Jesus. Christ. I swore a little rubbing my eyes. It only got worse. "Her name, Carter."

"Lucy. *Lucy* Devereaux. Has two apartments in the city. Wanna go check 'em out?"

"What?" Was she serious?

"Carter. What part of I am no longer one of you—"

"I know, I know," her voice took on a pleading whiny note. "I just *thought* since it's *you*, you'd want to be involved."

I didn't want to be involved but it involved Teo and my family in a way so maybe I could keep an eye on it.

What about Avani?

Talon would never know about Avani.

The same way Titan didn't know about me.

And my secrets were going to eat me the fuck alive.

"You're not going to kill Lucas, are you?"

That would be number one to confirm.

"Teo is good friends with him. Lucas went to school with Andrei."

And he helped us secure my damn warehouse that was almost done.

"Why would Lucas send his sister to steal anything for him? He works in real estate."

"Who knows," Bexley sounded like she was blowing bubbles. "We don't even think he did, but his father was friends with Malcolm so when I was coming I freaked him out a little." She giggled. "He told us he thinks his son or Lucy have it. Whatever the case, I thought since it's something related to you—"

"It isn't, Carter. It's not related to me at all."

Except in a way it was. I was kinda curious and the words felt hollow even as I said them.

But the Devereaux's were none of my business. Not anymore.

I wasn't Talon anymore.

I was just Thierry. Avani's boyfriend.

And I wanted to stay there even if a part of my brain wanted me to tell Teo about his friend potentially getting caught in the cross-fire of Bexley and Samara.

"As long as you guys don't kill Lucas, don't bother me."

"Poo," she sounded disappointed. "And here I thought you'd want to help out your old team." Help out?

The phrase made me think of the countless missions, fights, adrenaline and sense of…something. But I didn't want that.

I didn't need it anymore.

The one thing I needed was in school. I believed in letting things die, letting things go, moving on. Not chasing your past, not living in what could have been helped you move into the future.

Avani was my future. She was my world.

And I accepted it now.

It was the one thing I needed and my one thing was probably buried in another romance novel laughing with her friends.

Some part of me had calmed down with Avani. With her in my bloodstream? Her light was a prism.

All lush pink and in my field of vision all the time.

It cut through any shadow in me and lingered there, heating me up from the inside out.

It reflected me back in shards of goodness and all things safe.

She showed me things I hadn't seen before, and I protected her and opened her up to possibilities.

My senses were soothed. She was everything I wasn't which was something I had always known—but what I hadn't figured out until recently, Avani was my redemption.

My savior.

In so many ways, I helped her out of situations out of danger, but she saved me from myself.

I knew that now as I navigated paperwork, texting, and moving into the new reality with ease.

Had my confidence gone up since I read at a decent level now? Yes.

I figured out ways to make it easier day by day. Which meant, no more going backwards for the sake of doing so. Which meant no more shadows, no more hiding, no more existing—but living.

One day I'd introduce myself to her sister.

To her family.

Even Reed fucking Whittaker if he ever got over me holding a gun to him.

"Helping you guys means covering New York in blood."

"And you despise the idea of that so much," her voice was sarcastic but I got the point.

"Look," I huffed out a breath. "I need time and I need my own life. If shit get's interesting? Call me. But I gotta go right now."

I didn't have to go, but Mon cœur had a break in thirty minutes. And I suddenly needed to see her. Avani always reminded me I was more than a former monster.

Just Thierry was enough for her.

My phone rang seconds after I hung up, interrupting my thoughts again. Teo's name flashed on the screen. I suppressed a growl of frustration as I answered.

"Teo."

"The place you wanted is ready. I'll come and get you today to go see it?"

A noise of relief escaped me. Thank fuck. Avani would love the new place.

I needed to go do this. I met Teo across the street from the Brooklyn Bridge where the massive warehouse sat taking up all the space in the world.

On the outside it looked like a normal brick building, even

rundown. Teo's inky hair whipped around in the cold breeze as he motioned to it.

"I didn't touch the outside like you asked," he said. "But the inside is pristine."

That was the point. I wanted a place so much in plain sight nobody knew I existed. I wanted to hide away. Andrei's apartment was nice, but it was his. Memories of him and Talia everywhere. Not mine.

It never truly felt like mine.

Not unlike Avani.

I debated telling Teo about Avani, but why would I bother? It didn't matter if I did or didn't.

But he also knows Alisha and you're worried.

Maybe. I was a little concerned. I wanted her to myself. She was mine, my girl, my everything. I took care of her.

And right now, this was another way of making sure had our home.

It was three stories, the first floor being the living room, sprawling and enormous, vaulted huge ceilings with wooden beams and lights I could dim. Mahogany and wood and earthy finishes on everything.

The open plan kitchen just as big as the living room, the second floor holding the mezzanine bedroom.

The basement for the gym and garage and the top floors for the view into the city. Not bad at all.

It was a pretty penny that I had but solid.

"Teo, do you know your friend Lucas?" He nodded. "What do you know about his little sister?"

Teo's chiseled features frowned a little. "I always forget she exists." That might've been the point. "Don't tell me you're fucking her."

"No, why do you always assume that?"

He shrugged looking confused as to why I asked. "Why else would you ask?"

About that. He was watching me carefully.

"Lucy Devereaux…" his frown deepened. "Andrei has information on everyone. I know because he tells me."

"He knows her?"

"I think so. But I could be mistaken. She works for a private security company discreetly. Nobody is supposed to know."

"How does Andrei know?" No. Stupid question. "Never mind. He knows everything."

"He wouldn't dream of using the information against people. He just has…" Teo looked unhappy, his brows drawn together as he considered it. "Lucy…"

"What? What is it?"

He swore softly, his eyes widening. "I know *who* Lucy works for. I didn't think about it because I forget she exists sometimes. But I know."

I straightened to my full height not liking the look on my brother's face. "Who?"

"Gabriel Monroe." His eyes met mine.

Was that supposed to mean something? I didn't get it.

"And that is?"

"He works at Titan Security."

And just like that my heart bottomed out.

Oh. Fuck. Me.

Teo nailed it into me with his next words.

"He works with Reed Whittaker."

And that's who Talon was going after.

"Reed Whittaker is their next target."

CHAPTER 31
AVANI

Don't be upset. Promise I'm all right.

Something's happened to our old place. Reed said someone broke in and tried to go into my room.

Don't worry our things are fine.

Just some overzealous fan.

Promise. How is school?

That was text I got from Alisha.

And my heart broke a little more hearing about it since she hadn't mentioned anything about her fans being that insane since I left.

About our old apartment being broken into. Just like that. I told Thierry when he came to get me.

"And then she said she was staying with Reed," I told him sitting on our couch with my feet on his lap. "I mean, I just found out, how can I not be worried?"

A muscle tightened in his jaw. "When?"

I told him a few days ago but I didn't know. Alisha was keeping me in the dark for some reason.

"That's my old home. My sister and I moved there when we first lost Mum and Dad…" I wiped my eyes not even realizing I was crying. I felt him moving on the couch until I was inches arms.

"I know she's trying to protect me, but I don't feel protected," I told him, my voice muffled in his hoodie. "I feel hurt."

I just laid there on his chest a multitude of emotions; the grief of losing my home, my parents memories there, and Alisha being so scared she had to move in with Reed—all of it compiled into a mess.

"I'm a watering pot." I wiped my eyes as he chuckled low.

"You're not."

"But you're so calm about things and you don't let it get to you…"

His smile was soft as his eyes held a glint to them. "I wouldn't have you in any other way." His lips bushed over mine, once, twice before I whimpered as he kissed me more.

"I don't want to lose my sister," I whispered into them. A softer noise left him. That was the crux of it wasn't it? I was afraid of losing Alisha since the attempted break-in.

"You won't."

"But what if something, happens to her?" And just like that I crumpled. Around him? "I don't want to lose her."

I felt like a little girl able to tell someone she was afraid.

His hands held my face tight as he pressed his forehead into mine. "You won't, mon coeur. She's staying with Reed?"

"She said, they're staying at K2 together…" I told Thierry about Reed's building and his eyes narrowed a little listening to it. He listened and rubbed my hair as I told him. He was quiet as I talked.

"Your sister is gonna be okay, mon cœur ," he murmured. "But you haven't had any dinner, or anything. Let me take care of you so you don't run yourself to the ground while worrying over Alisha."

I pouted. "But I'm so good at it."

His grin was wide as he kissed me again.

But even as he did, I felt unease running through me. If a fan was bold enough to break into her apartment, how much danger was my sister really in?

～

THE WEEKS PASSED BY IN A BLUR BETWEEN MIDTERMS, PAPERS BEING due, books to be read, and Thierry.

He was keeping me together by not just being a supportive

boyfriend, between juggling me and his life, but by constantly being reassurance that everything

I was waiting for Marissa in class to start thirty minutes prior with Rosalie who frowned at her phone. "Bad news?" I asked her quietly.

She shook her head. "I auditioned for this modern historical drama. I don't know if you've heard of it, but it's called My Lady Grace?"

I did. Gemma and I binged season one two years ago.

"I loved that show, but they're taking forever because they are casting for season two aren't they? " At Rosalie 's nervous nod I blinked twice. And *then* it hit me. "Oh my Goodness, *you auditioned for season two?*"

She bit her lip looking a little shy, ducking behind her black bangs. "I may have."

Oh my God. "*Oh my God.*"

I had no clue Rosalie was an actress on top of being a model.

"That's fantastic! And they hadn't gotten back to you?"

She shook her head looking uneasy again. "It's been months and I'm debating if I just try for something else again."

I nodded listening to her tell me about her ups and downs as a model and working with beauty brands.

She reminded me of Alisha's struggles coming up.

Everyone always saw Alisha where she was right now—not where she had been years ago. It occurred to me people were easier to measure in terms of success all the time.

But nobody ever saw the girl struggling to feed me. I saw that girl.

"I feel so much pressure to be everything but myself," she murmured looking at her phone. "I feel hideous."

I gaped. "If you feel hideous I am a toad."

Rosalie was one of the more gorgeous girls on campus by far.

Her stunning dark hair always styled, her outfits like she'd stepped out a fashion magazine. She laughed a little.

"Nonsense," she looked around and then back at me a little shy. "Say, who's that guy that's always with you?"

Now it was my turn to duck my head. "Boyfriend?" I nodded.

She gasped swatting my arm now and I laughed. "*No. I didn't realize you were dating the prince of darkness.*"

I gasped whirling around to look at her. "What? Is that what

Marissa's been calling him?" I asked her when I saw the twinkle in her eyes.

She grinned ear to ear. "Where is he from? Does he have friends? Brothers? He looks a little familiar, but I can't pinpoint from where."

A blonde walked up to our table unrecognizable and Rosalie gaped. "Marissa, what the hell did you do?"

I almost didn't know it was her besides her green eyes. Her hair was now the whitest shade of blonde I had ever seen.

White to the point it matched computer paper. She rolled her eyes.

"Bad dye job. It looked like I was a cabbage faced doll instead of me so I ended up stripping it all this weekend. Safe to say ladies I've been busy."

"That is not your natural hair color," I was stunned and momentarily forgot Rosalie had asked about Thierry as Marissa explained her hair was blonde but not this blonde.

"All right, class."

The professor walked in and we all turned around in our seats. Back to reality even if Alisha's texts worried me.

I texted her again discreetly.

> How is everything? Haven't heard from you in a few days. Are you okay? How is Reed?

Reed ended up getting in touch with me a few weeks later.

He still texted me from time to time and he took me to Butter scotch's to get cupcakes and lunch.

They had the best sandwiches in the city which Reed agreed on when sitting with me.

"How's class?" He asked eating quietly listening to me talk. "Are you still taking your three classes a day or something?"

"I am, but only twice a week, then I have…" I told him about my other courses as I watched him, Reed's eyes softened, but I noticed the bags under his eyes.

The shadows darkening in the stormy grays. When I first Reed he seemed lighter around Alisha. Now, he looked like something was bothering him.

"Is everything all right?" I stopped talking. It didn't look like it. Worry lit up every bit of my body. "Is it Alisha?" It felt like an ugly snake wrapping around my stomach and my limbs until I couldn't breathe at imagining anything wrong with my sister.

"No," he murmured. But something was wrong. "No, she's… she's good. Did you get the books I sent you?"

I smiled slowly. "I did…thank you for getting me the entire series, and the limited edition sprayed edges editions too…they were really hard to get a hold of. How did you do that?"

Reed had been secretly spoiling me. If I so much as mentioned something through text it arrived in my apartment. If he knew anything about me?

He was going to turn me into a spy with how many secrets and products I hadn't told Alisha about.

Turns out, Reed had enough money to go around he wasn't spending for himself.

He had already told me that several times that he didn't have family.

He considered me and Alisha his family. So naturally, I didn't worry about him or my sister.

A genuine smile spread his face. "One of my clients was an author, super popular, her publisher hired my company for her events and they had copies in stock so if you ever need them? They have them."

I grinned at his expression. "Are you at work today?"

"Yeah, we have two offices. One in Greenwich, and one here. I sit at the one in Midtown. It's closer to Alisha." He paused as he said it. "Closer to everything."

I frowned. "K2 is close to Titan Midtown?"

He nodded taking a bite out of his sandwich looking distracted.

The back of my neck prickled a little and I talked to Reed about everything under the sun.

He was really good at listening and by the end of lunch, we walked to his car so he could drop me off at my apartment.

The expensive looking luxury SUV sat in a private garage and when I got in, Reed reached into the backseat and handed me something.

A jewelry box shaped present.

"What is that?"

"This is for you," he said looking shy. "Your sister mentioned you like sparkly objects. So I figured this would nice."

I blushed a little embarrassed. I had been a little raccoon growing up taking shiny things from my parents and Alisha.

And now Reed knew it but he decided to do something about it which warmed me from the inside out.

I beamed taking the box. It looked generic enough and I opened it as Reed started the car. He didn't look at me.

Inside was a gold charm bracelet. With tons of cute little gems and charms. "Reed, this is so cute. Where did you get this from?"

He didn't look at me as he said. "Antique shop. Wasn't much."

I grinned. "I love vintage stuff. It looks so pretty."

"I thought you might like it," one side of his mouth quirked up at me as I tried it on. It was really pretty and despite being a charm bracelet it didn't overwhelm my wrists.

Reed grinned at my happiness.

"I do love it."

When Reed dropped off, I saw the weight of something unfamiliar in his eyes. "Let me know if you need anything at all."

I laughed at his eagerness. "Reed, you're going to spoil me rotten."

His smile was warm as he agreed. "That's the point." But there was something in his eyes that made me reluctant to leave him.

"Is everything okay with you and my sister?"

He nodded looking emotional. "Yeah," his voice was gruff. "It is, I promise. We're good."

I didn't know why I felt the urge to hug him and I was in his arms a second later feeling his breathing hitch, a shaky exhale leaving him.

Something was wrong but maybe it wasn't Alisha. He wasn't telling me. And I didn't know what to do for him.

I told myself I'd talk to Thierry about it.

Maybe he could ask Teo and they could help Reed?

I didn't know what to do.

I couldn't imagine anything taking Reed away because all the material things aside?

It felt like I had Mum and Dad in my life with him in Alisha's life. I didn't want to lose it again. Ever.

"I love you, Reed."

I felt him release a shuddering breath. "Love you too, kiddo."

CHAPTER 32
THIERRY

"Lucy Devereaux *is* employed by Reed Whittaker."

Jace Lawrence, Teo's IT guy, looked like he'd just gotten out of jail. There was a hardened edge to the man's face, with his shaved head, tattoos and hard grey eyes.

He was six feet of pure muscle in his white button down and slacks and not what I would've expected someone from Teo's IT team to look like.

But Jace worked downstairs in the basement with no windows in Roadsters.

Teo broke the news to me as we both stood in that tech room while Jace sat there quietly. It was just the three of us.

I turned to him often, and I knew he kept his mouth shut about almost everything. When I reached out for him to help me with Avani, I didn't think it would get back to Teo. Mostly because Jace didn't speak.

He just relayed information. What Teo didn't know—he didn't know to ask.

I didn't feel like journeying out to Andrei's since Avani's school wasn't far from Teo's work place.

I wanted to be close to her when she needed me.

The doors were locked and he had cancelled his day to lay out the facts. Documents. Files.

Hard copies and nothing digital for me. And I sat there flipping through some of it with Jace sitting next to us on his computer ready to pull up whatever was necessary.

Teo stood with his jacket of his suit off, white dress shirt and tie on stretching over his lean chest as he motioned to the documents in my hand as I sat on his couch.

"This is information on the Titans?" I held up on the documents.

"Yes, sir." Jace was polite too. I knew the guy had been through some shit by the look in his eyes. Teo had an iron-clad NDA his guys signed and so nothing would be repeated out of this room.

"I talked to Bexley in the last few weeks," I explained. "They just got settled here. We have some time to figure this out."

Teo frowned. "So far this is all Andrei has. Jace got us this much, but at a cost. Over the summer someone on Gabriel's team killed off some of the informants we had on the ground. All we can get our hands on is that. Reed is discreet to say the last."

Reed Whittaker had a lot of secrets.

Too fucking many just like me.

And if I wasn't careful, the web I was weaving was going to catch me and him in it.

"Every one Andrei hires always turns up dead so the Titan's are not stupid." Teo's voice was low. "Andrei was interested when he heard a rumor about Gabriel Monroe not liking Lucas Devereaux, but Andrei couldn't figure out why."

Teo paused. "Jace," he turned to the other man who sat quietly waiting for instruction. "Pull up the map you made."

And then behind me the screens blinked on. I blew out a whistle. It was over eighty plus inches of monitor space with the information about the Titans all blown up.

"Jace, pull up Lucas Devereaux," Teo murmured. "Andrei thinks it's just a stupid grudge. I haven't told Lucas any of this, but Lucas isn't stupid. He's aware of things as well. Especially if someone is against him. He's got his people. I have mine."

Because if Teo told his friend his sister was a jewel thief who stole from a powerful beast of a unit?

All of Teo's secrets including me, would unravel.

And *nobody* wanted that.

He crossed his arms over his chest. "Jace, pull up the singular shot of Gabriel." Teo pointed at a blurry shot of a blonde-man taken in what looked like him getting into a nondescript car. I caught a side profile of him and that was it.

"You only have one shot of him?"

Why? This made no sense.

How was he so under the radar?

"He's listed as Lucy's employer on paper, but she technically works for Reed," Teo explained. "Andrei found out his alias is Raphael Santos. Rumor has it the Agency sends people to the Greenwich manor time to time. He's got a temper and they end up dead. This summer one of his guys killed off a few informants in the city when Gabriel got a little whiff of information being passed along."

Teo was playing in too many games. All thanks to Andrei.

"Why?" I asked. Why fuck with a former operative? Gabriel was former CIA. "Just to fuck with him?"

"He's a ghost," Teo looked at me as he put down more images and photos. "His team? They're broken up in a way that most of them? Don't use their real names. Andrei knew because he has a connection in the Agency that said Gabriel Monroe is his real name. But his alias the Agency created was Raphael Santos. A history professor at Astor University."

My spine stiffened and my blood began running colder.

Avani's college in particular.

I tucked that fact away to keep my eyes peeled.

"Jace, pull up the files on Gabriel Monroe originally. The beginning." Teo waited until Jace pulled up photos of a younger man. Blonde. Youthful. "He's a former Navy SEAL who joined the Agency young. Too young. He was decorated, held a lot of promise, and he had the world. Only, seven years ago, he quit after an assignment gone wrong."

"What happened?" I asked Teo. He looked at Jace.

Jace spoke for the first time his eyes meeting mine. "I can't get the exact information. Someone's locked the files down. I have to do some more digging but the Titan's are hiding him."

"The Titans are hiding everything." I shook my head. "What do you think happened?"

Jace paused for a second before looking at Teo who looked a little uneasy. "The rumor is…everyone on the team was pronounced dead."

I gaped. "Everyone? But him?"

Teo shook his head. "Every single member of the team, was marked as dead according to the contact Andrei has in the Agency. That means—"

"Every single member might be alive under a different alias?"

Holy. Shit. Teo nodded. "Jace."

The other man looked at me. "I suspect something happened on the assignment. Either they all are dead. Except for him. Or people made it out and the Agency made it go away."

Teo nodded looking grim as he watched me. "You're not going to like where I'm going with this. But Andrei was interested in Gabriel's old team because turns out they were hunting a man named Marcus Hagen. Sound familiar?"

Just like that, my blood ran to ice.

I looked at my brother's eyes a mirror image of my own.

I swallowed, feeling my throat constrict.

"That's Malcolm Nash." Talia's father had alias's. That was his most popular one.

Teo nodded looking at the files. "Andrei thinks Malcolm was in New York and he had Gabriel's team killed. All of them. Except for Gabriel. Somehow he made it out. As you can imagine, ever since he had Drew, any threat to Talia or him is a threat to Drew."

And Andrew was going to make sure nothing touched his family. "Andrei looked him up."

Jace spoke up. "Mr. DuPont requested a file on every single Titan possible."

"Gabriel was hunting Malcolm Nash seven years ago?" I dared to repeat it. Because everyone knew what I was thinking. "That was a suicide mission. Talia's father wasn't known for mercy."

That meant Gabriel had been hunting a man who he didn't know or understand.

Because even I couldn't fathom how much of a monster Malcolm Nash was.

Talia never talked about him like that.

To her, he was her father. But Andrei despised him.

"Not to mention Gabriel despises Lucas. Who happens to be dating Evie Monroe. Jace, pull up the photo of the girl."

I watched a photo appear on screen of a brunette with deep auburn hair and bright brown eyes.

"*That* is his sister. Lucas told me this summer he was dating her in secret. On paper she's listed as Reed's cousin. My guess is, because Gabriel isn't real—neither is she. I can't find a connection. It's a clusterfuck. But like I said," Teo muttered. "The Titans have a clusterfuck of secrets. Jace, pull up every single Titan on the main team."

Teo explained it as Jace pulled up three separate photos.

One was a man with features like he was a biker, dirty-blonde hair, navy eyes, a smirk on his face in the photo.

"This is Nathan Wyatt, he's currently guarding Gemma Marchand. Non-issue for us. Innocent. Jace, pull up the girl."

The next shot was a woman.

It was a passport shot of a brunette with bangs and the kind of green eyes on a woman I'd have a hard time forgetting. She was too pretty like a pageant queen.

Those eyes were cemented into my brain. Eerie bright green like emeralds or jewels. "Her eyes are wild."

"Insane," Teo murmured.

Jace spoke up. "This woman's alias is Maria Santos. She just appears randomly in time a few years ago. I don't think that's her real name. When I found anything on her? She was wiped again. And again. Like she was a ghost. Every single time I find her, she vanishes. Like her identity populates into someone else. She's got seventeen international passports."

"She's a Titan?" I asked Jace blowing out a whistle.

He tipped his head. "However, I got a Cuban passport out of all her passports and that one has the oldest date. My guess is, she's Cuban."

"She's a Cuban *operative?*"

"I think so," he said. Teo was quiet as I asked Jace more questions about whoever Maria was. "And no surveillance photos of her either. She's like Gabriel Monroe. But she's got multiple international passports for Titan so Mr. DuPont thinks she's important to Gabriel. Titan looks like it's split into two units. One is Reed's. One is Gabriel's."

"And Gabriel is the shadow?" I asked them.

Teo nodded finally. "Remember Raphael Santos?" His alias. "Not only is he employed at Astor University. Raphael Santos has two women who work under him. Maria. And a one Lucy Devereaux." He turned to me. "Bexley doesn't have this information."

"No, she only knows Reed."

Teo grinned. "She won't find anything else. Jace removed as much as he could find. Every single time he finds anything, he's instructed to wipe it. So nobody else does."

Fucking. Genius.

Because information was power. And Teo held enough of it.

And nobody was any wiser.

"So we don't know why Gabriel Monroe hates Lucas. But Lucas is secretly dating Gabriel's sister. Who might not be *his* sister."

Teo smirked nodding. "Correct. Lucas's sister Lucy works for Reed. And Lucas has no idea she stole an object from Talon."

"Correct. But Reed does." I repeated to him. "Bexley doesn't have any of this information save for Reed and Lucy."

Teo held out his finger. "And their families."

"And their families." I repeated. "So Reed is the target for Talon. Jace, I need every bit of information on Reed Whittaker you can get your hands on."

"But the real target is Gabriel." Teo finished. "The last time I sent someone after him, he killed them in his backyard. I can't let anyone else in. Jace has tried to dig up more information on him. He doesn't exist."

Teo looked at me with a glint in his eyes. "He's got connections. Mafia. Police department. Someone in his pocket higher up. Andrei thinks even if he is a ghost? He knows the right people to pull the right strings. So Titan is elusive. My guess is, they're going after Reed. Reed is a public facing figure. That's why everyone attacks me. Not you or Andrei."

I let out a breath. "Alma's going to go after Titan." She probably already had. "And their families."

"Tell me everything," Teo murmured. "I can help and keep it off Andrei's plate."

"Because of Drew?" My brother had his reasons.

Teo shrugged. "And because Lucas is involved. They cannot kill Lucas. He has done nothing wrong. I don't think Lucas is behind any of this. The only thing he cares about is Evie."

"And if Gabriel finds out Lucas is dating Evie—" I started.

"Lucas is a dead man on multiple fronts. I need to keep my friend alive." Teo finished. "He helped you too. We need to keep Lucas alive."

But I knew Talon.

I fucking knew how they operated.

"If they don't kill him, they're going to watch him first."

He nodded not looking pleased with that. "And weed him out if he isn't guilty. Tell me the information you have. We can put it together. Lucy stole something? And now she wants what with it? Did they even tell you what it was?"

"No."

"And you don't find that suspicious?" Teo asked. He looked at Jace. "Can you keep an eye on everyone listed here?"

"Yes, sir." The other man was already on his keyboard. "Anyone in particular we want surveillance on?"

"Reed," both Teo and said at the same time.

Teo looked at Jace. "When you do a deep dive on Reed Whittaker, I want you to pull up Alisha and Avani Malhotra. The older sister is dating him so Talon will make her a target first."

And I would protect my heart. She was covered.

We shared a look. Teo looked at me. "You failed to ask the most important question."

"No," I shook my head. "I was already thinking it."

Why would Reed Whittaker want anything Alma had?

Was it related to her or Talia?

I needed to go see Talia after this.

Not to tell her about Talon. But to see what she knew about Gabriel. About anything at all.

I could go see her after this and better me than Teo.

We talked for a while and he frowned over the pieces.

"It's too many secrets. We're missing a piece of this puzzle. Why does Whittaker or Monroe wants Alma or any of the Nash's unless it's revenge?"

"I don't know," I said honestly. That's the part that bothered me the most. "Talon is hunting for Lucy and I gotta go and figure out a way to talk to Bexley without her suspecting anything. Or her figuring out that we keep hiding information from everyone."

"Keep me in the loop. If it involves Lucas, I want to know. He's done nothing wrong. He would never put his sister up to this." Teo still loved Lucas like a brother. But he had many cards in his hand like me. "You'll go to Talia, I'll sneak through Andrei's office. I have to go see him now."

I hadn't talked to Andrei since I erupted on him.

And with everything going on, it was probably best that I didn't speak to him.

"And he's still avoiding everything?"

Teo's face went blank. "I don't think it's that simple anymore. Maxine is livid you are in our lives. He's trying to make sure the foundation we stand on doesn't erode. It isn't as simple as we think being a family man—"

"He doesn't show up for Drew—" I snapped stopping as Teo cut me off.

"He showed up for us. Look I'm not on his side, I'm not on your side. I understand where both of you are coming from."

He leaned forward his elbows on his knees as he watched me.

"He raised you and me. With her. Do you think he might be working on something to make sure nothing threatens our lives again? He has a hard time talking about anything. She's not talking to him. He's not talking to her. As much as you want to blame him because you love her, they need to get together like adults. They've been together for eighteen years, I feel like asking for a fucking conversation, isn't that big of a deal."

I was confused. "I thought you were against him avoiding Drew and Talia."

"I still am. And I can be. But I also understand everything you and she has, comes with a price. Why do you think I do not settle down? Do you think with my schedule I have time for a spouse? Andrei messed up. But so did she. Part of being healthy is under-standing—*they are both wrong."*

Teo's eyes held mine. "They are both. Wrong." He repeated it.

Out of everyone in the world Teo was not the person I imagined settling down. But he looked uncomfortable even as he said it.

My brother was not interested in women the way Andrei and I were. No, Teo liked trouble more than he liked anything else.

"I didn't even know you wanted to settle down," I shook my head in disbelief.

He shifted a little leaning back discomfort in his eyes. "I don't."

I was twenty.

Teo was seven years older than me.

He had experiences I didn't and I had experiences he didn't.

We used to fight a lot growing up but now? Not so much.

Now, he brought ideas to the table and I listened.

"I'll go and settle it with Talia."

He nodded looking at me with an interesting expression on his face.

Just like that my brother's eyes became eerily perceptive darting between me and the words in front of me.

"What is it?"

His lips quirked up as he narrowed his eyes. He turned to Jace who didn't look at me or him. His facial expression remained nuetral.

"You're dating the woman who taught you to read."

And just like that I felt my house of cards crumbling.

Teo's smile grew wider turning wicked. "I was wondering who you would spend time with until Talia mentioned you had a tutor over the summer. I printed those documents for dyslexic friendly readers and yet you were able to do so well."

His smile turned downright devious.

"Who is she? I thought it might be the tutor. I didn't say anything to Talia. But I am curious who she is now."

I looked away uncomfortable. Jaces eyes flickered up to me. He was keeping my secret. Even if Teo was his boss he wouldn't say a word about Avani. He already knew. When I sent him that audio to fix, he knew then. He knew her name. He knew who she was.

And I caught when Teo told him Avani Malhotra was connected to Reed Whittaker his eyes had darted to me. He knew.

It wasn't that I didn't trust Teo.

But Teo knew Alisha.

Who knew Reed.

Who was currently being targeted by Talon.

This wasn't the *best* clusterfuck to be in.

This was one hell of a web.

I swallowed feeling my own emotions threatening to choke me out as I said it. "I'm not." My eyes held Jace's. "I've been studying on my own."

I'd heard about lies tasting bitter but the taste was now permanently etched into my tongue from the lies I told everyone.

Teo snorted. "Well, your girlfriend's perfume smells nice."

Shit. Fuck. Jace smirked a little looking down at the keyboard.

I placed my ball cap squarely on my head taking the files with me as I left. Teo had a copy for himself. In the meantime I'd comb through it at the warehouse.

Where Avani couldn't tell I used to be Talon.

At the thought of her, and her perfume my mind immediately drifted to memories of her in the morning rushing out with me.

Laughter in the car. Her honey and pink and smiles all over me as I teased her.

I wasn't being rational when it came to Avani at all. I didn't want to be.

When it came to her, being sensible, disciplined, and rational, didn't exist.

I was letting this girl into my life while simultaneously lying to her about my past.

Avani might not care. Or she might care so much? I lost her.

And losing Avani wasn't a part of the equation. Ever.

I WENT TO GO TO SEE TALIA THAT AFTERNOON WHILE TEO DID HIS half of the job.

Working with Teo was easier than dealing with Andrei.

And when I went over to talk to Talia about Gabriel Monroe and Reed, Drew was asleep.

She opened the door in a bathrobe looking more tired than I'd ever seen.

The darker shadows under eyes more prominent telling me she wasn't getting much sleep.

I needed to text Teo to tell him we should both just find Andrei and tie him up to the apartment with Drew and give Talia a break.

Her usual tanner skin was pale as she crossed her arms over her chest.

"You don't look good," I kept my voice down.

"Just long nights. He needs to eat every three hours and I am currently every meal."

She motioned to her breasts.

"Nobody warns you about postpartum in the States. In Hong Kong I could have a stay at home nanny but in the States that culture isn't the same."

Talia had grown up in Hong Kong initially before moving to Europe and then finally the States.

"You miss it?" I dared to ask moving to the kitchen island with her while she moved around making us some tea.

"I do. Sometimes I wonder…" she trailed off not finishing her sentence. "Listen, I have to make a call. Did you need anything?"

I didn't know where to start.

So I started with what I knew. "Talia…do you know who Gabriel Monroe is?"

319

The cup crashed out of her hand into the floor and she hissed as hot water splattered.

I rushed to move to her swearing as I moved her out of the way.

"Shit, I burned my fingers a little." She looked down at her hands. "And I think my toes…" I swore grabbed towels and checking her out. Small stings. She would be fine. "Sorry," she murmured. "It slipped. I've been clumsier lately." But her eyes were a little lost.

"It's all right," I didn't come at a good time and she was sleep deprived.

She swallowed as she plotted and dabbed her burns running them under cold water while I cleaned up.

"W-where did you hear that name?" She murmured.

"Through the grapevine," I said thanking the universe my head was down while I cleaned up broken glass. "Do you know it?"

"No," she shook her head and I couldn't see her face. "No, I don't." Her throat worked as she turned to face me her eyes wide a little and red-rimmed. "Thank you for cleaning up. Is that all you had to ask me?"

She just looked off. Was she lying?

"Talia…" I didn't know where to start as I threw out the glass. "I…I know his team died six-maybe seven years ago while they were hunting Malcolm." Her face paled. "Do you know anything about it? I know you came into Talon then."

She shook her head but the look in her eyes confirmed my suspicions. The worst ones. I knew what Talia had been. What she done.

"No," her face was straight her eyes on me. But I knew a mask when I saw one and it made a shiver break out on my skin because Talia would only keep secrets from me if it was bad. Really bad. "I don't know who that is. Why do you ask?"

Because he was alive.

And I think he might be going after Talon. Right now.

For some reason.

Stealing from Alma, involving the clusterfuck of characters. It didn't make any sense to me. At all.

"I was curious," I murmured watching her struggling with her sting as she dabbed the marks on her skin. "It isn't important is it?"

"No," she said too quickly. "No, it isn't. My father never spoke of a Monroe." But she was lying.

She knew him. She knew Gabriel Monroe.

I swallowed hard feeling unease move through my gut. The cold knot was growing tighter and larger by the second.

"Talia…" I didn't know how to ask because she was my sister-in-law first and foremost. *"Did you kill his team?"*

Her eyes went wide and she whispered it looking horrified I would ask. "No. I would never do that to."

And she was telling the truth. I took a step forward. "So then what happened that night? What happened to the team?"

She shook her head looking distraught. "Why do you want to know? *Why are you asking these questions?"*

I dared to say it then. "Because Talon is back in town and they're hunting for Titan Security's heads. Gabriel and Reed."

She frowned. "Gabriel Monroe is dead."

So she knew something. She knew.

Talia was there that night. I was sure of it.

"You know what happened."

She looked away again looking like she was fighting her emotions. "Look, I don't know what is going on. Or why Alma is after Titan Security. But what I do know—" she turned back to me. "Gabriel Monroe was shot and killed that night. His entire team was murdered. I know this. Not a single member made it."

But there was something about the way she said it.

Someone made it.

Someone survived.

My chest was heaving as I processed what she was saying both of us watching each other then.

"Who survived?" I dared to ask.

She paled. "Nobody. None of them. Now get out of my house. I have ninety things to do. One of them is not entertaining questions about a dead man."

"Talia, if you know something—"

"I don't know anything—"

"I saw a photo of Gabriel—"

"Then it's a lie," she snapped, her eyes flashing wildly.

This was no longer Talia Nash.

This was the head of Talon.

The one raised by Malcolm Nash, and became his warrior.

Her voice cut through the air between the two of us like a knife. A blade.

321

"He's *dead*. He was *murdered*. His entire team was murdered. I don't know how. I just know that. And I'm done with this conversation because I refuse to entertain lunacy abut a ghost."

She looked unsteady as she wrapped her robe around herself breathily heavily.

"*Talia—*"

She moved away from me and walked out of the room looking unsteady.

What the fuck happened?

What the fuck was she hiding?

CHAPTER 33
AVANI

"*You seem distracted.*"

Avani sat across from me, chewing her lip, at the diner we went to for brunch.

"Is everything okay with you and Reed? You looked a little upset when you saw him."

I had seen Alisha and Reed at a cafe I had gone to with her and Kellan earlier that week. Now?

Sitting under the brighter lights of the retro diner we were in I took in my sister's expression.

Her every breath seemed to be a little off. She looked a little dazed and barely listening.

Did something happen to her and Reed?

But since I had met Reed and Alisha they seemed really strong, and Alisha hadn't mentioned anything about her weird fans.

She had only said that Reed had taken apart the old apartment and everything had been moved into K2, his building which was nice of him.

Now, she sat across from me, and her ever present bodyguard a cute blonde man named Kellan sat with a letterman jacket on the barstool not too far from us.

Close enough to hear our conversation but far enough sometimes I forgot he was with her.

"I'm sorry. Yes, everything is fine. I just have a lot on my mind."

She always did though. Ever since she started dating Reed I saw less of my sister.

But you're dating Thierry. You never told Alisha.

Between Reed, her stalking, losing our old apartment, and everything else?

I didn't know how to tell Alisha now because how did I tell my sister about my boyfriend when she'd lost so much? I wasn't cruel and I wasn't insensitive. I understood Thierry and I had our bubble. But right now?

While she looked haunted?

I didn't know how to say it.

Reed had sent a keycard to my apartment after Alisha had moved in saying should I ever need a home his door was open.

He really did think of everything and it made me wonder what else he had going on.

The vinyl seats beneath me felt warm in the diner, the smell of burgers and fries around us as I sipped my milkshake a little.

Her eyes darted to Kellan as the waitress walked by with more coffee and Kellan sat up more. She turned back to me with a small smile.

"It's nothing, tell me about you. Any cute boys I should be aware of?"

Tell her. Tell her about the boy.

I was sure my cheeks heated. Where did I start?

"I don't think I like college boys."

Not technically.

He wasn't in college.

And he was twenty but I was turning eighteen soon and it didn't matter to me.

He never took advantage of me.

In reality, out of the horror stories I heard I had gotten lucky. Really lucky.

Alisha mock gasped. "Let me guess, between the chlamydia and drinking binges, it's hard to find a decent man?"

We laughed as Kellan choked on his drink across from alisha.

"It's not that," I lowered my voice. "I just haven't found some-one...you know what Mum used to tell us about? The kinds of men in her stories, the kind that sweep you off your feet and love you more than life?"

Liar. Liar. You have.

But maybe I was gauging Alisha a little to see if she would be open to me screaming at the top of my lungs.

I have a boyfriend.

He's Matteo's younger brother.

I hate keeping him a secret.

I want to tell you so freaking bad.

But I'm scared with your life, your new world, you won't understand mine.

Instead what I said was. "Do you remember when Mum hadn't gone back home in ages? I asked her if it made her unhappy. Why did she stay? She said Dad was her home. She had no reason to go back when she'd been blessed with so much. Sometimes I think Reed is like that for you."

That's what he felt like.

"I feel like after Mum and Dad died, I realized recently you stopped living your life. You stopped being happy. Because of me —" There it was. Me. Slowly telling Alisha the truth.

"No—" she started looking at me a little horrified.

But it was true. It was my fault.

And that was why I never told her about my boyfriend.

"You've never looked happier. Even after you became the brand ambassador for EllaBeauty. Reed, he's been so good for you. Good to you. You look healthier."

It was true.

With Reed she looked more relaxed.

She looked like she had less stress on her plate even with a stalker.

She hadn't looked exhausted and genuinely her body looked different, like she glowed from the inside out.

"I'm so grateful he's a part of our family now. I'm so glad you finally gave him a chance. I wish we hadn't missed out three years."

I meant it. We had missed out on Reed.

Because of me.

Alisha wasn't with him because of me.

And she had lost three years of her life, if not five raising me. I wanted to be good to her, to do right by her.

I couldn't form the words. I have a boyfriend. It was so simple.

But another voice in my head argued, what right did I have to be happy—if my sister gave up the world for me and she had happiness now?

Would I be unfair to her to bring up my boyfriend when I was even younger than her?

Did I have the right to be happy?

Did I allow myself permission to forgive myself and feel something more than guilt around Alisha?

I didn't know the answer.

I just knew, happiness made me feel guilty. Even when I was with Thierry? Sometimes I struggled with that guilt.

I watched Alisha looking at me with a tender but broken expression.

Her eyes look haunted.

Alisha's hazel eyes softened on me, and Kellan turned to us a little watching her.

Like he knew what it meant for me to say it. Like he knew her.

"I'm really glad after everything you've been blessed with so much," I continued, my smile widening. "Mum would've had such a huge crush on him."

A watery laugh escaped her.

Her eyes drifted to my turtleneck as I reached for my coffee.

I looked down following her gaze to the bracelet Reed got me. On the outing Alisha didn't know about.

Drat.

"Is that a...?" She was watching it confused.

I shifted a little in my seat. *Oh no. Here it comes.*

I couldn't say it out loud about Thierry.

But I couldn't keep how wonderful Reed was a secret for much longer.

"I have to tell you something. I don't think you'll like it."

Her eyes met mine.

"Anything. I'd never judge you...but you might have to explain why you're wearing a thirty thousand-dollar bracelet I didn't buy for you."

"*Thirty—?*" What did she just say? Thirty? Thousand? Like zero's? "*Reed said he got it from an antique shop?*"

What on Earth is happening?

"*Reed?*" Alisha's eyes went wide as Kellan turned around to face me fully frowning.

"*He said he was browsing antique stores—*"

"*Reed doesn't go antique shopping.*"

Of course he doesn't. He's a CEO. I thought he sent his secretary to go antique shopping.

Or something.

"I know you'd know since you're his girlfriend. But he told me it was cheap."

Her eyes widened at the bracelet and I didn't know it was designer. There was no label on it.

How was I supposed to know?

I always took it off before my shower at home and Thierry hadn't said a word about it.

"He paid my tuition. *All of it.*" It rushed out of me as I told her everything. About the books, cards, brunches, allowances, and dorm swaps. Her jaw dropped.

"He said he didn't want me to tell you because he didn't want you to like him with any outside influences. He wanted you to like him for who he was. And he told me to keep it a secret so you can focus on you."

Oh my gosh, I love Reed so much. The more I spoke the more my sister looked ready to have a breakdown. Her eyes were wide and stunned. Kellan looked at Alisha a little worried now. More than that.

"But I paid…" she sputtered.

I gripped the table to keep from reaching out to Alisha so I could finish my thought.

"He said he sent it back and switched it with his account. He said even if things don't work out between you guys, which it won't ever happen, he's paying for me to go to school until I finish my PhD."

"Please don't be upset, I just wanted to tell you since our last lunch he said he wants to take us somewhere nice. I told him we hadn't been back to Calcutta in years….thirty thousand? I have to give this back to him. Are you okay? You don't look so good—"

And then I broke off when Kellan moved to Alisha, sliding into the booth quicker than a man his size could even move, holding her tight to him. Alisha broke down in his arms.

I gaped. *Dear Lord, I made my sister cry.*

Again.

"It's okay. It's all right. I'm just—" Alisha sputtered something and Kellan gave me a soft look that told me she would be all right.

She was just emotional. But I was…I felt the tension in my chest constrict further and further at seeing her break down in front of me.

Alisha never cried in front of me.

The pressure in my chest rose and rose feeling like Alisha's sadness was a consequence of me.

I felt my breathing shallow a little bit as she wiped her eyes and Kellan didn't move from his seat as he asked me if I was good.

I numbly nodded feeling horrible. The back of my neck prickled a little as I blinked back my emotion.

I didn't want to feel bad. I didn't want to feel like I was lying to Alisha about everything. She was like my Mum, I should tell her.

But after making her cry? The words didn't form.

Because I felt like all I did was hurt Alisha.

I ducked my head and didn't bring up Reed anymore.

I just wanted to go out and I numbly made up and excuse about a college party.

The only person I wanted to go home tonight to was Thierry.

As guilty as it made me feel.

As soon as I stepped out of the diner I walked to the corner of the near empty street feeling a chill down my spine.

Goosebumps skittered down my skin, my arms in the pre-winter chill of the city.

New York winters were unforgivable sometimes.

I took a few steps down to the corner of the street texting Thierry.

> I'm coming home soon. Just finished dinner.
> Love you.

> Should I come get you? I can be there soon.

> No, it's okay. I'm not far.

BESIDES, RIGHT NOW I JUST NEEDED A MOMENT TO THINK FOR MYSELF for a little bit wiping my eyes at disappointing Alisha.

Again.

I looked up for a second at the bright burst of moonlight on me, the crescent shape in the sky and waited for Thierry to text me back.

I saw the bubbles typing.

> Send me your location, Mon cœur. I'll come
> get you.

So I did.

> I'll wait for you here.

I heard footsteps to my right and I didn't even notice I'd just gone into the side of the darker building.

Closing out of the app, I turned on my flashlight.

I thought I saw someone and was about to stumble out into the light of the street lamps again.

Gasping a little, I saw the person moving quickly.

Taking a few steps back I thought I'd let them pass. Instead, my eyes widened at the sight of our doorman from our old building.

I went to scream but he was on me in another second. I shrieked muffled into cloth.

It smelled horrible and I felt the panic descend in my body as my phone clattered to the floor.

Oh my God.

Thierry!

CHAPTER 34
THIERRY

Someone was in Andrei's apartment.

I could feel the arctic chill inside of it.

Which meant someone from *Talon* was in Andrei's apartment. It wasn't just the breeze outside.

No, someone *colder* was in my apartment.

And there was only one person in the world who held that much energy.

Alma.

My heart beat sped up a little because Avani was out at the movies with her girlfriends.

She wouldn't be home. No. Thank fuck for smaller mercies.

Keeping the lights off, I slowly crept into the kitchen to find— blonde hair.

"*Nat?*" I thought it was Natasha. I was dead wrong.

Sitting at the kitchen island with a bowl of fettuccini in front of her was Alma. Blonde.

Bright-eyed with pale blue contacts making her look terrifying. She was wincing at my gun.

"Really? You did not know it was me?"

I felt a reluctant grin tugging at my lips. I had a heart attack a little. If Avani had been here, she'd be terrified. But also?

Talon would know I was dating their enemy now.

I blinked several times flicking on the lights to make sure I was seeing it correctly. The head of Talon was in my house.

"*You're blonde?* Are you in the city pretending to be Natasha?"

That's the only time she switched up her looks.

The girls were pulling the good old switch.

Everyone thought Natasha was in town when she was in Cape Verde running the show.

She looked at me holding up her fork a grimace forming on her beautiful sculpted face and high cheekbones.

"This is horrible food. It has no seasoning. I'm ashamed to have ever thought you'd be related to me."

I snorted, tucking my gun away. "I'm not Mexican, Alma, I can't keep my figure if I eat like you."

"Nobody said flavor was illegal," she quipped grimacing at the pasta. "How can you make noodles with no flavor? And there is nothing sweet in the house."

I motioned to the cupcakes on the island and stopped.

It had been so long since I even stopped to refill them, they'd gotten moldy. *Gross.*

I needed to pick up Avani some more. But she hadn't mentioned anything too busy in her life too.

Mon cœur had been busier as of late. Mid-terms. Papers. Exams. It was hectic. I was doing my best to support my girlfriend.

Alma set down her fork at the look on my face. "You are not happy to see me?"

"No, I'm exhausted. I've been out all day." I walked up to her.

Alma had no idea I was keeping secrets from her. She knew I knew enough about her. Bexley would tell Alma everything.

Nobody had any idea how many fucking secrets I've been keeping.

Not with Jace working over time to erase me.

Bexley had no idea I was working with Teo.

And oh, my fucking girlfriend had no idea I was looking out for her and her sister's lives.

I wasn't a double agent.

I was a triple agent.

I had left this life behind so many months ago, I forgot what it was like seeing her and her haunted eyes.

"You are busy with your new life?" Her eyes softened not looking upset at all. "I don't expect you to be involved. But I do want what is mine back."

"What did they take?" I kept my voice lower. "I know Carter

talked to you about me. I know Reed or Lucas took something from you. Why won't you tell me what it is?"

Something crossed her eyes then.

And for one fucking second, she looked exactly like Talia did when I asked her about the death of Gabriel Monroe's team.

She had her secrets. I had mine.

I couldn't dispense with any that I had without letting Alma know how much I knew.

She shook her head. "Come, let's go for a walk."

I bit back a sigh.

"I USED TO LOVE THIS CITY," ALMA LOOKED OUT ON THE BROOKLYN Bridge.

The night had fallen and I needed to be quick with Alma.

I was going to pick up Avani and now that I knew how easily Alma got in?

I needed to change out my fucking locks or move Avani somewhere safer away from the eyes of Talon.

I was so fucking frustrated right now.

The moment they'd shown up my life had been upended and even if I didn't want anything to do with Talon—they were threatening Reed. Which threatened my family. My heart.

And I couldn't have that.

We had gone all the way to Brooklyn where Alma said there was a halfway decent pizza spot Carter talked about. But I wasn't in the mood to eat.

She munched on the last bit of her slice as we walked on the bridge.

Finishing it she looked out the water wiping her hands. "I think at least."

"You've been here before? I didn't know you ever left Cape Verde besides missions." I was walking with her.

We'd stepped out in all black like I always wore except Alma was dressed for war now.

Both of us were always armed, but now she smiled as she looked over the expanse of the illuminated bridge.

"I don't remember," she said with a smile. I could tell when her eyes crinkled. I shook my head.

"You're getting old, sis." I teased. "Memory loss, what's next you tell me to hold your teeth while you brush them?"

She laughed outright then the sound musical.

Alma had some memory issues. Like Natasha she'd been in an accident as well only I think it was her brain and her heart that were an issue.

From time to time she forgot things. Memories. All pointing to a brain injury from the past.

My eyes drifted across the bridge to a lone figure walking on the other side. Dark hair. Bangs. Did I know her? I think I'd know if I knew her...

I never forgot a face though. Dyslexia didn't mean I was a total idiot. No, I thought she looked familiar.

"Oh, now I'm old hm?" Alma laughed lightly. I grinned ear to ear at her teasing. It wasn't always she cut back.

"Does Talia know you're in town?"

She shook her head. "Nobody knows. Just me and Carter. But Samara wanted to come. Said she would murder Cole in cold blood if she stayed around him."

Got it. Which meant she was keeping her secrets a secret from everyone. Just like me.

I grinned ear to ear at that. "How are they?"

"Decent."

I looked across the bridge and the brunette had turned her head. And then I knew how I knew her. Nobody had those eyes. Not that green. I knew her face.

Maria Santos. A Titan...hmmm.

Did she know me?

Probably not. Nobody knew who I was. I was half-listening to Alma who was looking over the bridge.

Did she know there was a Titan walking past us?

I knew the lady by her eyes.

Nobody had green eyes like her. Long suede boots. Jacket. She looked fierce.

But Alma would kill her in maybe three seconds if she knew. If.

Which meant Alma didn't know Maria or whatever her fucking name was. I internally sighed as I raked my eyes over her.

And then I had an idea. Just because I was a double—er, triple agent—didn't mean I couldn't relay it to the Titans.

If anything happened to Reed or his family, Avani would be devastated.

"So what's the plan?" I asked Alma casually figuring I'd throw the Titans a bone.

It might be fun and while my concern was all about Avani, even I couldn't resist.

"You go up North and take Whittaker and I help you guys with what you need?"

"Ideally," Alma murmured her voice lower than usual as she stared out to the sea. " I don't want to kill him until I know why he's playing cat and mouse games. I despise men for this very reason. They can't just say what they want, they have to play games." She rolled her eyes.

I snorted. "Talia says the same thing."

I eyed Maria Santos who walked by us.

Maybe she heard me. Maybe she didn't.

Either way I hope she was a good Titan who ran back to her home with her tail and told her leadership we would come for them.

Nothing like a good hunt.

"How is she?" Alma murmured. "How is Drew?"

Not good.

I hadn't spoken to Talia lately but I knew she was done with Andrei. Plus, the last time I scared her?

I didn't want to push her in her state.

Teo had been doing research on postpartum depression. Andrei wasn't helping Talia.

She was all alone in a new world with her baby.

Not ideal.

I hadn't helped but I didn't want to make it worse.

Not when I knew the source of all information was right here.

"They're all right. As they can be. Talia misses Hong Kong—"

"I do too. I miss the East Side of the world in general. Way cleaner and better food," she shrugged at my droll expression. "What? They put flavor in everything. And spice."

I grinned at that. Alma and Talia would ironically get along very well with Avani. Even Nat. The Talon girls had some of Avani's fire. Maybe that's why I liked her so much too.

As the cold breeze shifted around us, I felt something different coming off Alma.

I swallowed a little grateful she couldn't really dissect me right now thanks to my own outfit.

"What do you want from the Titans?" Besides her object back.

"Answers." Her eyes met mine colder than ever, the air around me frigid. "I want Reed to give me the answers I have waited years for."

"What are you talking about? Why would Reed have answers for you?"

She shook her head. "I don't know. But he took something of mine. And I know why. He won't win against me. But it's nice of him to think he can last."

And then I asked the one question that I knew would fire like a loaded weapon. "Why did you come to me? Do you want me to do recon for you?"

She shrugged. "If you want," her smirk was evident. "I wanted to see you. It's been forever."

That it had. "That's it?"

Her smile grew. "I cannot see my brother?"

I grinned. I was her little brother.

Years ago, Alma told me about how her brother had died on an assignment. She said once she lost him, there was nothing in her past worth sticking around for. So she'd become Talon.

She said I reminded her of him—*Liam*.

"I'll do what I can for you, I'll take care of Whittaker and his goons."

She chuckled. "Hardly. Have you seen them? Pathetic. Weak. It's funny because they think their professionals and then they go and steal things from me."

She said something in Spanish about weak men and I shook my head. There was a reason why Talon was good at their job.

Reed Whittaker wasn't prepared for what was coming for him. And I had to make sure she didn't kill everybody.

She wouldn't kill him right away. No, Alma was fond of mind games. She was going to drive him insane. And then she was gonna finish them off.

"Tell me where you're staying so I can find you."

Her grin was wide and a little terrifying.

"You can have my number instead."

Because Alma would never give out her information.

But now I had a way to reach her.

335

Even if I had to change my locks and warn Avani about not answering the door for guests.

I swore internally as I walked into the night with my old mentor.

I didn't trust anyone anymore.

Not with Avani in my life.

THE NEXT NIGHT, I HAD TO PICK MON CŒUR FROM THE DINER SHE was at with her sister.

But she wasn't there.

I was there in a few minutes after she texted me.

In the car when I drove by. I parked near it but enough for me to walk over in my ball cap and hoodie on.

The streetlights were bright enough that I saw a glint of metal on the ground.

A pink butterfly. Avani's phone case?

My blood immediately ran cold and my heart began pounding out of my chest. *Mon cœur ...please be nearby.*

I picked it up praying to anything it wasn't hers.

It wasn't my girls.

But it was. I opened it and it was a photo of her and Alisha staring back at me. Just like that my panic began to lose it. The moment I knew something was deadly wrong was when Reed Whittaker burst out of the fucking diner.

I swore internally ducking into the shadows. On his trails was a blonde in a Letterman jacket. What the—

Does he know where she is?

Dashing inside the diner I didn't waste a second. I flashed the phone to a stricken pale faced man behind the counter clearly frozen in place.

I held up her phone. "I'm with the idiot that just ran out. These two girls? You know them?"

"He-he's going to find them…" he sputtered looking horrified. Confirming my worst fears. Find them.

Someone has Avani. Someone hurt Avani.

And just like that my blood ran cold. My brows knit together as I ran back out to watch Reed Whittaker speeding off into the night. I needed to follow him. I needed information.

He knew. He knew where she was. I ran to my car ready to do just that.

Someone hurt my heart.

And I was going to fucking kill them.

CHAPTER 35
THIERRY

I followed Reed to a location Downtown, parking my car a few cars behind his.

He didn't even notice probably too far gone in his own turmoil, I turned off my car and sat quietly. It didn't take long at all for people to emerge like wraith as my palms heated and heart pounded.

He knew where Avani was? Why wasn't he moving in?

I bit back the urge to shake him and break into his car and tell him we needed to get our girls together.

No.

He was a Titan.

I was Talon.

He was still the enemy. And he stole from Alma. None of those things were erasable information.

Gabriel Monroe aside? Reed Whittaker wasn't exactly not on my shit-list. But he was good to Avani. Which was the only thing I cared about.

She was in that house he was around. I knew it. I fucking knew it. I watched as people materialized silently and the more they did just hanging out around me, the more I knew—I fucking knew—she was there. But I needed a way in. I couldn't break in. I couldn't take anyone down.

No. But I needed—

Alma's voice was in my head.

Breathe Grim. She might be your heart. But you are not stupid. Think. You need a—

"I need a vantage point." I felt it rush through me as I began looking around the area. I was still far enough from the operatives to be undetected but close enough to know they would know if I moved.

I slipped on a balaclava I had in my car as I looked around the buildings. I needed one facing a window inside. Anyone. I didn't have much time.

Mon cœur ...

The idea of anything happening to her? Sent an unfamiliar terror ripping through me and when I swallowed it felt like I had shards of glass down my throat.

Was she there? I could do it. I could save her.

I just needed a point. I slowly got out the car to not draw suspicion to myself. With the way I dressed? I blended right in with my ball cap. Nobody could see my eyes and I fit right in. Nobody would know.

I looked around at the building.

My money was that house was built like every house on the block. Which helped me. Because now? I knew exactly which building I needed to be on.

Reaching into the trunk, I pulled out a duffle bag I kept underneath the flat surface. And quietly as I could, despite people swarming the area? I fit right in. I looked like another operative. Nobody blinked twice about me.

Act like you belong, act confident. Reed Whittaker is going to do his thing.

You do yours.

"I got this Alma," I muttered. "Now is not the time."

But it works, si?

Yes, Alma it works.

I was rushing out to the nearest building climbing the stairs two at a time.

The house was two stories. *I need three. Just three.*

I burst into the rooftop, my heart beating out of my chest, gravel under my feet crunching as the moonlight beat down on me.

I could do this.

Assemble the gun. Breathe each time. Do it, now.

I'm on it, Alma. He has my girl I'm scared.

I know. But right now? She is not yours.
You are on a job. That is it. Do you copy?

I stilled, looking down at the pieces of the Barrett M82. Fastest and deadliest gun I could get my hands on as I sank to my knees and tore into assembling it.

It took me exactly one minute and thirty three seconds I didn't have to put it together. Rushing I loaded it with the generic bullets. Not the Talon ones since I wasn't killing for them anymore.

She is not your heart. She is not yours. Not right now.
Right now? She is in danger. Breathe, Grim. You can do this.
I need to find her, Alma.

I would find her. I eyed through the scope looking out trying to find a window into the house. Anything to tell me anything about who the fuck took my girl.

The scope was live revealing the house everyone was surrounding, right now, with my mask on—the Titans thought I was on their side.

For this second? I was. For my heart. I was.

My finger hovered over the trigger restrained as I looked through the window to see shadows. People. And I watched and waited.

It took a few moments, long ones, for me to see a man and a woman through the window. I peered through the scope.

My heart thudding at the thought of it being Avani.

I stilled my breathing until it lowered and I could feel the ice cold breeze descending into my blood stream. I was focused. Locked in.

That dark shadow inside the house has my girl. I saw a female talking to him. Who was that?

I narrowed my eyes.

Not Avani. Alisha…she was—my stomach soured. Why was she taking her clothes off?

Grim.

If by magic, an imaginary Alma appeared next to me. Her eyes in my vision.

You will take the shot.

"I can't," I muttered. "That's my girlfriend's sister. I can't hit her."

You won't hit her. Take the shot. Kill him.

I breathed out. "Alma, he's too close. I'll hit her, she's blocking the window."

Take. The. Shot. Now.

I let out a breath as Alisha stripped down to nothing. She was shaking. I could see how hard from here.

Shit shit shit shit. If that was Alisha? Where was Avani? What did he do to my heart? Did he hurt her?

Was she dead?

And just like that, that was the thought, the final thought in my head—all it took was that thought—and I was done.

I felt a calm descend over me and imaginary Alma vanished. Avani knew me as her man. As someone good. Someone who spoiled her and humored her eating habits and loved her.

I did love her.

But I was also this. The specter in the night.

One of the Reapers of Talon. Something I often forgot with her.

I felt something shift in me, something moved and my vision focused in as the chill descended into my blood stream.

I aimed the rifle at the man who was choking Alisha. I didn't even breathe. The Titans were plotting. I could see them.

But right now, they faded into the background.

On the rooftop I was invisible. A ghost.

The Grim Reaper. Again. For my heart. To the world I was a killer.

I never told Avani the truth because I was afraid it might shatter her views of me.

Now, I had never been more grateful of my past.

She saw my darkness, the chaos, and through the shadows of my soul, Avani believed my goodness was possible.

She was my light.

Without her, spring never would come.

Without her, I wasn't me.

Without her, I was death.

The faint mist curled in front of my mouth. And ice formed around my veins as I focused.

I didn't hesitate.

Inhale.

Exhale.

Alisha. Avani. I got you both.

I promise.

On the third exhale, I saw Alisha struggling through the scope and my heartbeat slowed.

341

The night held its breath the cold everywhere now.
The metal ice in my hand.
I felt it in my ear drums.
Now or never.
I fired.

CHAPTER 36
AVANI

WHEN MY EYES FLEW OPEN, THE WORLD WAS A BLUR OF DARKNESS, shadows, and the smell of…blood.

And the sight that met my eyes, made me want to scream.

That's when the shaking began.

I was tied to a wooden beam as I looked around the dingy old room. The first thing my eyes landed on was blood.

Lots of blood.

I felt a noise leave me as I looked at the form of a woman…and my stomach lurched at the sight of blood, matted hair, and bruised skin and—when I realized who it was, I almost threw up.

That is Selena. I knew by the boots.

And then even more horrifying—my eyes landed on Alisha, slumped in a corner and a noise left me. Until my eyes kept moving. We were…kidnapped?

Someone took me.

Oh God, Thierry was supposed to come and get me...

Oh God. Alisha. Selena...

Someone hurt me. Someone hurt us.

I forced myself to breathe even if it felt like my heartbeat had gotten so loud in fear? I heard nothing else.

"Didi," I felt my vision blur as I looked at a passed out Alisha. "Please don't be dead. Please be alive. Didi, wake up!"

I kept going whispering and struggling against the ties. "Wake up!"

It took several attempts but Alisha moaned softly waking up. Oh, thank God, she wasn't dead.

"Didi wake up! Selena's hurt. Please wake up."

Alisha's eyes opened then confused and a little hurt in them as she looked over at me. I heard the sound of footsteps overhead and ignored them focusing on my sister. I motioned to Selena.

"She was already here. What's happening?" I whispered. "We need to find a way out of here."

"I'll find a way out of here," Alisha's eyes despite looking worn down held a glint of determination as she looked around. Pulse-pounding fear raced through my body.

Alisha's eyes landed on the tiny window along the far wall.

"You can fit if we can get it open."

"No," I hissed, knowing exactly what my sister was thinking and my eyes welled up more. Alisha would do that for me. "I'm not leaving you."

"You have to." Her eyes turned back to me bright and wide now like she just realized the magnitude of our situation. "You have to run when I give you the chance to. Go find Reed."

I heard the creaking increase. He was coming back. *Oh God.*

"He's coming!"

"I'll distract him. Run, Avani. Look at me," I felt my eyes blur on Alisha. "I love you so much—"

"Didi—"

"Listen to me!" Alisha snapped. *"Find Reed. Reed will love you so much. Always. I'm so proud of you.* You are the smartest woman I know, and I am so honored to have been your sister. Thank you for making me better. *I promise, I love you.* Run for your life. Do you understand me?"

Nonononononono. Thierry. Where are you?

I couldn't stop breaking down now. I didn't want to lose her. Not like this. I wasn't going to leave her. Not her.

Alisha. I can't.

"Avani, run."

But if I didn't run what if Reed never found us? What if Reed never knew where we were? What if nobody knew? I could go outside and call Thierry. Get help from him.

I felt my resolve as I nodded to find Reed. And Thierry. I began to shake in my bonds just as the door to the basement open and bone-chilling fear swept over me.

Terror like nothing I had experienced was in my bones now as I felt the anxiety constricting around my throat as I saw him. That man from before. I wanted to upchuck everything I ate at the diner.

"Nice to see you're finally up." He was focused on Alisha. I lowered my eyes since he clearly had never been interested in me.

That was the man who always stared at my sister.

The one she had never noticed.

"Thought you got rid of me?"

"What do you want with us?" Alisha puffed out she was trying her hardest to hold her composure, and I saw the defiance in her eyes.

I would never again ever think my sister being a model meant she couldn't handle herself.

I heard nothing he said. It all felt like a fever dream. I couldn't even focus.

I prayed that Thierry had gotten to the diner and realized something happened to us.

Or Kellan. Kellan could call Reed. Someone had to be coming for us right?

Someone had to know we were trapped.

"You always take everything."

He was griping about something to Alisha.

What was he talking about?

I could see the confusion etched on Alisha's face. "What?"

He was clinically insane. "Don't play dumb with me, you little cunt. You know exactly what you did." He started towards me, his voice dripping with venom and I felt myself beginning to shake. "Don't worry, one of you will pay."

And I couldn't hold it back anymore squirming in my ties feeling the scream trapped in my throat ready to emerge.

"You're right. It is my fault. I'm so sorry!"

He stilled in front of me turning back to my sister. What was she talking about? In the darkness I could only make out Alisha's haunted eyes, raven hair matted to her face.

"How could you ruin my life?" He said to Alisha with a hint of insanity in his tone. I felt myself shaking, trembling, violently.

What the bloody hell was this man even talking about?

"Please, untie me. I'll make it up to you." What on Earth was Alisha talking about?

"Why should I believe you after you slept with Whittaker?" The man said.

"I didn't sleep with him," Alisha shook her head. What? What was happening?

"Don't fucking—"

"I didn't," Alisha's voice was stronger and in that horrifying moment I understood was Alisha was doing. Again. She had always been the type of person to sacrifice herself. Always.

"He was annoying me. I don't love him. Maybe I want you instead." *ALISHA.* I wanted to scream at her because I knew he was going to hurt her and kill her—and then me and my eyes drifted to Selena still passed out.

Reed. Thierry. Where are you guys?

"I want to be with you," as Alisha said it her voice trembled. And I realized my sister was going to give herself up in the hopes of someone saving me and Selena. And I didn't know if Selena was alive.

"Is that so?" And then he dropped the bat grabbing Alisha and I held back my scream barely. Barely.

"Or is it a lie because I already killed one of you bitches?"

Selena.

I couldn't stop staring at the blood. I had woken up first. I had seen her and my heart had dropped to my stomach.

"Untie me. Take me upstairs."

I heard nothing else. Absolutely nothing else.

"No, take me! You can't—"

"Shut the fuck up! You're next." He aimed the bat at me.

And then I watched in horror as he took my sister upstairs. More like dragging her and I felt my fear exponentially rise as I realized I had to find someone.

Reed. Thierry.

Anyone.

"I can't lose Alisha!" I cried. "If anyone out there is listening! *Help me! Help her!"*

Struggling against my bonds I growled in frustration as I called for Selena to wake up. *Just wake up.*

And I felt my heart completely shatter and break as I knew what he might've been doing to Alisha.

How he might hurt her. How he hurt Selena. I couldn't look away from her.

I was trapped in a nightmare and I wasn't sure how to get out of it.

My heart was aching.

"There's so much I haven't done. I don't remember if I told Thierry I love him. Did I tell Lish?" I looked at the door she'd gone through and I couldn't stop crying.

My sister was through that door. I needed to get out of here. I began looking around for something. Anything.

Broken glass? Wood splinters? Something. I slowly lowered myself onto my knees to grab something off the ground, glass and I rose up again.

"Selena, if you can hear me, please wake up." I used the glass to slowly start chipping away at the bonds.

It was about halfway my descent into madness and dark shadows I heard a shot. A crack.

It sounded like a small explosion upstairs.

And I felt my eyes go wide, my mouth dropped.

And I began to scream bloody murder.

"Alisha!"

I DIDN'T REMEMBER ANYTHING AFTER THAT. NOT QUITE. ONE moment I was screaming.

The next, the door burst open and the brightest pair of amber eyes like headlights landed on me.

I was in the man's arms a second later, briefly aware of Kellan behind him, his eyes haunted on me.

Kellan.

This was Reed's. Oh, thank God.

The man was cutting me loose and tucking me into his arms.

I couldn't breathe. Was my sister okay? *"A-Alisha."*

The man with amber eyes practically hauled me out of there moving quicker than I thought possible, my head tucked into his neck as I cried out. *"Alisha."*

"I know. I know she's okay."

I hadn't stopped crying and I didn't see my sister. And even in my worst nightmares? I couldn't have predicted *this*.

"Close your eyes, close your eyes." The stranger kept whispering. *"Keep 'em closed. Don't look."*

347

I sobbed into his neck as he held my head tight to him. His grip felt like iron. "I gotcha. I know. I'm with Reed. It's okay." A sob of relief tore through me as he was racing out with me.

"I know, I know." He was getting into a car then and we were off and I was crying harder than ever. "Don't turn, don't open your eyes."

"Alisha!"

"Reed has her. I promise he's got her. But I got you. Okay? I got you, it's okay."

He kept reassuring me in his deeper voice until I felt my heart racing uncontrollably.

The panic rising until I couldn't breathe. He pulled me back then and I saw his eyes wide as he took me in.

We were in an ambulance.

"Hey, look at me. Look at me, Reed has your sister. I need to let the EMT's look at you." The man holding me said.

I turned my head to find two women watching me with empathy as one of them began tearing out IV bags and other things.

"Look at me, there you go." I focused on his eyes. "Focus on me, while the girls work, okay? Reed has Alisha. Reed has her." He kept repeating himself and reassuring me as I shook too wildly to do anything else.

All I knew was I didn't know if Alisha was all right, if Selena was dead, and where Thierry was. Did he know what happened?

I was shaking so hard, when the EMT's brought me to the hospital, he took me in his arms again and carried me in. In the distance I heard more sirens. I must've made a noise because he moved my head into his neck again telling me not to look.

"Don't open your eyes. I gotcha. I promise."

CHAPTER 37
AVANI

I DIDN'T KNOW HOW THE DAYS PASSED.

But my mind was on Alisha.

I didn't even know day or time it was anymore. I didn't have my phone and I didn't want to speak to anyone.

My head hurt all the time. My entire body ached and I felt like I wanted to throw up with the nausea I felt.

I just made it to the hospital and Kieran, the man who was by my side, stayed there like glue.

I felt numb to *everything*.

I couldn't stop crying.

Everyone said Alisha was injured but nobody said what happened. I hadn't seen her in days. Or Reed. I cried in my room unable to eat properly or do anything.

A doctor came into the room to examine me at one point.

Dr. Whittaker. Adam.

Was he…related to Reed?

He certainly looked like him.

I barely heard the words coming out of his mouth. I was uncomfortable, in pain, and I just wanted my sister. Thierry. My family.

Kieran was there the entire time on the other side of the curtains when the nurses had helped me with my clothes folding them into a pile.

I didn't feel any of my injuries. I felt pain all over. It wasn't localized to one spot.

Like the agony I felt at almost losing my sister. I barely remembered the conversation. In that time, I didn't have my phone. I didn't know how to get to Thierry. He must've been worried.

Did he know how to find me? I couldn't stop freaking out.

And it only got worse the day a blonde-haired man appeared with pale blue eyes on me. He was over six-five and enormous. Bigger than Reed. He took up all the space in the room and took the air with it.

Kieran immediately adjusted us ducking his head when the man walked in and I knew something was wrong when I saw the folder in his hand.

I felt my heart racing.

My panic never-ending it seemed in the last few days.

It was endlessly colder in the room when he sat down across from me and Kieran watching over us as he murmured his words, barely speaking above a whisper.

He was so intense, I was sure if he spoke beyond that it would've terrified me even more.

I heard his words through a fog, his pale blue eyes on me and my heart was racing even more.

"I work with Reed. My name's Gabriel. I thought I might come by and give you some paperwork. I don't even need your signature for it, I can handle everything. But this is…" he trailed off looking at Kieran and suddenly his eyes hardened like a predators before he looked back. "This paperback is for you to have in case anything happens to Alisha—"

And just like I knew. "She's not okay."

My words came out as a whisper and he shook his head.

"No, she's all right. She's going to be. This is to cover our bases…"

He kept speaking but I didn't even hear him. I couldn't.

I felt like I was in a spiral of never ending chaos and pain.

My chest rose and fell harder and if he knew his words sent me into a panic attack he just stopped talking.

I didn't see or hear anything or anyone.

I just kept on crying.

And finally, I didn't know how long time passed—but finally Kieran came in one day and told me the one thing I waited to hear.

"Your sister's awake. Do you want to go see her?"

I was scrambling up before he even finished his sentence.

～

It took Reed twenty-four hours to get Alisha and me out of the hospital and into K2.

The blonde man from earlier, Gabriel, he explained to us what happened. That Alisha's overzealous fan was actually a stalker turned killer. It was our former doorman.

The man who gave me the creeps all the time. Alisha didn't even remember but I had.

He had been out to get her and me.

He had hurt Selena. Who was alive, but barely. That made me break down since I genuinely liked Selena when I met her. She'd been a pretty and nice woman who had occasionally checked in on me at school.

Gabriel calmly spoke to us while Reed looked on stone-faced. Kieran stood outside giving us all privacy.

I had hugged Alisha and held onto for a long time crying. I'd almost lost my sister and the panic had been terrifying. My head felt off.

I felt like I was navigating life in a fog.

"Reed wants us to stay at K2," she murmured brushing my hair back while I laid on her in her hospital bed.

Reed and his friend Gabriel had left us to ourselves thankfully. Kieran stood outside our door.

"I want to stay with you."

I had my own apartment and sometimes I went to Thierry's but the thought of finally being able to text him again—he must've been worried sick—filled me with relief.

Which was fine with me. I didn't want to let go of Alisha ever again but my mind couldn't stop racing about Thierry.

How did I get in touch with him?

As we left the ward we were I was a little overwhelmed by the sweet fragrances of flowers everywhere.

In all shades of pink covering the halls, the desks, the windows.

To the point where I thought it was someone's wedding.

They were everywhere. And cupcakes. Cookies. Sandwiches.

Someone had gotten catering?

I recognized the sandwiches.

They were from Butterscotch's. *My favorite bakery...*

I nabbed some red-velvet cupcakes with Alisha in tow wearing sweats and sunglasses looking out of place with Reed beside her.

Kieran smiled down at me as he handed me a bag for my cupcakes. It was all free grabs for everyone.

"Who sent these?" I asked him.

He shrugged handing me some more in a case. "Nobody knows but they keep coming in by the dozens with a note that it's for everyone."

He handed me a note. At the bottom of it was a pink heart.

I blinked a little astounded a little by the sheer amount of pale pink flowers everywhere.

It was seas of pink.

"I love pink carnations." *Thierry knew...could it...no.*

Why would he send this many?

How would he know where I was? How did he...

No. It couldn't be.

I swallowed my emotions. "I need to get a phone."

Reed who had kept an ear out for me turned to me as we walked out explaining. "I can get you a brand new set of everything when we get back to K2, is that all right with you? I know Gabriel is working out your school situation right now. He'll be in touch with me once he's got that figured out."

School situation?

God...my degree...I didn't even think about anything but feeling the loss of Alisha as I nodded dumbly.

Reed's smile was tight, his eyes usually bright now tired on his sleep-deprived expression. He hadn't left Alisha's side.

Reed put an arm around me as he held Alisha's hand walking out with us. He held me close enough to him that I snuggled into his warmth. Taking strength from him.

We piled into K2, Alisha going in Reed's car and I was in Kieran's. I didn't want to say a word as we got there. My eyes kept searching for Thierry everywhere. But he wasn't here.

I didn't even speak until we got to K2, the imposing structure Kieran took me too.

I felt my hands curling into my lap, my fingers colder than ever now.

I didn't even focus on Kieran saying something to me.

"You good?" Kieran had a slight accent like he was from somewhere that wasn't New York.

I nodded ducking my head aware I looked awful from crying, from freaking out, from everything.

A headache was blossoming behind my head and I felt it throbbing behind my right eye.

"Reed lives up at the top floor, I have a key card from him so I can show you how to get to him if you ever come alone…" he began walking me through the process from the garage. The back of my neck prickled as I looked into the darker section of the garage.

I turned over my shoulder expecting to find Thierry in the shadows. But no, nobody was there.

Where was he?

∼

REED'S ENTIRE APARTMENT LOOKED LIKE OUR OLD APARTMENT.

He had clearly done his research.

From the colorful throws, to the white couch and artwork. Alisha gaped as I walked around.

I was staying with my family for the next few days. I didn't want to leave them ever.

Eventually I could go back to school since Gabriel had told me he had gotten it to where I could do all my classes online.

And I had a therapist I could check in with for what happened. It took Reed a few hours to hand me all the things I needed.

A new phone, an e-reader I could use his card to purchase books on.

I was more concerned with getting to my room.

Reed showed me and Kieran around and the idea of not taking a shower in the hospital again was the most enticing thing. Well, second most enticing.

Using my new phone the first thing I did was dial Thierry's number. I had it memorized.

It had been almost a week since I had spoken to him.

He was supposed to come and pick me up…now where was he?

The moment I had been waiting for approached as I sat on my new bed for now and began typing in his number.

The phone didn't even ring. *The number you have reached has been disconnected.*

What?

I tried again. And again. And again.

Same thing. Maybe I had the wrong number.

I probably missed a digit. Maybe two?

I was wrong.

He wouldn't…why would he drop off the face of the Earth?

And I completely shattered at the fear coming in waves through me.

It grew and grew until it was suffocating.

"Thierry?" I croaked. *"What happened? Where are you?"*

I tried again and again until I heard a knock at my door.

"Avani." It was Kieran. "You good?"

"I'm fine!" I croaked out dropping the phone from my hands like it was an offensive object.

What just happened?

Where was my boyfriend?

CHAPTER 38
THIERRY

I DROPPED OFF THE FACE OF THE EARTH THE FIRST WEEK AVANI WAS in the hospital.

Disconnected my number. Erased my presence off everything.

After months of domestic bliss, softness, and almost…a lull in my life?

It had kicked back up to the insanity I knew it was.

The moment I shot the guy attacking Alisha, Reed and his team was bursting in and I ducked.

Moving so fast I didn't think twice about escaping. Except my car was fucking parked near the scene. And my only thought was to see Avani.

Only Avani.

Reed was moving with Alisha covered in his jacket in his arms. *Where was Avani?*

This anxiety in me was new, twisting my heart like a wet rag as I waited for my girl to appear. Anything. I searched the sea of people for her. Until she did.

Alive. Crying. I rushed to the edge of the rooftop staring at her in the night. I knew her anywhere, her shape. In the arms of another operative.

I narrowed my eyes. It was dark but I could make him out. Didn't I know him? He looked awfully—*O'Hara.*

I knew Teo's fucking friend.

Oh. Motherfucker.

355

He was a fucking Titan?

Shitshitshitshitshit.

I saw him put Avani into an ambulance. Was she hurt? Was she all right? I didn't wait to find out.

I moved so fucking fast calming down when the agents and operatives around me moved.

I got to my car and thankfully, I'd parked far enough towards the end of the street to not get stuck with the paramedics.

I started my car tossing the duffle into the backseat tearing off to the hospital. On the drive my mind was a mess. No longer what it used to be.

Whatever logic and reasonable thoughts I had, had been erased, leaving only Avani's eyes in my vision. Her laughter. Her scent in my car.

The pink gloss in the cupholder between us. Her cupcakes on my kitchen island. Images of her began playing back to me. Over and over in my head like a loop.

I couldn't lose her. I can't lose her.

I'd find her again. I could talk to her. I could tell her...

What? Tell her what?

Oh, sorry Avani I'm the sniper who killed the man who shot your sister? No big deal. Just my former day job.

Oh and by the way? I'm a fucking assassin.

Right. I had a better chance of scaling a ladder to the Moon.

I followed them close enough parking on an upper level to watch as Kieran fucking O'Hara carried Avani out into the hospital.

I recognized it from the documents Teo had. That place was owned by Reed. I couldn't walk in there and expose myself.

Alma's voice materialized in my head. She had trained me for years to be a tougher solider.

It doesn't matter if she is. Breathe.

You cannot walk in there and worry about her without fifty agents surrounding you.

This is not the time for your love story.

"Then when?"

But the voice in my head that was my trainer's? Was correct. I need to have a plan.

The first part of it was vanishing for a little for security. I needed to erase my location. My phone.

356

Wipe it clean and pretend like I didn't exist. Lay low until otherwise.

I was back to being a ghost.

Because no fucking way Reed Whittaker could know about me. *Not now.*

Teo raised a brow as he watched me in his office now one week later. I was miserable.

mon coeur was out there without me. At K2. And she hadn't left in a week.

"It's been a week since they were attacked...Jace says..."

I barely heard registered his voice in my mind as he relayed information Jace had. The fucking doorman attacked them.

Even after Alisha moved out.

I should've just fucking killed him that night. Avani was asleep, Alisha would've been tipsy.

"I could've killed him and buried him half alive and made him scream," I muttered absently.

I knew ninety different ways to kill a man. And I'd never get caught. I've been so caught up in her, I didn't even think about killing him that night. But I should've.

"What?" Teo asked looking up from his notes. "Did you hear me? Jace says someone shot at Lucas."

I sat up. "What?"

Teo nodded. "Someone shot at Lucas. He says he picked up the footage from the parking garage before someone else wiped it." He passed me a surveillance shot. "Recognize this woman?"

I looked down. And swore rolling my eyes. "Why the fuck am I not surprised trigger happy Samara would shoot at him?" I recognized that lean form and the braids anywhere. She wasn't even covering her face.

She was too cocky. And I was scared she'd get caught.

Teo swore. "You need to talk to her. If she's the crazy one, she needs to calm down. She can't just go shooting him in public parking lots even if Bexley is erasing her footprints—Jace says it's risky. Can you talk to Bexley and make sure her idiot friend doesn't kill mine?"

"Yeah." Because of having to ghost, my girlfriend temporarily wasn't bad enough. I was now currently juggling two different organizations who are at war with each other.

Fucking.

Fantastic.

My thoughts were of the last image I had of Avani who was thankfully alive. I saw her shivering. I saw her awake.

My heart.

"They just got back to K2." He rolled his eyes. "Kieran is with them. I could always just really ask him for information. He's guarding the little one." My little one. My girl. Not his.

"I don't trust your little friend as far I can see," I muttered. "Isn't he mob?"

"Former mob," Teo said. "His brother's Killian and Aidan are in charge. You'd like him. He's a little older than you but he's a younger brother—"

Not likely. I didn't like the sight of my heart in his arms. I didn't care if he helped her. I saved her.

I raised a skeptical brow contemplating murder if he did touch my girl when she was vulnerable. "I doubt it."

Teo chuckled. My jaw clenched involuntarily.

Kieran O'Hara would lose fingers before he touched my girl.

But I masked that emotion because if Teo caught a whiff of my desire he'd never let me live it down. And I was toeing my lines finely.

All of my secrets were like cards in my hand. Jace hadn't told Teo about Avani.

He'd also been the one to use a patsy to get the girls whatever I recommended from Butterscotch's and enough flowers to hide it all from us. Jace had enough patsy connections around town.

And whatever mental condition she was in? I couldn't get close enough to her to help her. I knew better. Titan territory was off limits for me. All across the board.

That didn't mean I couldn't be there for her.

Nobody would know it was me.

"Bexley and Samara are going to stir up trouble, if someone doesn't get involved."

"And Alma?" Teo asked. "Where is she?"

Teo was pissed off with Reed, but I only cared about one thing.

The last week of my life had been a blur.

I shrugged, pretending to be casual about it but I knew it bothered me.

"Bexley won't tell me where she is. But I'll figure it out. Alma can't be far. She left the Kindcaid brother's with Natasha. Which means she isn't worried about a *fight*. And we both know Samara is trigger happy enough to shoot a Titan to send a message."

"Jace says he's looking for a connection between Gabriel Monroe and Lucas," Teo murmured. "Jace thinks something happened in the past to link them together. He thinks if he can find what the link is between them, it'll be another piece of the puzzle."

"Evie Monroe/Whittaker is a secret."

Teo nodded. "She's definitely related to one of them. But I don't know which one."

"Any luck on finding Lucy Devereaux?"

Teo shook his head. "She's hiding. She's good at what she does. But you'll never believe who she was last seen with."

I frowned as he explained. "Jesus. Christ."

Teo laughed. "And the web get's bigger. Lucy Devereaux is dating Reed's brother, Adam Whittaker. Well half-brother."

"There's no fucking way Reed doesn't know this."

Teo smirked. "The two brother's don't speak. As it turns out, the younger one is a doctor. His father passed away a few years ago. But his father is not his father."

I was going to lose my mind.

"Why the fuck is everyone from this organization a fucking secret? Why does everybody have nineteen different names? Why is this also confusing?" I was snapping. "Lucy is dating Adam!"

Teo laughed at my expression. "And her brother is dating Evie."

"Those fucking—" I swore louder to Teo's laughter. I huffed out a deep breath. "I'm going insane. Does Jace know what Lucy stole?"

Teo shook his head. "Negative. But he says she was with Adam, which means—"

"Talon knows she was with Adam Whittaker." The doctor. "And let me fucking guess, he works at the same hospital Alisha was taken to."

"As the American's say, 'Bingo," Teo smirked. "You need to talk to Samara. She cannot kill Lucas. It doesn't matter what Gabriel thinks, the fact that he's around the Titans and dating one of them if Samara kills him, they'll wage war against Talon. Objects be damned."

I knew. I had to go now and pay them a fucking visit.

∼

I drove to the Primrose Hotel in Midtown to visit Bexley Carter. She would know where Samara was.

The entire drive over there something about Evie that was bothering me. There's something about that girl. And I couldn't put my finger on it. But something about her rub me the wrong way.

It was her eyes. I got the feeling someone was hiding her from the world...but why?

Who was she?

Nobody had two different names to be normal.

No. Whittaker and Monroe were hiding her. Not to mention, Talon was now threatening Lucas's company. Probably Natasha from Cape Verde. The Nash Group was in the heart of the city.

Because Natasha couldn't walk properly, she used her brain.

The strategist of Talon.

Whatever the object was that Lucy stole must've been important enough to Alma to slowly start driving everybody insane. She wouldn't tell me what it was, but I knew that it must've meant a lot to her because most of the time, she didn't really bother anybody. She pretty much kept to herself, and Talia really liked her.

Talia had no idea Alma was in town.

Because of Drew.

Nobody wanted to tell Talia. And I sure as fuck wasn't about to open yet another entanglement.

I left Andrei's old apartment fully and Teo cleared it out of all signs of me understanding full well why I wanted my space.

I packed all my photos and my memories up...for the ninetieth time. Only this time when I had packed...I felt a crack where my heart was.

Because Andrei's apartment had turned into my home with Avani there. My memories on the fridge.

My dates with her marked off. Her handwriting. My vision blurred a little at the idea of losing mon coeur.

I couldn't let that happen. I refused.

But the moment I had seen the fucking Polaroid's in that box—I lost my fucking mind.

Just because I couldn't talk to her right now while she was at K2 didn't mean I wasn't planning on seeing her.

The moment she got back to her apartment I'd be on her. She hadn't moved out. Jace said she was still a student.

I had never considered it a possibility that Avani might drop out of school. Not her.

Not when I knew education was the most important thing to her. But then again, she had been kidnapped. My hands gripped the steering wheel imaging for a second what my heart went through.

And the agony was back. The image of her photos in a cardboard box. All of it just wiped.

The empty fridge was the worst part of Andrei's now scraped apartment. All signs of life gone.

I packed anything Avani left behind myself. A pink sweater. Her chunky socks. A hairbrush she left with me.

I packed it into a box and moved it with me to the warehouse I now lived in.

Location change. Check.

For safety and my secrecy, I knew as much as it gutted me—I didn't need fifty Titan operatives blowing up my door to take me in for crimes I may have committed while working for Talia.

Avani was under Reed Whittaker's protection, Teo told me as much. I didn't need it traced back to me. In any way. As much as it didn't sit right with me?

Avani was vulnerable right now. If she brought me up?

She'd be bringing up a Thierry Mattison that no longer existed. Nothing real.

Jace had scraped me from any location I had been to tracking my GPS.

Reed wasn't the only professional who was good at his job.

I needed to figure out how to safely talk to her, explain to her potentially what I was and what I'd done. When she was out of K2. I knew my heart—I knew she might be staying with her sister. This wasn't about Reed.

It was always about Alisha.

Retreat. Regroup. Re-assess.

I made it to the Primrose and went upstairs the elegant feminine hotel to see Bexley.

At nineteen, Bexley was a prodigy.

She was good at what she did for Talon. She'd been trained by several people within Nash Group before emerging on her own in her own right.

I knocked on Bexley's hotel room door twice hearing K-POP

music from inside. Avani would get along with Bexley too, but I didn't trust Bexley since she was Alma's little hacker.

Through the music I heard the sound of something falling and then the patter of footsteps.

"Coming!" Opening the door wide stood a maybe five foot tall blonde with two space buns and a romper.

I only knew what it was called because Bexley only wore rompers. The ones that flared out like skirts so she looked perpetually like a child.

Big blue eyes bright and wild landed on me and a smile stretched her lips revealing rows of white teeth and the two fangs she had on either side of her mouth she'd gotten shaved into her teeth.

"*Grim!*"

"*Don't bite me.*"

It wasn't my first time seeing her in person here. But every single time I saw her she lit up.

Light laughter filled me as she hugged me tight. My nickname still held once Alma trained me and realized—I never missed a target.

"You missed me, short stack?"

"Duh," she rolled her eyes as I walked in her room and winced.

Now that she was alone, the room was technological chaos.

Wires everywhere and her laptop and speaker set up like some tech display of a wild nerd she was.

The feminine room looked at odds with her technology and the piles of candy she had at her desk.

"Please tell me you leave the room at some point?" I asked eyeing her dirty clothes pile. "At *any* point in time."

Bexley had been a stray Alma picked up from an orphanage, I was pretty sure she was a mix of South African and Dutch and something else.

But I couldn't tell. Everyone at Talon was a variant of multiple races.

"I got news for you," she chirped too happy. "One, I hate going outside. This city is cold. I hate it here. I only came because Alma wants her stuff back—"

"Which is—"

"*Nothing*," she said too quickly, her eyes darting to her computer screen as she sat down. Right. I'd figure it out.

"And second of all," she continued next with the voice of a narrator on a TV show. "Previously on this episode of Talon, Adam Whittaker *was* dating our ye old thief, Lucy Devereaux."

She stopped and turned to me. "Don't freak out. I think Samara fired a shot to scare Lucas."

Well. I had come here to talk to her about all this but she began relaying information to me. She thought I was here to help her.

I knew I was here for information.

Bexley waved her hands around in a staying motion.

"*No*. I said she fired a warning shot to scare him. We can't be sure which team Lucy is on. Lucas's father sold him out even though that idiot worked for Malcolm. So I think either Lucas is getting greedy because of who his father is, you know apples, trees, bananas—"

"*Carter*," I shot her a look. "*Focus*. Lucas Devereaux isn't a thief—"

"His sister is—"

"He's not close to her." I didn't think he was. By what Teo said? They hadn't spoken in years? I didn't know.

"Right," she gave me a guilty expression. "*So*, I don't see any reason why someone like Reed Whittaker would even dream of stealing anything from us. He has no ties to the Nash family. No ties to anyone we know. The most likely candidate is Lucas."

"Except Lucy hasn't seen her brother since coming to New York."

"Correct. Which means she's working for Reed. They met up in Titan Midtown. I know that much. But why does Reed Whittaker want a necklace? You know, Alma was posing as Lucas's secretary recently, and she wanted me to look up this girl."

Carter pulled up a file of Evie Whittaker. I read the notes.

"It says here she's Reed's cousin. But they look nothing alike. They don't have the same parents that are siblings. In fact, Evie doesn't have parents at all. Weird, much? Reed grew up on the East Coast. And then when Lucas mentioned her, he called her Monroe. Alma thought it had to be a slip up. In the system she's Whittaker. Until I posed the question. Why would one person have two names?"

Oh. Fuck. Me.

I looked at Evie Whittaker/Monroe. "*Someone's* protecting her."

And she has a third name they're protecting. I knew this. We were working on it.

Carter nodded. "Do you think she could be…" she trailed off her eyes downcast. I knew what she was asking.

"A victim of trafficking? No, unlikely. The Titan's aren't Malcolm Nash. They won't do that. Even I know they're not stupid." I pointed at Evie standing near Carter. "Does she look familiar to you?"

Carter frowned. "I thought so when I saw her, but I don't know where from."

That's what I said.

"But I feel like her third name is important. Because they're hiding it. I think Alma knows that too. I'm curious so I started digging but I keep getting shut down by their hacker."

But I couldn't get Evie out of my sight. Something about her bothered me even now.

I couldn't put my fucking finger on it.

"I feel like we're missing someone. She does look familiar to me." Bexley frowned. Bexley didn't know that Jace had more information. He was our team.

She didn't know he hid everything that was even remotely on the web taking it down before she got her hands on it.

Bexley didn't know I was playing chess.

Only I could see both boards.

And hers didn't have much. I felt bad, but I had to protect more than destroy now. I kept my voice neutral. "Alma doesn't recognize her?"

Carter shook her head. "Alma said she doesn't know any of the Titan's. Have you seen Adam? I know he's technically with Lucy but, he's cute." She chirped over her shoulder.

She pulled a photo of Adam Whittaker. And I bit back a laugh. "You have a crush on Adam Whittaker?"

She grinned. "Isn't he adorable? Look at his face. Look at his smile…" she let out a dreamy sigh. "I might be sad if Samara actually kills him, but check this out, ever since Lucy went missing, he's technically single." Her smile turned devious. "Bwauahaha."

"Careful, you go falling for a Titan and Alma might ex-communicate you."

"I never said I would fall for Adam," Bexley grinned. "I said he's cute. You got news for me?"

Nothing I could tell her.

"None. When you decided you wanna tell me where Alma is, let me know. And let me know when you dig up Evie's real name."

"I think Reed Whittaker has someone on his team fucking with me."

I turned back to her as she pulled up her screens.

"He's got a hacker on his team. Keeps sending me this."

She clicked on her screen and it opened up to an image of a jack in the box.

"A little creepy but you'll see."

When it pop open it held up a sign that said.

Nice try, shortcake.

"He calls me shortcake. Who the fuck is this?" Carter looked peeved. "I'm not that short. I don't even have a camera on this laptop. How does he know who I am?"

A sickening feeling entered my stomach.

"Can he see you?"

"Impossible," she said. "I locked this bitch down when I got here. He hasn't cracked anything on my end. He's fucking with my head."

That he was. But he was doing it to everyone.

Earlier Jace had mentioned to Teo that *someone* was covering the Titan's tracks. The Titan's had their own personal hacker. Someone good.

Someone knowledgable enough that Jace was aware Reed had someone on his team that was *good*.

He hadn't figured out who.

I chewed on my cheek as I considered what I did know.

"Tell Samara not to kill Adam or Lucas. We don't want war in this territory. I'll find out what I have to. Send me what you have on Lucy Devereaux. I'll go and check out her apartment and the Locksmith Pub."

Bexley pouted. "I have to make sure the Titan's hacker doesn't chew my network out. Reed Whittaker's hospital and Midtown location are locked down. I found a tiny weakness in K2's security but the hacker locked me out again."

"So they're good." Jace said as much. He was working on getting under their network now.

Her eyes looked wide at me. "He keeps sending me a jack in the box like a present every time I hit his walls. But I know I get further every single time. I feel like he's testing me." She turned back to her computer. "I feel like…he's waiting to see how far I'll go. And then he might attack me. Which is why I haven't been able to get much info."

Which was why Jace was hiding himself.

She bit her lip. "I know Alma wants to tear Titan out but… they're good at what they do…"

"But you are too."

She nodded looking proud. "I miss you, Grim."

"I miss you too, kid." I rubbed her hair between her space buns. She was adorable. A little insane. But adorable. "Don't cause too much trouble. Now tell me where Samara is."

"She's out hunting. She's got eyes on Lucas."

I frowned. Not good. Samara wouldn't listen to anybody. Except Alma.

She turned back and pulled up a photo of Adam Whittaker and gave a dreamy sigh. "Ahh, if only I didn't hate hospitals. I'd love to meet him."

"Tell Samara she cannot kill Lucas."

Bexley's eyes turned up to me. "She won't kill him first. Probably torture him."

I was afraid of that.

And then when I stepped outside the hotel I called Jace.

"Bexley just told me the Titan's have a hacker. He keeps sending her a jack in the box image, it moves and it pops up with a message."

He was quiet on the other end. "A jack in the box?"

"Yeah, are you familiar with it?"

"No, but Reed Whittaker has someone working for him, he's good. He can't see me. I made sure of it. I can see where Bexley is trying to enter his network. I found her, she needs to be more discreet because I've been tagging on her trail…" he mumbled about how he was following Bexley into the Titan's network. I wasn't an IT guy, but basically what Jace was saying was—he was hiding behind Bexley.

"The jack in the box sounds familiar," he muttered. "I have to look into who that is. For now, you might wanna tell Bexley to take a step back. He is testing her. And if she walks into his traps—"

"He has her and everyone else."

"Exactly." Jace didn't sound pleased as he paused. "You said the Titan hacker called her shortcake?"

"Yeah, why?"

Jace swore a little. "If she's got the camera's locked down, how does he know?" That's what I was worried about.

"I don't know. Do you have any idea how you're going to find out who the Titan hacker is?"

"I'm working on it. But I'm trying not to get too close. I think whoever he is, he might be aware I'm there as well. I wouldn't put it past him to be taunting me too." He paused. "I have an update for your girl. She's taking online classes now." I let out a breath.

"Is she…" I trailed off. "Is she coming back to her apartment?"

"I saw a note in there that said she might return in a week or so, after her birthday."

Her birthday. I'd miss that too. *Motherfucker*. I swore.

"Thank you. Any more updates on them let me know."

"Yes, sir."

One key thing hit me on the drive to my new warehouse.

Carter kept mentioning Reed.

She never mentioned Gabriel. She only has the information she was able to dig out.

Jace had more. Teo and I have more.

And for now, Gabriel Monroe and his mysteries would stay a secret. For now.

Jace was putting together a timeline for us to review.

Right after I figured out how not to get Lucas killed, Evie's real identity, why Reed and Lucy stole the object from Talon, and oh managing to keep my identity hidden from everybody.

I sighed and took a deep breath in my car. "mon coeur, I have bitten off more than I can chew. And I miss you."

I looked down at her lip gloss in my car.

"Gabriel Monroe is the epicenter of all this. I just know it." I turned back to the road. "But how?"

Soon. Eventually, I'd unravel everything Gabriel Monroe was hiding.

All his secrets.

And I'd get my girl back.

CHAPTER 39
AVANI

THE FIRST WEEK AT K2 PASSED IN A HAZE.

Kieran became my constant companion through it with Alisha and I spending more time together there.

It felt so good to be under the same roof as her…but I also felt displaced.

Alisha had done a few voice acting roles in her past. I was now acting full time. Pasting on a smile. Putting my hair back. Wearing decent clothes.

I felt dead on the inside.

It wasn't just about being kidnapped.

This went beyond that. I had lost my apartment, my life, almost lost Alisha, lost my boyfriend, and now I was…acting my best role of younger sister in K2.

Everything felt surreal to me like I was watching my life through those blurry windows they put in offices for privacy.

Kieran often spent time with me in my room or outside on the living room couches talking to me everything and nothing at all. I stared off into space aware if I even remotely uttered a single word —I might shatter.

I knew Kieran was hired by Reed. He was a Titan.

I knew he was my guard and he was keeping reoccupied to make sure nothing happened to me.

Like now while he sat next to me and was eating peanut chocolate candies and popcorn while watching a show with me.

I went to go grab one and Kieran without looking at me handed me some of the orange ones.

I smiled a little as I took it munching on peanut m&m's.

Objectively, even if my heart ached Kieran was handsome. Tall, tanned skin, handsome with his curling chocolate hair and tattoos scattered on his body.

I caught a glimpse every so often.

Now I blushed at the thought of how I had clung to him when he'd been with me in the hospital during the worst moments of my life to date.

Back at the hospital, I had been in a manic state grabbing at him like he was my lifeline. His face had been the first thing I had seen. And I latched onto him.

Now, with my hair up and long pajamas on, I sat watching some mystery movie Kieran said Reed had. Reed loved murder mysteries.

"Do you want some more s'mores or a heated blanket?"

He was also attentive.

I glanced over at him and he smiled easily.

"I'll go and make some tea." I stood slowly as he motioned for me to sit. "No, I insist, I need to get up. If I keep eating like this I'll become a s'more." I joked weakly.

Kieran grinned his teeth flashing. "Fine, but don't tell Reed I didn't do it because he might fire me."

My lips stretched wider as I walked into the kitchen to grab some tea for myself. "I wouldn't dare."

My eyes watered as I focused on the task the ache intensifying from losing someone I loved. Again. I had Alisha. But I lost…my boyfriend? Had it even been real?

Reed and Alisha had gone out for a quick date leaving me with Kieran who was good company.

Over the past few days Alisha had been more attentive to me, more than she ever was.

Almost like losing each other had stirred up different emotions now.

She sometimes fell asleep next to me and Reed found us together all the time.

When she wasn't home, Reed was working with Kieran letting me Reed while they walked the building.

I checked my phone like a compulsive addict on my spare time.

Marissa and Rosalie blew my phone up and I carefully omitted out any excess details in the group chat. I avoided talking to them. If I spoke out loud? I might break.

The official story was I had gotten sick.

The specific request came from Gabriel.

When I had first met him at the hospital, he had been a force of nature in my room. I met him and again since coming to K2. Since Alisha would go out to brunch sometimes with him, his taller handsome form taking up all the space in the room as my sister spent time with him.

This was the Gabriel handing all of my paperwork, my school-work which now I had via online classes.

It had been a trip explaining to my friends why I had been missing for so long. But Gabriel had been the one to sit me down alone in the guest room at K2. Alone.

"I know you have a life outside of Alisha, but I'm asking you to not mention anything about us to anyone."

His tone had been gentle and firm as he explained that Reed's company operated on discretion.

And that it wasn't common for civilians to even be this close to them. Ie, me and Alisha.

He sat with me for a bit quietly telling me about Titan. I was surprised it wasn't Reed.

"Reed and I do better splitting our personal lives letting the other handle it. He takes care of my half and I take care of his."

"I'm sorry I freaked out on you," I murmured to him feeling shy under his gaze. But his gaze was warm on me like Reed's.

Gabriel reminded me of the demon pirate king Damon's old mentor, Raphael.

He was blonde and charming handsome angel, but Raphael was a notorious womanizer who taught Damon everything and secretly helped Damon.

"You don't have to apologize," Gabriel looked almost affronted I would.

It snapped me back to reality instead of imagining a shirtless Gabriel wielding a sword and wings.

This Gabriel had had taken off his grey suit jacket leaving him in his white dress shirt and tie off.

His wheat-colored hair reminded me a little of Kellan's.

But his eyes were the iciest pale shade of blue one could get.

"You should never apologize. It isn't wrong to feel things."

"I still feel bad—"

"*You* thought you almost lost your sister." His eyes softened tremendously as he said that. "It's a lot. You don't ever have to apologize for feeling anything. If you need me, you have my number."

Back at the hospital he had been a little terrifying but up close, Gabriel Monroe was awfully soft and sweet. I imagined Gabriel gave good hugs with those broad shoulders of his.

I nodded and Gabriel smiled politely at me his eyes watching me with something there.

"That paperwork you signed still stands even after you turn eighteen which I know is in a few days. If anything ever happens, you're still his family. So you never have to worry. Nothing will happen to Lish. You're all right."

"Thank you," I murmured unsure of what to say.

"If Reed isn't there for you, if you need anything—call me." I had his number. "Anything at all. No matter what time. No matter what. Do you understand?"

At his tone, I blinked up at him. I was sitting against the headboard and he had pulled up a chair but right now I felt it like he was staring into my soul with those eyes. I nodded dumbly.

"Anything," he repeated. "Call me."

Ducking my head almost embarrassed around him, Alisha chose that moment to knock and poke her head in, her eyes landing on us. Gabriel straightened a little as he saw her.

Alisha grinned at us, her hair swinging loose around her. "Dinner's ready both of you. Come on."

And that night I had dinner with Gabriel and Reed and Alisha.

The three of them got on well and I got some time to ruminate. Once Gabriel was around me like a normal man, I didn't panic much. He came over with snacks and spent time with Alisha more than anyone else.

Reed got together with him and the three of them sounded like good friends.

Gabriel had been the one at the hospital to explain what happened to me and Alisha. And Selena.

We weren't allowed to see Selena, not technically, but Kieran had convinced his older brother Killian, whose girlfriend was Selena's nurse. Nisha Graham. A sweet faced woman who told us we could have a few minutes and the three of them watched over me.

I had seen Selena briefly and she looked like half of the person I had met weeks prior.

Life was moving on around me.

But me. I

had hid inside of K2 curled up next to someone or another.

Sometimes Reed spent the evenings watching episodes of mystery shows or crime dramas.

And he just let me curl into him while we both watched until I fell asleep. He didn't say much to me but held me tighter.

I made some tea mechanically until I saw Kieran at the door.

I didn't realize I had been standing at the counter staring at the empty cup with a tea bag just sitting in it.

"Hey, you good? Not spacing out are ya?"

His eyes were concerned as he watched me.

But the ache where Thierry vanished filled me like a gaping wound. Some parts of me healed. Other parts of me had nightmares.

All of me needed a heart it didn't have.

I couldn't even go by myself to visit Andrei's apartment. And look like a crazy woman? I had left my hair brush with him, but Reed had not only given me a new phone and laptop and everything else.

Anything I needed he told me to order or Kieran to order. I should've been so grateful. Nothing was off-limits. But all I felt was an aching loss.

I felt nervous at first until Kieran teased that Reed had billions to give and his wallet could use a little workout.

Reed's not exactly buying himself Roadsters every other week, you know what I mean? A few million here and there he won't miss it.

I'd purchased books to drown out the rest of my emotions. Reed volunteered Kieran to build me a library in the guest room, and some pajamas, which then led to candles and flowers, and then led to chocolates—it was endless, but Kieran encouraged me to shop my heart out.

"I'm all right," I finished making my tea as I looked at him. He was handsome. But…not for me. "I'm finished. Can you grab some more s'mores and we can head back to watching someone get chopped up?"

His grin widened. "Yeah. I can."

Kieran spent more time with me than he did not with me and having a friend was nice.

He reminded me a little of Ben.

Someone who was nice to everyone. Someone I didn't really feel anything for. He wasn't Thierry. Nobody was. And I didn't know how to tell Reed how devastated I felt.

~

"Happy Birthday!"

Alisha came into my room one morning with streamers and balloons.

I rubbed my eyes to see Reed grinning behind her, his tall frame in his hoodie filling up the doorway of my room at K2.

Reed had it designed like my old room which was comforting as much as it made me a little nauseous.

"Lish, I think we woke her up."

Alisha let the balloons go and pounced on me smattering kisses all over me. "It's fine, she'll live. Now take that."

I giggled feeling warmer than I had in weeks with her hugs. Reed sat on the other side of the enormous bed he had in the guest room.

Reed grinned at me. "Happy Birthday, kiddo."

"You're finally eighteen!"

Was I?

I didn't feel it. The thought was like a bucket of ice water that someone flung on me.

Shouldn't there a momentous moment where I felt oh hooray I'm not a "child" anymore on paper?

Because I had felt like this since Mum and Dad died. Lost. Hollow. Stuck.

Unable to be useful to anyone around me.

I didn't feel any different.

If anything? I felt worse. I felt younger.

Like I was twelve. Dependent on Alisha and her support. And now Reed's.

I felt my eyes blur again as Alisha cuddled next to me.

She was recovering and she was worried about me. I got that she was keeping me here too. Making sure I was okay.

"How do you feel?" She brushed my hair back. "We're a little worried about you." I blinked rapidly at that looking away and slowly sitting up.

"I'm all right. Just tired." I could feel the emotions bubbling to the surface and I shoved them down again. They weren't welcome. Not now.

After working to go to university where I could live my life—I just started living—and my life felt upended.

This feeling never truly went away. Thierry had been a breath of stability, protecting, good things for me.

Now? With it gone…even with Lish…I felt…inadequate and lost. I didn't know how to talk about my heartbreak.

I didn't know how to tell Alisha how I felt.

I just remembered at some point Gemma came to see us and I cried into her as hard as I could've. Dimly I was aware I was living in a fog. A dull fog.

"Darling," Alisha brushed my hair back again. "What's wrong?" Her hazel eyes watered a little. "Are you okay?"

"I think your body is suffocating me." I teased. She laughed falling over next to me propping herself up on one elbow and Reed grinned at her.

"What do you want to do for your birthday?"

"Hmmm, can we go out to…Chocolate Factory?" I injected the actress into my voice. I was going to drop out of school now and be a professional actress like Rosalie. That was the only solution.

"Where's that?" Reed was on his phone already as Alisha grinned.

"Midtown," she said. "It's a fully chocolate themed restaurant. Avani loves it."

I did. I thought it might cheer us all up.

Reed took Alisha me out to eat brunch there.

On the way back we stopped by a bookshop and Reed got a few things for both of us.

"Reed always spoils us," I whispered to my sister who was watching him softly. She turned me with bright eyes.

"He says he has a hard time explaining himself or his thoughts, but if you need him for anything at all, he is always there."

She motioned to the brand new e-reader that just came out in my hand.

"Don't buy that. He bought you two in case you lose one."

I gaped and Alisha laughed at my expression.Her eyes softened though as she watched me. "Are you afraid right now?"

I felt caught in that moment by her eyes.

"You can tell me," she whispered. "I know this is a—"

"It's not," I cut her off. There was something in my voice I didn't recognize. "It's not a lot."

I didn't want to speak to her abut it. I didn't want to speak to anyone.

I swallowed and Alisha's eyes widened at whatever she saw in my eyes.

"Avani—"

"It's not, Didi." I injected something into my voice I didn't feel. "Please, just drop it."

Because the last thing I wanted was her being aware of the mistakes that I had made. Of how I felt. How useless I was.

How helpless I felt.

I hated who I was.

I hated my existence.

I hated everything.

And I was pretty certain I had reached the anger stage of my grief.

Reed came back with a smile on her. "We have one more stop on the way and we can head home. You guys all right?"

Alisha kissed him lightly, her worry shifting to something softer, and I ducked my head looking away giving them some privacy.

On the outside, in public, I managed to put on a good appearance. I moisturized, put on normal clothes Reed had gotten me matching Alisha, and I pretended to be okay.

On the inside? I was dying.

Alisha had a brain injury. Reed was hovering over both of us as a concerned boyfriend and pseudo-brother to me.

Kieran spent time watching movies with me and being an emotional teddy bear when he sat by me.

I was in a play. Pretending with everyone. Smiling. Nodding. Going along with it. All the while I felt shards of glass in my heart where it used to be.

Now it felt ripped out.

By the only person I wanted near me. The only person that truly mattered. He was gone.

375

I walked outside with both of them to Reed's SUV and I felt my neck prickle.

But when I turned around I didn't see him.

I was imagining it.

Just like I had been stupid enough to think someone like that—could love someone like me—just Avani.

Useless. Not Alisha—Avani.

I let out a breath blinking back my emotions and got into the car.

IT WAS LATER THAT NIGHT, ALISHA AND I HAD CUPCAKES WHILE Kieran dropped by with balloons and more cupcakes.

The apartment was covered in flowers. Teo even sent Alisha and me some flowers for my birthday. Reed had scowled the entire time as Alisha brushed it off.

Reed shook his head at Kieran being in the apartment, but Alisha swatted his arm. "Just let her live."

He didn't look happy about it and for some reason it made me giggle. Without having Papa around Reed had turned into a father figure more than a brother.

I honestly thought they might've thought something was going on between us.

But I didn't like Kieran.

I was done with boys and heartache.

Kieran and I sat quietly in my guest room. Both of us leaning against the headboard while he put on a movie.

I didn't even know what was happening I was so numb.

"How's your birthday so far?" Kieran muttered.

"Good," I looked down at the pink swirls on my cupcake. "We went out to lunch."

"How do you feel?"

I swallowed feeling thorns in my throat as I did. "Can we not—" I broke off unable to even formulate the words.

The way my fingers clenched, my jaw followed, I closed my eyes to compose myself. I had nightmares.

Of blood.

Of Selena dying. Alisha dying.

Me being alone and alive and tormented at being *useless* Avani.

"I don't want to talk about anything."

He was quiet. "Do you want me to leave?"

No. I didn't. Because oddly enough as much as I knew I wanted to be alone, I was terrified if I was—I might snap into pieces. And I didn't want that anymore.

I wanted to be around the people who cared about me.

But not feel any of my emotions around them.

My therapist called it emotional paralysis. I wanted the liminal space of being physically there, but not there at all.

"No. You can stay. Unless…I'm holding you up."

"No." Kieran's voice was gruff. "No, I'm all yours."

I swallowed at that as my eyes darted to the screen finally focusing on the movie. "Are those flying cats?"

He chuckled and I looked at him grinning. "You're always drifting off so I found the most ridiculous video I could find and played that."

A reluctant smile curved my lips at his attempts. "Thank you."

"Don't mention it. You want some pizza or something?"

And just like that my walls slammed back down.

"No." I shook my head. "No, I'm good." Instead my mind drifted on asking Alisha to get Kieran a cat since he wanted one so much.

∼

IT WAS THIRTY MINUTES LATER REED CAME INTO THE ROOM AND HE looked at Kieran motioning for him to come outside. Kieran dutifully left.

I followed him outside wondering why Reed looked like that. I found Alisha in the kitchen wringing her hands.

"…Lucas Devereaux in his apartment…I need to call Adam. Gabriel is there right now helping Lucas, but he's bleeding…" Reed was saying to Kieran. "Stay with my girls. Do not leave. Tell Stephanie downstairs to call for the Delta team downtown to come here. Do you copy?"

Kieran nodded. Something was happening.

"I gotta go, Angel." Reed kissed Alisha hard in front of me and I watched her eyes go wide. "Something happened at work. I love you." He then turned to me and kissed my forehead holding my face in his hands in a way that made my eyes water in worry. "Love you too, kid. Stay here. Neither one of you leave, okay?

Reed rushed out not looking back on his phone as he ran.

"What just happened?" I looked at Alisha who stood a little open mouthed and she came over to hug me again.

"I think something bad just happened…"

And that was his life.

This was normal for Reed. I looked at the concern on her face.

"Is this all right with you?"

She nodded slowly. "It is. He's got this. I don't worry. I just think…he's had a rough few weeks…months…" Her eyes held a wealth of worry. "If he's gone for a few days, do you mind if I go check on him? He might be in the city or Greenwich…"

My sister didn't look all right. Not in the slightest.

"Not at all. Do what you have to, I'll be fine."

CHAPTER 40
THIERRY

It was the third week Avani was in K2, that I followed her around long enough to know Kieran O'Hara was a fucking thorn in my side.

He had two older brothers. The oldest Aidan O'Hara, current head of the family crime syndicate and the other one, Killian O'Hara, scary motherfucker with mismatched eyes.

He made me look friendly.

But to my fucking relief, Killian O'Hara had a girlfriend he was *obsessed* with and all over her whenever they were together. She was adorable like Avani so I left her alone.

Aidan was in Chicago. So I was straight spying on Kieran for the time being.

Every second was an eternity without her.

One where I didn't know how to even make what I felt about her. I thought I knew I cared about people.

I cared about Andrei and Teo. Talia and Drew. Alma.

I had my life.

But somehow my love for Avani encompassed beyond all that. It was like something had taken over me, painted my soul over with streaks of light from her.

Not just from the summer we spent.

But from every single conversation, every single moment we had, every dinner, every bit of snuggling, every time she fell asleep on me.

I was madly and irrevocably in love with my girlfriend.

And I wanted her back.

Now.

I needed to tell her the truth. It had been almost three weeks and her birthday was coming up.

"How often does he need to hold her fucking hand? *Get your hands off my girl.*"

I growled low and feeling no better than some wild animal, as I watched Avani walking with Kieran into Butterscotch's where she looked exhausted.

Did I make the right choice?

It took every inch of my self control to not kidnap her off the fucking street. I sat in my car grumbling and growling eating my sandwich without my heart.

This was her favorite food. Not mine. I didn't even like pesto.

I found myself sniffing her perfumes.

Her lip gloss still in the center console. Her books in the backseat of my car. Her sweater there too.

Every single part of her wrapped around my soul. And none of it compared to her.

It was one of my first times seeing her like this.

She looked…haunted.

And the sight of it made me want to kiss her again. Broken, lost, it ripped into my soul.

Because the last person in the world I had ever wanted to hurt was Avani. Ever.

I wanted to hold her, hug her, kiss her. I felt like shit ghosting my fucking girlfriend for three weeks now.

She was probably pissed at me.

Her birthday was coming up soon. I had her present in my warehouse. I built it into my warehouse figuring she'd want a space there for herself.

Teo had been confused by the last minute changes but agreed because I asked. That's it.

Now, I had to watch my girlfriend who probably thought I was dead or something on a fucking three—whatever date with Evie and Kieran.

I couldn't even walk in without drawing suspicion because she would know me. She would.

I couldn't see them and I felt myself simmering.

Boiling with jealousy, frustration, anger, the need to go in there and kiss her and reclaim her.

But I sat there fucking waiting.

Waiting. For my moment.

I GOT THE PHONE CALL FROM JACE ON AVANI'S BIRTHDAY.

"Sir, Lucas Devereaux was shot tonight. He was taken unconscious to the Titan hospital. Camera sightings found Samara on the rooftop on the other side."

I swore launching up from my couch.

"Motherfucker. Keep your eyes on her, tell me where she's going."

"Yes, sir."

I rushed to put my clothes on and run out with Jace on hold. He was guiding me through where she was moving. Even with Bexley hiding Samara, once Jace got her on camera? He could follow the path Bexley was blocking off.

Just because people couldn't use didn't mean that that couldn't follow the anomaly patterns in cyberspace.

I followed his directions until she stopped.

At the Nash Group tower.

"She's going to the top," he muttered. "She's fast."

"She's insane and if Lucas dies tonight, she's starting a war for no fucking reason. There is no *evidence* Lucas and Lucy met once since Lucy came back to New York. Keep your eyes on her in Nash Group."

"I'll do my best." He stayed on the phone with me as I drove to the tower.

I would call Alma.

After I confronted Samara's psycho ass.

I made it there, parking underground and racing up to the top offices. With Natasha in Cape Verde, Samara had access to her office.

It took me fifteen fucking long minutes to find her in Natasha's office. I entered the code and the moment I did, she spun around from the open safe and aimed her gun at me. Too bad I was just as fast.

I held my gun on her shutting the door on both of us.

"What the fucking fuck is wrong with you! Why would you shoot Lucas—"

"I didn't—" she snapped, her eyes flashed fire. *"I was watching him tonight! I owe you nothing! You're not one of us!"*

"I will never stop being one of you, you stupid bitch. Are you trying to get everyone killed—"

"What the fuck does it matter?" Samara's growl was savage.

I saw how insane her eyes were then as she held her gun trained on me. "You wouldn't fucking understand anything. How the fuck did you even find—"

"Why did you shoot Lucas when he didn't meet with Lucy?" I shouted back at her. *"You knew he didn't meet her. He didn't have anything!"*

"He has information!" She shot back, eyes wild. *"Why the fuck do you even care—"*

"Because he's innocent!" I roared back. *"We don't kill innocents!"*

"I didn't kill him! Some idiot in a grey suit was trying to kill him instead! I shot the fucking whiskey glass until Lucas jumped in the way. I never killed anyone!"

She was puffing out her breath. "Someone else is invested in Lucas Devereaux. Not me."

Grey suit? Who the fuck was trying to kill Lucas besides Talon?

"You what?"

"Are you hard of hearing? Someone was trying to kill him. Already. Before me. Blonde. I don't know who he is. But he tried to choke him out. I can't have my asset dead," she shot back.

We were both still holding our guns.

"They were fighting. I wanted to get the blonde off him. That's it. I didn't kill him. I think I grazed him. At best. He's alive. Breathing. EMT's took him and his girlfriend. The EMT was Adam Whittaker. Safe to say, I can clear all of them off the list now."

I huffed out a breath and dropped my gun. She took a second and dropped hers.

I eyed the vault behind her. Nash Group was where they kept their weapons.

"You drove your bike here." It was a statement.

Samara rode her motorcycle everywhere. Now I saw why with how fast she was.

"Do you have *anything* useful to say? Because I have to report to Alma now and tell her what happened."

And Alma was gonna rip her a new one.

She was clearly pissed. But Samara was always pissed.

Her dark hair braided back, eyes melting into the night. She was spooky. Like all of us. Half-dead humans masquerading as real people. Ghosts and shadows.

Reapers.

Having a baby had humanized Talia, but all of the girls were frightening in their own way.

"Do you ever get tired of being bitter?" I had to ask. I was just as annoyed as her. "Or do you guys just shoot everyone for an object nobody is willing to say what it is?"

She rolled her eyes at me. "Get out of the fucking office, Thierry before I decided you're not worth leaving alive."

She turned away and opened the vault to put her sniper back.

"Lucas is cleared. Your brother's friend is a non-issue. But his sister is a different story."

And Reed Whittaker.

Fuck my life.

CHAPTER 41
AVANI / THIERRY

WHEN REED CAME BACK HE LOOKED EXHAUSTED.

He'd hugged me pressing his lips to my forehead and muttering if I was okay when I greeted them at the door.

I was. Was he? He didn't look it at all.

"He's just tired," Alisha murmured taking him back to their room.

Alisha had made sure he'd at least showered and passed out instantly. Kieran had stayed with me the entire time. Something had happened to Reed.

"Didi," I whispered when Alisha came out of their room. "How is he?" Now, the worry cut through the numbness.

Kieran wasn't allowed to leave until Reed was doing better.

"He's all right, you remember Evie? You went out to brunch with her and Kieran a week ago?"

I did, I had. I nodded. Evie Monroe was Gabriel's younger sister.

"Something happened to her boyfriend, Lucas." Alisha said it carefully as she hugged me. "So, Reed had to go and help him out for a few days."

"Is she okay?"

Alisha nodded. "Everyone's fine, darling. I promise." She held me tighter as she said it but even she was trembling. "Kieran's going to drop you off to your place, right?"

I nodded dumbly. She looked a little reluctant to let me go even as she did.

She pushed my hair back behind my ears. In the time I had stayed here at K2, Reed had been determined to feed both of us so much.

We'd both gained some more weight despite having left the hospital. Her cheeks were rounder and flushed as she nodded.

"Please come back to us if you need anything. We're always here for you."

I understood.

I heard her. I did. I heard the words coming out of her mouth.

And none of them mattered.

Because I was tired of feeling twelve. Tired of feeling like a child. And tired of depending on her and Reed so much it felt like I was latched on.

Kieran was dropping me off to my apartment. I'd be back to my old life. Sans…everything else.

∾

Thierry

AND THEN FINALLY. *FUCKING. FINALLY.*

The day came after her birthday where Avani came back to her apartment.

At this point? I was a mess. I was a wreck.

Lucy's Locksmith Pub had yielded a secret hideaway.

It was probably a speakeasy in the past. All types of weird costumes and stuff were in there and suddenly I knew—Lucy Devereaux was hiding.

As a brunette. Hmm. I'd get Jace to work on that one.

Her apartment yielded research she was doing on Talon.

I didn't touch her things.

No, Lucy was collateral.

I filled in Teo in the meantime. And he and Jace kept his ears out on Reed.

By some fucking miracle Adam Whittaker dropped by Teo's office saying he had a girlfriend. My money—Lucy had never left his life. I wouldn't say a word.

I told Bexley what I could safely tell her.

I kept Lucy's information to myself. Teo played dumb with

Adam and used my car so I could securely spy on Avani without drawing too much attention.

I was stalking my fucking girlfriend.

Fuck.

I swore under my breath as I waited for fucking Kieran to leave Avani's apartment.

Leave, motherfucker. Leave, so I can see my woman.

The longing in me mixed with the guilt I felt for hurting her. I knew she looked distressed. I had caused that. I didn't know what happened to her.

Jace and Bexley couldn't hack into the hospital. And Jace had let me and Teo know that Reed was aware of what we were doing.

As soon as I saw Kieran walking out with a stupid smile on his stupid face. I was fucking *moving.*

I waited until he left the parking lot and I waited for a few more minutes after that. And then I implemented my plan. Grabbing my ball cap and pizza boxes.

Nothing was more invisible than delivery drivers.

And then I started moving. I tore off to her the moment Kieran was out of the way.

The moment I reached for her I was grateful for the pizza boxes, thanks to her camera in front of her door.

Given the recent events, I fucking should've known Reed was monitoring it. I was being risky. Too risky.

I knocked hard on the door.

It took her a second. "Hu—hullo?"

"Delivery!"

Fuck my life.

I was hiding my face but I hoped to fucking God Avani either opened the door for me holding the damn pizzas.

Or she knew I was someone to be feared and didn't.

I hoped for my sake it wasn't the latter.

"I didn't order pizza."

"Name on the box is Alisha." Why the fuck did I sound like I swallowed a bear? I cleared on my throat. "She your sister?"

"Oh," I heard the sound of her clicking open the door, and then there she was.

After three long eternal weeks of waiting patiently for my girl.

Patiently.

The door opened to her in nothing but a towel wrapped around but that wasn't what caught my eye.

Why was she crying? She sniffled as she said. "Yes?"

And then her eyes opened wide.

Comically wide. *Oh, my heart.*

I was on her in a fucking heartbeat.

Plowing through the door like an Avani seeking missile as she gasped and stumbled back.

Tossing the damn pizzas on her coffee table and knocking things down.

I was on her, one hand slamming the door closed, the other tangling in her hair and yanking her lips against mine.

The moment I had her against the door, my entire being sighed as her mouth opened in a gasp.

I was on her in a heartbeat.

I dimly registered her shock as I kissed her over and over, hungrily, like a man starved for a drop of water in a desert.

Like I would die if I didn't kiss her, and she moaned a little taking my tongue before she pulled away with a sob, her mouth gasping for air.

I pulled her back hungrily, licking her face like some animal, her neck, all over and she gripped my shoulders tightly as I found her mouth again.

My mouth hot on hers. Seeking more. Her gasp swallowed by me as I thrust my tongue into her mouth. Not even giving her a chance. Not once.

The taste of her soothing my brain which had lost its ever loving mind juggling Samara trying to hit whoever had been with Lucas.

Juggling everyone else. But. My. Girl.

No words came out of me as I kissed her over and over and over. I didn't want to stop.

I ate at her practically tearing at the flimsy towel around her until I felt her bare skin on me.

I groaned as I felt every lush curve on that body mold against mine. Fucking. *Finally.*

She gasped into my mouth and she was tearing up with shock so I did her a solid.

Holding her face in my hands I said the words that would seal my fate.

"I shot the man who tried to kill Alisha."

CHAPTER 42
AVANI

IT WAS LIKE WHIPLASH.

But ten-fold.

I felt like every word out of his mouth hit me like a stun gun.

I thought Alisha sent me pizza. I didn't know Thierry would be on the other side of that door.

Even now his lips pressed into my face, everywhere he could reach with me clinging to him like I was drowning. I felt his skin on mine like a hot brand against me.

A lightening strike to my soul would've been more delicate compared to staring into the wild blue eyes that had kissed me so many times only now he was telling me a truth I couldn't even wrap my head around.

What did he just say?

"W-what?"

I shot the man who tried to kill Alisha.

And I am in love with you. I love you. I love you. I love you. I'm so sorry I stayed away. I am.

I love you, Avani Malhotra. Look at me, baby, look at me. There you go.

His hands held my face tight, his touch soothing and electrifying sending shockwaves through as my grip on my towel tightened.

"I'm sorry," he was saying over and over again. "I'm so sorry."

My heart felt like it was ready to leap out of my chest from the fear and how hard it was *pounding*.

"I swear I didn't want to stay away—"

My brain physically could not process the level of shock I was going through.

"Tell me you're all right. You look like you're getting to—" his words were laced with concern cutting off abruptly as my knees buckled.

In an instant, I was in his arms, like iron holding me securely into his chest as my heart continued to thunder holding onto him. And that was when I realized the towel had hit the floor and the horror of the moment sank into me as I made a noise and went to cover myself.

Instead of grabbing it, he whipped off his hoodie and pulled it over my head. Gratefully, I was shaking as I slid my arms feeling like he was a dream I might wake up from.

He sat on the couch, whispering apologies into my temple, his lips moving rapidly as he held me tighter.

His fingers tangled into my hair and I was drowning in his scent. Dark shadows. Spice. Sin. Thierry was dangerous. I'd known it from the day I met him. But now?

He was absolutely the reason why I felt like I was floundering in a sea of rolling emotions and I didn't know what to feel next.

"I'm sorry, there's so much to tell you—"

"What do you mean you shot the man..."

He turned my face to me. "I was the sniper. On the roof. I saw your sister with him. I saw it. I swear. I followed Reed. I followed you. I saw O'Hara, he carried you out. I saw them take you to the hospital. I just couldn't go in."

As he spoke my eyes and mouth dropped in horror. He was...he had...he was...I couldn't even breathe.

"You...you—"

"I worked in private security for Talon, I know how to shoot, Mon cœur. I did it. I swear I never left you. I never left. Did you get my flowers? The cupcakes?"

My jaw dropped wider.

At this point, I was gone. Stunned.

I fucking knew it. *"Oh. Bloody hell that was you."*

I knew it.

I knew it.

I knew it.

He nodded fervently. "You got them."

The entire hospital got them.

I felt like something had imploded in my chest. I was shaking harder now a little overwhelmed as he spoke.

That was *him*. He had *saved* my sister. Gabriel had told Alisha and I what had happened.

"You're the sniper…" my head was reeling. "You shot the man…"

He saved Alisha. He saved my family. That had been him…

His eyes held mine. And I processed as he said what he did.

"Why didn't you…why are you—"

"That's a long story and I promise I will tell you, but right now you look like you're going to faint. Why were you crying?"

He wiped my eyes as I drew back a little processing him. Kieran had just left me…and he had been there.

Had he been watching me the entire time?

"I never left," he shook his head. "I never left you."

"I waited for you," I whispered wiping my eyes feeling the cracks in the numbness in me. "I thought you forgot…about me."

"I would never forget about you." His eyes held mine as he shook his head. "You have been mine since the day I met you and you leapt into my arms trusting me to take care of you. I would die before I let anything happen to you. I promised you that day and I will keep all of my promises to you if you let me."

"I d-d-d-idn't think you knew—" Oh. Now, those cracks were growing.

"I knew. I wouldn't let you go. I knew the entire time and I was coming for you. Tell me you understand. Tell me you believe me."

I did. Because he had to have been there to know those details. He had been watching me the entire time.

"Why didn't you—"

"Reed." He said simply. I was so confused now. A swirl of emotions filled me.

"Reed…"

What does Reed have to do with him? He doesn't know Reed. Does he? Besides the one time they kind of met…

He nodded with a grim expression. "I promise I'll explain everything I swear. Let me get you something to eat, let me take care of you—I promise."

I couldn't stop shaking. " I need a minute."

While I looked down at the hands on my lap I felt his eyes on me. Every so often he wiped my eyes and kissed my cheeks.

He couldn't keep his hands off me as I felt my world tilt. I felt something unfamiliar bubbling to the surface of my skin. An emotion I rarely felt. But one I had been feeling all too often lately.

It was too much. I felt like I couldn't stabilize after my kidnapping let alone, now.

Images flashed through my mind of the last few months of meeting him. Teaching him. Spending long hours at the library with him.

Thierry had always saved me.

But I didn't feel like the same girl I was in the past. In the summer. That girl felt so far away from here.

It felt like a different world. I felt shaken up. Terrified. That emotion continued to bubble higher to the surface.

My entire world upended and now, my sister had a head injury and my boyfriend was telling me he had shot the man who tried to kill her.

Saving everyone. Taking action.

I looked at him watching me with wide blue eyes brighter than I had ever seen them. He was taking me in, every so often leaning in to kiss me and cuddle me to him.

Being on his lap, being in his arms, everything felt right again.

I had a long time to think about the last three weeks.

He had made me feel safe and protected. Sensations I hadn't really felt even with Alisha. Her love was different than his. But his love made me feel alive.

I felt like Avani.

Not someone's little sister. Not something to be coddled.

But like a woman.

He saw me as a woman.

But do I see myself as a woman?

Did I like myself? Was I living in Alisha's shadow so much I was just grateful to have the attention? Or was this something I actually wanted?

I had been lamenting deep down I hadn't gotten to kiss him one last time or tell him I loved him or hear the sound of his voice.

And the idea of *not* having that had been agonizing.

"You saved my sister…and me…"

My entire body was screaming. It had been the one place I wanted to exist in—his arms—for three weeks. I needed him.

I needed him more than anything.

Kieran who was much older than Thierry had been there. Yes, did I understand he worked for Reed?

I did.

But this was the second time I got the feeling Thierry was making a choice *without me*.

When I had needed him the most he had made a call that affected *both* of us.

He had made the decision to spend the last three weeks without me when I needed him the most.

I had wanted him for so long. For months.

I felt like I had been waiting an eternity for him.

When the emotion finally broke through my skin I realized why I felt the way I did.

I was angry with him. Angry for ghosting me. Angry for abandoning me. He had left me.

He had made the choice to leave me and then show up to my place now like it hadn't happened. As though I would just accept him and take him back—like the last few days of my life hadn't happened.

I heard him.

I did.

I also heard the twelve year old in me crying in her room over Mum no longer being there screaming too.

And she didn't want to be hurt anymore.

Because the girl I was…I kept hurting. I kept hurting and hurting everyone around me. I didn't want to be that girl anymore.

My head was spinning but I knew how I felt. I knew what I felt.

My entire life had been filled with everyone making choices for me. Maybe I did need to grow up. Maybe I wasn't enough. Maybe I wasn't…Alisha.

I didn't get the same happiness she did.

And even if my eyes watered, and I understood what he said—it had been weeks without him at my darkest moments.

That darkness lingered. It was embedded into my soul now.

I kept seeing Selena dying.

I kept seeing Alisha passed out.

I kept reliving the moment Alisha sacrificed herself.

I kept seeing Reed freaking out.

I kept seeing Alisha at twenty crying.

393

I kept seeing eggs over rice.

The world around me moving on.

Without me.

If Alisha had died…if Thierry hadn't been there…I would've been useless like I had always been. Like I always was.

Thierry couldn't make decisions with me.

Logically, I understood he had saved my sister. He had never left me. He had always been there. He took care of me.

I understood it in my brain. Logically.

Emotionally?

I felt abandoned. Again. I had spiraled too far into somewhere darker. I was learning to rebuild myself without him. Or anyone. I had shut down too far.

Even if his intentions were good?

Even if he meant well?

He had decided by himself—that I wasn't and I couldn't make my own decisions. And in doing so, he reinforced my deepest fears about being powerless and dependent and not worthy of that place in his life for him to have called me in K2 and simply told me the truth. Whatever it may have been.

"You'll give me anything?" I whispered barely able to breathe right now.

"Yes. I've been here the entire time. Should I get something? I brought pizza with—"

"Leave."

CHAPTER 43
THIERRY

IT WOULD'VE BEEN THE SAME AS HER SLAPPING ME.

"What?"

I felt that word like a gunshot.

"Leave." Avani whispered it not looking at me. She slowly stood in my hoodie and motioned for me and the door. "You need to leave. I can't do this. I don't want this."

Her…she sounded different. What happened to my girl?

"Avani…"

"Leave." Her voice sounded completely different.

That light laughter, the warmth, I didn't catch it at first, but the bright sunshine behind her eyes—it was gone.

Now, her eyes…they reminded me of Alma's. Dead. Cold. Dark.

"What did he do to you?" I whispered horrified at her expression. She looked blank. I could tell she was hurting but she looked at a spot with those dark eyes now.

"Losing my Mum was the worst feeling in the world. I remember b-b-b-reaking down because I really n-n-needed her…I needed you. *I needed you.*" Her voice rose to a higher pitch. "And you dropped the ball the last second. Without even considering that maybe just maybe I might want to know why shot that man, why you sent bloody flowers—"

"Mon cœur —"

"I'm not finished!"

I had never heard Avani raise her voice at me.

"Do you have any idea what the last few weeks of my life have been without you? Do you have any idea how I felt? I thought I lost you. The w-w-way I lost my p-p-parents. You made me feel like on top of almost losing Alisha, *I felt that for you.*"

Right now? That slightly higher pitch told me how much fucking trouble I was in.

"Thank you for saving my life. Thank you for the flowers. I'm sorry your life hasn't been what you expected—"

I felt my heart snapping when I knew what was coming. I knew.

"But I cannot do this. I will not. I don't care what issues you have with Reed. I don't care what's happening in your life or his. I don't care. I want to be left alone. Do you understand me?"

In front of me I watched my girlfriend splinter. "Get out!" She screamed. *"Get the fuck out of my house!"*

"Avani." I stood slowly aware I was watching her fall apart. I didn't know what happened. Jace couldn't hack into the files at the hospital. I didn't know what the fuck was happening there. It was a dark zone. But right now—whatever had happened to my heart— she was completely dark. "Avani, breathe for me—"

"You broke your promise to me," she shouted. "We were part-ners. My parents were partners. You promised me to tell me—"

"It's not that simple!" I felt the word leave me. But it was the wrong thing to say. "mon coeur, you are my heart. There is nothing in this world I love more than you. I do everything I do for you. Every single thing." The words ripped from my throat. "There is no me without you, mon coeur—"

"Then why did you leave! It was a simple text!"

Because she was right. It was simple.

It was a simple heart or gif. It was a simple unknown number to call her phone number every single day.

But it wasn't at the same time. The duality of it warred in me.

Oh. I. Fucked. Up.

"Why!"

"Mon cœur ," I held my hands out. "Don't do this, please let me explain—"

And then the doorbell rang.

Both of us froze.

My eyes widened in horror at who it could fucking be because I couldn't get caught.

I lunged for her covering her mouth so she couldn't say a word.

"Please don't tell whoever that is I exist, I swear I know you're angry with me. I know you hate me. But I can't get caught right now. I'm juggling too much and I still have to take care of you. Even if you hate me."

Her eyes widened as I said the words and I swore I fucking saw a hint of that spark in them. But I couldn't be sure because the fucking doorbell rang again.

Oh, I fucked up.

I fucked up so bad. In that moment I realized two things. I underestimated my girl. I underestimated Avani's emotional needs. And I fucked. Up. Big. Time.

My skin burned where it touched hers and she padded to her door checking the little camera.

Fucking O'Hara.

"Mon cœur," I dropped my voice to a whisper desperation clawing it's way up like a rabid beast in my throat. "Please, don't—"

I had to hide.

If he saw me, Reed would know, my whole fucking plan would be blown to pieces.

I needed to get Alma out the city, and I had no fucking clue how to do it.

And then I realized one thing, Avani. My hoodie which thankfully covered her. No panties.

Oh, fuck.

Answering the door for O'Hara.

I couldn't even stop her as she opened the door a crack.

My blood boiled at the thought of him seeing her like this.

"Kieran?"

Oh fuck me. I hid knowing she couldn't even open the door fully. Standing behind it I hid still able to look at her as she shyly peered out.

"Yes?"

"Hey, I forgot to drop off your duffle. It was in the passenger seat. I think you forgot it." He handed her the gym bag she used to travel.

I wanted to growl in frustration as she spoke softly to him. How the fuck did I get here? Fucking up beyond repair.

I thought I was doing what was best for me and her.

"Thank you," she laughed low as she took it at something he said.

Oh, this motherfucker. Who the fuck—

"I promise I am. Actually, I got pizza so I promise I'm perfect."

Yes, she is. She was perfect for me.

Not O'Hara.

I felt my jaw tighten almost painfully. But Avani never once let him in. I saw how her right leg tapped on the floor and her fingers clenching the doorknob in my hoodie. My clothes.

The image of her naked body for a flash, her lush tits, her softly rounded stomach was carved into my retinas until I gave her my clothes.

But even if she was angry with me, she wouldn't throw me to the wolves, and she wouldn't out me.

Whether she knew it or not Avani wanted to protect me. She wanted to take care of me. She always would.

I had left my gun in my car knowing it would freak Avani out. I wish I'd brought it now.

"I promise I'm good."

And then he fucking said it.

"Did you wanna go to Butterscotch's again sometime?"

Again? How often did they go?

Avani's low laughter shot through me like a hot knife.

Serrated and jagged the ends digging into the parts of me that missed her laughter with me.

Missed her all over me. Now, my girl was laughing. At him.

With him.

And I never considered that Avani...might've liked him.

That thought went through with me the grace of a thousand needles digging into my skin. Is that why she was kicking me out? Because he had been coming over?

Something akin to rage flared hot in my veins. Is that why she was moving on? Without me? She liked him?

"You did like my cupcakes." What the fuck did that mean? Her cupcakes? I wanted her cupcakes.

He laughed. *Stop laughing.* "It's way better stealing it from you."

She laughed low. "Yeah, I can message you when I'd like to go."

"Yeah?"

Mother. Fucker. She did like him. Is that what happened? A searing hot pain went through me at how badly I fucked up.

I failed to tell Avani the truth.

And in the few weeks she had been at K2, at her most vulnerable, he had been there. He had saved her.

In her eyes it hadn't been me.

He had carried her out. Stayed with her at the hospital.

Avani had been terrified for her sister's life.

He had been there through every single difficult moment she had.

And I hadn't.

I fucking failed. And he had stepped up.

And even though I logically knew this shit? Another part of me, the jealous demon in my soul refused to even comprehend losing my heart to anyone.

My eyes snapped open, jealousy surged through me like molten lava, it was enough to make me snap the door in half, shut it, and take Avani with a violence I didn't think I had in me with her.

"I'd like that," Avani murmured. "That sounds good. I can ask Evie if she wants to come and maybe Ben and the girls too. It'll be fun."

And the fire that had been burning turned into a raging wildfire now. A supernova of rage and desire.

She'd. Like. That? Make it a fun date? With all her new friends? In her new life?

That didn't include me?

Not anymore.

"I was going to go shower, otherwise I'd invite you in, but I promise I'm good." She said it softer now.

"Yeah, just let me know what you need and I'm here."

I saw her smile.

Oh. Fuck me. I was so pissed now. "I will. Thanks again."

Avani would not be dating O'Hara. I knew O'Hara.

I knew exactly who he was.

He would tear his fangs into her and sink in so deep she'd become darker—I couldn't even fathom her being anyone else's.

Just mine. She was mine.

She had been mine for so long. Would be mind until my last fucking breath.

Consume her into me until nothing was left behind but smoke and shadows and darkness. My soul with hers.

She was my light. Kieran would destroy her.

I would remake her to my Queen.

Avani was my love. I wasn't losing her.

The idea of anything else was…inconceivable.

She was tempting the devil. Because I'd held back with her so many times. So much. And now? Now I knew, I'd almost lost my girl once three week ago.

I wasn't losing her again.

I'd held back long enough. Been her Prince Charming. Soft. Safe. Her protector. But now?

My careful control, my meticulous mask, the normality—crumbled like sand-castle in the ocean. It was obliterated.

As Avani said her goodbyes and shut the door those doe eyes landed on me. Soft. Sweet.

A little stunned. Good. She saw it too.

I was on her in another second, my hand around her throat and my lips on hers. Determined to brand myself into her skin.

"Is he the reason why you wanted to kick me out?" I lowered my voice.

Her eyes flared on me. I saw the way she grew stunned at my expression. And her hands came up and shoved at me until I shifted off her.

"This is why I am done," she hissed. "This is why. You only react when you lose me." There was nothing but fire in her eyes now. "You left me at my lowest. You abandoned me. You betrayed me! And you have the gall to say anything about Kieran—"

That's all it took. Her saying his name. That was it.

I stamped my mouth over hers unable to hold back.

I was gone.

"I never lost you," I growled into her mouth. "Not once. Not for a second. Ever. Not to him. Not to anyone. You have been mine since the moment I met you." I was done holding back. "I protect you. I take care of you. I fucked up. Yes. But I loved you then, I love you now, and every single thing I have ever done has been because I love you. And I am sorry, I fucked up. I did. I swear I was trying to protect you. I swear—" I broke off feeling unhinged and feral for this woman.

I always would be.

"You have no fucking clue how I feel about you. There is no me without you."

Her lips parted under me and just like that I fucking knew

Avani felt the same. She felt for me. Her pupils dilated. Breathing hitched. I wasn't holding her hard at all.

No.

I would be rougher with her now.

Those eyes haunted me for weeks.

The Reaper never misses. Never loses.

I will never lose.

Especially not her.

"Tell me you want him more than you want me, and I will walk the fuck away." My eyes met hers. "Say the fucking word."

Her throat worked under my grip. "Or else what?"

"Or else I fuck you."

Her throat felt tighter as she took a shuddering breath.

"Say it."

A beat passed. Another. I felt something in me rising to the surface. Bubbling over until I couldn't get enough.

"Say it." I bit it out. Waiting for her to break. I wasn't kidding. I would leave. If she said it—I would walk.

I would never do that to her.

But if she didn't? Something in me rose up. All bets were off.

Her eyes were wide on me like she didn't recognize me. I didn't recognize myself. I felt like I was on the brink of something I had never felt.

Loss.

I had never lost. I never cared enough to lose.

I never missed. Never.

And now I had.

Did she want him?

Avani's throat worked, the delicate lines and the little wobble of her bottom lip gave her away.

Me. I was her choice.

I didn't even hesitate.

I stamped my mouth over hers.

CHAPTER 44
AVANI

His hand moved so fast, wrapping around my throat lightly I knew I was caught.

Thierry didn't kiss me.

He consumed me, burning me out from the inside with every stroke of his tongue.

I didn't know who moved first. Didn't know how we were fumbling, his hoodie yanked over my head, him picking up my naked body in his arms, my legs wrapping around his waist. Instinctively. I knew.

I moaned into his mouth, his hands everywhere then, as I heard the clink of his belt. He was darkness, midnight and sin and all mine. And in that moment a ravenous hunger went through me.

He lifted me up into his arms, turning a few steps to the couch. Dropping us both onto it.

I felt his body moving over mine.

"I wanted to be patient, wanted to take my time."

He could barely speak, I could barely think.

Fully naked, I felt the head of his cock slipping against my pussy. I stopped thinking then as his mouth moved down my neck, latching on.

A moan left my lips as the cracks inside of the ice inside of me began to thaw. He hungrily worked down and the first stroke of his tongue against my nipples—I yelped a little.

All thoughts in my head faded to the sensation of him.

It felt like the feeling was returning to my insides like ice thawing out in the summer. My body arched into his, every nerve ending sizzling as he sucked and played with the other.

Oh God, this was already too much. And not enough all at once.

I was gasping and writing as he switched with a groan. "God, I've waited fucking forever for this."

Every single wall I had crumbled with each stroke of his tongue. Sending lightning into my bloodstream, almost shocking me back to reality.

For weeks I had been in this fugue state.

And now I was coming alive. I wanted him more than ever. All the way he rubbed the head of him against me.

"Open for me, mon coeur, I promise I'll always take care of you."

I whimpered feeling hot soaked I was. He kept slipping and we both groaned as he did. My fingers tangled in those inky locks as he sucked harder and I screamed a little.

"Get up here," I tugged on his hair. He shook his head not looking at me as he pressed in. I didn't understand until I felt him stretching me.

I fell back flat on the couch as I breathed out. The moment he thrust in I groaned.

It felt like a searing hot pain inside of me. An animal noise left me as I closed my eyes.

"Keep going," I whimpered. "Don't stop."

There was this deep innate part of me that demanded he keep going. Demanded to feel him.

His length splitting me in half claiming every bit of me I didn't know he could.

I wanted to be consumed. Destroyed. Re-made from the inside out. A noise left me as he let go of my nipples and slowly rose up, lips moving over a spot in my neck he'd found earlier that made me gasp.

Something in me *had* changed.

Instead of feeling numb. This moment made me feel more awake than I had in years. I wanted it. *Needed* it.

His voice was dark in my ears and I clenched instinctively as the sound of it. "Look at how hungry you are, you take me so well, mon coeur. *Your body knows it belongs to me.*"

I felt another rush of moisture and my body clenching wildly at that releasing a groan from him.

This was sex?

This felt too intense to survive. This felt all-consuming and even still I couldn't deny the feeling of rightness that flowed through me.

"You're perfect, stretched around me, trembling..." he kissed that spot on my neck that made me lose it and a dark chuckle left him.

Was I? I didn't feel it. I felt like I was so full I couldn't move.

Completely helpless.

"I think you can take more, can't you?"

I was struggling I was. We both groaned as he did something with his hips shoving forward more and I whimpered gripping his shoulders tight, nails digging half-moons into his skin.

"Oh God, stop," I whimpered. And opened my eyes slowly to find burning blue ones watching me, brushing my hair back, his entire expression drowsy and soft as he pulsed inside of me.

Quite frankly—I didn't think it got anymore honest than this.

Now buried deep in me his mouth whispered over mine. *"Did you want to get rid of me? So your new man could pay you a visit—"*

What right did he have?

"What right do you have over me?" I gasped aware I was tempting him. Aware of what he had done. Aware of myself.

A ferocious look entered his eyes. "Your pussy strangling my dick says otherwise."

I felt myself clenching down on him even more as he said it.

"This is sex," I whispered not feeling it. "That's all it is—"

"Wrong." His voice was gravel. "You and I both know it isn't sex. You can be angry with me, mon coeur, you can be as pissed off as you like. I fucked up. I know it. But don't think I won't spend every single fucking minute of my life making up for it."

He chuckled sounded defeated. "I'm the one you let into your home. Into your body. Into your heart. I know it because it's my heart. I know you."

I was leaking at the sound of that.

My eyes were low as he watched me.

"You thought so low of me."

I felt like I was drugged and vulnerable and still powerful at the same time the duality of emotions raged within me. Lust and anger. Love and self-hatred. Confusion and understanding. And he was my anchor.

"No," he shook his head as I adjusted to him. "No, I thought low of me."

I frowned as he brushed my hair back, his arms bracketing my head. "I promise I will tell you, I promise. Something tells me you won't be mad when I do."

His eyes flashed an unholy blue. His mouth dropped to my ear as he drew out enough for me to close my eyes, every sensitive nerve-ending alight with pleasure as he did. Like he was testing me.

We both let out a sigh.

"Now be a good girl and scream my fucking name while I show this pussy who owns it."

Instead of feeling terrified with it, I felt a rush of heat in my body.

Every inch of him pressed to me.

"Open your eyes, Mon cœur. I want to see you."

But even I tried to disobey, my body had other ideas.

She knew him. And she loved him.

I felt his lips over that sensitive part of my neck that made me clench tighter. Drawing him so deep he felt like he was permanently a part of me.

"If you want to play games with me, I can play them too. I can stay buried so deep in you forever. I'll live inside this pussy. Make it my new home. You won't be able to do anything." His chuckle was dangerous and low. "I can keep you pinned down, desperate, aching, just like this. You like that. I can feel you losing it."

Oh God.

"I'll stay right here until you break. Until you beg. Until you remember me. I've walked through hell these last few weeks without my heart, I'm letting you go now."

Don't.

"Should I keep going?"

Yes. Yes. Yes. Yes. A thousand times.

"I won't ever move, mon cœur. Just stay here until you beg me to move. Until it drives you insane. I could do that. Plant my seed so deep you're mine forever."

A whimper left me as my eyes almost fluttered open.

I arched my hips a little suddenly realizing the situation I was in. Trapped and pinned by over two hundred pounds of a very jealous boyfriend who for all intents and purposes had messed up. Sort of.

Was this *me* punishing him?

Now I knew why he said he wouldn't move.

Because now I *needed* him to move. Something in me building, feeling the tension coiling.

Now that the pain faded completely it left me stuffed to my throat and panting. Wanting. Twisted.

I take it back, forget slow burn, sexual torture is way worse.

"Are you upset that I didn't tell you my truth, or are you upset that I wasn't there?" His voice was low as I felt the desperate need clawing at me. I felt his lips brushing over mine and I squirmed a little.

"Both."

I was struggling. I was trying to shift, move, anything but he had settled so heavily down on me—I was trapped.

"Look at me," he whispered. "Give me your eyes."

I forced them open to find him watching me again with his low-lidded soft ones. His blues looked warmer than they ever had and full of emotion. Raw stark emotion.

I felt my bottom lip wobble, the cracks turning into full on tremors that were threatening to break through to whatever I had been protecting these last few weeks.

"Do you need me now?"

His brow furrowed a little at his hurt. I felt hurt.

But the pleasure was overriding it, my heels digging into his legs.

He was using my own body against me, keeping me on the edge, demanding honesty from me.

That thought lit a fire in me. Tiny but there.

"You don't get to demand from me," I choked out.

My resolve, my fear, my anxiety was so high right now even with him. I was terrified. I could feel it warring with pleasure. Terrified of loss. Of pain. Of hurt. Feeling that ache again.

"I'm not going to lose anymore."

His eyes went midnight, feral and downright dark. "I'm going to spend the rest of my day and my life, showing you just how sorry I am. I won't break your promises again. But right now?"

His hand gripped my throat lightly as he drew out of my body mercifully and my eyes closed.

"Right now, I'm going to show you exactly what happens when you try to run from me."

The first raw thrust inside of me reminded me he wasn't wearing anything, but at the hospital I had gotten on birth control —I wasn't worried about anything. Not with him.

Because deep down I did trust him.

The moment he hit somewhere deep a ragged noise left me and I felt him adjusting, moving my legs higher, pushing some of the throw pillows out of the way.

Every thrust after that I was certain was designed to drive me insane. Noises escaped my lips that sounded completely helpless as his eyes held mine.

"Give me those eyes, mon coeur." His fingers wrapped around my throat tighter but I could still breathe.

I closed mine feeling the cracks in the armor inside of me.

I didn't want to break down with him like this.

Every single thrust began to unlock a part of me I didn't want to let go of.

And I realized in that moment he would do whatever to make sure he ripped her out.

"Is that how it's going to be?" His voice was guttural in my ear as he squeezed my throat and rose up a little above me.

My eyes flew open wondering if he was going to leave.

He wrapped an arm around me, taking me with him and I squealed a little at the position so I held onto him. Scrambling to grip his t-shirt suddenly aware of him being fully clothed and me completely at his mercy.

He moved something around me and then I was set back down my hips pressed up on a throw pillow…

What the—

The angle of this was completely different, my legs even higher than before, and when he ground down I felt him even deeper inside of me, it felt like he had sank even further.

And then he hit somewhere even sweeter while grinding into my clit. Pure white-hot fire burst inside of me.

I couldn't hold back the scream.

"That's my good girl."

407

CHAPTER 45
THIERRY

I was trying not to lose my fucking shit.

And failing.

In this position that wet tight heat of hers wrapped around me like a glove. And I was dying.

I hadn't been with a woman in forever and now?

I felt like a teenager trying not to tap out with the first thrust.

And then she let out that little scream and I knew I had her.

"That's my girl," I growled in her ear, bending my body over hers making sure to do it again and again. Avani went wild under me as I knew I hit that spot in her. "There you go, scream for me."

She let out this whimper that unraveled me at my core.

"Oh God, Thierry."

"That's the spot, isn't it?" I fucking knew it. I drove deeper into her and she screamed again. "Every single fucking time you got around me, I thought about this."

I closed my eyes at my name from her lips. I dreamed of that little fucking moan. I thought about her endlessly for days. Nights. Months.

And I felt her clutching my back, holding on for dear life as she tightened reflexively.

She wasn't going to last very long like this.

I knew enough to know if she came I'd absolutely fucking die. I was hanging on by a thread.

Thinner than I could see. More fragile by the moans leaving her.

Her lush beautiful peach tipped nipples shaking with every slam. I bracketed my arms around her head, looking into those eyes.

My girlfriend's eyes had changed.

She was encased in this ice. I never thought I'd look into that warmth and find nothing. I held onto her as I pounded deep, my own vision hazy with pleasure. My lips parting over hers.

Come back to me.

How do I wake you up?

They batted up at me all soft and full of surrender.

"Tell me you feel this. You feel me?"

She nodded fervently bringing a cruel smirk to my lips. I knew she did.

"You don't get to hide from me, you don't get to run. Not when I've spent the months chasing you. Not when I know, I would chase you across lifetimes to see you like this."

The words fell from my lips, sounding completely demented as I fucked my girl with a fervor I felt. Her eyes glazed with even more hazy pleasure like never before.

I dreamt of her like this. With that look in her eyes as she whimpered over and over.

It was her first time, but with how her heels dug into my thighs urging me closer, I got that Avani wanted me as desperately as I wanted her.

I took her with a violence that should've freaked out both of us and yet, the more I did, the more she urged me on.

"Harder," she gasped into my mouth. "Right there." She desperately grabbed me. "Right there, *please.*"

"I gotcha," I buried my head in her throat, finding that spot her pulse fluttered and bit down. Hard. I pinned her down, making her take every inch of me, angling deeper, thrusting harder—until I couldn't think of anything else. All I could do was feel.

She screamed as she came apart under me. I held her down the moment I felt her hips bucking up, her back arching.

It was explosive, and she tightened so hard around my dick, I lost it.

I groaned into her neck as I came unable to hold it back. It pushed me over my edge.

Shitshitshitshitshit. I tightened my grip on her holding us fused together as I breathed out.

It took me a long time to calm down not because I was out of breath but because it felt like the emotions I had been holding for three weeks had all bubbled to the surface.

And now more than ever I was aware that I felt just as vulnerable as her. I lifted my head a little to make sure she was okay, but I felt her hand gripping my head close to her, her other arm wrapped around me.

A sniffle came from under me. And another.

I swore softly but she held me tight to her.

"Stay," she whispered, her voice hoarse now. "Stay right there."

I didn't move a muscle, just tugged the fucking pillow out so she wouldn't be stuck in this angle tossing it to the floor.

"I'm not going anywhere," I murmured back. "I'm not leaving you anymore."

She didn't say anything but I felt the hot wet tracks of her tears on my skin.

IT TOOK US FOREVER TO GET OFF THAT COUCH.

Her perfume was missing. She smelled like nothing.

Clean. Sterile. Her eyes lost that light in them. And she was crying quietly this time as I slowly, reluctantly, rose up.

"Let me get you up," I murmured. "Let me take care of you."

I didn't know how to process the ache in my chest at her expression. She looked freshly fucked and vulnerable.

She needed a bath. She'd be sore. I needed to get us off this couch and somewhere softer.

The moment I saw the blood on my cock, I knew the guy I shot didn't hurt her like that. But there were other ways to break someone's spirit. I had seen Alisha struggling with him. I saw things she didn't.

I tore off my shirt and helped her up pausing as she blinked at my tattoos on my chest. And then she blinked at the rest of me. Her eyes widening in horror.

"W-what happened to you?"

There might have been a second reason I didn't take off my shirt for Avani ever.

Until now this was the first time I had. Her mouth dropped

open, her trembling fingers brushing over one of the many scars I did have.

Turns out, being a Reaper didn't mean you were unscathed.

"Got into my fair share of fights and scrapes, mon coeur."

I told her I worked security. I didn't tell her how brutal of a business being a mercenary was.

I had a few cuts and scrapes, but some old scars from the one time I'd gotten caught in a bomb. A burn scar on my arm. A few on my chest and back.

While I might've been prettier from the neck up, the rest of me was blatantly aware—I'd been through shit.

I didn't mind it though. I just didn't like the look on Avani's face.

"You've kept so many secrets from me," she whispered her voice hoarse.

I tipped my head, taking her naked body into my arms and standing up with her. "I have," I walked us to the back where her bathroom was. "But I intend to tell you every single thing I can today."

But first, I needed to find out what happened to her.

In the tub I settled with her in my arms cuddling her and she quietly filled me in while I soothed her. We both had a lot to catch up on. My fault.

Since Avani and I could've done this three weeks ago.

I swore internally as she spoke crying silently and telling me what happened.

And so long long hours later after cleaning us up, eating together, I began explaining everything to a wide-eyed Avani who listened.

With both of us on her bed, I covered us up with a comforter and turned on her heated blanket so she'd be less sore.

Her eyes grew progressively wider with every confession. I told her *everything* in that moment.

I didn't want to keep secrets from her anymore.

I spilled on every. Single. Thing.

Including the Nash sisters.

Including my siblings.

Even Andrei and Talia.

"Good lord," she whispered, her eyes wider than ever now. "That's what you've spent three weeks doing? Juggling everyone? Everything?"

I saw Avani doing the math as she looked at me.

Keeping her safe. Her family safe. Her sister's man alive.

I told her about Lucas and she gasped. "Alisha didn't tell me he was shot."

"I don't think she can," I explained the entire thing to her. And then I dared to say it. "I don't think it's just Reed. When you were at the hospital and when you were at K2, did you meet someone named Gabriel?"

She nodded looking bemused. "I can't even fathom what he's been through. He was really kind to me." Avani knew everything now and she looked at me like I had three heads. "You think he's in it with Reed?"

"I do. And I think he's the key to everything. He's the one at Titan with the most secrets. The fact that he's been using his real name, but he doesn't exist, he operates with confidence in knowing that he'll never get caught. I think that he and your sisters man, stole something that they shouldn't have. And now, I have to figure out what this cluster fuck is."

"Teo and your family don't know about me?"

"No, the same way the Titan's don't know about me." I knew with confidence after Avani protected me from Kieran, nobody knew we were together. Jace protected me from cameras around the city tracing my phone to erase me.

In turn, I would have to hope nobody was watching Avani. I doubted it. She was the least likely to be watched.

I told her about my suspicions. And then I told her about Evie.

Avani munched on her pizza a little bit more than stunned now. "Why is everyone lying?"

"I don't know, mon coeur, but I will always tell you the truth. I only held back because I didn't even know how to start. And then that happened to you…"

When she'd been kidnapped.

We were sitting against her headboard eating pizza as I finished. Everything. Every last thing. She knew it.

"I can't believe you chased me down."

"I would always chase you down. I have from the start."

"I know," she murmured her eyes softer. "Thank you feels silly now."

I smirked. "I accept."

"Reed…he stole…an object," she muttered searching her room,

412

the comforter pulled up high to her chest. "That doesn't sound like him. Why would he ever…he has money…"

"I don't think Alma would give this up. Whatever it is."

She frowned. "Alma didn't say what it was? She's the new head of Talon…"

I shook my head. She looked deep in thought.

"What is it?" I asked.

She shook her head. "Is it a sentimental item? Related to the sisters or her family?"

I nodded. "Has to be for her to go so hard."

Avani's eyes met mine now with a glimmer of fire in them.

"Do you think it could be family jewelry?"

I blinked. "What?"

"It's something sentimental. She's a woman. My Mum had her hairpins. The one I was wearing the day I met you? The one I lost —" she hadn't lost it. "It belonged to her Mum. And now me. Unless Alma has the same, it has to be a sentimental piece of jewelry. Reed has no need for art, and he wouldn't steal just anything—I think it's jewelry. A ring maybe? A necklace perhaps?"

I paused in chewing. I never *considered what* the object was.

It could've been anything.

"Why do you say that?" I liked the way Avani's mind worked. Because what she didn't have in the same level of experience, I think, she made up for with her intellect. And what I had an experience, I filled in her caps. She was my partner.

"Because she's a woman. Maybe the object belonged to her, but if it did, it seems logical it belonged to someone else before her. It's not about the value of the object, it's about the history. Like every diamond is valuable, but a diamond worn by the first Queen of a nation? Is priceless. This isn't just about Alma. That object, a piece of jewelry had to belong to someone else. Why else would she want it so bad?"

"Like her mother?"

Avani nodded. " Or her sister. Or *someone*."

"But she's a Nash."

"I know, which doesn't make sense your sister-in-law didn't want to answer questions. I think Talia knows what she's hiding," she murmured. "I didn't know Gabriel's team died. I didn't know any of this, so I'm processing this as well. This is insanity, Thierry. And you're sure you don't want to speak to Reed?"

I shook my head. "Not after he threatened Teo and I almost shot him."

Avani's face fell when I explained to her the entire thing about that day and she looked a little hurt and broken.

"This is madness."

"Yeah, you're telling me." I said. "Sorry for…dumping it on you."

"No," she shook her head. "It's like a textbook. It's okay."

She sat there her red pepper flaked pizza slice in hand.

"I can't believe this. Do you think Alisha is aware of this?"

I didn't know. "Jace doesn't know how deep the rabbit the hole runs. I was hoping you might help me fill in some blanks."

She shook her head. "Hang on, you didn't tell me this months ago, because you thought what? If I knew you did the same job Reed did, I might judge you?"

I swallowed not considering that Reed Whittaker did in fact do the same things I did, but for some reason it felt different when I did them. It felt worse. "Well, now that you say it like that, I sound stupid as fuck."

She frowned. "You're not stupid. I understand where you're coming from, I just think this mystery you've landed yourself in, requires some level of trust. Of course I will help you solve it. Is Reed in danger? My sister should know if he is."

"I think Reed knows." I told her. "I think he's very aware because of that hacker. Someone's been ten steps ahead of everyone."

"It's not Evie, she's with Lucas. Though Evie does work IT for Titan," Avani frowned, processing everything calmer than I expected. And didn't I feel like an idiot not realizing my girl would be calm about this stuff.

"Do you think I can show you some photos and maybe you recognize these people?"

She nodded again. "Of course. What are you going to do about all this?"

"I need to figure out what the fuck is happening. And then," I let out a breath hating the words coming out of my mouth. "I need to figure out how to get Talon out of the city before they start killing even more people. Lucas is the only small casualty that can be allowed. The moment Samara's trigger happy ass gets to a Titan?"

"Trouble," she murmured looking at me with a different look in her eyes now. "I will help you."

I paused. "Are you still mad at me, mon coeur?"

"A little. But I need time to process this information too."

Right. Because both of us had been through a rough few weeks.

"I have something…I wanna show you," I ducked my head slowly leaving the bed.

When I found my pants in bathroom I dug out my phone and that hairpin of hers.

I trekked back to the bedroom where she set our pizzas down on her dresser and straightened.

Her eye tracked down my body and I tried not to feel satisfaction at the dark look in them.

I set my phone down and held out her pin that had burned a hole in my pocket. I chuckled at her jaw dropping, eyes widening.

"I knew you took it, you scoundrel!"

And at her laugh and the way her eyes lit up I felt my heart crack open.

There it was.

Her eyes sparkled as she laughed a little taking it. "You have no idea I was so upset with myself when I thought I lost it."

"You can have it back," I was aware of giving up my lucky charm. But I didn't think I needed it when I had the real reason for it in my life.

"Why did you keep it?" She shook her head. "After all these years?"

I told her sitting at the edge of her bed not giving a shit I wasn't wearing anything.

"I didn't even realize I was carrying it around everywhere, and then I was in Nairobi and the hotel I was in blew up. I almost got caught in that blast. I almost died that day. My buddy, Cole dragged me out. I blacked out and when I got back to my room I saw that I never took this with me. I used to carry it everywhere and the one time I didn't? I almost died so I ended up keeping it. Most Reaper's have short life spans given our career. Every time I had that, I never missed, nothing bad happened. And I was safe. So I kept it."

Her rapid blinking told me she understood what I was trying to say. Her entire face crumpled.

"You should keep it," she whispered brokenly handing it back after last look. "Here." She pressed it back into my hands. And then she frowned at my hands as she pressed it in.

"Gabriel…Alma…" she whispered it as she took the pin from my hands. She looked it over. "If someone stole this why would you be upset?"

I answered with zero hesitation. "Because it's yours. It's a piece of you—" I stopped talking. "Oh, fuck."

Her eyes widened. "You have to talk to Alma about this object. I think Gabriel stole it, but it's not about her—"

"It belonged to someone before her."

"And that person was important to *both* of them."

I kissed her swiftly taking the hairpin back. "Have I mentioned you're a genius?"

"I may have heard it once or twice," she laughed low again looking so damn beautiful with all her chestnut hair waving and curling and her eyes on me.

A little hint of light there now. Better. Much better.

"I was worried about you," I admitted feeling the ache intensify as she watched me. "I didn't know if you were gone. I stayed until I knew you were alive."

Her throat worked, her eyes wet again.

"You know," she said softly. Her eyes raked down my chest. "I'm still pretty upset with you."

My heart clenched as she said it.

"So if you want to get up here and convince me to not be upset," she said primly looking away tracing a circle on my skeleton tattoos. "I won't mind."

A slow grin curved my lips. "You're not sore."

She thought about it with a flush on her cheeks. "A little. But…I want you too much."

I grinned. "I can think of a few other things."

Her brows rose.

My lips stretched wider as I kissed her. "Lay back, *mon coeur*."

CHAPTER 46
AVANI

I ALWAYS BELIEVED IN LOVE. I DID.

Mum and Papa taught me that.

But with Thierry? It transcended what I thought possible.

He laid me back and dipped between my legs eating at me until I came so hard. He had been my first time many times. In many ways. I was a little embarrassed.

But it got better and better.

This time when he slid into me, he didn't move.

Thierry kissed me, playing with my body until every nerve ending felt alive with sensation. I came just like that and he marveled a little as he followed,

"Mon coeur," he murmured over my lips. "Please tell me you're on something. I think I forgot with how excited I got."

A smile tipped up my lips.

I told him I was on birth control after the scary incident.

His eyes shuttered a little whenever I spoke about it.

But I understood it was more about me almost dying at the hands of a mad man than him being upset.

We talked for long moments, my hairpin on his side of the bed as he fiddled with it. All these years he kept it.

I was more or less reeling as he fell asleep next to me with my thoughts.

Gabriel and Alma the two heads of two different organizations were connected. I was sure of it.

Reed had no reason to steal anything.

And even he had?

I had no reason to doubt Reed when I had seen the lengths he would go to for my sister.

Logically, Reed was in love with Alisha—not whoever this Alma woman was.

If Lucy Devereaux, Evie's boyfriend's sister, worked for Gabriel? He was single.

He was a likely bet.

But…I looked at Thierry and I thought about everything he had told me. Everything he was juggling. It sounded intense and insane. It sounded absolutely mad.

He was lying to his family, he was lying to his old team, he was lying to me initially—to protect me. How on Earth had he lasted so long?

My eyes took in the shadows under his eyes. His features clouded with worry even in his sleep. He was juggling so much and once he had explained and I heard him out? It made sense.

Part of me was recovering from my kidnapping and at how I felt. Another part of me recognized…I was wrong. I had been enough. I always had been. He just needed to give me agency too.

Once he had? I wanted to help him. I wanted to help unravel… whatever was going on at Titan.

Mostly because…I didn't want Alisha and Reed in danger.

Even as collateral. Part of me wondered if I could just go and talk to Gabriel and ask him for all of the answers I wanted.

But another part of me wondered if he would either give it to me, or he would just lie to my face and tell me that everything was fine.

Because there was a moment when we were at the hospital, when he came and told me that I had to sign the papers in case something happened to Alisha, and I remember thinking in that moment, that he was lying to me.

Gabriel lied when he looked at me and said Alisha was fine.

I knew it then.

I didn't know how but I did.

And this was such a big deal. There was no way they would tell me. Which meant I would have to work with Thierry and figure it out.

From the beginning.

The sun was going down outside when I found my phone in the living room and went through my messages. Alisha. Gabriel. Even Reed. Kieran.

Thierry's jealousy over Kieran was nothing because I didn't actually feel anything for Kieran. I kinda thought he would be good for Marissa.

She was a little mad and I thought her wild child attitude would be good to keep Kieran on his toes, which was why I thought a group date might be better.

I texted everyone back to let them know I was fine before sitting down on my couch in Thierry's hoodie to make a map of everything.

In between me writing my thoughts down I kept thinking about Thierry's scars. His life. His upbringing.

Talia.

She knew things. She wasn't saying anything because she didn't want us to know.

Hmmm.

I began to formulate a mind map while he slept.

I always thought better with color.

I would help him get to the bottom of this.

Privately I knew Reed and Thierry now, didn't get along. Which meant I couldn't tell my family about him.

And the last thing I wanted to do was keep him a secret any longer. Every time I had gone to tell my family, something had happened. And now I realized I was grateful that I didn't tell them, because I would've exposed him.

One day I would have to.

I would.

Because...this man not only loved me? He had been kept a secret by everybody his entire life. I don't want our want to be a secret.

Which meant the sooner I solve this case with him, and I helped him, the sooner I could stand by his side and tell Alisha I was dating Thierry.

CHAPTER 47
AVANI

"You got me a birthday present?" I asked Thierry a few days after we'd left my apartment.

"I built it," he said with a smile as he walked me with my eyes closed somewhere in his warehouse.

Because all of my classes were online. I was able to actually get more work done in less time. Ahead of schedule. Which meant Thierry drove me out to his new apartment. A warehouse located across the Brooklyn Bridge.

After spending days wrapped up in each other in my apartment, we finally went to his.

The imposing structure looked terrible on the outside. A bit broken down and eerie like a haunted house. Weathered down a bit with brick and industrial vibes.

On the inside? It soared four stories high. The basement level beneath us where he parked completely hidden from view.

It was lavish and stunning with enormous mahogany and gold trim everywhere reminding me of Andrei's old apartment.

High vaulted ceilings with massive windows led in warm lighting despite the chill outside the place was warm and cozy.

Wooden beams from the second and third floor showed me to the mezzanine bedroom.

There was a straight staircase leading to it, but the artfully placed vintage industrial fixtures around it lent it an otherworldly quality.

"This looks like Andrei's place, but better."

He grinned and pointed to the fridge in the open plan enormous kitchen spanning into the living room.

"You put our photos on the fridge."

"It's your home too."

I tried not to trip over my own two feet surprised as he said it on my way to the kitchen. He had put all our photos up. Our memories.

And he said he had to show me the third floor. In his personal elevator.

"This is insane. How much money do you have?" I realized how shamelessly forward that was, but for Gods sake the man had an elevator in his warehouse.

"Plenty. Spend it how you want to." He chuckled at my expression. "I was jealous when Reed paid for your things. I knew you'd never use his card, but I wanted to take care of you too. I'm comfortable. Not as much as my brother's but enough."

Enough to have an elevator. I was blinking as he handed me an eye mask. "You have to put this on for my surprise."

I eyed him and he chuckled. "Not that kind of surprise but if you want I can after."

I blushed turning violently red. Even after days of rolling around my bed with him, I still wanted him. I quickly put the mask on as he helped me walk out.

"It's got so much space I never have to leave it. Take a step there. Okay almost done. Almost."

"I swear to God if this is just a room full of cupcakes—"

"It's even better. One second, I gotta turn the lights on."

I waited with the blindfold on.

He rushed back to me, the air shifting around me then. "Okay, ready?"

"I am quite frankly dying."

He chuckled as he took it off. And my jaw dropped.

"Oh. My." *God. My brain is going to explode.*

This wasn't real.

I looked at him and back at the room I was in. It was a library.

But not like…Andrei's library or study. It was a library. The entire room. The long length of the third floor. Entirely.

Walls to walls of books, floral chandeliers, soft plush couches, coffee tables with globes, books, golden decor, rolling ladders to reach every shelf.

"This is like something out of a fantasy…"

The entire place looked too exquisite to be real. Like it belonged in a fairy tale. I looked around unable to even breathe.

He nodded. "And it's all yours."

What? My jaw hit the floor. What did he just say? The air whooshed out of my lungs.

You built me a library…

I couldn't breathe. My chest tightened at the space, my heart overflowing. *He built me a library.*

"I was going to show you on your birthday because I wanted to move out of Andrei's place. When I found out about Talon," he explained with a soft expression on his face. "I had to move fast. This was the last bit of it. It wasn't too difficult to get it all up here. Come on, there's something here I want to show you." He moved down the long hall to the end of it where I saw the entire wall dedicated to romance. "I thought this might be a solid touch."

He handed me a copy of—"This is the first print of House of Midnight and Shadow."

I couldn't breathe. "Where did you—"

"I just asked Jace. He found a seller with the copy. We got it."

I blinked. "This is a fortune." All of this was. "You built me a library."

I think I'm going to pass out.

"I thought it might be a good place for you to spend your time when you move in with me." He looked embarrassed as he paused. "Happy Birthday, mon coeur. I'm sorry I missed it."

Something wild exploded in my chest. I practically threw myself in his arms kissing him until I was tearing at his clothes overcome with emotions.

"When I move with you—"

"If you want—" he broke off as I kissed him harder.

"I want—" I broke off dropping my sweater on the library floor. "I do."

"Here? In your library—"

"Our library," I whispered frantic stripping down to nothing. "It's our home."

His eyes were midnight dark as he kissed me hungrily taking me down to the floor in a toppled grace that only he had.

"You need me?" He backed me into the shelves and I gasped a little.

"*Yes.*"

His smile was wicked. "I've dreamed of having you here, like this, in our home. In every room."

"Take me," I whispered arching into him as his hands traced trails of fire down my body. "Please."

"Please what?" His lips moved over mine, down my jaw, my pulse. "Say it."

"Please, fuck me." I whimpered it as his fingers slid up my skirt tearing at my stockings.

A soft noise left me. "I love listening to you beg." His voice was dark velvet over my skin as he brushed over the slick heat of my body. My knees almost gave out with the force of it had his hand not slid further.

My mouth parted in a gasp, helpless and pinned as two of his fingers slid into me.

"You're always so soaked for me," he crooned. "Such a good girl."

My vision went hazy as I held onto him while he curled those fingers in. He'd done it before but he'd been eating me out every single time. Now, the sensation was different.

Noises fell from my lips as he moved his fingers against a spot so sensitive I bit back a scream.

"No," he growled. "This is our home. You can scream as much as you like."

A broken noise left me. "Take me. Please, fuck me. I need you—" I broke off when he withdrew his fingers and turned me around.

"Put your hands on the wall."

I obeyed as I heard the snap and clink of him working at his pants. We both groaned at the first press of him behind me. In this position he always felt bigger than he was. Enormous. Stretching me impossibly open. I whimpered as his hand moved around to my clit.

It was electric when he started playing with me as he slid in.

I'd barely adjusted to his size when he drew out still rubbing my clit and began a ferocious ruthless rhythm.

"OhGodOhGodohGod," I cried. My orgasm wrecked through me so much faster than before.

My legs shook wildly and he wrapped an arm around my waist to make sure I didn't fall over.

My hands slipped from the wall as he held onto me, both of us still wearing clothes as he almost picked me up never stopping. I screamed a little as he bent me over a larger table.

His hands tearing at my sweater, dragging it up to unsnap my bra.

The moment they were free, his fingers were on them, the skeletal tattoos on my skin, rough and possessive. The sounds left my throat then as he slammed into my sensitized pussy over and over. Tugging at my nipples at the same time.

It was electric.

"Look at you," he growled in my ear. "Taking me like a good slut."

I screamed as his rhythm never faltered drawing me frightening closer to my second orgasm. I barely recovered from my first one.

"Does my good girl like her little pussy fucked?"

"Y-yes." I was struggling. I was dying right now. "Right there."

The obscene sound of him slamming into me over and over filled the air.

"Scream for me," he growled. "Tell me what I wanna hear."

I obeyed as his thrusts turned wilder. *"Fuck me."*

"Harder?"

"Yesyesyesyes, harder. Don't stop, please."

His tongue traced my neck and I felt my knees tremble a little almost collapsing. "Careful what you ask for mon coeur. I'm half tempted to keep you here forever, put a chain around your neck and drag you around the place whenever I want you on my cock."

Oh. God. I clenched so tightly at the thought he chuckled.

"I think my heart loves that—"

"I do. Yesyesyesyes." Every single thrust I cried out. I didn't have to hold back here. This was our space. My home with him. I felt a little more than emotional.

I wanted that. I wanted to be his. I screamed a little as his thrusts became almost brutal.

I cried out holding onto the table grateful for how solid it was right now because I was going to come.

It was building so fast, I couldn't stop it.

Words left my lips that sounded like they were coming from someone else. "I want you to destroy me." A groan left his lips as I gasped it. "I want you to break me. Tear me apart."

Behind me Thierry groaned. "You wanna be my slut?"

"*Godsyes.*"

I wanted to be fucked. Devoured. Consumed from the inside out. I wanted to be possessed by him. Erased of my identity and branded into his skin.

The romance novels lied to me. I didn't want a hero. I wanted to belong to the shadows.

In the in-between with this man.

Everything else paled in comparison.

"Gonna tear into this pussy and give you what you asked for." Oh. Thank. God.

I was right there. Right there.

"Harder, please."

He gave me exactly what I needed.

I squealed as it drew closer and closer.

"*OhGodohGodohGod.*"

He licked down my throat as he rolled my nipples and I shattered right there. It imploded through me like a supernova and I couldn't breathe anymore.

"*That's my fucking good girl.*" My eyes rolled back at the sound of that. "Come for me, little love. Let me feel it."

He groaned as he drove deeper and I felt myself rising up off my toes.

One of his hands came up and grabbed my throat to keep me still, as he pounded in harder and I could hear the obscene noises coming from me.

"Keep coming for me. Let me feel that pussy lose it."

I was losing my breath like this. A squeal escaped me as he pounded into my sensitized body.

I was brainless. Fucked. Burning from the inside out.

"Nobody's gonna save you from me."

I whimpered as my orgasm felt prolonged now. "I don't wanna be *saved.*"

"No?" He crooned. "What do you want?"

Just you.

Oh God.

"Just you," I whispered unable to stop shaking now. "Please—Please." He bent me over the table and I held on for dear life as he pounded into me so hard then.

Fuckfuckfuckfuckfuck.

That was so good. And I wanted nothing else but this forever.

I think I was turning into an animal.

A horny wild animal.

That was it. Because I was on him all the time. Reaching for him at night. Waking him up with his cock in my mouth in the mornings.

Thierry returned it. Taking me everywhere. In every room in the warehouse, in the pool, in the shower, in the garage and everything in between.

I felt depraved. Almost like I was making up for lost time.

We finished one round and it turned into another. And another. Until we were both panting and even then?

I felt hyper aroused.

I couldn't stop reaching for him. Sinking to my knees whenever he was around and taking him into my mouth for so long he drew me back and asked me if I was all right.

I was.

Just needing him.

He bent me over on his pool table and took me there one night like a savage. Another time I rode him on the bar. I was aware I was turning into a wilder woman. And I loved this part of me.

And I honestly thought he had a mental list of everywhere he could and couldn't take me.

One night he sat on the bed while I was grinding on his lap. He was buried deep in me and I was adjusting to his size.

"We should make a list," I whispered.

"Whatever you want," he panted around my nipple in his mouth. "Whatever."

I bit back a wild laugh that bubbled up.

"Of things…places…anything we wanna do."

He tugged my nipple and I whimpered a little. "Anything?"

"*Anything.*"

"Like?" He suckled harder making it difficult to think.

"Like I want to try anal." I giggled at his reaction as his eyes widened comically."What?" I didn't stop grinding and I watched him struggling.

"Avani—"

"Don't tell me you haven't thought about it."

He groaned. "You're going to destroy me at this rate."

It made me laugh a little more as his cheeks flushed. He groaned a little. "Make your list, mon coeur. Just give me a heads up so I can get what you need."

I kissed him the entire time I rode him.

~

"W<small>E SHOULD REALLY STOP DOING THIS</small>," I <small>MOANED</small>.

"Stop, what?" He popped his head up from licking a trail down my body. He looked comically horrified.

I grinned feeling joy fluttering around in my chest. "Why are we like this?"

"Making up for lost time," he muttered working his way down until he ate at me. I lost all train of thought until I tugged him up on top of me.

In his car. We'd gone to see a movie.

Or we tried to.

Both of us sat there for twenty minutes before we took one look at each other and left. Before making out like wild people in his car.

He was tearing at my skirts and stocking so much he just promised to buy me new ones as he ate at me in the backseat.

"Get inside me." I moaned. Thankfully, he had tinted windows and parked in a darker part of the lot. "God, I wish we could go home right now."

A wicked look entered his eyes as he rose up over me. A grin spread his lips.

"Do you want to try something with me?"

I blinked at his devious grin. He adjusted his clothing and climbed to the front turning on his car and I already knew where he was going.

"We're both incorrigible." I whispered climbing on his lap as he entered in his address. His car was one of the only Roadster models with the self-driving feature Teo had installed.

"Maybe," he whispered as he undid his pants taking his cock out for me to sit on. "But you fucking love it."

I did. I grinned into his mouth as I felt myself stretching over his thick stalk until I moaned.

"There you go," he crooned as the car started moving. For a second I thought about the windows and the worry people might see me having sex with my boyfriend and I had to remind myself to calm down.

"This is terrifying." I whispered against his lips. "But so hot."

He moaned into my mouth as he kissed me and I ground down on him. "Ride me, mon coeur."

I did and when we got to the highway I completely understood why people did risky things.

"I love this," I bounced on him over and over slamming myself down and he threw his head back with a groan.

"Just like that," he swore grabbing my hips and helping. We were going the speed limit from what I saw Thierry hadn't wanted us to be too risky.

A beeping noise filled the air and we both stopped making out for him to look at the dash. He swore a little, wild blue eyes meeting mine. "Cops."

I looked around feeling a little panic as I stopped moving on him. "They're not on the road."

"Oracle has a sensor. She tells me before we even see them." He tapped something behind me to make it stop. "We can stop if you want. In case they pull us over, I'm not driving any faster than this with you in the car."

I clenched at that.

"No," I kissed him picking up my hips again feeling on edge. "I don't want to stop."

He groaned a little closing his eyes. "Slow down, at least. I can't think when you do that." And then he seemed to have second thoughts. "Oracle, this is Grim."

"Yes, sir."

I gripped him so tightly never getting used to his AI embedded in his devices. He rarely spoke to her and when he did, her human voice scared me.

"Take the nearest exit and find a fucking parking lot."

"Certainly, sir."

I laughed at the look on his face as he went back to kissing me. He shook his head. "I've created a monster."

"A scoundrel." I corrected. "Now I am too."

His grin was wicked on me. "Still so proper."

"You love it." And I began to move again loving the way he threw his head back with another groan.

428

"You broke my dick."

"I did not break it." I giggled. My chest felt almost buoyant with him and his warmth. "You had no problem with me earlier."

"I think I'm dead," he whispered dramatically. "Killed by my mermaid."

We burst into laughter as we laid in his enormous King sized bed after what felt like the fifteenth time I'd come. Thierry laughed outright as he teased me. "We're both—what's your word, mon coeur?"

"I can't think," I panted. "Words are words."

He laughed rolling onto his side and I did the same looking at him. "You're a pirate, mon coeur. Like your books."

"Says the pirate himself." *Hang on. Mermaid. Pirate. How did he know about*—I gasped suddenly wide awake. "You did not—"

"I *did*." His grin was wicked, his eyes twinkling with glee. Electric blue met mine. "I listened to all the audiobooks. Every single one. And *you* are a filthy little slut."

He grinned as he said it.

I giggled feeling warmth in me at that.

"I like it. I know." I grinned brushing my fingers on his tattooed chest. "Isn't it great? It's rather raunchy."

"It's basically just sex. With demon pirates and mermaids who have legs on land." He pulled me closer to him to kiss me.

"It's hot." I argued feeling a little protective of my favorite fantasy book series. "You liked it. And it's not just sex. There's a huge plot. The sex softens the stress."

There was plot. Feathered with hot scenes. I think a few weeks had gone by where Thierry juggled his life and I juggled mine and these breaks were the ones I craved.

"But there is sex," he reminded me, brushing my nose with his. "You love it." He brushed his lips with mine.

"I love you." I finished feeling calmer than I had in years while also being surrounded by the most chaos. His eyes softened.

"Your eyes are back to normal," he murmured. "They're not dark anymore."

"Were they different?"

He nodded looking almost relieved. "I'm glad you're back, mon coeur. I was worried about you for a second. Do you feel better?"

I nodded slowly. "I do. I'm getting better."

More of me felt thawed out. Less dark.

I knew his nickname. Grim.

Ironically, Thierry's presence, his love, taking care of me, and giving me our home—gave me back life.

The more I spent with him, the more alive I came.

I was healing.

CHAPTER 48
THIERRY

"I KNOW WHAT THE OBJECT IS."

"What?"

Teo had wanted to meet me quickly before he drove off to his penthouse.

His voice was downright dark as he stood in my basement garage.

He'd taken his car and came over one morning and he hadn't bothered to go upstairs. Said it was too urgent.

Avani was with her sister right now at K2, but I was aware if Teo came upstairs to my living space? He'd see our photos. Our life.

Her pink sweaters and dresses, my darker clothes right next to hers.

She existed in her apartment on campus like it was a halfway crash house.

My home was hers. Ours.

"I know what the object is," his eyes were a little bloodshot and he looked...

"Why are you covered in bruises?" I frowned at him despite his excitement. Teo was covered in *hickies* and bruises and scratch marks. "Did a woman do that to you?"

His grin was wide enough for me to realize why Avani told me not to smile like that.

My brother looked like he'd spent the last few days all tangled up in bed.

"Your girlfriend is possessive." He motioned to my hickies. His expression turned feral. "Is she upstairs right now?" He leaned back almost triumphant. "You know I never thought you'd share your little hideaway with a woman. You love her."

Jesus fucking Christ. I snapped. "Get to the point."

"It's a *necklace*," Teo said looking downright devious. "With Gabriel Monroe's name on it. Your Alma has been keeping secrets. If that's even her real fucking name at this point."

"*What?*"

And just like that Avani's words came back to me.

A present. A memory.

We were using her hairpin as a stand-in.

But now? Mon coeur was right.

Alma's object wasn't just any necklace.

"Why would a necklace owned by a Nash have someone else's name on it?"

"Exactly," Teo snapped his fingers. "And you have her number, but you don't know where she stays?"

I shook my head my mind was reeling. Gabriel Monroe stole Alma's necklace for what? "But don't worry, I have a plan to get the necklace back."

And then I listened to Teo tell me how he had found Lucy Devereaux the thief. He had met her. And he was going to—

"You're going to fake a break-in to K2, with Lucy and Jace to get the real necklace back on paper. But you want to make a fake necklace for me to give to Alma? Are you insane?"

"I am brilliant, no?" Teo grinned wide. "And then you will deliver the necklace to Alma and her associates and they will leave New York. Forever. Good riddance."

I blinked at my brother's logic. "You want me to lie to Alma to get her out of the city? Hang on—" I held up a hand. "First of all, how the fuck did you find Lucy Dev—"

"I didn't." He was grinning wider now. "Remember Adam?"

"Reed's brother." Whittaker.

"He came to me." Teo pointed at his chest.

"And he just told you his girlfriend is a thief who he is *still* dating—didn't they break up?"

Teo looked like it was Christmas morning. "No. They didn't. Adam came to me over something that happened with Kieran, and I met Lucy and—"

Oh. *Motherfucker.*

"And *naturally* you slept with her? Lucas is your friend, you just slept with Adam Whittaker's girlfriend who also happens to be Lucas's little sister behind his back?"

"*Non*, I slept with Adam Whittaker's girlfriend *with* him."

I blinked. Call me surprised because that was one curve-ball I didn't see coming. My brother looked like a cat that ate all the canaries. In this case, he caught one canary for sure.

The jewel thief.

Well.

Shit.

I knew my brother and his expression turned downright red. For once. I raised a brow.

"He…what? Did he just walk into your office and ask you to fuck his girlfriend—" I broke off at the look on Teo's face. *"Jesus Christ."*

He had.

I underestimated the Whittaker boys. *Especially* the younger one.

Laughter bubbled in my throat at Teo's pleased expression.

"And now you wanna pretend to steal the necklace back from Reed who you know has it because Lucy fucking turned it over to him. Was it when she went to visit Titan Midtown?"

"Exactly," Teo nodded looking uncomfortable for once. It was a rare sight and it made me shift.

Of fucking course my brother would have a threesome with the jewel thief and her man.

I swore a little letting out a breath.

"This is insane." mon coeur was right. This was insanity. "How are you going to recreate it?"

Teo explained Lucy had a photo from a few months ago when Reed had sent her on the assignment. To fucking Senegal. She'd taken it and she memorized almost everything about the damn thing. And she had admitted it belonged to Monroe.

"So Gabriel Monroe stole it back?"

Teo shook his head. "I don't know. I just know if she's here for the necklace, and the necklace alone. She'll go away if we give it back."

"But what if she knows it's not the real one?"

The universe better fucking help me then.

He made a noise.

"Lucy says it's *just* the necklace. There's nothing else about it. Alma will never know. I will make it the best. And then you can introduce me to your girlfriend."

"Absolutely not. Absolutely *not*." Did he even realize what he was asking me to do? "I can't lie to Alma! She'll know."

"*How?*" He raised his brows. "How would she know? She trusts you like you're her dead brother or something. She knows you. She likes you. Lucy and I are going to pretend to break in to K2. This should alert Bexley that the necklace was stolen *again*. Titan will think it's done by a third party. Talon will think the necklace is theirs. They will leave. Titan will hunt a ghost. And you and I are free."

"*When you say it like it sounds fucking foolproof.*"

"*That's because it is.*" He looked at me like I was insane for not considering it sooner. "I don't know why I didn't think about it sooner."

"You're juggling Durand and Roadsters—"

"*Oui*," Teo switched to French. "*But relying on a thief like Lucy is brilliant. She will pull off the stunt. But I can get us free.*"

As my heart would say.

"This is insane."

"I am insane," Teo pointed at himself. "I have to do this. For all of you."

"What if you get caught?"

"I won't," he made a noise gripping my shoulder. "Jace will block out all the camera's. Nobody will see me or her. Nobody will ever know I was with Lucy. Even now Jace blacks out my location."

He had been pinging mine across the city through his program.

"I promise. I can do this. Give me a week. I'll stage it perfectly."

I shook my head. "I need to go and lay out the groundwork with Bexley, otherwise, it won't be believable."

Because Talon didn't know I knew.

Motherfucker.

Things had been eerily quiet. Something had happened to the Talon girls. Something to make them stand down. Bexley had left me alone, Alma had gone quiet, and Samara had all but vanished.

I explained that to Teo. His frown deepened listening to me.

"A third variable has entered," he murmured. "Something's going on with them."

434

"And I need to figure out what."

On my drive to the Primrose while Avani was with her sister, I ended up running through scenarios in my mind.

Talia was hiding something. I hadn't heard from her in ages. Her calls went to voicemail after that confrontation. Andrei had asked Teo to juggle a few things on his own.

Now Teo was handling a staged break-in.

And I had to go and finesse information out of a nineteen year old.

I called Jace and asked him for the one thing I'd never imagine I would ever do. "Can you look up information on Alma Nash? I want everything you can find on her."

"Yes, sir."

"Matter of fact, run me through every single person I know in Talon. Get me all their info."

Jace agreed and went to work. The man was a fucking national treasure with what work he did do for my family.

"Yes, sir."

I had to go and finesse Bexley now and get information out of her. I fucking prayed mon coeur was having an easier time getting any kind of information about Titan out of her sister.

I got to the Primrose and I went straight to Bexley's room.

K-POP music blasted out again and when she answered the door she was in a robe and the television was blaring some anime at the loudest volume it could go.

There were snacks everywhere and the room was a mess. Something in my chest tightened.

"Please tell me this isn't your first time alone," I looked at her blonde hair matted and messy and she looked a little wide-eyed at me.

"What the fuck happened to you?" Bexley Carter had seen better days. Her space buns undone, a bathrobe that had seen better days. Her entire room looked like a hurricane had gone through it and she smelled weird.

Clothes. Tech cords. Her eyes were wide.

"Ummm, things have been kinda quiet on our front so I've been hanging out."

I looked around the room again. "I know, but where's Samara? Alma?"

She let out a breath as she wiggled her bare toes like a child as she watched me.

Sometimes I forgot, Bexley's entire life had been in the Talon compound. She'd learned everything from the girls there. Which meant, she didn't know how to be alone. She never had been.

Did they forget about her?

No. They wouldn't do that to Bexley.

I felt an unfamiliar sensation in my chest while watching her. No food containers from room service. Just instant ramen and lots of candy and snacks. No fresh clothes.

Just a sign that nobody bothered to check on her.

A hot flare of something went through me.

"When was the last time you showered?"

"Well," she started those big blue eyes wide. "Samara keeps to herself unless Alma needs her here. But Alma…" she looked a little uneasy. "She made a friend…and he's been spending time with her."

I frowned. "That doesn't sound like her." Out of all the people I knew, Alma was the one least likely to be involved with anyone.

"Yeah," Bexley didn't sound enthusiastic stretching out the word. "She kinda paused the whole search for her stuff and they hang out a lot now. She said she's catching up on lost time or something? I don't know."

"Who is it? What's his name?" Now I was curious.

She shook her head. "Alma just said he's an old friend."

But that didn't make sense. I was still staring at the piles of her clothes in the room. I need to go talk to her now then. This was not what I thought they were coming here for.

Something was deeply wrong.

But I had one problem to fix at a time.

"Listen," I started in on her. "I'm going to help you clean up, and I'm gonna call the hotel to get their laundry service and some decent food in here." Like veggies. And limited sugar. "And then I want a few things from you."

She blinked up at me. "Like?"

"Like for starters? I want to know where Alma is. Is she here with you at the Primrose or somewhere else?" On the drive over I had a sneaking suspicion Alma wasn't far.

Bexley squirmed under my gaze.

"Bexley, this is not normal for her. Or for you. All of you need to leave New York and go back to Cape Verde. I know you haven't left this room since you got here. And I know you hate it here. *So let me help you.*"

She was looking at me like I promised her a birthday present now, the hope blossoming across her face let me know she really didn't want to be here.

She was here out of loyalty to Alma. And right now Alma wasn't showing loyalty back. "Really?"

Really. "But first, shower, change, I'll call housekeeping. Is Alma staying here with you?"

She nodded.

"Where?"

"Top floor. End of the hall."

"And you have the key?"

She pointed to her desk her voice a whisper. "You won't tell anyone?"

"No."

But I would pay her a fucking visit. And she better have one hell of an explanation to what the fuck was going on around here.

CHAPTER 49
AVANI

"I'm so happy you're here," Alisha brought me some tea at the kitchen island in K2. "I have missed you. How is everything?"

"Interesting, safe to say there's still plenty of things I had to get done when I got settled..." I kept up conversation for the sake of it. But I was here on a mission.

I was determined to get the answers I needed. I initially told Thierry I was going to talk to Evie but I realized, she didn't know me well.

Thierry and I had a hunch though, Alisha might know something. If not everything.

And so I was here to test out my theories.

I loved my sister to pieces.

I also wanted to make sure I could actually protect her and Reed who I knew had been busier since I couldn't remember the last time I had lunch with him.

He did text often but he let me know he was juggling many things. Which didn't bother me so much.

I was hiding my boyfriend. It worked out.

"Really? What on Earth can a person talk about for forty pages about rice?" Alisha blinked confused a little. "Academia is appalling."

"I have no idea," I laughed, the sound musical in her kitchen. "But I just have been drowning. I do intend to finish up the term earlier than usual and I should be free for the holidays."

She beamed. "You'll have to come over then. Reed and I miss you, he's very sorry he hasn't been able to make it to lunch."

"No," I brushed it off feeling an anxious skitter across my skin. "Speaking of Reed, how is he? And Gabriel? Are they at the manor?"

I wanted to be alone with Alisha when I did ask her my questions.

For some reason she turned pink. "Yes, they're both at the manor. Working on something." Alisha was fidgeting with her cup a little. "Did you want something to eat?"

So she was alone at K2?

"No, I'm fine. How's Selena doing?" I wasn't manipulative but I wanted my sister to really think I was genuinely going in this direction. "I haven't heard from her in a while."

Alisha brightened, her shoulders relaxing again. "Well, I think Gabriel said Selena and Kellan are currently in Miami. On a couples retreat I think." She bit her lip. "They're just decompressing from everything that happened."

"I didn't know that. I haven't heard from her. Do you know when they'll be back?" Because that meant Reed had two less Titan's in New York.

"No," Alisha looked down at her teacup. "I spoke to Kellan last night and he likes it down there, but he also misses New York."

A couple retreat did sound really nice. Maybe Thierry and I could do that once this madness blew over.

"Say, Didi." I dared to just go for it, fiddling around in my chair a bit. "I was spending some time with Evie and she mentioned she was Gabriel's little sister."

She nodded, her raven hair swirling around her and eyes bright on me. This was it.

"They look nothing alike, I thought she was more related to Reed."

"Oh," Alisha looked almost shy as she said. "Evie is definitely more like his daughter. Don't let the sibling title fool you. He's much older than her and he's taken care of her for most of her life."

"And their parents?" I kept my voice light like I was here for Evie. I mean, I was, but I was here for any information at all. "I was curious because I know her birthday will be around the corner and I didn't want to get her something and be insensitive. She mentioned her family was Mexican, but I didn't think Gabriel was."

Alisha's eyes widened and for some reason my sister cast a glance at the hallway.

When she looked back her expression changed a little. A little protective and more closed off.

"Darling, I know this doesn't go anywhere and while I'm not okay with repeating someone else's life, I think it's sweet you want to be good to Evie. I know she'd love to have sisters," Alisha said, her voice was measured and softer.

I nodded eagerly like I meant it. I did. "I love Evie so much, she's such a sweetheart."

Alisha smile was gentle. Almost like..she was upset about something. "Gabriel adopted Evie at fifteen. Her Mum passed away from cancer. She is Mexican. I don't think Gabriel is anything but from the East Coast. I believe so."

My heart was fluttering rapidly. Evie was adopted.

Well, that made sense considering she was posing under two different last names.

"And her family?"

Alisha looked like she was thinking deeply about something. "Evie doesn't have any family but Gabriel. They're very close. You know she settled with Lucas in her apartment."

I knew. But…how did he adopt her? Why?

"But was he related to her then if he adopted her at fifteen? That's a really big gesture to her."

My sister's eyes softened. "It was a tremendous gesture." Her voice was lower as she said it much much much quieter. "Do you promise me you won't tell a soul?"

She held out her pinky. Oh no.

I was going to break her promise. I was. Because I was here to finesse information and my sister thought I was here for a birthday present idea. *Please, forgive me, Alisha.*

I crossed my fingers behind my back and the other took Alisha's pinky. "Promise."

"Gabriel was married to Evie's elder sister. When she died, he found Evie who had lost her mother and he adopted her to honor his wife. He loved her tremendously. To pieces. Evie is a product of that love. It's why he regards her more of a daughter than a sister. She reminds him of his wife."

The one thing nobody told me about trying to be a spy for information was how real it felt to find things out.

I couldn't school my shock. I couldn't hide it as Alisha said the words. "He was married?" I whispered it. "Gabriel?"

She nodded and I saw something else in her eyes then. Alisha's eyes held a wealth of sadness. She knew him. She was good friends with him. What she shared was to make sure she could protect him and by extension—Evie.

Which meant I could tell Thierry, but I would have to tread lightly and make sure nobody else was hurt in the process.

"Evie resembles her sister a little. Just enough for him to see his wife whenever he looks at her. Evie is Mexican but I think her family in general is Latin. But the only thing you should really get her is lots and lots of plant fertilizer." Alisha smiled at my expression. "You haven't been to the manor or to her apartment but she has plants on every inch of her space. I promise she'll love it so much."

"Plant food?"

Alisha laughed lightly. "Trust me, when you get a chance from your schoolwork, pay her a visit. She'd love it."

I intended to. But now I had a critical piece of information.

Gabriel had been married to a woman who had died. So what was Alma?

"Gosh," Alisha whispered her eyes held this look to them that I knew she felt almost guilty telling me.

But she trusted me to not tell anyone.

My sister, who had always held back and been better at keeping secrets trusted me out of respect for her new extended family.

I couldn't hurt her or let her be hurt.

But I also had to figure this out. Because some part of me understood there was a much bigger picture here at work. Secrets Reed and Gabriel were keeping. Secrets I was keeping.

Did I think about turning to Alisha and just telling her the truth?

I did. I definitely did.

But I also knew, there was information Thierry didn't have on the Talon side. Until we knew everything, we couldn't do anything.

One day, I would introduce Thierry, I could come clean to Alisha. But for right now?

I needed to protect her to. It was the only way to.

"I am ravenous. Should I make us some lunch?"

"Umm, no. I actually have to go soon I'm meeting my friends Rosalie and Marissa. I think I mentioned them when I was here."

"Oh yeah…how is that going?"

I talked to my sister for a bit my head reeling with this new information on where Evie stood in the mind map of the secrets in Titan.

"Say, Didi." I asked quietly when Alisha got up to grab herself a sandwich. "Just out of curiosity, is Evie a Devereaux now? Or?"

"Well, I think Evie's waiting a tiny bit before changing her name again."

Alisha didn't even look as she said it. "I think after going from her first name to Monroe she's tired of all the documents."

I kept a smile in my voice as I asked. "What was her name before?"

Alisha turned to me then her eyes thoughtful. "You're putting too much thought into presents for Evie."

I squirmed a little. "Well, she just seemed alone. I want to make her feel special too. I don't think she has anyone now that Selena is gone."

And Alisha's entire expression softened. "This is true." But I also knew Alisha was protecting them.

"Evie's name was Santos. It means Saint in Spanish I believe so you could always get Evie something related to wings."

Santos.

And so Evie's *real* name, the third name she was hiding was Santos.

"Perfect," I whispered. "I'll think about wings shaped like plants." Alisha chuckled. "Or perhaps wings made up of ivy."

"Ohh that's romantic, Evie loves lingerie—"

We both looked at each other.

"Emerald green lingerie sets!" We said at the same time. She laughed, the sound of it in the kitchen louder than before looking lighter.

"With wings," I added with an easier smile. I had missed my sister, but now?

I knew we might be looking for someone that wasn't Evie.

No, it was clear the person who held the key to the information we needed was Gabriel's wife.

And as long as Reed and Thierry didn't get along?

I couldn't tell Alisha about my boyfriend. And nobody knew about us. It would have to stay that way.

I tucked the bit about the Santos sister's away to tell Thierry.

CHAPTER 50
THIERRY

After I helped Bexley get her life together, I asked one of the maids to check on her at all times.

She'd gone and showered while they'd come and taken her laundry. I ignored their looks as they tidied up as a team.

I'd ordered real food that wasn't candy.

Tidied up her space to the point where I didn't recognize it.

Only then when she was sitting in the bed cleaned up and eating, did I sit with her for a bit checking on her.

Giving her a list of ways to take care of herself and I'd make sure I checked in with her daily.

"Thanks, Grim." She bit into a broccoli and grimaced.

"Text me if you need me. And when I get my hands on the necklace, I'll give it back to you guys."

My stomach soured at the expression in her eyes.

Bexley was in over head. She might've been Talon, but she was still nineteen. A year younger than me. But she seemed like she was twelve sometimes, younger than me in many ways.

I sat next to her, my longer legs hanging off the bed while hers barely touched the floor. "You don't look so good, if you get sick? Call me."

She nodded looking so innocent I didn't know what else to do but hug her. "Thanks."

"Don't mention it. I gotchu too. I gotta go yell at Alma now but I'll check on you more often, yeah?"

"Yeah." She smiled up at me looking brighter than before now that she was clean and had sets of clean clothes coming. "I'm bad at taking care of myself."

"Yeah, but you can practice, right? And you got me."

"Miss you, Grim."

"Miss you too. Let me know."

"Are you going to check on Samara?"

"Probably. Unless she's with her boy toy?"

"Boyfriend," Bexley corrected looking all of ten. She ducked her head spitting out her broccoli as she said it. "This is not real food."

"It's definitely not that clay you eat as candy, kid."

"I don't like broccoli."

"Well, it likes you so keep eating."

"You're a bully." *The best kind.*

I bit back a sigh. *Couldn't win 'em all.*

I did make a detour to Samara's room on her floor. And I paused before I knocked at the sound of something creaking, furniture slamming.

A masculine groan following a feminine scream came muffled from inside the room. *"Shane..."*

"There you go, beautiful."

"Shane, don't stop. Don't stop."

"I'm not gonna..."

Merde.

Samara was getting laid? I thought she was celibate.

"I need to bleach my ears," I muttered. "Alma owe me so bad."

When I got to the top floor the elevator let me off in a hallway that went left and right in a T-intersection.

There were massive pillars that made the ceilings look ten times larger up here.

And what looked like a rooftop staircase.

The Primrose was high end and stunning.

Right up Alma's alley and I guessed she might be at the top considering she liked the towers in the compound at Talon.

But not like this.

I needed to talk to her.

I walked down the hall to her room and knocked even though I had an extra keycard. Might as well be polite.

To my surprise Alma wasn't there.

Frustrated I looked both ways before swiping the keycard and breaking into my former mentor's room. I loved Alma, I did. But right now?

She was getting on my ever-loving nerve.

The place was white and pristine. She was always really neat. A trait that Bexley did not have from her.

But the first thing I noticed off the bat were the two coffee cups on her table. Someone had been here with her.

I cleared the entire suite in a few seconds. Making sure I was alone.

There was quite frankly nothing personal in Alma's luggage.

Nothing on her bed. No dice.

Until I got to the men's jacket on her couch.

Not her size.

Someone taller. She did have a man in her life?

Or? I sifted through the jacket and found nothing off about it. There were some sequins on the thing but that was it.

A cane sat next to it and a book about…martial arts?

Who did this belong to?

My phone buzzed with a text from Jace.

I set the jacket down and went to read it when I heard the sound of the door.

I bolted retreating into another room. *Fuck.*

She was back and I was breaking in. Double fuck. I bolted, hiding in a closet in the guest room while I read Jace's text.

I got your info.

Perfect.

And with Avani hopefully getting me something else, I could piece it together with her.

I heard the door to the hotel room shut and a male voice said. "I fucking knew I left my jacket here. It's chillier outside now."

I immediately started to hit the record button on my phone.

Jace could figure it out later.

"We have time," I heard Alma's voice and her light laughter. I held the phone closer to the door. "You can stop rushing."

"Absolutely not. I see you again after all these years and you don't think I'm going to live it up? You're out of your mind, sis."

Alma's laughter filled the air sounding lighter and easier than before.

After all these years?

Sis?

No. She said Liam was dead.

Alma *did* have a brother.

Years ago, she told me she lost Liam in an assignment.

But now? I was beginning to ask all the questions I could—even about dead people.

"I told you, you'd like the brunch here."

"I did, hey, did you move my jacket?"

I froze. My heart stopped beating. *Shiiiit.*

"No, who wears all that leather? I thought you outgrew after Papi told you it made you look like a sinner."

His laughter came through clearly. "That's exactly why I wear it. I'm still a sinner."

Alma said something in rapid-fire Spanish that made him laugh louder.

She hadn't said his name though so I didn't know who it was.

My heart was racing and pounding hoping they'd leave or I would have to figure out a way to get the fuck out of here.

"Are you ready now?" She asked him. "You are so dramatic."

"Yeah let me grab my things from the guest room and we can head out. It's not my fault, I gotta look good."

"You are so stupid even now—"

"Yeah, says you. We gotta fix your hair."

He was coming here.

Shitshitshit.

I quickly checked the closet but it was empty.

I breathed out a quiet breath of relief as I peered through the shutters of the closet, slowly getting to my knees to see him better.

Most people expected someone eye-level. I fucking prayed he hadn't left his things in here.

I crouched low focused on seeing who this guy was. Who Alma was…ignoring her team for.

He walked in with his cane leaning on it as he grabbed something off the side of the bed. "I almost forgot Lara's presents."

Lara?

I heard another set of footsteps as I peered out and saw a taller man, with black hair, glasses. I couldn't see his face clearly but he had paler skin than Alma and I did.

"At some point I am going to have to meet Lara," Alma's voice was at the door. Shit. Fuck. *Oh my God.* "You cannot hide your girl-friend from me forever. I want to meet the woman who swept up my brother. You used to be such a manwhore."

"Don't ever say that around Lara," he laughed lightly. "I'm loyal to one woman now. And that's her. Well, you but you're my sister so it's different."

My heart bottomed out. It didn't sink—it plummeted into the depths of the ocean.

Both of them were in the room. And he. Was. Her. Brother.

My heart was racing and I forced it to calm down only focused on watching the man and Alma.

I took notes mentally about a woman named Lara.

Why was that name familiar? Did I know a Lara?

"I know, I'm trying to figure out how to explain it to her, okay? She's been worried and I don't want her to think I'm cheating on her with my fucking sister. But I have no fucking clue where to start." He shuddered making a face and she laughed. "*Gross.*"

"You're the one stalling, *Liam.* I told you I wanted to meet her. Do you know how I feel hearing someone finally got you? I never thought I'd see the day."

Liam.

Oh.

Mother.

Fucker.

Shit.

FUCCCCKKKK.

He grinned at her. "Yeah. She's something else. But I'm waiting for the right time to tell her. It's not every day my sister comes back from the dead and I have to tell my girlfriend now? I'll pass."

Forget the ocean.

My heart leapt out of my chest.

Out. Of. My. Chest.

What?

Alma said Liam was dead. Did Liam think she had been dead too? What the fucking fuck was going on?

Because now I knew it was Liam. And he was alive. Alma lied to me.

Why?

"Come on, at the rate you move, everything will close." But Alma's voice was soft with him.

"You still love to boss me around."

"I never got tired of it, stupid. Now let's go."

"Just for that? I'm gonna make you carry me, shortcake."

"Don't you dare—" Alma squealed as Liam carted her up over his shoulder.

"Easy, shortcake, I'm still weak in the legs—"

"Don't remind me, I will always feel bad—"

My spine stiffened despite being crouched down and I almost fell out of the fucking closet.

Shortcake.

Why would he call me, shortcake?

A jack in the box?

A hacker?

Oracle was Liam's design.

Alma told me years ago her brother and her had figured out an AI program. Oracle was...his baby. Bexley was using Liam's program. Bexley didn't know Liam was a hacker. Bexley didn't know Liam. Was. Alive.

Alma suggested it for Talon.

Titan's hacker called Bexley shortcake.

Titan's hacker...is Liam.

Liam...oh.

Mother.

Fucker.

My was going to explode. Liam Sullivan was a double agent for Titan and Talon.

Because his sister was the head of Talon.

I was going to explode.

What were the odds?

I needed to call Jace. I couldn't confront Alma.

As her and Liam left the room laughing about something I was frozen.

Because I was ninety percent sure of a few things.

Alma Nash wasn't who she said she was.

Liam was alive. He was a Titan.

He was the hacker messing with Bexley.

He was the reason Titan didn't know about us.

Mon coeur—the mystery just got a little more interesting.

Part of me wanted to confront them. Another part of me wanted to play the long game now.

The one where I found out just what the fuck was happening around me.

Because I was one hundred percent certain now—Alma and Liam—Titan and Talon were more than connected, they were fucking related.

But Alma wasn't two-faced which meant she had an insider. Liam must've recently found her.

Because Bexley said something changed in Alma recently. Recently. What the fuck was going on?

I waited until the door closed to the hotel room. Another ten minutes before sneaking out.

Alma would never turn on Talon.

Which meant she had an insider in Titan. A mole.

Her fucking *brother*.

Those two were keeping secrets from everyone.

And I needed to know why and who Alma really was.

Mon coeur we have a lot to talk about.

CHAPTER 51
THIERRY

"Her brother is alive!"

Avani cried out in my arms as I held my heart tight to me in shock.

I was in shock.

"And he thought she was dead! And Liam is a Titan! A double agent! Good heavens! That means he's betraying Reed *and* Gabriel!"

"I know, mon coeur. I think I like seeing your Brit side outraged."

"This is preposterous," she sputtered. "What on Earth is happening?"

"Tell me about it—"

"What a rude man!"

"Complete fucking dick—"

"And she's awful as well—"

"She's lying to everyone—"

"Why on Earth can't they just talk to each other?" Mon coeur's accent grew thicker as she grew more prim and proper as she spoke. "This is so terribly cruel."

"And fucked up. Bex is sick and I gotta check on her, my heart."

"I do love being your partner," she murmured. "I'm sorry about your friend. Tell me her hotel room so we can send her some things. The hotel does delivery if it's the Primrose. My sister loves that spot."

I made it out of the Primrose and quickly left to get Avani from K2. Picking her up, I drove us both to our home.

She'd leapt into my lap the moment we did, both of us grumbled for a bit about humanity taking comfort in each other.

Avani had grabbed a blanket and cuddled me in it while we talked.

And then Avani told me her half.

"Evie's real name is Eva Santos."

It was my turn to be shocked.

"I have a fucking headache. So now we have people who thought they were dead. Evie's real last name. And a dead wife Gabriel obviously loved. Alisha wouldn't say her name?"

Avani shook her head. "No, I my sister was protecting Gabriel. She said that Reed and Gabriel were at the manor. But when I was leaving? I saw Gabriel's suit jacket on her couch."

"You think he visits her?"

She nodded her expression solemn. "I think Alisha knows everything and she's protecting Gabriel and Evie. Because the necklace is somehow connected to him. No, that doesn't make sense—"

"Unless the necklace was his wife's." I watched her. "He gave it to his wife."

"So then how does Alma have it?" She tipped her head. "What did Jace say he had for you? None of this makes sense and we're missing something. We are still missing how Alma is connected to Gabriel."

"Jace said to call him but I was waiting to catch up with you before I did. Should we call him now? Or do you want to go see him?"

"I think we need to go see him," she muttered. "Even if I don't want to do anything but you right now."

"Let's go solve a murder mystery."

Avani and I got dressed to visit Roadsters where Jace sat. It was late enough for me to know Teo wasn't there.

And Jace never went home.

I didn't know where he lived, I just knew he existed in Roadsters like a cog in Teo's wheel. An intelligent cog.

I was polished in slacks and a sweater, and Avani wore a new pink ankle length dress I'd gotten her, even with the chill in the air, she'd put on nude stockings and heels that made her legs look endless.

When she stepped out I blew out a whistle.

"Mon coeur, I think I take it back." My voice was gruff. "We can spare twenty minutes. Maybe an hour. Murder can wait. My dick can't—"

"You will have to—"

"Mon couer—"

"No. Don't you dare," she breathed out. "We have to go. After, I promise. Come on."

We rushed out together to go see Jace in person.

I grinned at Avani adjusting her lip gloss in the car and applying the last touches to her perfume.

I kept a smaller bottle in the car for her to apply whenever she needed it. Watching her through sideways glances I grinned as she frowned over her lips.

"Can we order pizza when we come home?" She said conversationally as if we weren't on our way to uncover conspiracies that were beyond us. "All this mystery makes me hungry."

"Anything you want," I turned into Roadsters. "Whatever you want."

She smiled over at me easily. "I'm really curious about this Liam gentleman…" as she spoke I watched her expressions and her frown. "I wonder what he's thinking right now and why he's making the choices he is."

"I don't know, mon coeur, but double agents rarely make it out alive."

And that's the other thing that worried me. Reed Whittaker had a mole in his organization. Did he know? If he did, was he drawing out Alma? Why?

Avani continued to brainstorm with me.

From the day I had snatched Avani up in her apartment and she'd come back from K2 upset with me?

I'd been nothing but honest with her.

And once I had explained everything to her, because she was an intellectual, she forgave me pretty easily.

As long as I told her the truth.

The more I told her, the more I respected her, and it was like a circle of trust that we had now.

One that I valued more than anything else.

Her partnership. Our teamwork.

She was my equal. And somewhere along this relationship, the more I had of her?

The less I thought in blacks and white. I was no longer shaped and marred by shadows and darkness.

And she was no longer as pure and innocent as I found her.

No, together we'd merged into something else.

If I lived a thousand lives, in another world in another alternate reality—she was mine in every single one.

I would give her whatever she wanted. Peace of mind. Love.

And somehow it all worked out.

I took her hand as we got out Avani chattering low about her theories and I listened in all the way to go see Jace.

I'd given a heads up I'd bring her here so he wasn't startled by her.

We walked down to the basement and I held Avani's hand aware it wasn't the first time we were out like this in the open, but for the first time—we were in a setting that belonged to my family. Again. After years.

Jace stood the moment Avani stepped in his grey eyes widening a bit.

I realized, I never actually saw him stand up in his tailored black suit.

Teo's house rules were that you dressed for respect in Roadsters.

Durand was even more uptight, but Teo held up the DuPont name well.

Avani smiled and introduced herself to him holding her hand out.

He looked slightly uncomfortable with it and I realized, he never actually touched anyone. He was tall, a little over six feet. Lean and clean shaven head.

And when he took her hand and offered her a polite smile I realized one little thing—he wasn't much older than me.

Eyes like winter steel fixed on Avani with an intensity before turning to me.

"Mr. Mattison."

Avani blinked like she'd forgotten at some point my real name.

I grinned not feeling jealous entirely of him, but he was watching Avani. The focus of his eyes a little different, not appreciation but something like curiosity in them.

Was it because she's a part of our world now?

I got it. My girl was gorgeous.

I knew as much. Chestnut hair, wide soft brown eyes filled with warmth now, and a smile that lit up everything in me, now aimed at me.

I tugged her close to me as Jace looked a little anxious around her. I was protective of Avani even in my own territory.

I wondered if she made him nervous. And why.

"You said you had updates," I reminded him carefully. "It was urgent."

He looked away a little more nervous now. "It is. I think I solved your case."

Avani and I exchanged a look of concern as we followed him.

He handled million-dollars of tech operations and dealt with me and Talon and Titan, but around Avani he looked off.

If she caught it she didn't show any signs.

"I do," Jace said. "I did some digging. I found an interesting correlation to that name. Santos. And you mentioned Alma had a brother named Liam?"

I nodded. Jace moved to his computer and I had Avani in front of me so she would see the screens too.

Jace pulled up an old report. "This is the file your brother, Mr. DuPont has of Gabriel Monroe's final assignment in the CIA." He pulled up two names on the screen.

Isobel Santos.

Liam Sullivan.

I frowned at the two names.

"There are no photos of anyone in these case files. But Isobel Santos and Liam Sullivan were two operatives on that assignment. It was a five man team, the six of them being a woman named—"

"Selena!" Avani gasped. "That's Selena Tavares." Avani rushed to explain Selena and I realized that was Maria Santos's real name. "She worked with Gabriel!"

Jace spoke up. "So this team existed seven years ago. It looks like they were pronounced dead before Selena Tavares made it out to them. So she's alive. We know this. Her alias is Maria."

Avani blinked up at the names. "Isobel Santos is she Evie's sister?"

Jace looked at both of us then. "So I tried looking for a sibling. And I traced Isobel Santos's identity back. Way back." He pulled up multiple files. "When she was twelve, her parents split up. Her father is Portugese. Her mother is Mexican. But they divorced and they took their daughters to opposites sides of the globe. Isobel's dad took her to the East Coast. And then," he pulled up another file.

This time it was Evie Monroe. Or Santos.

"This is Eva Santos. Her mother did die at fifteen. And she was adopted by Gabriel Monroe. Her last name is Monroe, if you dig deeper. Whittaker is a cover. Once I dug past it? She's a Monroe."

"But she's Isobel's sister?" Avani whispered.

My mind was already connecting the dots. "Gabriel Monroe went on an assignment with his wife. That doesn't make sense. Who is Liam Sullivan? He can't be Alma's Liam. And why are there no photos of anyone?"

"Someone hid those," Jace muttered clicking at his keyboard. "Too deep for me to pull it out. But Liam Sullivan is where the story gets interesting. Because he was on that assignment as well. And on that night, every single members was proclaimed dead, including him."

Avani nodded. "But that can't be true. Because Gabriel is alive. And Thierry saw Liam with Alma."

Jace smiled softly. "Which is why I ran with the assumption of one thing—what if *everyone* was still alive?"

And Avani and I turned our heads to look at him as he watched us.

"Liam *Sullivan?* I ran him back. He was adopted by William Santos. Isobel Santo's father. His name is Liam Santos. Or it was for a bit. Those files are buried. Sullivan is his old last name before he changed it."

My blood ran cold. "Isobel's *brother* is Liam?" And suddenly an eerie sensation crept down my spine. Isobel's. *Brother.*

"Not a real brother." Jace corrected. "William Santos, adopted Liam Sullivan at the age of thirteen. Isobel Santos and Liam went to the same school. They went the same college. They joined the CIA together. They were siblings, but not by blood. William adopted him out of an abusive household. Changed his name to Santos. But when Isobel died according to the case files? Liam

Santos changed his name back to Sullivan and he reappears on the grid. My guess is, Isobel's death right after the death of his adoptive father? Ruined him. He erased them from his life. And he moved on. Guy's a hot fucking mess."

Jace motioned to the records he had. "Liam Sullivan guy works in software. IT. He owns a smaller company on his own but it's private. Just to make cash flow." And then he pulled up the logo of a jack in the box. "Recognize this?"

"Holy fucking shit," I whispered. "He is the Titan hacker."

Jace looked grim. "It gets a lot worse. After I assumed that Liam was alive, if Gabriel was alive, I dug into Isobel. She doesn't reappear at all. But you know who does appear after Isobel is pronounce dead? At the exact same time?"

"Alma," Avani and I whispered at the same time.

Alma. *Nash.*

Who might not have been a Nash at all.

Jace looked downright miserable. "Isobel Santos vanishes from the grid. And Alma Nash shows up. This is where your sister Talia comes in." He looked at me. "I'm not supposed to tell you this, because I have never spoken a word about Miss Avani to anyone. But when I discovered this connection, I realized Talia Nash is connected to the disappearance of Isobel Santos. She has to be. She was in New York at the time. She knew about her father's operations. Talia might know exactly what is happening right now."

Jace kept going like he didn't drop bombs on me right then.

"Talia is extremely efficient and connected, and somehow, Alma ended up in the universe at the same time Isobel went missing. Talia's documentation inside Talon, I have access to, because of your brother. Gabriel's team was hunting the Nash family. Under the name Marcus Hagen, which was always the alias of the next head of Talon—"

"Talia," I whispered.

Jace nodded. "Talia won't tell you the truth. I can't just go to my boss's wife and ask her for answers."

Jace gave us a look that said he knew better.

"Mr. DuPont is strict. Both of your brother's are. But I serve each of you individually. And this information is critical. I buried it back. But I dug up information of a few of the Titans."

I was reeling now for a number of reasons.

457

Jace looked remorseful. "Alma Nash now exists in the world and Isobel Santos is never heard from again."

Avani spoke for me then. "But can you verify Alma and Isobel are the same person? How do we do that?"

I could do it.

I could fucking do it.

Jace pulled up a photo of surveillance footage.

"This is a blurry shot of Alma Nash in South Africa a year ago." He zoomed in on it. "That is the necklace she wore. That is the object Gabriel and Reed stole. It has his name on it. For some fucking reason she wears Isobel's necklace."

But it wasn't a good photo at all.

Even with her hair back when it was dark. It wasn't clear. But the necklace was on there.

"And you know who else was in South Africa at the time?" Jace asked. Dropping down a photo of a blonde with bright blue eyes. "This is Lucy Devereaux your resident jewel thief who stole the necklace. Lucy scoped it out because Lucy works on paper for a man named Raphael Santos."

"Santos," I muttered.

"Exactly," Jace continued. "This name kept popping up."

I huffed out a breath realizing how deep this ran.

Avani spoke up. "Gabriel Monroe goes on an assignment seven years ago. His team is killed. He leaves the CIA. He comes to New York. He starts Titan with Reed, Selena, Evie, and Nathan. The original five of the Titan's. Selena was using the last name Santos as an alias. But she has no relationship to the Santos sisters, it's just…a name to her."

"Correct." Jace looked at her with a hint of pride in his eyes. "Selena Maria *Tavares* has no relationship to the Santos sisters. She's a former Cuban trained spy who joined the Titans with Gabriel Monroe. But Gabriel does have a connection to both of the Santos sisters."

"But Gabriel's wife was never listed on the paper. Gabriel goes on this mission with Isobel and her brother Liam." Avani continued. "Everyone dies on this mission and when it's all said and done —everyone's identity is obliterated so they have to change their names and become new people. For safety? Or to hide."

"Probably both," I held her hand needing her warmth against

mine. The pink dress seemed out of place now among all the darkness and tech.

"Don't forget there were two others on his team," Jace added. "Two other people were on that team. They're both *legally* dead."

"As far as know," Avani said. "So now we have a woman named Alma Nash who joined Talon masquerading as a Nash cousin. But she isn't a Nash. And tonight, Thierry heard her with a man named Liam who she called her brother. We have no photos of her. We have no proof of existence prior to seven years ago. And that is the only connection Alma and Isobel have. Along with Liam. He is the common denominator. And one can only assume—*Alma Nash is not who she says she is.*"

"Don't forget Liam said to Alma that he thought she was dead, so he hasn't introduced Alma to his girlfriend Lara," I added.

Avani looked concerned as I said it her jaw dropping. "Lara *Ford* is my sister Alisha's best friend. If it is the same Lara, then Liam Sullivan is Alma Nash's *Liam*."

"Correct," Jace said.

Avani looked at me then excited. "*But why steal her necklace?* Why not just find *her*? If Gabriel's team was hunting the Nash family, why would Alma be Isobel even if she called Liam her brother? *That doesn't make sense.* Why would she switch sides? What did Talia do? Because you know Talia was there that night. She had to be. *Thats why she was so afraid when you asked her.*"

Jace spoke up pointing at me. "Even if Alma called this man Liam her brother, even if we assume it's Isobel Santos masquerading as Alma Nash, Miss Avani has a point. Why would she lie? Why would she hide? Her husband was on that trip? Why did she leave Liam behind? Wouldn't she have taken Liam with her? Why would Liam be a double agent in Titan? Why would she wear Gabriel's necklace and avoid him for seven years? *None of that makes sense.*"

No. It never made any sense.

Avani looked at Jace. "Jace, you said those photos are buried, can you do me a favor? Did Isobel Santos go to high school?"

"I know where you're going with this. You want me to find Isobel Santos's yearbook photo."

"No," Avani shook her head, her intelligent eyes gleaming even as my hands shook. "I want Thierry to tell me if that woman in the yearbook photo is his Alma Nash. All we need is a photo. The name

Santos was the key to unlocking this. But a photo is all he needs. And once we confirm it? We can figure out."

And my heart pounded rapidly as Jace went into a deep dive of Isobel Santos. Before the CIA.

He found it relatively quickly.

"I got her." He pulled up a photo and I stopped breathing.

But it looked off. She looked…off.

Her hair was mahogany. Her eyes lighter than Avani's.

And she looked…alive.

Not half-dead like she always did.

"She looks alive," I whispered my heart plummeting to my depths. "She looks different."

"Thierry," Avani breathed. "Is that her?"

I knew that face anywhere. I knew my mentor.

She trained me. Guided me. Made me better.

I learned from her.

"She said…I was like her Liam." I whispered feeling my vision blur. "Jace, give her black hair and make her eyes darker." My voice sounded gruff. As he did my heart sank.

Holy. Fucking. Shit.

Not Alma.

Never Alma.

Isobel Santos, formerly Alma Nash stared back at me with a smile on her eighteen year old face. Jace pulled up a photo of Liam Sullivan next to her matching the man I saw in the Primrose but his eyes were brilliant green like Talia's. Like Tavares.

My jaw dropped.

"Never Alma," I whispered. "They're siblings." Which meant Liam Sullivan was Gabriel Monroe's brother-in-law.

She was Gabriel Monroe's wife. And she was currently at war with her husband's team. Two sides of the same coin.

Every single moment, every lesson, every conversation, was a lie.

She wasn't real.

"Alma Nash is Isobel Santos." I croaked out feeling my vision blur. "That's what this has been about. That's why nobody gave me answers. They were never hiding Evie. They were all hiding her."

Talon vs Titan.

Isobel. Versus. Gabriel.

"This has been seven fucking years in the making."

Nobody said a word and then Avani looked up at me as I said it.

"Gabriel Monroe isn't hunting a stranger. *He's hunting his wife. That's what this is all about.* And she's alive. And he knows it. He stole the necklace to bring her out. This isn't a feud. This is an angry couple who haven't spoken to each other in seven years. Do you know what this means, mon coeur?"

It meant everything I thought I knew. Talia. Alma. My very foundation of what it meant to be in Talon was a lie.

They'd all been playing a role this entire time.

I barely heard Avani's voice.

"We just solved the case."

CHAPTER 52
AVANI

IT HAD BEEN A WEEK SINCE THE REVELATION AT JACE'S.

It was early in the morning that Thierry and I lay awake.

Teo was coming to drop off a necklace…that wasn't real…

For a woman who was pretending to be someone else. With her brother. And Gabriel who was keeping all his secrets.

My head was *reeling*.

We should've been happy it was over once Bexley had the necklace.

But all I felt was dread. Anticipation. Anxiety. And Thierry had lain there processing how his entire life had been…this.

I held onto him tightly juggling studying for my finals with this.

This was insanity. Even for me.

"I still have questions," I whispered to him. Thierry was laying on my chest, my fingers threaded through his hair.

"Liam said he just found out Alma was alive," Thierry muttered. "That's one."

"And Bexley is doing better?"

He nodded into me. "I think she has the flu, so I sent her some soup and other items."

He'd texted Bexley every day to make sure the girl was good.

We needed to go see her and actually introduce me to her so she wasn't completely alone.

It was too many secrets. Too many lies.

And not enough talking.

I was half tempted to send everybody an email and tell them to come to the warehouse just so we could hash it out between the two organizations.

Urgent. Mandatory Meeting between two covert operation group to actually behave like adults. I wanted to roll my eyes as I held him closer, rubbing his scalp. "Better?"

He groaned into my skin. "You have no idea."

Because at this point it was getting on my ever loving nerves.

Thierry came home with me and curled into his bed looking stunned. He'd been quiet the entire ride home that night.

Jace had glanced over him worried and I'd brought him home where he'd stayed processing it.

And now finally, Teo was getting the stupid necklace to us.

Two adults fighting over a bloody necklace. I had it up my neck with everyone around me acting like a conversation would kill them.

Neither one of us had spoken to our families.

Thierry had shut down a little processing his reality and I just wanted to know one thing—Did Evie know her sister was alive?

A suspicion in me doubted it.

Because Evie genuinely believed she was gone. Why else would Gabriel have adopted her? Did she know? If anything happened to Alisha I would be devastated but from what Jace explained—Evie didn't know her elder sister.

Did Evie know, Liam was her brother? At least on paper, they were related. Because Gabriel was her brother-in-law.

Once we had some of the mind map figured out and the lines connected? Even if there were a thousand more questions?

One thing was clear.

Once Teo gave us the dupe?

Thierry turning it in to Bexley would send Alma home. With or without Liam. With or without Gabriel.

And all I could think of was introducing Thierry to Reed and Alisha.

Oddly enough, I knew with all my heart, I knew and I had realized this the more I loved him, the more I spent time with him, the more I *knew*—he was my favorite part of every single day—I would walk away from Alisha and Reed if it meant being with Thierry.

I hoped it wouldn't come to that. I really did.

But he was my heart. I wouldn't lose him. I couldn't.

Lying here with him in his house, in his arms, nothing else mattered to me. We'd make it work. And the idea of losing Alisha? As much as it ached through my entire soul?

There was also something in me that picked this man.

I chose him.

I did.

He was my soul. Whatever our hearts were made up of?

His and mine were the same.

And I was never losing him.

THIERRY GOT UP EVENTUALLY TO SHOWER AND CHANGE INTO something other than his pajamas while I made breakfast.

It was the least I could do with both of us running on anxiety.

I knew Teo wasn't actually breaking into K2, but the nuances aside I was a little anxious. Just enough to need the distraction of cooking.

Setting aside the pancakes and bacon and juice, I went to call him from the back, but when I came back in?

I saw his back to me sitting on a barstool in his signature black hoodie and backwards ball cap.

"You got here so fast," I laughed lightly. "Did you run here for pancakes?"

My laughter turned into a moan when I kissed him wrapping my arms around him, my eyes closed and I just saw his lips.

He tasted different as I brushed my tongue against his mouth, he stiffened a little.

"You definitely stole a pancake or two while I was gone," I kissed him again playfully. "I made enough for both of us, darling."

I pulled back with a smile and it turned into complete horror when I saw just *who* I was kissing.

"*Oh my goodness!*" I shrieked and jumped back.

"Mon Dieu," Teo sat in the kitchen staring at me like I was a poltergeist. "*Avani?*"

Oh. My. GOD.

"*Why are you here?*" He whispered horrified. "What are you—"

"*Why didn't you make any noise! How did you get in here!*"

"*Me?*" Teo looked at me like I had three heads. "*What—You—He —YOU. This was about you. You're the reason he's been like this!*"

He looked just as stunned as me and both of us looked ready to have a heart attack.

He covered his mouth in horror and I wiped at mine.

"You're his tutor. You're the one he's been seeing."

"Oh my God I just kissed you," I was horrified.

He sputtered in French and the horror only increased when I turned and saw *Thierry* rubbing his hair walking into the hallway shirtless in his pajama bottoms. And nothing else. All muscled abs and pecs and tattoos.

His head snapped up and his smile turned into a frown at the sight of Teo. And then me.

His head looked back and forth between us, registering the scene and then it snapped to Teo. *"What did you do?"*

Teo looked speechless. "Why does *everyone* blame me?"

"I swear I didn't mean to," I croaked. "I kissed him."

Thierry's head snapped to me in shock. I rushed to explain.

"I thought it was you, I thought you finished your shower. He ate our pancakes." I covered my mouth in horror pressing my hands to my burning face.

Teo looked like he was imploding as he looked at his brother and pointed at me and said something in French. Thierry looked furious at his brother.

"Are you insane?" He was on Teo in another second hauling his brother up. And I realized how similar they were in size then.

Seeing the two of them side by side was a little eerie.

"You kissed my girlfriend?"

"Girlfriend?" Teo growled in frustration shoving Thierry back. *"You're sleeping with—"*

"Dating. I'm dating her. She's mine. There's a difference between her and your thief."

"Titan has no idea she's with me. And the thief has a boyfriend—"

In that moment Teo looked nauseated and he went back and forth with Thierry in rapid-fire French.

"You kissed her!" Thierry shouted back at him. "You're not one to talk after sleeping with Lucy! If anything, that's *exponentially* worse since she's your best friend's sister."

Teo pointed at me and yelled something back at his brother that suspiciously sounded like 'baby.'

Which naturally made me furious.

"I am not a baby," I shouted at him. "I'm a grown woman and I can make my own choices!" His head snapped to me horrified with me. "You slept with the jewel thief?"

Good. Heavens.

Teo looked at me like I had three heads. And I moved to Thierry's side to hold his hand.

"You two are *together*," Teo's throat worked as he swore a little. I hadn't ever seen him so completely distraught. "I need to go to Lucy. When I come back, which I will, I want to know *everything*."

His eyes landed on both of us as he held out the duplicate necklace to Thierry.

"*Everything*."

CHAPTER 53
THIERRY

TEO DID COME BACK AND SAT WITH US CALMLY NOW, LISTENING AS WE both explained everything to him.

His usual playful demeanor had been erased leaving behind a harder, calculating version of him.

Things went from bad to worse.

It took Teo time to come by where Avani and I quietly processed that everyone in our lives was actively lying to each other. It took him another week of juggling ninety tasks.

Including us, but we were protecting our bubble.

Our love.

Everyone else? Not so much.

When we finished he shook his head.

"I knew Jace wasn't saying *everything* to me, but I didn't know he would protect you."

The edge in his voice was there and it made me and Avani next to me tense as we sat there like two kids in trouble. Even if we weren't. Teo wasn't going to stop me from being with her.

Nothing would.

Not a single thing in this lifetime would keep me from *my* heart.

"It's not Jace's fault," Avani spoke up with a fierce expression in her warmer eyes and her pink nightie. "Don't fire him. He was doing his job. And we solved the case."

I had taken the necklace to Bexley who was sick. She'd taken it anyway to give to Alma. And I needed to introduce Avani to her and check in with her.

Because the only reason none of us had stepped out of our lines was because this wasn't about Gabriel Monroe.

This wasn't about his wife or her secrets.

Now, this was about two *insanely powerful* organizations, lying to everyone around them, lying to protect others, and now those carefully constructed lies were beginning to unravel.

The threads expanding until I knew it was going to snap apart. The only question was—*when?*

I hauled *mon coeur* into my arms.

"Don't fire him," Avani looked at Teo with wide pleading eyes and Teo looked at her like she was three-headed alien.

He was usually playful and my brother. I knew Teo was a genius disguised as a drug addict.

Now, he was Matteo DuPont the billionaire businessman who ran a successful company and I saw a shrewd look in his eyes I had never seen before.

Next to me Avani shifted.

"While I do love seeing you," Teo began carefully. "If my brother dies because of you, I won't stop at calling you names."

Her eyes widened as he said it and I went to step in. Because Teo and Andrei were cruel when they wanted to be. I knew that much.

"*You've* been with my brother since this summer?"

"*Yes.*"

"And you're aware your family will kill him if they find out?Teo looked at her with a hard expression, one I'd rarely see him wear. "*You think Reed or Alisha will let you—*"

"*It doesn't matter what my family let's me do,*" Avani cut him off her voice rising on him as she faced him head on.

All five-foot nothing of her squaring her shoulders in her pink nightie looking like a pissed off fairy, and facing off against my brother who dressed in his best suit looking like a dark god.

"I'm not leaving him. I'm never walking away from him."

Avani's voice held a hint of steel in it I would catch whenever I'd test her.

"In fact, I appreciate you helping us but I have a bone to pick with you as well. Don't think for a second you will make me feel the least bit guilty for loving him. I won't. And should my family ever come after him, I will handle that. I won't let them hurt him, Teo. I love him. Nothing will ever hurt him."

Something unfamiliar burst in my chest at the sounds of her words.

It cracked open like warm rays of the sun on my skin as she defended me. Time after time.

She stood by me.

I always thought I lived in the darkness, everyone's secret, but Avani...she was my girl.

She stood by all of it.

"I haven't told Alisha about Thierry even when I knew he was Talon. I've known the entire time. I didn't care. *I still don't.* I've been helping him and gathering intelligence and making sure nothing happens to both of us as well."

She crossed her arms over her chest as she spoke and eyed him down.

"I solved the case with him. I knew your sister-in-law was lying to you both. Your elder brother has anger issues. And you all neglected Thierry, I mean sure you financially supported him, but there was nothing else there. I was his tutor. I did teach him to read. Something apparently two multi-millionaires could not accomplish!"

Her voice rose and I saw Teo blink like he had seen her for the first time.

She looked extremely proper and pissed sitting there. And Teo looked impressed as he watched her.

"If you think you're going to come after me for loving your brother more than you and I'm going to sit here and take your judgment, you're out of your mind. I'm not going anywhere. I'm here to stay by his side. And even if I haven't told Alisha about Thierry, frankly, your side of the family could use *a lot* of therapy."

He choked a little as she said it and I felt a reluctant grin come to my lips. *Mon coeur.*

She settled back. "Well, do you have anymore information for us? And are you done being angry?"

She blinked all innocently at him and my brother watched her carefully.

"When did you grow up?" He muttered. "I feel like you were twelve the other day."

A giggle escaped her sounding adorable. "I should thank you for

469

letting me into your brother's study all those years ago. That's where we met."

She motioned to me and Teo leaned back in his seat swearing softly, the shock written on his face. He ran his hands down his face muttering about fate and luck.

Now I grinned wider.

"Do you two want to talk while I go make us lunch?" I asked the two of them.

Her chestnut hair spun wildly around her and her bright mocha eyes batted up at me.

When I kissed her softly before getting up I thought my brother —the one who had threesomes with everyone—would faint.

He swore softly and looked stressed again. I knew what he was thinking about.

He wasn't worried about Avani.

He was worried about Reed Whittaker killing me when he found out I was fucking his future sister-in-law.

Or the Titans coming after me as a whole.

It would never happen.

Not only would I not let it, I had faith *mon coeur* would tear into them with her bare hands if she could. Lucy Devereaux and Teo brainstormed to get Alma a fake. It looked like the real thing enough. I needed to take it to Bexley.

That was how I was going to get it to Alma.

Isobel.

Fuck my life.

My phone pinged one morning.

Jace.

> We have a problem. Reed Whittaker was seen at the Primrose Hotel.
>
> I think he's going after your friends.
>
> He knows.
>
> I can't block him because he's got the place locked down. Him and the Titans.

I stopped everything I was doing. *Bexley.*

"*Mon coeur!*" I rushed into the living room as both Teo and Avani stood.

I looked at Teo's wide eyes so similar to mine. "I need to go to the Primrose. I think Reed Whittaker knows about Alma too!"

"I'm coming with you!" Avani protested. "If there's anyone that's going to stop my family from hurting you ever—it's me."

Teo looked at her and then me. "Normally I would argue, but she's not wrong. It is her family. And they will kill you if you don't take her."

"Mon coeur—"

"No," Avani stepped forward. "I can be your shield! Let me!"

"Let her, mon frere, she know's what she's doing." Teo adjusted his shirt. "I'm coming to. If *anyone's* going to be hitting Reed Whittaker it's going to be me."

CHAPTER 54
AVANI

I hadn't even gotten a chance to throw on anything.

I was rushing to grab my white sneakers and running out the door in a pink nightie out of all things. There was *no* time.

Beside me Thierry tucked a gun into his back and Teo tore off his jacket rolling up his shirtsleeves like he wanted to fight Reed—right now.

I was fully aware we were about to up against my family.

I tried calling Gabriel in the car but he didn't answer. Not him. Not Reed. Not when they were going after Thierry's old team.

"Bloody fucking hell!" I cried. *"Why won't they pick up?"*

"Probably because they're tearing the place apart," Thierry growled.

I frantically called Reed. Anyone at this point. And then I remembered my sister. My heart was racing, my palms sweating.

"Didi, pick up the phone."

"Avani?" My sister answered, she sounded like she was running.

"Oh thank God! Didi call Reed! Tell him to stop!"

"What?" I heard Alisha practically leap up. "What—How do you—"

"I'm dating Thierry, Teo's brother! I know about you guys. I know about Talon. And I know Gabriel is looking for his wife! Please stop them!"

Out of all the ways for Alisha to find out?

This was *not* the way I saw it going down.

"We're here, mon coeur." Thierry was grabbing his gun.

Alisha shrieked sounding completely panicked. *"You're what! Avani! Are you insane! Gabriel!"* My sister was screaming at him. "Stay on the phone with me!"

"I will." I whipped my head around to the boys who shot me the same look of shock. Only both of their eyes held mischief. "You two are devious."

Teo's grin was wicked. "Don't hate me for killing your brother-in-law."

"He's not married to Alisha."

"Not yet."

The moment Thierry pulled into the parking area, we bolted out only to be swarmed with operatives.

In another second both brother made a noise and Teo had me in his arms.

"Don't get yourself killed," he growled at Thierry.

"I won't." Thierry looked viciously at me. "Stay with Teo."

And I knew then he was going to fight them. And he wasn't going to win.

"No!" I screamed. "Don't you dare! I can stop this!"

I could stop Reed. Otherwise they'd kill Thierry. But I couldn't hear anything.

"Reed is the reason why we are here," Thierry growled.

"Hands up!" One of them roared aiming his gun at me. At me. Just like I felt Thierry move with a growl. But I knew better. There were dozens of them. *Dozens. Swarming.*

The panic was real inside of me. This was the scariest thing I'd ever felt. Black-clad emerging from the shadows of the lot on us and all of us froze.

The visceral fear was still there when the operatives still moved to the DuPont's.

"Nononono, Thierry!" I shrieked. "Don't do it!" I was grabbing for Thierry as one of them reached for him. Behind me someone swore and growled. "No, don't touch him!"

Teo snapped at one of them who cocked their gun at him. "Get your hands off my brother, scum."

I felt someone else grabbing Thierry and I lost my mind. "No!"

And then *everyone* lost their ever loving mind.

Teo swung at someone with a growl not giving a shit. An operative moved at Thierry and I screamed grabbing him.

No, they won't take him from me.

"Avani! Stay back!"

I didn't even know Thierry could move like that, rushing towards two of the operatives and kicking them down. His movements were fluid and fast as he went after them.

To my left Teo was grunting as he took out one of them the other one putting him in a chokehold.

And then two figures were running to me, ripping off their masks. I saw a familiar pair of blue eyes hit me and blonde hair.

"Kellan!" I cried out.

He shouted at everyone in a booming voice I didn't know he had. His expression was ruthless. *"Get off! Everybody off! All of you down!"*

Everybody froze and ducked including Teo, who took me down with him, and Thierry.

Kellan's gun was trained on Thierry. "Hands up, DuPont!"

"Nice try, it isn't DuPont," Thierry smirked.

"Stop!" I screamed scrambling up, grabbing both of the DuPont brother who looked like they had a penchant for trouble. *"He's not the enemy!"*

I had never in my life felt terror like this. Until now. Not until I saw Thierry lifting his hands up to his head. I was wrapped around him as Kellan's eyes looked horrified.

"Avani," Kellan spoke up with concern in his expression and confusion. "What are you doing?"

"He's my boyfriend!"

CHAPTER 55
AVANI

As I said it his jaw dropped in horror.

"What the fuck are you idiots doing?"

Reed. I saw his long leaner form cutting through everyone as he rushed downstairs my sister right behind him rushing to me.

"Didi!" I called for her, her dark hair flying behind her as she looked like she hit a wall when she saw me, Thierry, and Teo next to each other. I was holding onto Thierry with one arm, and Teo held my waist.

"Jesus fucking Christ—" Reed swore. *"Watts, put your gun down. Avani, sweetheart—"*

"Avani, you're dating him!" Alisha looked stunned at Thierry. *"He's a murderer."*

"He is not! I am with him! He isn't the enemy! He is not Talon! And he's my family!"

"Even if I am, I have discretion."

"Thierry, you are not helping," I cried.

He held up his hands innocently looking more amused at me as Alisha looked ready to pass out. Reed wrapped his arm around her if he noticed the same thing when she started hyperventilating.

"Didi," I spoke up. "Please. Stop this. Talon isn't the enemy—I know everything. Don't hurt him. Or his friends." I looked at Reed pleading with him.

Reed swore looking at Thierry then me with horror dawning in his eyes. *"What the fuck is happening right now?"*

"Did you take Talon?" Thierry growled at him not giving a damn about the black-clad members of Titan around us. "Did you take Bexley?"

"We took your friends into custody," Kellan answered looking pale still at Thierry. Like he knew something I didn't. "The dark-haired girl, Samara is with Shane. And your blonde friend was taken to the hospital." He was looking back and forth at me and Thierry like he couldn't comprehend it.

"Avani." Alisha's eyes searched mine. "Please tell me that's the truth and he isn't holding you hostage!"

I wish her words didn't cut into me the way it did.

"Didi," I felt my eyes well up. "He's *mine*...please don't hurt him."

Alisha covered her mouth and looked at Reed as Kellan moved around us motioning everyone back. I rambled rushing to explain I was seeing him.

"...all summer," I rambled. I held onto him and Teo who didn't look like he was letting me go more worried about me than the clear men with guns around us. *"He saved Alisha's life!"*

I quickly explained how Thierry saved Alisha and nobody had known.

Reed and Alisha's jaw dropped like Kellan's.

"*You* shot Alisha's stalker? You're the fucking sniper!" Reed looked at Thierry like he had three heads now. "*You* sent the flowers to the hospital? No fucking wonder nobody could figure it out."

This entire time I realized it had been a mystery.

Thierry had been moving like a shadow in-between everyone for me. Always me.

I loved him. I was *never* letting him go.

I kept going about Thierry sending me flowers and it was incoherent to me, I couldn't stop shaking even held up by both DuPont's.

I was babbling incessantly nervous and shaking in the cold parking lot as Thierry took his jacket off and wrapped it around me.

Teo next to me scowled at Reed who didn't look at him with an ounce of care. I didn't understand why they despised each other so much. But it didn't even matter to me.

Reed closed the distance with Alisha and blew out a breath staring at Thierry like he was a dinosaur from a different realm.

"You're dating her?" He asked him, lowering his voice. "You've been dating for *months*." Reed's stormy eyes met mine. "Months."

I felt the guilt sinking in now. "I'm sorry. I would've told you but you guys hated each other…" I squeezed Thierry's hand. "And I love him, so much. Please don't hurt him."

My voice broke as I begged.

"Before I knew about you and your stupid necklace," Thierry shot back at him his mouth turned down about me. "Before you tried to attack Teo in his office. And before I got involved with her serial killer." He motioned to Alisha.

"Didi, he isn't a villain. He saved your life," I added. "Please." I looked around at the agents. "Please tell me everything is all right."

Reed blew out a breath. "Everyone they're clear. Kellan, you're gonna wanna take Thierry to his team." He eyed Teo. "What the fuck do you want?"

Teo smirked. "If you killed my brother tonight, I was going to kill you."

The two eyed each other as Alisha stepped in between them drawing Teo's attention down to her.

"*Avani*," she held my face. "You didn't say a word." Alisha's eyes watered. "*Why didn't you tell me?*"

Now, I felt the guilt. "I'm *sorry*," I licked my lips. "*I thought if I did, you would think ill of me—*"

"*Me?*"

This was what I had been dreading. Her betrayal was written all over her eyes.

"Not because you're a bad Mum. You're wonderful. I just felt so bad. I was going to tell you after Reed came into our lives, I swear, but then we both were kidnapped…Thierry saved you. He's been making sure Talon doesn't come after Reed."

I sniffled as Alisha hugged me then and drew back to look up at Thierry.

"They have been after me," Reed muttered. "Your team was hunting me and my family."

"No," Thierry shook his head. "They were never a threat. You met Bexley, she's at the hospital you said? She wouldn't hurt a fly. Teo over there was watching out for Adam. We would never hurt you or anyone around you."

"Bexley bit Garrett," Kellan spoke up. "That's about it. We were worried you were going to kill us."

"Why? She bites everyone," Thierry rolled his eyes. "I need to make sure my team is good." And then his eyes landed back on Alisha who looked up at him. Instantly, both of them looked uneasy.

The air was thick now as my stomach twisted at the two of the most important people in my life now finally meeting.

"Thank you," Alisha murmured. "Thank you for everything. This might take some getting used to. I'm still not done processing your reputation for saving me." Her throat worked as she watched him. "Did you kill all those people in New York?"

"Just one." He shook his head looking embarrassed. I knew what he did.

But I also knew…Reed did the same thing.

They called it different things.

Contractors. Mercenaries.

Titan. Talon.

Two halves of the same coin.

Controlled by two *former* lovers.

"The only person I killed in New York was the man who took you. Everything else is orders from above. For other operatives. Not me. I'm with her."

He motioned to me as we held on.

Alisha nodded. "Okay, I think I'm ready to pass out now…Reed, he saved our lives…"

If it wasn't for Thierry—Alisha might not have made it…

That was the most important thing to Reed.

Reed was there wrapping his arm around her. Reed looked at us for a quiet moment processing us. Processing this. He shook his head then like he made a choice.

"Both of you go with Kellan to see Thierry's team." Reed eyed Teo. "Why are you here?"

"Are you done trying to scare everything?" Now Teo looked ready for a fight. *"You attacked my brother's friends—"*

"Your brother's friends are a black ops unit designed to kill everything—"

"So is Titan you hypocrite!"

"The only reason you aren't dead is because Alisha stops me every single time I try to kill you."

"That's because like Adam and Lucy—she actually likes me."

"Oh, for the love of God, both of you!" Alisha snapped. "Reed, his

brother saved my life, the least you two can do right now is be civil. Teo stop provoking him, you always do this—"

"I would if he wasn't so fucking easy—" Teo's eyes flashed a violent blue.

"That's it." Reed lunged at Teo and I stepped back as Kellan went after both of them.

"Oh my goodness," I covered my mouth.

"Bexley is sick right now. I need to make sure you didn't scare her to death," he murmured looking unconcerned. "Mon coeur, I need to go."

"I know," I looked at Reed laying into Teo then and Teo giving it right back. I winced again.

Kellan, now yanking at Reed as another operative tried to separate Teo. Both of them were relentless despite Teo in his dress shirt and Reed in black gear.

"This is why your brother came to me—" Teo growled. *"Because he knew he couldn't turn to you!"*

Reed's eyes widened for a split second and he whipped around holding Teo down on the ground and looked at Thierry. "You motherfucker, *you* were the connection. *You two were working with Adam and Lucy?"* Reed looked beyond stunned now. "That's how you guys are connected!"

As the dots clicked for Reed?

Teo got in another hit and Reed slamming him down before punching him. I winced along with Alisha who wrung her hands together worried.

All the operatives looked around unsure of exactly who to pull off as Kellan yanked at them. *"Both of you cut it the fuck out!"*

Teo spat out blood. *"I've been waiting for this day—"*

"Of course you fucking have—" Reed and Teo were polar opposites with one thing in common.

"Waiting for Alisha to realize, you're shit—" Teo growled and Alisha sighed.

"Guys—" she started.

"You don't say her fucking name—" Reed growled smashing his fist into Teo's chin. I winced a little.

"Are they fighting over you?" I asked Alisha. "I thought you didn't like Teo—"

"She *doesn't.*" Reed was vicious as Teo laughed outright.

Good. Lord. He was evil.

Alisha looked between Thierry and Reed and then back at my boyfriend.

"He's been on edge for a few months now because of Talon. He thought you guys were going to kill him and his brother. We thought you were working with them." Alisha shook her head at me. "I *cannot* believe you two have been secretly dating. This makes Evic and Lucas sneaking around look like a joke."

"Evie and Lucas snuck around?" I asked. "I thought they were married?"

"Lucas Devereaux?" Thierry raised a brow. "He was an accident by the way. Bad shot."

Alisha turned bright red. "It's a long story. You might have to fill in Gabriel." And then she gasped. "Good Lord. I need to get to Gabriel. Reed! Stop fighting Teo!"

"Okay," I held out my hands. "First rule of thumb. No more secrets. From anyone. And second of all? I thought Gabriel was with you? What is he going to do about his wife?"

"I don't know yet. He's working on it," Alisha looked uneasy. "Gabriel's going to address all this."

"You son of a bitch—" Reed growled interrupting us. *"I can't fucking believe you were with my baby sister—"*

Teo laughed manically and Thierry scowled at his brother. "You're supposed to be the CEO, you fucking joke—"

Alisha looked at Thierry. "I didn't realize how young your friends were. Or you…I didn't know you were…helping us. Helping her."

"I swear, Didi, he isn't a bad man." I would defend Thierry forever.

He looked almost embarrassed interacting with Alisha who looked torn between crying and hugging me again.

"Good lord," Alisha whispered. "I think the stress has gotten to both of them."

Thierry looked unimpressed. "You don't say?"

CHAPTER 56
THIERRY

I did finally get to Bexley who was sick in the hospital.

"Please, get me out of here," she coughed. "He's holding me hostage."

"You have donuts," I motioned dryly to the three boxes under her bed. "Would a guard get his captive donuts?"

She turned pink at the mention of her guard Garrett Fuller who sat six feet away pretending to ignore us.

I knew he was listening to every single word she said. The fucker was massive. Six-six, all hard edge of blonde and green eyes.

"He can be a jailer with donuts," Bexley eyed me with those big blues.

"He can't be a jailer and get you donuts. If he didn't like you he would've gotten you potatoes. Are you hiding chocolate milk behind you?"

"No."

"I can see the carton."

"No."

"She's hiding snacks under the bed," Garrett grumbled looking amused. "She's like fifteen."

"I'm nineteen, Jack in the Beanstalk!"

"I prefer the giant," he muttered.

"You would."

I covered my mouth as Avani blinked. Bexley eyed her suspiciously now. "Your girlfriend is the enemy."

"No, my girlfriend is my heart, don't talk to her. Talk to me. How's Samara?"

"Samara is dating the enemy too. Her boytoy Shane is a Titan," Bexley grumbled eyeing Garrett her cheeks turning pink. "I'm with the enemy too."

"Shane didn't know Samara was a member of Talon when he was with her. Trust me, they're both in shock." Garrett looked like he was fighting laughter. "Give me the donuts back, shortstack."

"Go kick rocks." Bexley dissolved into coughing fits and I had to step in with Avani who wrapped a blanket around her.

"Bex, this is Avani."

"The *enemy*." She grumbled. "When can I go home? I hate being a hostage."

"You can go after you're better," I eyed Garrett Fuller. "Isn't that right?"

He tipped his head. "Her friend on the other hand is sedated. Don't look at me like that. She tried to kill Shane. She was so angry she fought him."

"Where's Samara now?"

"In her hospital room," Garrett muttered motioning out the door. "Shane brought her to make sure he didn't hurt her. Just sedated her enough. I think he's in more shock knowing she was one of you guys."

I did go check on Samara to find Shane Alves sitting by her bedside looking torn up.

"You told her you were a grad student?" I asked him and he looked shaken up to see me and Avani side by side.

"She told me she was a tourist."

I shook my head. "I'm so fucking done with spies."

First Alma's husband? *Now this?*

We left Alisha and Reed at the Primrose because Gabriel had gone to find his wife. Confront her.

Or whatever the fuck they wanted to do after seven years.

To be fair?

As long as I had mon coeur at this point? I was so exhausted I wanted to crawl into my girlfriend and stay in her arms forever.

"Mon coeur, I miss you," I muttered.

"Now that my sister knows about us, and Gabriel found his lady, want to go home?"

I sighed holding her hands over my heart.

"I never want anything to do with Titan ever again."

Thats exactly what Reed did as Alisha came over to us.

"I am sorry, Reed has been pushed to his limits, Lucy almost broke in to K2 scaring him, Adam and him had been fighting, and it's been a hectic few months for him. When he realized this was the last opportunity he had to catch Talon, he took it. He's usually not this mad."

Andrei watched her carefully as she looked up at me and I realized how tiny Alisha was compared to Avani.

Her eyes shimmered a little.

"I need to call my wife," Andrei said in the background moving to do that.

"My brother's won't forgive you guys," I shook my head. But I didn't know how I felt. I understood their desperation. But I had also felt it. Bexley. Samara, even if I didn't like her, and then Jace. I felt my world under a threat. And I was pretty sure I'd choked down one of the operatives downstairs.

I hoped they weren't dead but—

"Reed's agents attacked the DuPont's," Avani came to my defense. "I know you guys were desperate and I know you didn't know what we did. But...there had to have been better ways to handle this."

Alisha looked remorseful as Reed came back while Gabriel turned to the five agents. "I need to go with him to make sure he doesn't murder Liam."

Alisha nodded. "Shall I come to?"

He shook his head. "Not this time, Angel. But I love you." He kissed her soundly. And he turned to Matteo. "We'll fix everything in the building before we leave."

But Teo's eyes were hard on Reed. "I have never liked you. I dislike you even more. You couldn't have spoken?"

"Would you have answered any of my fucking questions?" Reed looked Teo. "You think me breaking into your company is fun? Like I did it with reckless intent? Like I didn't factor anything in? Your family is Talon. You guys hid my best friend's wife for seven years. I just found out from Lucy she gave the fake necklace over and that means she's going to go underground again. I had one shot. One fucking shot. I took it."

Reed's eyes met mine. "What the fuck am I supposed to do? Ask you if you've hid Isobel Santos?" He looked annoyed with us. "Get fucking real. You motherfuckers started this shit seven years ago. I'll be damned if I don't end it."

There was an intense wildness to his eyes I always knew lurked there but he'd been fed up with us.

Why else would he make a reckless choice like this?

"Talia Nash is still someone we're interested in," Reed watched Andrei. "His wife holds the rest of the secrets. She's the only one who knows what happened. And we can't get a hold of her."

"Because Talia isn't an idiot," Teo scoffed. "If she saw you coming, she would take Drew and hide."

Which is what worried me.

Andrei was on the phone texting Talia now. Talia who kept her secrets for so long. So many years. Isobel while she wasn't in the room? I felt her presence in Gabriel. Mentor. Wife. Leader of Talon now.

Her and Talia were the keeper of all secrets.

Somehow my sister-in-law was central to this too.

"I need to go to her," Andrei said to Teo and me. "She isn't picking up. If anything happens to her," he squared his eyes on Reed. "I will rip your little company apart. In the foreseeable future, stay away from my family."

His eyes landed on Avani and I could tell he was struggling with hating Titan and accepting I was dating her. I tugged her closer and shook my head.

"You can stay away from Titan," I said my voice hard. "But she isn't a Titan. She's mine. She's a part of us now."

And I felt Avani tremble because out of everyone, she had been caught between two worlds too. We had been hiding, but now?

My family hated her. And she was my family too.

Andrei didn't say a word as he left everyone moving out of his way as he rushed home—for fucking once.

Teo looked at Jace. "Anyone else in the room you know?"

Jace shook his head with a little smile on his face as I looked down at Avani.

"Part of you?" She murmured looking at me with a smile.

I tipped my head to her brushing my lips over hers despite the dozens of guns in the room. And one angry Reed. Gabriel still there with his team.

"Mon coeur, did I tell you what that means?"

"You said it meant sweetheart," she blinked up at me with wet eyes.

"It means *my* heart," I muttered into her skin pulling back to watch her eyes widen. "You've always been a part of me. Nothing was going to stop me from being with you." I glanced up at Reed and Alisha. "Not even you two."

"I cannot believe you guys have been hunting my boyfriend," Avani said to her sister. "He's here to stay."

Alisha looked a little uneasy but she nodded. "I think it just takes time adjustment," she said softly to me. "I'm sorry for months I thought you were a deranged killer."

I was. But I was also Avani's.

I grinned at Alisha's expression.

Reed looked at Alisha then with a contemplative expression. "When you invite him for dinner at K2 with Lucy, he's going to freak Lucy out. I just know it. With how jumpy she is around men."

Avani giggled then softening the tension. "You want us over?"

"If he doesn't hate us as well," Alisha nodded to me. "You look quite devious with that smile. This may take some getting used to."

I grinned at Alisha. "Nice to finally meet you."

CHAPTER 57
AVANI

THIERRY WANTED ME TO MEET HIS FAMILY. AND I WANTED THIERRY to meet mine.

Not just Teo this time.

But Andrei and Talia.

I slid into a pink dress he had picked out for me with an elegant bodice and florals embellishments on the straps. And he stepped out of his closet in slacks and nothing else.

Both of our jaws dropped.

"Aw, hell, mon coeur, nobody's going anywhere now…" he groaned as he tore his belt off and I squeaked.

"We're going to be late!"

"I don't give a fuck when you look edible."

"Thierry—"

"Bend over for me, mon coeur, I need this—" he broke off, his kisses trailing down my neck making me moan as he bent me over the edge of the bed.

Desperate hands, tearing silk, and then I felt him pressing into my body. I moaned gripping the sheets for dear life as his cock stretched my inner walls.

"Thierry—"

His hand snaked around my body and tugged my bodice down, both of his hands cupping my breasts. I cried out as he slid in deeper now.

"There you go, mon coeur, let your man in."

I sobbed into the sheets aware he was absolutely ruining my makeup and my hair and I couldn't even plead for him to stop because I wanted him.

"Fuck, look at you pressing back on me. Such a good fucking girl."

"Thierry—please…please…" I gripped the sheets tighter not realizing I was pushing back on him. For long moments he worked into me until he bottomed out and I arched my back. One hand kept tugging on my nipples, as the other curved up to my throat where I felt his lips grazing my ear.

My eyes rolled back as he began drawing out while murmuring in that dark voice. "That's a good girl. You're gonna take my cock before we do anything else, aren't you?"

"Yes." It was breathless leaving me. Automatic. He plunged back in a smooth drive and we both groaned.

I closed my eyes as I knew how he moved.

"I'm just getting warmed up, mon coeur—"

"Late—" I gasped.

His chuckle was dark. "Yes, we are going to be late." He sounded completely dry about it. "And you're going to take every single fucking inch of me the entire time. I might just fuck you the entire way there. Let you sit through dinner with my cum leaking out of you—"

I shattered just like that, the clenching, the pressure, the tugging on my nipples too much for me.

He groaned as he drove in deeper and harder fucking me through it.

Every single time he did this, it prolonged my orgasm beyond what I thought was possible.

And he kept going. His grip on my throat tighter as I came harder crying his name out as he worked between my legs like an animal.

"Spread those fucking thighs for me. Wider." I obeyed as a shriek left me at how deep it got him. *"That's my fucking girl."*

"Oh God."

He held fast to my breast and my throat while working into me like an unrestrained menace.

Every single thrust is deeper, harder, until I muffled my screams into the bed as he drove into me—if it wasn't for him holding me steady my knees would've given out and they almost done as my orgasm reaches a different height.

A broken noise left my throat as he groans at the ruthless force he's taking me with. The pleasure pulsing through my core is too much.

"Right fucking there, I know it's right fucking—"

I screamed louder than I ever had exploding, a rush of my orgasm coming out of me. Down my thighs. Down my legs. I screamed even louder at the sensations coursing through me.

My knees gave out and he held up by my waist bringing me flush against him as I shook wildly.

"Oh God—"

"Damn, that's hot as fuck…" he murmured into my ear as I trembled so wildly, I couldn't stand.

"*Thierry*." A low moan left me as he slowed his thrusts down. "Sensitive."

"I know, mon coeur, don't worry. I'll take care of you."

He pulled out of me and in another instant he had the dress of me, flinging it to a chair in the side of the room as he spun me around, drowsy and lethargic. Laying me back on the bed as I trembled.

When he slid back in I could barely keep my eyes open as he began moving again in my sensitized body.

"Fuck, that was beautiful," he murmured over my lips. "You're beautiful, my heart."

"Oh God," I whimpered feeling him hitting somewhere deeper and I began to shake. "God—I can't—"

He groaned sealing his mouth over my throat. "Yes, you can. And you're going to come for me. And take me with you this time."

I sobbed into his neck feeling utterly dominated by him, thrusting inside of me with the rhythm of an unhinged god.

"Ngghhh."

"There you are—"

I lost it as it built so quickly this time I screamed into his neck as he groaned fucking me through it.

As he collapsed into me he laughed lightly in my neck. "Mon coeur, you've killed me."

I managed to mumble incoherently.

It took us a longer time to clean up, clean me up, the floor which was no shortage of embarrassment for me when Thierry realized I could do that one night. He'd been a feral animal in me ever since.

Including tonight.

While we were getting dressed to see his family.

I grumbled as he tidied me up and laughed as I kissed him back. "Scoundrel."

"You love it, mon coeur," he raised an elegant brow. "Want me to fuck your little hole with my tongue?"

I clapped my hand over his mouth. "We are never going to make it to your siblings."

His eyes twinkled deviously as I shooed him away picking up my dress—now ruined and stained. I pouted.

"What am I going to wear?" The pretty pink chiffon and silk was ruined. I peered over my shoulder as he held up an elegant black number.

"Option B."

"What is that?"

"The black version of that dress," he motioned to the pink one. "I know you had that color laid out for weeks, but I thought this one might suit you better."

It was gorgeous. Even more so than earlier. This time he helped me fit myself into it after changing into pristine black lingerie. Lace. Silk. Patterns.

"You look beautiful, mon coeur," he murmured, his eyes meeting mine in the mirror as he zipped it up.

Thierry who was invested in the air I breathed pinned my hair up with my Mum's pin. The one he stole all those years ago.

"Ready to meet my family?"

"Where is your shirt?" I laughed lightly still a little shaken up as he knelt to help me with my heels. My hair. Offering me my lip gloss.

The man knew how to win me over.

He grinned. "I was thinking I'd go like this—ow—mon coeur—you wound me."

I laughed easily feeling it bubbling up in my throat with him. "Please, go change. Thank you for helping me." I admired his tattoos and his muscled body slipping into his dress shirt.

"You won't get me in a tie, mon coeur."

"I'll let you use it on me after dinner," I tossed out casually.

His haste to get to a tie made me laugh harder as he put it on efficiently. And I did feel even after all those intense orgasms my core clenching as he did it himself.

"Where did you learn that?"

He winked. "A gentleman never tells his secrets."

"You are no gentleman."

"Non? What am I then?" He turned around smoothly and came over to me, bending down until his lips brushed mine. "Besides yours?"

I couldn't even breathe around the way he made me feel like a dark Queen next to him. My heart was racing, its pattern erratic.

"Mine. You have always been mine."

"Mhm." He kissed me slowly and I pushed him back.

"No, we can't—"

"I wasn't—"

"Yes, you were, you're playing with my bra—"

"You're not wearing a bra—"

"Thierry. We are going to be late—"

"We already are."

He laughed, all sharp-teeth and sin and I all but pounced on him.

"I despise being late—"

"Mon couer, my brother isn't on time to anything because of Talia, you'll be fine."

"Are you sure?"

He wasn't. I could tell.

I would've grumbled in annoyance had I not been sure he'd flip me over immediately and take me.

AFTERWORD

Thank you guys for making it this far into the
     Titan Security Series.
I would like to say the next book is the final
     book in the series.
And it's been years in the making.

STROKE OF LOVE

Gabriel Monroe and Isobel Santos go head to head

Titan vs Talon

In

Stroke of Love

ABOUT THE AUTHOR

Lilah Lance writes for every girl who just wants to be loved for who she is.

When Lilah isn't writing she likes to travel and spend her downtime on the beach.

For more info, check out www.lilahlance.com where you can subscribe to her newsletter for all things exclusively Titan.